WITCHY WOMAN

I peered out, straining to discern precious details. Dimly I could make out a glint on the asphalt drive below. Marcus's motorcycle. So he'd not left yet. I leaned closer to the window and tried to look straight down.

Without even the slightest hesitation or stab of conscience, I found myself sliding the latch to the right and carefully sliding the sash upward, inch by inch.

Cold swept into the room like a marauding invader, invisibly, insidiously. I shivered and dropped to my knees, resting my hands on the sill. They were right down there, all right.

A ring of light edged into view, rippling like water. An oil lamp or flame of some sort. The light moved, and then I could see the two of them, glowing like fairy people in the darkness of night.

They were heading for the woods.

I watched the swinging lantern and shadowy figures disappear into an invisible treeline that I knew must be there. I stayed at the window, despite the fact that I was shivering to beat the devil, and kept scanning the far distance for some sign of what they were doing. I saw a pale glow lighting the treetops.

Fire? And voices, wafting to me on the wind.

Chanting.

Adrenaline zipped up my spine. I hastily closed the window and climbed into bed, dragging the soft blankets up to my chin. No wonder Marcus and Felicity were an item. They were magical partners. Did they work with others? A coven of witches? Were they out there now?

What had I gotten myself into?

Berkley Prime Crime titles by Madelyn Alt

The Trouble with Magic

Madelyn Alt

BERKLEY PRIME CRIME, NEW YORK

THE BERKLEY PUBLISHING GROUP
Published by the Penguin Group
Penguin Group (USA) Inc.
375 Hudson Street, New York, New York 10014, USA
Penguin Group (Canada), 90 Eglinton Avenue East, Suite 700, Toronto, Ontario M4P 2Y3, Canada
(a division of Pearson Penguin Canada Inc.)
Penguin Books Ltd., 80 Strand, London WC2R 0RL, England
Penguin Group Ireland, 25 St. Stephen's Green, Dublin 2, Ireland (a division of Penguin Books Ltd.)
Penguin Group (Australia), 250 Camberwell Road, Camberwell, Victoria 3124, Australia
(a division of Pearson Australia Group Pty. Ltd.)
Penguin Books India Pvt. Ltd., 11 Community Centre, Panchsheel Park, New Delhi—110 017, India
Penguin Group (NZ), Cnr. Airborne and Rosedale Roads, Albany, Auckland 1310, New Zealand
(a division of Pearson New Zealand Ltd.)
Penguin Books (South Africa) (Pty.) Ltd., 24 Sturdee Avenue, Rosebank, Johannesburg 2196,
South Africa

Penguin Books Ltd., Registered Offices: 80 Strand, London WC2R 0RL, England

This is a work of fiction. Names, characters, places, and incidents either are the product of the author's imagination or are used fictitiously, and any resemblance to actual persons, living or dead, business establishments, events, or locales is entirely coincidental. The publisher does not have any control over and does not assume any responsibility for author or third-party websites or their content.

THE TROUBLE WITH MAGIC

A Berkley Prime Crime Book / published by arrangement with the author

PRINTING HISTORY
Berkley Prime Crime mass-market edition / January 2006

Copyright © 2006 by Madelyn Alt.
Cover illustration by Monika Roe.
Cover design by Judith Murello.
Interior text design by Stacy Irwin.

ISBN: 0-425-20746-3

BERKLEY® PRIME CRIME
Berkley Prime Crime Books are published by The Berkley Publishing Group,
a division of Penguin Group (USA) Inc.,
375 Hudson Street, New York, New York 10014.
The name BERKLEY PRIME CRIME and the BERKLEY PRIME CRIME design
are trademarks belonging to Penguin Group (USA) Inc.

PRINTED IN THE UNITED STATES OF AMERICA

10 9 8 7 6 5 4

The universe is full of magical things,
patiently waiting for our wits to grow sharper.

— EDEN PHILLPOTTS

Chapter 1

I don't know what it was that made me abandon my usual path to work on that particular October Tuesday. The morning had dawned misty and gray—my favorite kind—and it made me groan all the more about heading into the grim Collections job I had desperately come to dread. Four-plus years of pressuring-slash-coercing-slash-browbeating tightfisted customers into paying our invoices, working to solve problems and inconsistencies *ad infinitum,* and pouring a never-ending stream of coffee for a boss who viewed every female in the office as slave labor—well, it was enough to drive anyone over the edge. Lately I'd been having to drag myself out of bed in the morning . . . but it was futile to resist. I was nothing if not responsible.

That morning the whispers of reluctance proved too insistent to ignore. Despite what I considered near-saintlike intentions of swinging into work early (my boss, more commonly known as The Toad, would have inserted a snide *for once* at that point), I found myself cranking the worn steering wheel of my old 1972 Bug at the next intersection, leaving the straight and orderly procession of Main Street to veer off downhill on the lesser traveled River Street.

A blatant avoidance tactic, granted, but sometimes a girl's gotta do what a girl's gotta do.

Stony Mill, Indiana, is your typical Midwestern town, with typical Hoosier idiosyncrasies. Staunchly proud of its position in the Bible Belt of the north, it is a place where going to church on Sunday means you're forgiven for your visit to the hooter bar on Friday night. I know this town like the back of my hand . . . or at least, I used to. A shadow had fallen over my hometown; I hardly recognized it anymore. They say that change is good. That it keeps a place from stagnating. In the case of Stony Mill, that meant opening our arms to a flood of big-city expatriates who saw my quiet town as a way of building their expensive homes free of the burden of city-sized taxes. With them came problems. Too many problems. Why the interlopers all seemed to feel this town owed them for the honor of their presence was beyond me.

Behold, people, the Me generation is alive and well.

One good thing to come out of it was the district along River Street, the oldest thoroughfare in the county and a once thriving trade center whose ancient and rustic warehouses now sheltered a bustling antiques trade. I loved antiques, but I rarely allowed myself the luxury of even window shopping down this way. First of all, I worked for a living, and the shoppes (someone had added an extra *p* and an *e* to the word in advertising a few years back because they thought it sounded erudite) catered to those with far more padding in their purses. Second, I worked for a living; hence, I had better ways to spend my hard-earned pennies. Like paying the rent. Or if I was feeling a little crazy, squandering it on something really frivolous. Like peanut butter, or mac 'n' cheese.

As always, the storefronts looked like something out of a Norman Rockwell painting. Weathered gray clapboards and multipaned windows bordered with shutters and cascading flower boxes worked together to score major points with the yuppie crowd. (That would not be me.) Yet as much as I abhorred the bustle of the crowds, I loved the quiet dignity of the old buildings, the gentle whisper of the river currents, the riotous colors of mums and still-thriving geraniums spilling from the windowboxes, and the come-in-and-sit-a-spell hominess of the store displays. The combination was pretty hard to resist.

With a last rueful glance at the cheap digital clock Velcro-ed to my dashboard, I parked the temperamental car I laughingly called Christine and stepped out into the damp.

Just for a minute or two, I told myself. Just long enough to soak up the atmosphere of the place before it was overrun by the country club set that generally kept me at bay.

Designer separates and hundred-dollar-an-ounce perfume really try my patience.

Overhead, darker clouds had begun to gather, a warning of even wetter weather still to come. Ever hopeful, I dug behind the frayed bucket seat in the off chance that I had left some sort of jacket or—was it too much to ask?—an umbrella back there, but after two minutes of muttering beneath my breath, I came up with nothing more than a few desiccated French fries and an overdue library book I thought I had returned weeks ago.

I flipped it over, only halfheartedly considering. It was a thriller, and not a very good one. It did have a plastic sleeve on the cover . . .

I discarded the thought immediately. Somehow I suspected the library would frown upon one of its prized potboilers being used as a rain shield. Besides, my love for books wouldn't allow it, no matter how desperate I got. Better to get back in the Bug and drive on to the office.

I wanted to. I really did. It would be the sensible thing to do. But something inside me, some burgeoning impulse I didn't understand, prevented my feet from doing the sensible thing.

A little exasperated, and a lot bemused, I found myself stuffing my hands into the pockets of my slacks and hunching my shoulders against the wind and damp as I walked up the rejuvenated brick-and-concrete sidewalks, silently praising those few store owners who had thoughtfully erected awnings.

At first I scarcely looked at the shops. I thought if I just got out and walked around a bit, whatever it was that was compelling me to be there might leave me the hell alone and let me get back to the mundane existence I grudgingly led. Eventually the wind and mist seemed to lessen as I pushed on and I found myself pausing to gaze longingly at tall, Gothic cabinets and sparkling glass bottles, bookshelves and bureaus with lace doilies dripping from them, enormous earthen crocks overflowing with dried bittersweet, and more. So much more.

I looked. I dreamed. I lusted.

Suddenly, lightning cracked open the dark sky over Stony Mill, Indiana.

"Shit!"

I raced for my car, digging for my keys as my legs pumped, harder, faster. I hadn't found them by the time I reached the car, but through my wilting bangs I could see the telltale knob poking up from the door panel—I hadn't locked the driver's-side door. Laughing with relief, I reached for the latch and jammed my thumb against the chrome push button release.

Nothing. It didn't budge.

Christine strikes again.

I didn't even bother to curse this time as the rain plastered my hair to my scalp; I bolted in a blind panic. I was hoping to find an open store somewhere along the riverfront, but it was only a few ticks past eight. Most of the stores didn't open for another hour. I was doomed.

Shivering, I ducked into a small alcove, pressing my back against the old wood-and-glass door in hopes that the rain couldn't reach me there. My efforts were only halfway effective—raindrops still pelted my face, gathering reinforcements by the minute. I sighed, resigned to a long, cold, wet wait . . . but . . . there was a part of me that gleefully accepted the delay. After all, my boss could hardly complain if I came in looking like a wet version of my Great-Aunt Frances's ancient fox stole. And then there was that little niggle at the back of my mind that told me I was right where I was supposed to be today.

Confused, weary, I turned my face to the sky. *What?* I demanded in silence of the universe at large. *What are you trying to tell me?*

Without warning, the door I was leaning against opened

and I fell backward, pinwheeling my arms in a futile grab for balance, into a dark space that smelled strongly of cinnamon.

Hardwood floors, I noted as my all-too-ample backside made contact. Ouch. *(Mental note: Must borrow Melaine's Buns of Steel video.)*

I sat there a moment, wondering how my day had come to this. I'd started out with such good intentions. Really I had. *(Approaching the Big Three-Oh sometimes does that to a girl.)* Get into work early, make a serious attempt to show The Toad that I wasn't the lackluster reprobate he thought me to be, press my nose firmly to the grindstone, and maybe, just maybe, start working my way up in the world. I surrender to temptation for one brief moment of weakness and look what happens: I end up late for work, soaked to the skin, and sprawled on a scuffed wooden floor that might as well have been concrete.

Obviously something went wrong somewhere.

But self-pity serves no woman's purpose and we Hoosiers are nothing if not hardy, so I gingerly dusted my palms against my cheap black slacks (Wal-Mart, $14.95), wincing at the sting of scraped skin. I was about to scramble to my feet when a pale face suddenly floated into view before my eyes, swooping out at me from the darkness.

"Holy-Mary-Mother-of-God!" I yelped, scrabbling backward in surprise.

A gentle laugh halted my retreat. "Hardly. Are you all right, dear?"

All right? My heart was beating faster than Thumper's hind feet and I'd conked my right shoulder on something hard and unyielding, but all things considered, I was no worse for the wear. The woman's voice—my poor, numb brain worked to decipher its nationality . . . Irish? English?—was a soft coo, as soothing as a mother singing a lullaby. Well, someone's mother, anyway. Someone else's, that is.

I squinted as a match flared three feet away, the bitter odor of sulfur for a moment overpowering the cinnamon bun scent of the store.

"The electricity is out." The woman touched the match to a candle. The flame sputtered once then caught, casting warm light in a small golden circle. "That last bit of lightning must have taken out a transformer or some such nonsense. The gods are having a fine time up there this morning, if I do say so myself."

Seeing that my wits had fled and still hadn't returned, she extended a slender, beringed hand to me. I took it, gratefully, and scrambled to my feet. Only when I had let go did the heat of it register. My hand tingled with the impression of hers.

Something trembled on the edge of my awareness, the kind of watchfulness you get when you know something is about to happen. The hairs at the nape of my neck prickled. My senses perked. And yet, I felt no sense of danger.

"I'm terribly sorry to barge in on you this way," I began, finding my voice at last as I tried to make sense of the impressions battering at me from all directions. "I'm not sure what happened, actually. I'd taken refuge from the storm in your alcove, and the next thing I knew—"

"Ah. I have been meaning to get that lock fixed," the woman said simply, setting the candlestick on a wooden countertop. She opened a cabinet and took out several more, arranging them precisely in an arc, then used the first to light the lot of them.

Slowly the circle of light grew in circumference, warm, shimmering. Welcoming. For the first time I could see the woman who had for a moment scared the daylights out of me. Sleek coppery hair, liberally streaked with silver, was combed away from her face in rich waves that curved around her ears and tickled her nape. Her clothes were not the designer togs of the yuppie contingent, but they exuded a classic kind of elegance that I thought of as timeless, and they suited her to a tee. A pair of half-moon spectacles hung on a long silver chain about her neck. On her, I bet they looked magnificent. She was of average height, willow-slender, but from her emanated a quiet strength that had nothing to do with the physical and everything to do with character. On the whole, she was everything I wanted to be when I grew up.

"Do I meet with your approval?"

I snapped my gaze up to her twinkling blue eyes. Heat

rushed to my cheeks. "I'm sorry. That must have seemed terribly rude."

She waved aside my apology, her rings shooting sparks in the shimmering candlelight. "Rudeness is in the eye of the beholder. I would be doing the same if I were you, given the circumstances." She held out her hand to me. "Felicity Dow."

Hesitating only a moment, I took her hand. "Maggie O'Neill."

"Charmed, my dear."

I shifted, wondering what time it was and wishing I had found a way to afford a cell phone like everyone else in the civilized world. The Toad would be grinding his crowns to powder by now.

"I should be going," I said, gesturing halfheartedly toward the door. Actually, I'd rather catch my death of pneumonia standing out in the rain than go into work at this late hour, but I couldn't tell my benefactor that. I did, however, need to call in, and soon. Maybe if I tried very hard, I could muster a passable scratchy throat for effect.

"Nonsense. You'll catch your death in this weather."

A shiver went zipping up my spine as she echoed my thoughts. *Déjà vu.* "The rain is letting up."

It was a halfhearted attempt at best, and it received just as much attention as it deserved. She had been bustling about in the dark, just beyond the bowl of candlelight. Now she came forward, a delicate china cup held out toward me, complete with saucer.

"Here. You'll be wanting this."

She definitely was not from around here. No one slid saucers under their teacups anymore. In fact, hardly anyone I knew drank tea.

The spicy scent of Earl Gray wafted up on tendrils of steam. Bemused, I looked down into the clear brown depths. The steam swirled before my eyes like a cloud that had been stirred by the finger of an angel.

Her laughter tinkled on the air around me. "Don't you just love it when it does that?"

From the moment I had entered this store, nothing had

seemed quite right. I felt like Alice when she fell down the rabbit's hole, and I couldn't figure out why.

"If you're looking for a job—"

I stared at her, trying to focus. Had I said anything about looking for a job?

"—I could use someone here. Full time, of course. I can't promise you'll be a millionaire by the time you're forty, but I can say that the company you'd keep is delightfully effervescent." She flashed me an elfish smile. "And you'll never be bored."

Her clear eyes gently probed mine. I lowered my eyelashes self-consciously. Somehow I got the feeling that this woman rarely missed much.

Even so, a sudden swell of yearning rose within me, filling my throat with desire.

A job. *Here.*

I glanced around, thirstily drinking in as many details as I could make out. Neat shelves lined the walls, their bulging contents tidy and yet wonderfully chaotic. Delightful scents promised a trove of treasures to be discovered and experienced, one by one. Candles and antiques. Books. Trunks large and small, begging to be opened. It was as if the entire store had been created with me in mind. Who knew what wonders I would find when the lights came back on?

Temptation burned within me, steady and sweet. I longed to accept. Oh, how I longed to.

Did I dare?

"The hours?" I squeaked out.

In the blink of an eye, the benevolent stranger became the smart businesswoman as she strode briskly behind what I could now tell was a rustic antique counter with a scarred but well-oiled top. From a file cabinet hidden beneath the counter's ruffled chintz skirt, she withdrew a single sheet of paper.

She handed it to me. "This will detail the job duties, as well as the benefits. I can't offer much, but I do the best I can."

Matter-of-fact, not embarrassed or apologetic, and not arrogant. I liked that. It was more honest.

The letterhead showed the name of the store—ENCHANTMENTS—in bold, swirling letters, and beneath it in italics, *ANTIQUES AND FINE GIFTS.*

Enchantments. I liked that, too.

Outside, the line drive of wind and rain had begun to abate, a sign that I should let the nice lady get back to her shop while I got back to reality. Who knew, maybe I would be back.

Things were certainly looking up.

I gave her my thanks and told her I would give her a call that evening about the job, one way or another. Her nod said she had expected no less of me.

"Incidentally," she said in an off-handed tone, "I hope this won't affect your decision, but I should like our working relationship to be based on honesty and mutual trust. In fact, I insist upon it."

I nodded, sneaking a glance at my watch. Eight thirty-six. The Toad was going to kill me. "I appreciate the sentiment."

"Quite. You see, my dear, I am a witch."

The second hand on my watch might as well have frozen. I blinked at her, not quite sure what I should say. "I, uh, don't suppose you mean in the cranky, take-no-prisoners sense."

She smiled a patient little smile. "I mean in the metaphysical, magical sense."

A witch in Stony Mill. Holy crap, was she crazy? Trying not to stare, I dredged back through my hazy memory for all I'd learned about the American Witch Trials, thanks to a long-ago English lit lesson involving Miller's *The Crucible.* Paranoia, power plays, and politics came immediately to mind. I'd lived in Stony Mill my whole life, and from what I'd seen, your average, everyday Hoosier hadn't progressed much beyond that puritanical state.

But it was all make-believe anyway, right? No one believed in that kind of thing anymore.

In the end I decided not to hold it against her. It wasn't my place to sneer if she wanted to play Harry Potter. When Judgment Day came, everything was in the hands of God anyway, if you believed in all that, which, even after eight years of catechism I wasn't entirely sure that I did. Besides, what did it matter if she was a bit of a loon? She was a likable loon, didn't seem at all dangerous, and she was willing to hire me on the spot, which made her more than all right in my book.

I gave a magnanimous wave of my hand and smiled cheerily back at her as though I heard such claims all the time. "I could use a little magic in my life."

I couldn't have known at that moment just how true that was.

Chapter 2

Twelve minutes later I was standing stiffly at attention before The Toad, doing my best not to cry in front of my coworkers while he read me the riot act backward and forward, complete with red face and popping neck veins.

"Car problems . . ." was all I managed in my defense before he lifted his hand and pointed a finger toward the door.

"Miss O'Neill," he began in the same unpleasant, nasal tones that never failed to make me feel all of twelve years old, "your services are no longer required. Your final check will be mailed to you following next Thursday's payroll. I must ask that you leave the premises posthaste."

Posthaste? Nobody used words like *posthaste* anymore.

Pompous ass.

I swallowed the words with my pride, grimacing at the sour taste of public humiliation. "May I at least collect my things?"

His pointing finger never lowered. "One of the girls will bring them out to you."

The Girls. That's all we'd ever been to him. Never mind that the girls held his company together on a day-to-day basis. Some of the girls were old enough to be his mother, but it didn't matter. No amount of respect could be afforded The Girls.

My answer to him was short, to the point, and probably inadvisable, but I strode out of that sagging brick prison filled with more confidence, more joy than I'd felt in months. Years! It didn't matter that I'd lost my only means of paying my bills. There was something to be said for self-possession in the face of adversity, and the shock on The Toad's face had been worth it.

In the crumbling parking lot, I sat behind the wheel of my car, trying to decide what came next.

As I saw it, I had three options.

One, I could buy some newspapers and go back to my apartment to mope about in my scruffy pink bathrobe and fuzzy slippers while I scanned the classifieds.

Fun, fun.

Two, I could run home to Mother and Dad to take whatever comfort they were willing to offer. Dad would insist on feeding me chocolate—never a bad thing. Mom, on the other hand, would insist that I move back in with them.

Yeah, like *that* was going to happen. It might be a sin to say, but I'd rather join the black-habited commandos at St. Catherine's. At least as a nun I wouldn't be expected to date the losers Mom was always trying to hook me up with.

Three, I could contact the woman at Enchantments and accept her offer. Assuming she hadn't already come to her senses.

Three had always been my lucky number.

One glowing, ego boost of a phone call later, I was once again gainfully employed. The world was my oyster, life was a bowl of cherries without the pits, and my confidence was as puffed up as a blowfish on steroids with ridiculous clichés. Grinning broadly, I snapped on the radio and sped through my small town, my foot heavy on the gas pedal, my heart light as air, my voice as warbling-ly bad as ever as I sang along with Cyndi Lauper (gotta love the "80s Power Hour"). On top of the world, or as much of the world as could be in evidence in Stony Mill, Indiana, I stopped in at the Java Hut and splurged on a Cinnamon Latte topped with whipped cream and mocha sprinkles, then tooled back across town toward my sister's house, knowing I would find her home.

Melanie lived on the north edge of town in a subdivision with the ultrapretentious name of Buckingham West. Five years my junior, she was the standard by which my well-meaning mother measured the lack of success in my life. Married just out of college to the most prominent young lawyer in town, she was beautiful, the capable mother of two gorgeous little girls, perennially perky, and most importantly, married to the most prominent young lawyer in town. Which meant, of course, that she had risen above the modest expectations of our family and friends and had assumed a position of authority that she thought hers by default. Did I mention that she was married to the most prominent young lawyer in town?

"Does Mom know?"

I had just confessed the loss of my job and was overcome by her concern. "Gee, thanks, Mel. I'll be all right, really. Don't worry about me."

She made a face over the rim of her coffee cup. "Well, of course you will. Honestly, Mags, you can be so melodramatic about things. Now, answer me. Does Mom know?"

Doting as ever, my sis. "No. Not yet."

She gave me that measured stare that never failed to leave me defensive. Good heavens, when had she become so like our mother?

"It only just happened, you know. I thought I would postpone tightening the noose around my neck for a few hours."

"Mmhmm. So what are you going to tell her?"

I stared at her, trying to remember why I had come. For comfort? Hardly. No, I had come to brag about my change in fortune, and I meant to do just that.

I reached for my paper cup and lifted it to my mouth before dropping my little bomb. "That I already have another job. A good one, as a matter of fact."

"Well, well. That's wonderful. Where will you be working?"

If her tone was any indication, Mel was enjoying a bit of skepticism. Good. I planned to have fun with this.

"I bumped into the owner of a gift shop down on the riverfront. You know that cute little shopping area that's been doing so well?"

Mel lifted her artfully shaped brows in surprise. "I love those stores."

That much was evident just by looking around. Her home was filled with elegant and expensive treasures. Enough to make me just the teensiest bit jealous.

"Which one?" she asked, hardly skipping a beat.

"Ever heard of Enchantments?"

Mel actually gasped. "*You're* going to be working for Enchantments? That's one of my favorites! They have the most fabulous antiques there. And bath oils, and soaps, and . . . I don't suppose you'll get an employee discount?"

I responded with no more than a shrug and a mysterious little smile, basking in the glow of knowing I'd made the right decision. Perhaps this was the one thing I had needed to turn my life around. To make some real changes. To move forward.

I rose to pour the dregs of my latte down the drain and caught sight of myself in a lovely sunflower mirror over the sink: round face, too pale skin, flyaway shoulder-length brown hair and all. But my hazel eyes sparkled, and my skin had a glow of confidence I had rarely seen. I was happy. For once it didn't matter that Mel had inherited the sleek good looks of Great-Aunt Ceci, our late grandmother's wild younger sister who had disgraced the family by running off to New York City to become a Rockette, while I took after Grandma Cora herself, with a stubbornness to match. Today . . . today was different. Today was mine.

Mirror, mirror, on the wall . . .

"Mags, don't take this the wrong way, but . . . why you? I mean, you don't exactly have a history in retail."

The air in my bubble fizzed out, just a little. "Retail is about numbers, right? And accounting is all about numbers. Everything will work out in the end."

Mel's perfectly made-up face said she wasn't so sure. "Whatever you think is best."

Oh, yeah. She had Mom down pat.

I had arranged to start right away at Enchantments. The next morning, filled with trepidation (a last-minute keepsake from my mother—Mom had always been generous when it came to that sort of thing) but determined not to let it hold me back, I showed up at the store early and was forced to wait, chewing my thumbnail and shivering inside Christine's unheated confines until a low-slung black Lexus purred into the spot next to me. I grabbed my purse and keys and all but leaped from my car to greet her.

The car door swung open and Felicity Dow smiled up at me. "Oh, you're here already. Excellent."

I stood to one side, quivering like a nervous puppy as my new boss unfolded her legs from her car. She paused just long enough to throw the tail of a crimson wool wrap over one shoulder, then reached behind her seat to withdraw a slim black leather case and an old-fashioned velvet pouch purse that she slipped over her wrist.

She glanced at me. "Ready, then? Let's get busy, shall we?"

I still hadn't managed anything more than a squeaky "Good morning," but I followed her nevertheless, overcome by an excitement that was making my very skin vibrate. Felicity unlocked the nondescript metal security door and led the way inside.

I hesitated, unnerved by the sense that by crossing that threshold, my life was about to change forever.

Was I ready?

I'd better be. When it came right down to it, I was more afraid of my life *not* changing from what it had been before. Now was not the time for chickening out.

Holding my breath, I stepped into the back room and looked around. The smallish space was dark inside, but I could see the outlines of a sturdy roll-top desk. And shelves. Lots of shelves. Obviously an office. To my right a closed door sported a placard labeled STORAGE.

The lights came on with a snap that felt alive, and the room swam into focus.

"There we are. Storage, there. My office is here, but you are, of course, welcome to use it at any time. You may store your things here—" She indicated a coat closet I hadn't even noticed. "Why don't you make yourself comfortable while I fix us a spot of tea."

Felicity disappeared through dark purple velvet curtains to reveal the entry to the main part of the store. I slipped out of my coat, taking advantage of the time alone to have a quick look around free of scrutiny. I wouldn't say I was nervous, exactly. Well, maybe a little. It was just that I'd never known anyone who called herself a witch before, and it was more intimidating than I'd expected. In the back of my mind, I kept hearing Sister Agnes's waspish voice cautioning us against the evils of witchcraft. *"Thou shalt not suffer a witch to live."* Isn't that what the Bible says? Although I had to admit, with her salon-sleek hair and elegant clothes, Felicity certainly didn't *look* the part. Neither did the contents of the office offer a glimpse into a scarred psyche. Office supplies, file boxes, catalogs, inspirational tomes, items of nondistinction, all. They might have belonged to any businesswoman in today's fast-paced world.

Everything looked so . . . normal. Not a pentagram or inverted crucifix in sight. I felt the tension twisting my stomach muscles slip a notch.

"Here you are, Margaret." Felicity breezed through the parted drapes, carrying a steaming china cup in each hand. "I hope chai is to your liking. It's very soothing."

"Maggie," I said automatically, leaning into the fragrant steam rising from my teacup. I'd never heard of chai. It smelled faintly fruity, with a hint of cloves, possibly nutmeg, and other spices I couldn't place. "Call me Maggie. Only my mother calls me Margaret."

"Maggie, then. I am very glad you came today. I rather thought . . . well, that I had perhaps frightened you away."

I guiltily tucked my nose into the depths of my teacup, wondering again whether she was able to read minds. She certainly seemed to have a knack for echoing my thoughts. And for being direct.

"You needn't be afraid of me, you know."

I set my cup down, deciding to face the shadow of fear that had settled around my shoulders. "I'm not afraid. Just . . . curious. I've never met a witch before, and . . . well, I'm sure you know what people say."

"Were you wondering where I keep my pointed hat and bubbling cauldron?"

Laughter trebled up from her throat, the bell-clear sound hugging around us like a mantle of softest cashmere.

I grinned, sheepishly, in spite of myself. "Something like that."

"Well, my dear. I don't show my magical tools to just anyone. But if you are truly curious, ask me again sometime. Like persistence, curiosity has its own rewards."

It also killed the cat, but I wasn't about to bring that up.

A twittering peal broke the spell, and I waited while Felicity delved into the beaded velvet bag that she had left on her desk. She unfolded her cell phone.

"Liss here. Oh. Hello." Her voice trailed off, and I watched as her face stilled. "Oh. Has anything happened? You sound so strange. Well . . . yes, of course I can come out. Someone's there? Have you rung the police? Oh. Yes, I see. No, calm down. Do try not to panic. I need to make a few phone calls, and then I'll be out. Yes, straightaway. There is nothing to be afraid of. No. Don't *do* anything. Leave the house if you feel threatened."

I couldn't believe what I was hearing. What on earth was going on? I could faintly hear the tones of a woman's voice on the other end of the line. I chewed on the soft flesh of my lower lip as the tension became a palpable force surrounding us.

"All right, then. Do try to stay calm. I'll be right there."

Felicity held the phone in her hands with her eyes closed for several moments before looking up at me rather blankly, as though she'd forgotten I was there. "Excuse me for a moment, will you, Maggie?"

"Of course."

She left me in the office while she went through to the storefront to make her calls. I tried not to listen—really I did—but there was no door to block the sound of her voice.

"Right-o. It's only that she sounded so strange. Not at all right. Anyway, thank you, Marcus. I'm so glad I found you at home."

I grabbed a featherduster from the little cubby and tried to look busy dusting the shelves before she poked her head back between the drapes.

"Maggie, I hate to do this, but I'm afraid it simply cannot be helped. I'm going to have to leave you here alone for a while."

Alone? Eek. Nothing like being thrown into the thick of things straight off.

"A—friend—of mine has a bit of an emergency, and I've promised to help her. Don't worry, it's probably nothing. Everything will be fine. I'll show you how to run the cash register. Just ring up the purchases for any customers who may come in and don't worry about anything else for the time being. I'll leave you my cell phone number in case you run into difficulty." She patted my hand, her thoughts already a million miles away. "I'll return as soon as I can."

I nodded, my pulse quickening with the urgency I heard in her voice. "You go. I'll be fine here."

The brass bell at the front of the store tinkled then, and we both turned as one toward the sound.

"Liss? You back there?"

The voice was deep, a little gravelly, and alive with that riff of authority that could always be relied upon in a person of the male persuasion.

Felicity lifted her head. "I'll be right with you, Marcus." To me, she said, "Let's go up front. I have a friend I'd like you to meet."

I followed her to the storefront I'd not yet had the opportunity to explore. Standing in the doorway was a young man in what I guessed to be his early twenties, his long rangy body covered head to toe in sleek black leather. Dark wavy hair fell down below his shoulders, while his eyes were hidden behind a pair of oblong, Generation X–ish black shades. He looked dark, a little dangerous, and at the risk of making my dead grandmother roll over in her grave, a whole lot sexy. In other words, the last kind of person I would have expected to frequent a store like Enchantments.

A slow smile touched his lips as I emerged from behind Felicity. "Well, well. Who's your shadow, Liss?"

Felicity motioned me behind the counter. "Maggie

O'Neill, may I present a dear friend of mine, Marcus Quinn. Maggie is my new associate, Marcus. Maggie, Marcus helps me with one of my . . . pet projects."

As she walked me through the operation of the register, I couldn't help wondering what kind of project a twenty-something man could assist a forty-something-year-old woman with. The thought made me smile.

"Right-o, then," Felicity said, breezing back to pick up her wool wrap. "Maggie, we'll be back soon. My number is on the pad by the register. Ring me if you run into trouble."

Marcus followed Felicity out the back. I trailed behind them both, looking on from the doorway as Marcus held the door for Felicity. I might not have known quite what to make of him, but I couldn't help admiring the view. There was something about a man in black that made me think of all those things Grandma Cora had always warned me against.

Parked next to Liss's Lexus was a motorcycle, a sleek little foreign number. It seemed to perfectly suit Marcus's personality, or at least what little I knew of it. As he walked past it, he gave the bike's seat a fond pat before turning to duck into the waiting car.

He looked up as he swung the car door open and caught me watching him. Again that slow, delicious smile. Before I could turn away, he hooked a fingertip over the bridge of his shades to lower them, revealing eyes a startling shade of blue that surprised me all the more by aiming a saucy wink in my direction before he, too, disappeared into the belly of Felicity's car.

I stood at the door for several moments after they'd purred out of sight, wondering why I felt so unnervingly off-kilter. And then a laugh bubbled up in my throat. I had spent *way* too many years buried in that tomb called Suitable Employment. Marcus Quinn was the hottest thing I'd seen in ages, a vision in black leather, and he'd just winked at me. Innocent gesture or no, my pulse was tooling along like an Indy 500 pace car. I was grinning like a maniac. For God's sake, I was all but drooling. If he'd known how long it had been since a man had seen my bed, he would have run away in abject terror.

Too bad he was already taken.

For one self-indulgent moment, I allowed myself to envy my new boss—a lovely and generous woman who deserved a fling with a young studmuffin as much as anyone, I reminded my dark side. Besides, I didn't need a man right now anyway. Now was the time to get everything back on track, to figure out who I was and what I wanted to do with the rest of my life before I got all distracted by a soul mate with a bod for sin. And I most definitely did not need a dark and dangerous hell-raiser like Marcus Quinn.

By that time my conscience was raising holy hell, so with one last sigh I shut the door and returned to my post.

For some people the voice of their conscience comes in silent thought form. For others, it's more vocal, but always an extension of their own voice. Mine was the voice I'd heard so often as a high-strung and imaginative child—the stern, commanding voice of my Grandma Cora. Grandma Cora was the quintessential Hoosier farmer's wife. As a child I'd been terrified of her, a short squat woman of Irish and German descent with capable hands and a no-nonsense attitude. I had spent a lot of time with her when my mom went through her Tupperware Lady stint way back in the early eighties. While my mom spent her evenings burping plastic bowls at parties, I spent mine watching my grandma knead hundreds of loaves of bread and pluck countless chickens bald. She saw my childhood fears and imaginings as nonsense and often told me the best way to overcome them was to face them head on. Maybe that was what had prompted her to stick a big, fat tomato worm down my shirt when I had refused to help her knock them from the plants at the tender age of nine.

My grandma would have scared the crap out of Genghis Khan.

I knew for a fact Grandma wouldn't like this new direction my life was taking. Grandma thought good Catholic women found good Catholic husbands and stayed home to raise their scores of children into, you guessed it, good Catholics. According to Grandma, good Catholic women did something with their lives that truly mattered. Apparently working hard to keep one's head above water doesn't count. As it turned out, Grandma Cora and my mom had a lot in common. Thanks to some character defect I no doubt inherited from my dad's side, I've spent most of my life trying to prove them both wrong.

I wandered through the storefront, wondering what I should do first. It felt strange being alone in the shop when I'd only worked there for a total of, oh, ten minutes. Not uncomfortable, just odd. I decided now was the perfect time to familiarize myself with all of the merchandise without Felicity's all-knowing gaze on me.

First things first: music.

Beneath the counter I found a small stereo and a supply of CDs with names like *Ocean Waves* and *Earth Mother*. Most of the time I preferred my music with words, but these would do for now. I popped in *Green Rain*, smiling as the healing sounds of a gentle shower filled the room, and began a leisurely drift through the stacks of goodies.

I still couldn't believe my good luck. In addition to the lovely gifts and antiques, there was a bar for gourmet teas imported from England, specialty coffees, and fine chocolates. In one corner a monstrous Gothic cabinet held court. The bulk spices and herbs filling its pull-down bins made the entire area smell as exotic as a Marrakesh street market. Later I would take the time to go through each drawer one by one for a delightful olfactory experience, but for now I wanted to complete my storewide inventory. Lost in the moment, I opened decorating books and trailed my fingers across fabric swatches, delighted in pictorial compositions of the English countryside, sighed for a china tea set that cost about as much as my car, and daydreamed over a book about ancient Stonehenge.

Such lovely, lovely things.

But taking inventory of my surroundings turned out to be even more of an adventure than I had at first anticipated. Behind an unmarked four-panel door that I'd expected to reveal the bathroom, I found a stairway leading to an upper level. The stairs opened loft-style to a large well-lit space, easily half the size of the lower section of the store. Shelves dominated one whole end of the room, library-style, the windows above them displaying nothing but sky. The air in the room seemed unusually still to me, hushed in the way St. Cather-

ine's is during the day when there are only a few scattered
church members crouched on kneelers throughout the dimly
lit chapel. I moved forward slowly toward the shelves, quiet-
ing my steps upon the wide oak floorboards.

Something about this place . . .

The hairs on my arms stood up as I approached an enormous round braided rug devoid of furnishings in the center of
the room. Unnerved by the sensation, I stopped in my tracks
and ended up taking a circuitous path around it to the shelves,
never quite ridding myself of the feeling that I was intruding.

If I had any doubts as to the eccentricities of Felicity's religious habits, those doubts were entirely erased by the items
on the shelves in that quiet, quiet space. This was no ordinary
book collection. This was a glimpse into the hidden and mysterious world of occult practice. There were books on witchcraft by the hundreds, whose titles made mention of things
such as wicca, wita, pecti-wita, and strega, whose authors possessed names from the mundane, Raymond Buckland, to the
exotic, such as Zsuzsanna Budapest, to the strangely poetic
Starhawk. Other books referred to goddesses, from the Celtic
to Greek, Egyptian, even Sumerian. There were books on
Buddhism, Hinduism, and Shintoism. Qabala and Kabbalah.
Shamanic magick, ceremonial magick, sympathetic magick,
practical magick, crystal and herbal correspondences, and
your basic candle spells. Elements, elementals, spirits, haunt-
ings, stone circles, and yes, even crop circles. Enough woo-
woo topics to make your head spin, *Exorcist*-style. And then
there were catalogs for places with names like Lady Arwen's
Cauldron, Avalon Cometh, Nightshade Alley, and Magickal
Nights; places where you could get anything and everything
for the practicing pagan.

At first I felt . . . unsettled . . . by the realization that my
boss, who was practically my savior, was in truth and in fact
someone who did not worship God, who uttered spells in the
dark of night, and who would upon her death burn in the fiery
pits of Hell. At least, according to what I'd been taught.

Jerry Springer, come on down.

To follow my grandma's edicts, I should make it my life's
mission to save Felicity's eternal soul, to somehow find a way

to turn her away from the dark side and return her to The Light. But I had long ago begun to question the teachings of my upbringing. How could I possibly think to convince Felicity of the error of her ways when I couldn't convince myself that any of it meant . . . anything? Besides, the whole concept of foisting one's version of reality on every unsuspecting passerby seemed to me rather presumptuous and, well, rude.

Caught up in my musings, I wandered around the perimeter of the room, marveling over a jewel case of crystals of all shapes, colors, and sizes. Another held all manner of jewelry—all silver, all distinctive. One piece, a brooch in the shape of a serpentine Celtic knot with a large pearlescent stone set in the center, was a duplicate of the pin Felicity had worn on the morning we first met. A large pharmaceuticals chest contained drawers labeled with the old-fashioned names of plants and herbs like mugwort, vervain, mandrake, and yarrow. Spell components, I gathered.

Despite the strange and unfamiliar contents of the loft, I felt comfortable here. But one question remained in my mind.

What would make a woman as worldly and intelligent as Felicity believe in the superstitious world of magic?

I had no answer.

I found myself wandering back to the books, running my fingertips over the spines. An insatiable curiosity burned in me; I couldn't seem to help myself. Biting my lip, I screwed up my courage and hooked an index finger over the binding of one, tipping it outward. It fell into my hand, its worn binding allowing it to fall open to a passage by Dorothy Valiente.

I began to read:

I am the gracious Goddess who gives the gift of joy unto the heart of man, upon Earth I give knowledge of the Spirit eternal, and beyond death I give peace and freedom and reunion with those who have gone before; nor do I demand sacrifice, for behold I am the Mother all living, and my love is poured out upon the Earth.

That wasn't as bad as I would have thought. In fact . . .
I stared at the page, mesmerized by the words that were

strangely sensible. But that . . . that was crazy. An illusion. It was the author's voice, her lyrical turn-of-phrase. That's what had drawn my attention. That's all.

Normal people just didn't believe in magic.

From below, the front bell tinkled. The sound startled me from my reverie. Eyes wide, I snapped the book shut and held very still, hoping against hope whoever was down below would go away.

Typical hand-in-the-cookie-jar behavior. Inexcusably spineless.

I set my jaw. *Margaret Mary-Catherine O'Neill, this is your life. Isn't it about time you got it together?*

I responded to the mental admonishment in the way I'd always responded to Grandma's insights: quickly, and with the knowledge that the alternative would somehow be much worse. Getting to my feet, I straightened my sensible imitation-mohair sweater (Did I tell you how much I love Wal-Mart?) before descending the stairs as quickly as possible. It wasn't until I hit the landing that I realized I still had the witch book in my hand.

Damn.

As a last resort, I tucked it under my arm and headed toward my post at the register. I could ditch it beneath the counter when no one was looking. There was no way I was going to set it down in plain sight.

An elderly woman had entered the store. She glanced up when I stepped through the door, but only barely. It wasn't until I took a seat on a tall stool behind the counter that she acknowledged me.

"New here, aren't you?"

I smiled politely, ready to test my erstwhile submerged people skills. "Yes, ma'am. Today is my first day."

Her smallish eyes lowered, taking in my appearance. "Thought so. Didn't know Felicity was looking to hire someone. She might have said. I might have put in an application myself if I'd've known that to be the case." Having completed her assessment of my person, she sniffed and went back to pawing through a tall stack of crisp white linens.

My cheeks felt as hot as flame. The woman's sniff was an

obvious dismissal. Obviously she found me lacking. Probably in some way pertaining to Enchantment's employee discount policy. Despite that insight, I nudged the book beneath the counter before I gave her something else with which to take exception.

After an eternity of mauling Felicity's careful antique textile display, the woman brought a single handkerchief to the counter. It was white, plain, its only adornment a chain-stitch of white floss following within an inch of its hemmed border.

I rang up the purchase, doing my best to appear efficient. "Will there be anything else?" I asked politely.

Her puckered mouth pinched even tighter. "What is it about big business these days? Always pushing extras on hardworking folks like me. If there was anything else I had in mind, I would have said so, now, wouldn't I?"

My smile held. It was a struggle, but it did. "I'm sorry. I didn't mean to offend."

"Hunh."

"That will be three-fifteen."

Digging into a bag the size of Montana, she managed to come up with three ones after only five minutes. The fifteen pennies—yes, that's right, pennies—took slightly longer.

"Don't forget to initial my receipt," she commanded as I wrapped the scrap of fabric in tissue paper and placed it in a tiny paper sack. "I don't want any hassles if I decide to return this. It's overpriced as it is, and if I find something better across the street, I'll be wanting my money back."

My blood pressure edged a notch higher. I gritted my teeth. "Of course."

Tucking everything into her mammoth purse, she gave me a stern look. "And don't think I won't advise Ms. Dow that you were neglecting your post in her absence. Frittering about in the back room. I think she has a right to know the truth about her employees. My duty as a steady customer."

With that and a high-minded sniff, she slung the bag over her arm and turned up her nose before heading for the door.

I stared glumly toward the display windows, certain I'd just signed my own pink slip. *That* couldn't have gone any worse.

Maybe Mel was right. Maybe I wasn't cut out for a job with the public.

Thankfully my trip down Self-Pity Lane proved short and sweet. The rest of the morning flew by with a steady stream of customers with cash at the ready, and none so sour as the purse-mouthed biddy who'd been my first. Thank God. She'd nearly succeeded in ending my career in retail, but later customers cured my momentary lapse of faith, and I persevered. By the time the noon siren blared, I was knee-deep in customers and merchandise deliveries. An hour later, the lunch crowd thinned a bit and I finally had a moment to myself. I sat down on the stool behind the counter and gazed, exhausted but happy, at the deliveries piling up, waiting to be opened. What wonders would I find in their corrugated cardboard depths? Oh, but Felicity had said only to ring up purchases and never mind the rest for now. Sighing wistfully, I stowed them in the storage room, then went in search of something to assuage the growling beast of my stomach.

One PB&J and a snack bag of chips later, and I was still alone and needing to find something to amuse myself. I changed the music to yet another New Age selection—Celtic pipes this time. I dusted the merchandise. I cleaned the telephone keypad. I refolded the whites the Cantankerous One had left in a jumble. Finally there were no chores remaining. Left to its own idle resources, my mind began to wander.

Specifically, I began to wonder why Felicity had not yet returned. Or at the very least, called.

I frowned as I tried to recall Felicity's part in the phone conversation this morning. What had she said? Had she mentioned anything about whom she would be seeing? Where she was going? She'd been gone for hours without a word. While I appreciated her trust in me, I couldn't believe that I had done anything to warrant that level of confidence.

Should I call her cell?

All my life I've been a worrier, even when unprovoked or unmerited. But just then, at that precise moment, I felt a soul-deep certainty unlike anything I'd ever felt before.

Something was wrong.

Very wrong.

The bell above the door jangled again, sending my heart into apoplexy. I looked up and nearly choked on my PB&J. Standing on the threshold in the neatly pressed uniform of our local police force was a prime example of the boys in blue. I made some hurried mental calculations.

Age? Mid-thirties or I'd eat my featherduster.

Eye color? Undetermined.

Arms of steel? Oh yeah.

My stomach did some loop-de-loops of nervous appreciation. If I hadn't been so anxious about Felicity's extended absence, I might just have batted my eyelashes. As it was, all I could do was stare.

He came forward, his movements deliberate and slow. "Miss O'Neill?"

Could it be any more perfect? He knew my name.

Wait a sec. *How* could he know my name?

"Can I help you, Officer . . . ?"

"Fielding, ma'am. Deputy Fielding." He didn't move a muscle. I couldn't see his eyes, but from behind his mirrored aviators (a throwback to the eighties?) I sensed that he was watching me closely. "Your employer, Felicity Dow, asked me to bring these to you."

He held out his hand. A strong, capable hand, with calluses at the base of each finger. I couldn't help noticing.

I also couldn't miss the heavy gold band. Married. Damn and double damn.

With a wistful sigh, I shifted my gaze one inch south of the wedding band. In his palm he held a ring of keys. On the ring was a silver charm in the shape of a coiled Celtic knot.

Felicity's keys.

I frowned, trying to make sense of the offering. "I don't understand. Why would Felicity send me her keys? Is she all right? Has there been an accident or something?"

He didn't answer right away. Instead he turned slightly, making a slow sweep of the store from behind his sunglasses. "Miss O'Neill, how well do you know Ms. Dow?"

The question took me by surprise. "Not very, I suppose. I've only started working for her this morning."

"You may want to rethink that decision."

"Why would I want to do that?"

He reached up and slowly, purposely removed his sunglasses. "Isabella Harding was found dead this morning."

My eyebrows stretched to new heights. Isabella Harding was the wife of one of the richest men in town. "I don't know what to say. How does that affect—"

"The late Mrs. Harding is Ms. Dow's estranged sister. Ms. Dow is at the station right now for questioning in the matter."

Simple words. Straightforward. They might as well have been Greek. I stared into his unsmiling gray green eyes. "Are you trying to tell me that you believe Felicity was somehow involved?"

"I'm telling you she's being questioned," he replied without a trace of emotion as he slipped his glasses back on. As if that alone were explanation enough. "Let me give you a piece of friendly advice, Miss O'Neill. Find yourself another job. Get yourself far, far away from here, before Ms. Dow's secret world swallows you whole."

He nodded crisply and turned to leave. My head was spinning. This wasn't the first murder Stony Mill had seen, nor would it be the last. But it was the first I'd been involved in, however remote that involvement. There was something sobering about that, a gravity that took me by the throat and made me feel hot and cold all at once.

Could Felicity somehow have been involved in the death of her own sister? And what about Marcus? Where was he now, and what did he know about all of this?

Questions begged answers, and the only way I was going to get some anytime soon was to go straight to the source.

Before I knew what I was doing, I held up my hand. "Wait!"

Even as he turned to look at me, I had grabbed the keys off the counter and was shoving things into my purse. "Do you mind telling me why?" he asked.

"Because I'm coming with you."

Chapter 3

I waited, shivering, in the unheated lobby of the local cop shop for five solid hours for Felicity to be released. For the most part I was ignored, a nondescript lump of ice taking up space on one of the metal folding chairs that had been left stacked in a corner. Every once in a while, the Tic Tac–popping dispatcher took pity on me and brought me a cup of incredibly bad, watered-down coffee. It was better than nothing, but only just. The time wasn't a total waste, however. An hour into the wait, I discovered I had inadvertently shoved the witch book into my bag, so I spent the rest of the time going back and forth between eavesdropping on the banter and jargon peculiar to those in law enforcement and sneaking peeks into the strange and compelling world of magick, spelled with a *k*, I learned, to differentiate it from the optical illusions performed by sideshow magicians.

And what an eye-opener it was. Too bad it was all just make-believe. I had to admit, it would be nice to be able to believe in wishes and fairies and making things happen purely by strength of will. And it made me wonder, too, when and why our childish faith in all things magical suddenly abandons us. When had I stopped believing? What darkness had crept into my life that made me realize I was on my own?

At least the book accomplished one thing. It kept me from

thinking about my new boss, and whether the police were serious in questioning her about the circumstances surrounding her sister's death.

When Felicity finally emerged, dusk was casting long shadows across the institutional brown carpet. Two uniformed officers escorted her from the back room, that mysterious place they took all potential miscreants for questioning. Our town boys prided themselves on a ninety-five percent arrest rate. In my humble opinion that seemed a bit high, but if exaggeration kept the citizens of Stony Mill happy, who was I to quibble? Placation has its advantages. Just ask my mom. I've been placating her for years.

As I watched from my hidden vantage point in the corner, Felicity swung her wrap around her slender shoulders with her signature savoir faire before turning to her escorts.

"My thanks, lads. I appreciate your efforts. Truly I do. Despite your regretful tendencies to believe the worst of me."

Her eyes twinkled and she might as well have twitched her nose, à la Samantha on TV's *Bewitched*. One of the officers, fortyish and with the kind of ramrod comportment that screamed ex-military, flushed to his thinning hairline and shifted uneasily from foot to foot.

"Ms. Dow. I hope . . . I'm very sorry for your loss today. Very sorry. But God, God will see justice is done."

His voice trailed away, but I didn't need to hear his ineffectual stammering to realize the man was a little sweet on her. I wondered if Felicity knew. Then I noticed the little smile playing around her lips and the speculative glances she cast through her eyelashes. Oh yeah, Felicity knew, and she was playing it up. To the hilt.

Smart woman.

The second cop, whom I recognized as Jim Cowpin, Stony Mill High class of '88, stepped in to save him with a steadying hand to his shoulder. "We appreciate you coming in, ma'am. I'm sorry it has to come to this, but of course you realize we're only doing our jobs."

"I wouldn't have it any other way."

Cowpin paused. Cleared his throat. "I'm, uh, afraid we'll have to ask you to remain in the area."

Felicity's laugh was throaty and warm. "Don't leave town, is that it, boys?"

He held his ground. "I'm afraid so, ma'am."

"Very well, then. In the event that my presence is required elsewhere, I shall dutifully obtain the approval of the Stony Mill Police Department first. Fair enough? Then I bid you good evening, gentlemen."

She caught sight of me as she turned toward the door. Surprise flickered across her face, followed closely by gratitude. "Maggie! I cannot tell you how wonderful it is to see you! But you shouldn't have come, my dear. Nasty business, this lot."

The mother of all understatements. "How are you holding up, Felicity?" I asked politely.

She cast a barely perceptible glance over her left shoulder at the two uniformed officers who watched on, then gave me a meaningful look. "Let's get away from here, shall we? It's been rather a long day."

Outside, the evening air was crisp and smelled faintly of burning leaves. The yellow glow of the street lamps made our shadows stretch in front of us, unnaturally long and slender. Silence followed us out of the police station, broken only by the faraway buzz of a leaf blower. Now that we were away from the watchful eye of the police, I felt a little funny and more than a little uncertain. Questions kept popping into my head. Questions like, was I right to trust Felicity; and was I doing the right thing?

Get a grip, Maggie.

"Is your car here?" I asked to distract myself.

"My . . . ?" Felicity blinked at me. "No. My goodness, I'd nearly forgotten. It's at . . . the house. My sister's, I mean." She gave me a rueful smile. "I must be getting dotty in my old age."

My natural wariness thawed, just a bit. "Who wouldn't be a bit out of sorts after what you've been through today?" I soothed. I patted her on the arm. "My car's down this way. Come on. I'll take you home."

Some might question my afternoon vigil, much less my offer of a ride home to a murder suspect. But realistically I knew that if Felicity Dow *had* offed her sister, she wouldn't be likely to add fuel to the coals of suspicion by going on a deadly rampage. I mean, who would mind the store? Besides, I didn't want to believe she could be guilty. I liked her. And there was no way I was just going to leave her stranded. Not when she was standing there, lost and utterly alone. I would take her home, because that was the decent thing to do.

Not to get her car, though. Even if we were able to gain access to her late (I tried not to gulp) sister's property, I wasn't at all sure that I wanted to find myself at the scene of a murder a scant eight hours after it took place. Indiana might be cornfields and apple pie to everyone else, but it could be damned eerie after dark with the moon rising high and a fresh wind kicking at the trees. And with a killer running loose . . .

I shivered involuntarily, and my gaze slid sideways. Just for a second.

Oblivious to my nervousness, Felicity stood by while I unlocked her door, then she slid immediately into the old bucket seat with a sigh of relief and closed her eyes. Just as quickly my moment of unease was replaced by concern. She had been so composed before, and was so silent now. I hurried around to the driver's side and got in, locking the door behind me. Christine started on the first try for once. I fiddled with the radio dials in an attempt to tune in something calming, but tonight the only thing coming from the antique radio was static. Giving up, I turned at last to Felicity and touched her neatly folded hands.

"Liss?" The shortened version of her name flowed easily from my lips, as if I'd been calling her that for years. "Liss, you're going to have to tell me where you live."

"Hmm? Oh, sorry, dear. Victoria Park Road. About six miles out."

I tried to keep my protective instincts in check as I put Christine into gear and steered her up the hill toward Main Street. They tended to rear up whenever I saw an MLV (Most Likely Victim) singled out. That's me: Maggie O'Neill, Queen of the Underdogs. I just couldn't seem to help it. In light of recent events and by virtue of her spiritual beliefs, Felicity was in great danger of becoming Most Likely #1 in my book. Instinct told me I could trust her, but common sense was telling me to move slowly. I needed more information.

Victoria Park was a former Indian trail, a winding country road that meandered through farm fields and pockets of woods. It was lovely in the summer, with a shelter of leafy bowers overhead, breathtaking in autumn with a gold red shower of falling leaves, austere and commanding in winter and spring. I knew it fairly well, having discovered it on one of my solitary sojourns through the countryside on yet another date-challenged Saturday night. Not that I have a lot of those. All right, okay, so I do. Sue me.

I stopped at the railroad tracks to look for trains. We were approaching my favorite part of the road, where two expensive properties rested side by side, delineated by long lengths of elaborate limestone and iron fencing and grand security gates. The fencing styles had changed several times over the last few years, each time advancing in expense and splendor until the competition ended last September with the current models. Rumors had long circulated town about the quarreling neighbors, each trying to outdo the other. Like Dueling Banjos, on a more grandiose scale.

"There. Just there—turn right."

So of course it stood to reason that my new boss was one of the sparring fence owners. Good thing I hadn't spouted off about them.

Obediently, I cranked the wheel hard right and pulled onto a paved asphalt drive until the curlicued gate halted my progress. I paused uncertainly, wondering whether we needed to call someone, somewhere, to unlock it. Before I could ask, Felicity delved into the depths of her bag and pulled out a tiny handheld gadget. It made a funny *ptchew-ptchew* sound that reminded me a little of Space Invaders, then the scissorlike gates swung slowly open.

"You'll need to hurry through once they're open, dear. They won't remain so for long."

I managed to conquer this new challenge and eased up the winding wooded drive, through a darkness that was nearly complete. In the glow of my high-beams, the trees and underbrush writhed and twisted in the rising wind, like pale and spindly kokopelli ghosts dancing eerily around us.

Our destination remained hidden until I guided Christine round the last bend in the drive. A second soft *ptchew-ptchew* sounded to my right and security lights blazed to life. My mouth fell open. Situated in a shallow bowl behind the screen of trees was an enormous home reminiscent of an old English manor, complete with mellow brick and Gothic-style windows.

"This is yours?" I squeaked.

Felicity gave an odd half-smile. "Home sweet home."

"Nice place."

I tried not to think of my basement apartment, which in the cold light of day looked like, well, a basement.

We parked beneath a carriage port that sheltered a rear entrance. Poor old Christine looked desperately shabby in such exalted surroundings. I gave her a loyal, if consoling, pat on the hood and hovered nearby as Felicity unlocked the door.

"Well . . ." I said, not wanting her to think I was trying to overstay my welcome. I mean, I was dying to see inside her gorgeous house, and I wanted even more to hear what had happened today, but I wasn't about to foist myself upon her at a time like this.

"You will be staying, of course," Felicity cut in before I could finish my thought. Her tone brooked no refusal and displayed a bit of the strength that had slipped away from her for a time. "I'd appreciate the company."

"If you're sure . . ."

She smiled and swept her arm toward the door. "Welcome to The Gables."

We stepped into a large foyer, expensively finished with gleaming woods and sky-high ceiling beams. A single lamp cast a pale circle of light that barely touched the airy space. In awe, I tipped my head back to gaze at a chandelier that hovered high above our heads. Dripping with crystals, it shimmered and sparkled in the faint moonlight that drifted through a window above the door.

I was about to comment on the beauty of the room when a shadow peeled away from a deeper well of blackness near the stairs. In what felt like slow motion, I snapped my head forward, brought my hands up, and opened my mouth to scream before I realized that Felicity had also noticed the intruder and didn't seem at all alarmed.

"Marcus," she said, the pleasure in her voice understated, but very much in evidence. "I might have expected as much."

She moved forward to greet him with a tight hug that had me inspecting the details on the molding and wondering if I should announce my departure. It was one thing to suspect my boss of having an affair with a studly young bohunk. It was quite another to be faced with outright proof of it.

"Are you all right, Liss?" he asked, staring into her eyes.

She laughed softly and pressed her palm to his cheek. "Right as rain, ducks."

"I don't believe that for a minute. Hey, I parked my bike in the garage, as usual. You don't mind, do you?"

That would explain why I hadn't seen anything when I pulled Christine up underneath the carriage port.

"Of course not. Have I ever?"

He muttered something under his breath for her ears alone, and she nodded; then she turned and held out her hand to me. "Good heavens, we're being rude. Marcus, why don't you show Maggie around while I fix drinks. Maggie, what will you have?"

"Um, well, iced tea?" I felt myself blush, but I stood my ground. I didn't feel comfortable enough with the situation to lower my guard. If only to assuage my own uneasiness, I needed to keep my wits about me.

"Iced tea it is. Marcus?"

His fingertips lingered as he slipped her wrap from her shoulders. "Tea sounds good."

"Three for tea, then."

She disappeared through a door to our right, leaving me alone with her young studmuffin. In true guy form, Marcus tossed the cashmere shawl casually over an antique Windsor chair and held out his hands for my jacket, waiting. I took an involuntary step backward. The prospect of giving it up, of relinquishing even a shred of my security, heightened my already niggling feelings of vulnerability, and I didn't like it. I shook my head. "Thanks, but I'll keep it for now," I told him vaguely. "I'm a little cold."

He shrugged. "Suit yourself." But I couldn't mistake the speculative glance that he swept down my body, nor could I misinterpret the amusement that flickered in his eyes. "So. Would you like a look-see?"

I would. I did.

I had grown up firmly entrenched in middle-class America, with middle-class values and aspirations (although my mother would be the first to tell you I'm a habitual underachiever). What I found in Felicity's home left me boggled. Outside, it was all English Renaissance. Inside the mellow brick home it was simply fine living. The house was decorated in hunting prints and heavy moldings, massive hearths, and a masculine sort of elegance that didn't seem to fit Felicity's natural chintz-and-sunshine chic but was beautiful nonetheless. Straight from the ritziest decorating journals, the rooms were enormous, the ceilings high, and the furniture out of this world. Martha Stewart, eat your heart out.

"Nice," was all I could think to say.

"Yeah."

We were standing in the middle of an upstairs guestroom, near a massive bed with a velvet canopy and curtains, the fairytale room of a princess from a faraway land. I stretched out a finger to stroke the midnight blue velvet and caught sight of myself in the dressing table mirror, across the room. My face was alight with awe and wide-eyed amazement.

I shook my head. "Clearly I am out of my league here."

He arched a brow and gave me a quizzical smirk. "You mean the fancy trappings?"

A little embarrassed, I shrugged.

"Liss isn't like that. This house was her husband's dream. I think she'd be just as happy in a little cottage somewhere, just doing her own thing."

"Ah." I latched on to the nugget of information greedily. I knew so little about her. This was my chance for some inside info from someone who knew her intimately. I wasn't about to let it pass me by. "Why does she stay?"

"I suppose she feels she owes it to him. To his memory." He rested a hip against the high mattress and crossed his arms. The briefest glimpse of a tattoo tantalized me from beneath the sleeve of his black T-shirt, but it was his eyes that made me shiver. As blue as blue could be, clear as crystal, all-knowing. "Never mind why Liss is here. I want to know why you're here."

The directness of his approach took me off guard. I'd never been very good with confrontation. I stared at him while all of the smart answers flew right out of my head and I was left with nothing more than the truth to fill the empty space. "I don't know exactly," I admitted.

"I mean, I guess I'm here to find out the truth. And because I feel sorry for Felicity. Today had to be total hell."

"Yeah."

I let my eyes drop to his folded arms, to where I'd seen the tattoo peek out. It was a stylized Celtic knot, I could see now, with a star at its center. Something clicked in my head, just beyond my grasp.

"Liss is . . ." He paused as though struggling with his thoughts. "She's strong, but too independent. She won't ask for help. She likes to think she can take care of everything on her own. That's one of the reasons she made me leave her when the police wanted to question her further down at the station. I can be pretty opinionated, I guess, and she knew I'd have a hard time waiting around without kicking up some trouble. I guess she knows me pretty well, at that."

Ah. That explained why he had let her go through all of that on her own. I had wondered. At least I knew now that it hadn't been his choice after all to abandon Liss to the wolves.

"You're worried about her." I voiced the thought aloud before I knew what I was doing, but I knew instantly that it was true. I knew a lot of things that way. Always had. It was a particular talent of mine. I liked to call it reading people. Body language, eyes—both tell the undercurrents of a story most people are simply too busy to listen to. The times when I knew details I shouldn't were what really bothered me. Usually I chalked it up to luck, but sometimes I couldn't help wondering . . .

"She's been through a lot this year. She handles it well, but—"

He broke off abruptly as Felicity appeared in the door.

"There you are!" She beamed at us. "I've been looking everywhere for you. Drinks are ready belowstairs, whenever you are."

I smiled at her use of the Queen's English. I couldn't help myself.

"Have you eaten anything?" she went on, leading the way toward the stairs.

"You mean besides the LifeSavers I found in my pocket?" I quipped.

"No one should be forced to eat lint-covered LifeSavers at a time like this," she countered, proving she hadn't lost her sense of humor. "Come, come. Do you care for eggs? I scramble a splendid cheese omelet, if I do say so myself. Marcus?"

"I'd kill for one of your omelets. Kidding!" he said, holding up his hands in surrender when he saw my face. "Bad joke, never mind. I'm right behind you."

We followed her to one of the best-equipped private kitchens I had ever seen. Clean lines, slick surfaces, stainless-steel appliances that gleamed in the bright lighting. This was not your everyday Hoosier kitchen. Professional grade all the way.

"Cooking was my husband's favorite hobby," she said, catching the upward drift of my eyebrows. "He loved this room. I, on the other hand, scarcely know my way around a hotplate. Except for eggs and a good cup of tea, of course. Everyone should have at least one specialty."

And she wasn't exaggerating about hers. Within minutes I was wrapping my tongue around buttery soft eggs that made my tastebuds sing. I gorged myself like I hadn't eaten in weeks, reveling in the experience, then leaned back against my chair, satiated and happy. Marcus, on the other hand, scarcely touched his. All his attention was focused on the woman opposite him.

"You're not eating," Felicity said in a quiet voice.

Marcus glanced down at his plate. "Neither are you."

"It's been a rather trying day."

Typical English understatement, that stiff-upper-lip mentality we Americans found so alien, so . . . coolly detached. What secrets did it hide from the casual observer?

"Have you told her about what happened?" he asked, jerking his head in my direction.

Felicity's glance flicked to me. "Not yet."

"I think you should."

"I'm not sure where to begin."

I reached out a hand in encouragement. "I know that your sister was killed. What I don't know is how or why. Why don't we just go over what happened. Step by step. How did you get mixed up in all of this?"

Felicity sighed and stared down into the glass of tea she held with both hands. "Goddess if I know. Isabella and I . . . we didn't have what one would consider a close relationship. It pains me to say, but it's true. We'd scarcely exchanged two words since . . ." She paused, a pained frown marring her brow. "Since Gerald—my husband—left this world for the next."

I thought of Mel and her picture-perfect life, and the way my mother never let an opportunity pass by to draw my attention to it. "Sisters aren't always close. Sometimes water *is* thicker than blood. Sometimes blood gets infected. Poisoned by outside influences that are difficult to overcome."

Felicity nodded, lost in thought. "When she called this morning, however, none of that mattered."

The phone call. Of course. "What did she want?"

Felicity exchanged a glance with Marcus. "Maggie, do you believe in ghosts?"

I blinked. "You . . . you mean . . ."

"I mean precisely that. Ghosts. Spirits. Entities from another dimension or time."

"I don't know how to answer that."

"Yes or no would be a good beginning."

"Well . . . I suppose I've never really thought much about it. I mean, certainly I believe it's *possible* for there to exist things we cannot hear or see."

I was reaching here, but I didn't want to hurt her feelings. Besides, I hadn't completely written off the possibility of an omniscient, omnipresent force in the universe, and if one believed in God, then angels, devils, and ghosts weren't *too* much of a stretch.

"Isabella phoned me because she had been having trouble of the paranormal persuasion."

The ultimate in domestic disturbances. "What kind of experiences are we talking about here?"

"I'm not quite sure. All I know is that she was very much afraid this morning."

"Did she elaborate?"

"Not much. Sounds. A sense of being watched, of not being alone. What came into play in this particular instance, I have no idea, but I fear it very well could have killed my sister."

I was trying to keep an open mind, really I was, but it was all just a bit too far out for me. This was the twenty-first century, fergoshsakes. "Do you really believe that?"

"Yes. No. I'm not sure. I suppose it's too much to hope for. The thought that someone might have wanted her dead . . ." Frowning, she traced her fingertip thoughtfully around the rim of her glass. "I found her, you know. Lying crumpled and broken at the base of the stairs, her eyes open and glassy. A pool of blood spreading beneath her head." She lifted her eyes to mine. "Her body was still warm. You have no idea how . . . how difficult that was."

My heart clenched suddenly and I had to lower my eyes. If this was an act for my benefit, it was a very good one.

Marcus rose and went behind her, his hands strong and supportive on her slender shoulders. She reached up and covered one of his hands with her own.

"Liss . . . it may become necessary to create a sequence of events," he told her gently. "Did the cops give you any information? Any at all?"

She shook her head. "Only that they believed Isabella had been . . . dead . . . a very short time. And that the injuries to her head were not solely the result of the fall."

Marcus went still, his eyes shuttered. He cleared his throat. "They're sure?"

She almost smiled. "I assume they know what they're talking about."

"It seems awfully early to be making that kind of judgment call."

"They're the experts."

I wasn't so sure. Having lived in this town my whole life, I knew what kind of *experts* we had on our small police force.

Most were greenhorn young men, with little life experience and even less understanding of the world beyond Stony Mill. The rest were tired middle-aged men, a little soft around the middle, who'd escaped their killer nine-to-five origins for a lower-stress job passing out speeding tickets and busting high schoolers for being stupid enough to keep drugs in their lockers. They were *not* up to the challenge of a murder.

Not even the intense Deputy Fielding.

I cleared my throat. "So Isabella asked you to come out, then?"

"Yes. No—I can hardly remember." Her brow creased as she tried to sharpen the details in her mind. "She didn't ask me, I don't think. But she must have known I'd come. Ghosts, the paranormal. She needed no reminder that the supernatural is my area of expertise. Why else would she call?"

Marcus nodded in agreement. "Right. What next?"

"That must have been around nine-ten, I suppose. I called you then, Marcus. What time would you say that we left here?"

"Ten minutes to cross town. Nine-twenty, nine-twenty-five at the outside."

"We arrived at Isabella's no more than ten minutes after that. Nine-thirty-five or so. Marcus, you said that you saw something in the woods that separates the properties. I parked by the house, and you went to check that out."

I looked up at Marcus. "What did you see?"

He tipped his head back, staring sightlessly at the ceiling. "A flash of movement. Quick. There one moment, gone the next."

"And did you find anything?" I pressed.

"Nothing."

"Mmm." I tried to think of the most diplomatic phrasing. "So, really, it might have been the wind. A squirrel, or maybe even a deer."

"You might think that," he replied equably. "*If* you didn't feel what I felt."

"And what was that?"

He locked his gaze with mine. "Energy signature."

My eyebrows shot up. "I beg your pardon?"

"Someone had been there. Someone with very strong emotions."

Energy signature. Yeah. "I see."

"Marcus is quite correct." Felicity rose to her feet and began to scrape the contents of her plate into the garbage disposal. "When I went up to the house, I felt it, too."

I took a deep breath, trying to still the sudden snap of my nerves. "All right. All that aside, what happened next?"

"While Marcus investigated the movement, I rang the bell. No one answered, which seemed odd. I could hear the bell ringing inside, but nothing else. I tried calling on my cell phone, but that, too, went unanswered. I wondered whether she might have left after all. She had sounded very frightened; it seemed a distinct possibility.

"Something told me to try the doorknob. It was unlocked, so I thought . . . well . . . I could just check. I thought it couldn't hurt to do a quick walk-through and make sure nothing was wrong. She'd asked me to come because of the disturbances; even if she'd left, there might have been residual energies lurking about."

More woo-woo. It was all Greek to me, but Marcus seemed to understand perfectly. "So you opened the door . . ." he prompted.

"I opened the door and stepped inside." Her eyes fixed on Marcus's face, but no light gave life to them, only a haze of memory. "I didn't sense anything . . . *specific* . . . but my fear level had begun to rise. The shades were drawn; it was like twilight inside. Silent as the grave. I went to the kitchen. It was empty, but I could see she'd been having tea and biscuits. There was a wrung-out teabag and a rinsed cup in the sink; a saucer with a biscuit on the table. Her laptop was open next to it, but it had shut down." She took a breath. "I went down the hall. Past the laundry. The butler's pantry. Nothing seemed out of place, really, but it was so . . . bloody . . . quiet. The hairs on my arms and on the back of my neck were standing on end. The air, it felt . . . *wrong*. And then I began to hear the whispers."

Shock and fear spurted through me. "Someone was there?"

Marcus shook his head, his eyes locked on Felicity. "Spirits," he muttered. "Trying to guide her. It's what she does."

She nodded. "I tried to focus on them, but it was all too chaotic. I couldn't pinpoint . . . they were all so insistent." She paused and we waited for her to continue, not wanting to disturb the process that seemed to be taking her on a physical path through her memories of the morning. At length she went on. "I closed my eyes, trying to *feel*. Where to go. What to do. Upstairs? Outside? I remember asking my guides to help me. At that point I think I knew something was very, very wrong. I went down the hall to the foyer and . . ." Her voice trailed away.

"And that's where you found her," Marcus finished for her.

She nodded. "I stepped into the foyer and my eyes dazzled from the sudden glare of sunlight coming through the windows on the landing above. It was so bright that I had to squint and hold my hand out against the light until my eyes adjusted. And then I saw her, lying at the foot of the marble staircase. Not fifteen feet from where I stood. Her legs were twisted beneath her, blood pooled under her head. There were great smears of it here and there along the steps."

I placed my hand over hers, felt it quiver oh-so-slightly beneath mine before she regained control. Across the table, a muscle worked in Marcus's temple, but his face remained expressionless.

"I thought . . . I thought she'd cracked her head open when she'd fallen," Felicity continued, "but the police believe she was struck with something before she fell. 'Localized blunt force trauma,' I believe is what they called it. Pending the results of the forensic review, I'm sure. That doesn't exactly spell accidental death, now, does it."

I had begun to tremble with a slow swell of sympathetic adrenaline. Try as I might, I couldn't rid my mind of the image of Isabella Harding, broken and twisted at the base of the stairs.

A murder. Right here in Stony Mill.

Marcus got to his feet and crossed to the French doors. Despite his languid cowboy-slouch and hands jammed in the back pockets of his low-riding leather pants he looked like he might slam his fist against the glass in frustration at any moment. He stared out at the dark, his gaze darting restlessly back and forth. "There was someone there in the woods. I know it. They could be out there right now. Watching us."

"Oh, Marcus." Felicity shook her head.

"Um," I said, all senses on high alert as my gaze was drawn to the blackness beyond the glass panes, "what makes you think they'd be watching us here?"

"Didn't you know?" Marcus turned away from the window long enough to cast me a curious glance. "The trees—you can't see them very well at the moment, but—they connect with the Harding property."

My mouth went dry. That would mean—

That would mean Isabella Harding was the second half of Dueling Banjos.

Which also meant that her murder took place *right . . . next . . . door.*

Chapter 4

If I lingered over thoughts like that, I'd give myself a serious case of the heebie-jeebies.

I closed my eyes and took a deep breath, willing away the fear that had billowed up inside me.

"I don't think I feel comfortable with you being out here alone," Marcus was saying.

Felicity patted his hand. "I'll be fine."

He turned his hand palm up abruptly and captured hers. "You shouldn't be alone tonight." His chin jutted stubbornly.

"Well . . ." Felicity looked at me. "Perhaps Maggie would be willing to stay the night. I have plenty of room. If you don't mind, of course," she hurried to amend. "Please don't feel obligated if you have other plans."

I gazed back and forth between them, wondering how I'd managed to get myself into this kind of predicament. I didn't know whether I should feel honored by the invitation or maneuvered. Spending the night in a secluded mansion, miles away from town and police and other signs of civilization, alone with someone I wanted to trust but who had recently been questioned in an as-yet unsolved murder . . . well, let's just say it wasn't what I'd expected to be on my itinerary for the evening. But I had no real reason yet to mistrust Felicity, despite her professed dabbling in the Arts. I rather liked her and her nonconformist ways, and I doubted that I was in any kind of danger by staying. Still . . .

What to do, what to do.

In the end, good manners won out. It's just not nice to turn away the request of a friend in need. My grandmother, dead though she may be, would never let me live it down.

Marcus waited downstairs while Felicity showed me to the bedroom nearest the stairs, dimming the lights as we went along. I watched her movements a little nervously. Amazing how a house can take on a menacing quality when cast into shadow.

"The bedding was freshened just yesterday," she said, bustling around the room with a stack of fresh towels and a carafe of water. "I'll just grab something for you to sleep in, and you should have everything you need."

I looked skeptically at her slender figure. "I don't think you have anything that will fit."

"Oh, I think we can find something to suit." She paused, fluffing an already full pillow. "I hope you don't mind if I turn in straightaway. It has been quite a long day."

"Not at all."

She came back with a high-necked flannel gown that would have made my grandmother's heart go pitter-pat. Old-fashioned, but she was right, it could have fit two of me. We said our good nights and I closed the door behind her. As an afterthought, I reached down and turned the key in the lock. Better safe than sorry.

I sat on the edge of the bed a moment, listening to her footsteps echo down the flight of stairs. Going down to say good night to Marcus, no doubt.

I picked up the gown, fingering the soft flannel as I looked around the room. Crocheted lace dripped from the massive bed's lintels, while on the mattress itself a soft chenille duvet cradled me in goosedown comfort. An eight-foot secretary towered next to the window, while a three-way mirror and a dressing table with a chintz skirt completed the ensemble near the door. The room lacked nothing in the way of amenities, but I felt anything but comfortable as I found my gaze drawn toward the window and the darkness beyond.

I thought about the woods Marcus had mentioned, silent and secretive beneath the low-lying cloud cover, and the house that stood just beyond them. Was I crazy to stay here, so near to the site of the horrific deed? Now that I'd had a chance to think, it seemed a little too convenient that I was the one to stay rather than Marcus.

Why was I there, really?

It suddenly occurred to me that quite a few minutes had passed, but I hadn't heard the telltale rumble of Marcus's motorcycle dwindling into the distance. Nor had I heard Felicity's return up the stairs.

I couldn't help wondering . . .

Before I knew it, I found myself stretching my hand out to switch off the lamp, plunging the room into inky blackness. Holding my breath, I crept around the grand bed toward the window, my hands outstretched in the careful reach of a blind person in unfamiliar surroundings. I felt my way around the bench at the foot of the bed, until my fingertips bumped the cold, smooth glass of the window.

When I'd arrived with Felicity, the security lights had been on, flooding light onto the architectural details of the house and casting light here and there around the grounds. Now they had gone out, or been turned out. Why?

I peered out, straining to discern precious details. Dimly, I could make out a glint on the asphalt drive below. Marcus's motorcycle. He'd moved it from the garage, but he'd not left yet. I leaned closer to the window and tried to look straight down.

Was that movement I saw, there below?

It was. What were they doing? Without even the slightest hesitation or stab of conscience, I found myself sliding the window latch to the right and carefully sliding the sash upward, inch by inch.

Cold swept into the room like a marauding invader, invisible and insidious. I shivered and dropped to my knees, resting my hands on the sill. They were down there, all right.

"Do you have everything?" Felicity's voice was pitched low.

"Right here. Hand me the lantern."

A ring of light edged into view, rippling like water. An oil lamp or a flame of some sort. The light moved, and then I could see the two of them, glowing like fairy people in the darkness of night.

They were headed for the woods.

A part of me wanted to throw on warm clothes and follow them, but I was too sensible for something so foolhardy. What could they be doing? Trysting? Or perhaps their presence together had a more ominous portent. Maybe they were burying evidence.

They were together this morning, at the murder scene. What if tonight was just an elaborate sham to get me on their side? What if they were both involved in the murder of Isabella Harding and were out there now, trying to cover up their tracks?

I watched the swinging lantern and shadowy figures disappear into an invisible treeline that I knew must be there. I stayed at the window, despite the fact that I was shivering to beat the devil, and kept scanning the far distance for some sign of what they were doing. I don't know how long I sat there—at some point, I had the wits to grab a soft throw from the end of the bed—but I must have drifted off for a moment. When I lifted my head from my hands, I saw a pale glow lighting the treetops. Not in the south as I had expected, but more toward the northwest.

Fire? And voices, wafting to me on the wind.

Chanting.

They were chanting.

Adrenalin zipped up my spine. I hastily closed the window and climbed into bed, dragging the soft blankets up to my chin. No wonder Marcus and Felicity were an item. They were magical partners. Did they work with others? A coven of witches? Were they out there now?

What had I gotten myself into?

The wind continued late into the night, whining against my guestroom window. Wind was not uncommon here in northeastern Indiana, where the wide stretches of flatlands and shortage of forests provided little barrier to the more powerful forces of nature. Normally I found the sound comforting, like a soothing lullaby. Tonight it danced at the edges of my consciousness, taunting me as I lay there, tossing and turning and making a general mess of the bedclothes while I replayed the events of the day and evening in my mind. Over, and over, and over. My nerves were pulled as tight as my overstretched underwear elastic. I tried to make my mind a blank, but every time I closed my eyes, I saw an attractive, petite woman lying twisted at the base of a vast expanse of marble stairs, her eyes opened wide in sightless horror as she faced her killer in her last moments of life. Between that and the witchy rituals being practiced so near, was it any wonder that I was having trouble relaxing? Usually I considered myself a fairly easygoing person. As politically correct as possible—not because I wanted so much to spare those with the oversensitivity gene, but because tolerance seemed the best way to get through a world where one had so little control. Why try to control things you couldn't change?

Except when it came to an unknown murderer who walked free tonight behind a cloak of anonymity. Stony Mill could not allow that to go on for long. I hoped the police had an actual plan.

I also hoped, with all my might, that Felicity wasn't involved.

Lying back against the pillows, I stared at the ceiling and willed the proverbial sheep to come out of the woodwork so that I could get down to the business of getting back to sleep.

Deep breaths. Deep, cleansing breaths.

One . . . two . . .

Nothing.

Here, sheepy, sheepy, sheepy . . .

Lame, I know, but it was 2 A.M. and I was getting punchy.

From the hall, I heard a sudden stir, an odd series of clicks that seemed to be drawing nearer. My nerves were already on edge, and my ears immediately hearkened to the noise. Toenails on hardwood flooring. A dog, I decided. Probably big. Friendly, I hoped. Strange that Felicity hadn't mentioned owning one. The presence of a big, protective dog would have made me feel infinitely better about the impromptu sleepover.

Intrigued, I sat up in bed and slipped my feet over the edge. Cool air swirled about my bare ankles like the eddies of an unseen river as I tiptoed over to the door and pressed my ear to the crack. The animal seemed to have paused outside my door. I could hear it panting, a soft whine punctuating the occasional exhaled breath. It sensed my presence; I felt sure of that. I could almost feel its stare through the door panel.

I might be naïve, but I certainly wasn't stupid enough to open the door to a strange dog. At length it seemed to lose interest in me and continued on down the long hall, the clicks of its toenails fading into the distance. When I decided it had gone far enough for my peace of mind, I slowly, quietly, turned the knob and opened the door an inch. Nothing launched itself at me from the darkness, so I opened it a little wider and poked my head out as the doggie footsteps made their way down the hall.

At the end of the corridor, a mere fifty feet away, moonlight cast a silvery glow through a tall window. I waited for the dog to enter the light . . . and waited . . . surely it should be there now . . . for heaven's sake, it should be beyond the window by now, shouldn't it?

And then, in the blink of an eye, the sound was gone. Completely and utterly gone.

And in that moment I realized that the hallway was carpeted.

Fear lodged at the base of my throat. *Just your imagination,* I told myself as I pressed the door firmly into place. Ears playing tricks on you.

Just the same, I turned the brass lock and ran back to my bed, huddling with my knees drawn up to my chin until my heart had stopped its frantic thundering.

Chapter 5

Hours later, I dragged myself downstairs in search of a very large, very hot, very strong cup of coffee.

In the cold light of day, the frightening undercurrents I'd experienced the night before were gone and I was forced to acknowledge that I'd let my overactive imagination run away with me. Felicity's house looked normal even to my sleep-deprived sensibilities. Elegant, to be sure, and formal to a fault, but normal. I peeked in doorways as I made my way to the kitchen. So many of the rooms felt reserved to me, coldly masculine and devoid of the hospitality I associated with my boss. Only the library, full of wingback chairs and stacks of books, and an overstuffed sitting room in shades of apricot and terra cotta reflected Felicity's personality and beckoned invitingly to the casual observer.

I would have loved to accept, but I'd already decided that the best thing to do for now was to take things day by day as far as Felicity and my job were concerned. I didn't have enough information yet to condemn or to clear her, but she'd taken a chance on me when I had not an ounce of retail experience. The least I could do was try to keep an open mind.

I would have just enough time for a single cup of coffee (but nothing else—if our forefathers had intended for breakfast to appeal to the masses, they would have scheduled it at a more respectable hour) before I needed to head off to open the store. Today Felicity would need my help more than ever. She could hardly be expected to focus on the day-to-day details of running her business so soon after her sister's untimely demise, no matter how dedicated she might be.

I found Felicity ensconced at the table in the kitchen, looking like a million bucks. In one hand she held a fork over a plate piled indecently high with eggs and what looked and smelled suspiciously like fish. In the other, she held a pen, currently poised over a sizable stack of paperwork.

Felicity looked up. "Good morning!" she said in a tone that reeked of sunshine and daisies.

Felicity, evidently, was a morning person. Even on my best days, I could never be described as a morning person. Still, I did my best to put on a happy face and return the greeting in kind. Except mine came out slightly less perky.

Felicity's eyebrows raised. "Goodness, dear. Didn't you sleep well?"

So much for imitations. I headed straight for the coffeepot, trying not to notice that even *it* was burbling cheerfully away. "I couldn't seem to relax," I apologized, "after yesterday."

As soon as the words left my mouth, I wished I could call them back. I wasn't usually that tactless.

But instead of taking offense, she sighed. "Yes, it is difficult to put such things out of one's mind. One must try, however. Life is for the living."

I nodded, impressed by her ability to overcome. Terribly resilient of her. I, however, was nowhere near as evolved and had reverted back to a state of quivering confusion. "Where is your dog this morning?" I asked as I stirred several spoons of sugar into my coffee.

Felicity paused. "Dog?"

"You know. Furry animal. Sharp teeth. Sloppy tongue."

She set her fork tines-down on her plate and folded her hands in her lap. "I don't own a dog, Maggie."

I coughed out a nervous laugh. "Sure you do. You must. I heard it upstairs in the hall last night." At her curious stare, I prompted, "Big dog. Lots of toenails. It wanted into my room."

She shook her head.

Then what was it I had heard last night? Could a neighborhood dog have sneaked into Felicity's home somehow, without her knowledge? But if it did, how did it disappear so quickly, without me seeing it? I was getting that Alice-in-Wonderland feeling again. I took a big gulp of coffee to squash it into submission, yelping when the coffee burned my tongue. "Damn."

Felicity slid her plate away. "I think I know what you might have heard."

Her serious tone unnerved me. Part of me sensed that I wouldn't want to hear what she was about to say, but I wasn't the type to quail in the face of adversity. Most of the time. "Go on."

She laid her hand upon the stack of papers. "I had planned to broach this subject with you eventually, but it appears it will have to be sooner rather than later. Do you remember what I asked you last night?"

Something clicked into place in my head. I did remember. "Are you saying that you think—"

She looked me straight in the eye. "It was a spirit."

Ghosts—okay, maybe. I was kind of on the fence as far as that subject was concerned. But a ghost *dog*?

"My experience has demonstrated there to be several different types of paranormal disturbances. You see, I spearhead a research group that investigates paranormal encounters."

Witch-extraordinaire, and now Ghostbuster? Mm-hmm. "I see. Did you know you had a ghost, er, dog in your house?"

Felicity smiled patiently at me. Once again, I had the uncanny feeling that she could see straight through me. "You're skeptical."

I stood up and went to the sink, essentially turning my back to her. Operating, obviously, under the credo that if I couldn't see her, she couldn't see me. "I don't mean to be. This is all just a bit new to me. I mean, you practice witchcraft. And now ghosts, too. I've never known anyone who believes . . . well, in magic. The supernatural. And around here, as I'm sure you realize, it might as well be heresy."

"No need to worry, ducks. Few people start out believing in 'all of this,' as you say. It is just a bit woo-woo, isn't it?" She laughed, a self-deprecating chuckle that was entirely charming. "The thing is, the world is an amazing place, really. *We* are the ones who have trivialized everything, we are the ones who have stripped the magic from the world and left it a terribly mundane sort of place."

Something to think about, anyway. But the abstract theory so rarely applied to real life, in my experience.

"Most people walk around day by day completely blind to the wonder of the world around them. They refuse to see the signs of the divine in all of creation, in the very patterns of life. If they would only pay attention . . ."

"And you study these things?" I asked, trying to make sense of it all.

"With a little help from my friends," she affirmed. "Marcus, for one. You can meet the rest of them later, if you like. We meet at the store—"

The store! The clock above the door bore the truth of my suspicions. "Look at the time!" I exclaimed, dumping my coffee into the sink. "If I don't hurry, I'll be late opening the store."

"One of the greatest benefits of owning one's own business," Felicity remarked with a careless flip of her hand, "is not having to worry overmuch about tardiness."

"But the customers," I protested as I mentally tried to calculate the rate of speed necessary to travel the seven miles to the store.

"Will either wait or return later. Calm yourself, my dear. Five or ten minutes is not the end of the world."

I stared at her, blankly, and then couldn't help laughing. The Toad would never have held such a lenient view. How ironic that now that I had actually found an employer who did, she turned out to be (A) a suspect in a murder investigation, and (B) a witch. But what else could I do but try to keep an open mind? I just couldn't bring myself to go crawling back to the Toad to beg for my job. Even if I did, he wasn't the altruistic type. Besides, by doing that, wouldn't I also be admitting that I had been in the wrong? My mother would jump all over that. The last thing I needed to do right now was give her more reason to be disappointed in me. For now I was better off trying to forget any misgivings I might have about godless women and canine ghosts and accept that surprises sometimes come in mysterious packages.

My second day at Enchantments went much better than I had expected. Felicity did everything she could to make me comfortable at the store, and I found myself enjoying the easy banter between my boss and the regulars. Thursdays are our early night, so by the time the day ended at four o'clock, I was feeling quite at home in my new position. I didn't even mind when a couple of Felicity's *special* customers dropped in for a visit to the Loft. I recognized one of them: Helen Bradden, a soft-eyed teacher at Riverview Elementary. I'd had her in the second grade. She smiled at my open-mouthed surprise, gave me an impish wink, then made her way upstairs.

I was beginning to get a new picture of modern-day witches. Hardly history's version of big-nosed hags in pointy hats who cackled over steaming cauldrons, neither were they the crystal-studded and strangely robed versions seen in New Age documentaries. The followers of the Craft I encountered today were both young and old, beautiful and plain, dressed in jeans or cashmere or polyester, and all greeted Felicity like a beloved sister. Their warm reception made it obvious Felicity had the respect and admiration of her compatriots. A few days ago, I would never have guessed there were those who still believed in magic. Now I found that Stony Mill and the surrounding towns housed several. Most preferred to keep their beliefs to themselves, hidden from the paranoia and judgments of their more conventional, churchgoing neighbors. There was a certain safety in anonymity.

I left the store that afternoon thinking about Felicity and trying to sort out my feelings about the situation I found myself in. I was certain of nothing, but I couldn't deny that I was curious. I also couldn't forget the undeniable connection I had felt in the first moments of our acquaintance. That sense of familiarity. Of recognition. More than any other, it was that feeling that kept me there waiting to see what would happen next.

Rather than head home, I made my way toward the Stony Mill Carnegie Library, digging the past due library book out of my backseat at a convenient stop light. Time to face the music.

The library parking lot was nearly empty when I pulled in. I took a prime spot, put on my contrite face, and tucking the book under my arm, headed in through the front doors.

Head Librarian Marian Tabor spotted me right away. "I wondered when you'd be coming in," she grunted.

I waved sheepishly. "Sorry about that. I've been busy." I set the book down on the counter, carefully smoothing the cover.

"So I hear tell." At my suspicious glance, she shrugged. "I saw your mother at the grocery the other day."

Danger! Danger, Will Robinson!

Marian had been friends with my mom as long as I'd been coming to the library on my own, and she always seemed to know intimate details about my private life. Notoriously sharp-tongued to those patrons hapless enough to cause damage to one of the library's many volumes, she was in one way your quintessential librarian. But Marian, affectionately known about town as Marian the Librarian, departed from that prissy image with her affinity for leopard print clothing and her sharp eye for the male body. Never mind the fact that she was a plus-sized woman in a size two world. In Marian's mind, none of that made a bit of difference, and more power to her. Today she'd confined the leopard to a scarf, tied jauntily around her blowsy up-do and left to dangle behind her right ear.

"Your mom mentioned you hadn't had a date in a long time," she commented as she stamped the card in the back of the book with a resounding thump.

I felt my cheeks go hot. "My mom, as you well know, has a habit of sticking her nose into my business," I mumbled. "Unnecessarily, I might add."

"Honey, it's nothing to be ashamed of. We all have dry spells from time to time." Marian looked left and right before leaning conspiratorially over the counter. "I might have someone for you. My nephew. Just moved back to town last year. Military man, you know. Well, he was for a time. Tells his mother that he doesn't have time for that right now. If you can imagine. He's just licking his wounds. Got his heart broke by some pretty young Southern thing, God love him. Southern women can be so cruel." She shook her head, lamenting the fate of her nephew. Then she narrowed her eyes at me, silently appraising me. Her eyes twinkled above her reading glasses. "Might be a bit young for you, but young is good, trust me. Strong like bull."

I pictured some squat little He-man with long arms and hairy knuckles. "Erm . . . no thanks."

"It wouldn't be any trouble. I'd be happy to put in a good word for you."

"Gee, that's real nice of you, Marian, but I don't really have time right now, either."

She stared at me as if I'd grown a horn in the center of my forehead. "You're joking. Dollar twenty-five."

I dug in my wallet and pulled out five quarters. "Nope, 'fraid not. New job and all that."

"Marcus said the same thing," she said, shaking her head. "I will never understand the younger generation."

I felt myself go faint. "Marcus . . . Quinn?"

"Ah, so you do know him! I knew he'd get scoped out before long."

"I did not . . . never mind. You said he was in the military?"

She nodded. "Military intelligence. He can probably kill a man with his bare hands." She arched her brow meaningfully. I guess I was supposed to fall to my knees with longing.

Time to change the subject. "Hey, does the library keep old newspapers on file?"

Instantly she was all business. "Of course we do. On microfiche. Why? Something I can help you with?"

"I'm not sure. I was hoping to find references to Isabella Harding."

"The newspapers from this week haven't been filed yet. Unless you mean earlier references."

"Exactly."

She plopped her BE RIGHT BACK sign down on the counter and beckoned for me to follow her downstairs. "The 'fiche readers are all in the basement. The Dinosaur Collection. We don't get much call for them anymore, although we do keep up with the local paper. I'm afraid we simply don't have the server space to store scans, so we do what we can." She flipped the lights on and led the way to the tables with unerring accuracy even before the fluorescents blinked to life. Within seconds she'd dragged out a stack of films that dated back several years, and she showed me where the rest were kept. "I believe the Hardings first came to town around ten years ago. You have a lot of searching to do, hon."

My heart sank, but I recovered quickly. "That's okay," I told her, reaching for the power switch on the machine.

My disappointment must have shown on my face, because after a moment's pause she placed her hand over mine. "Listen, I don't have a date yet for this weekend, and I have more access to the resources than you do. Why don't I just see what I can find for you? Now, no need to thank me," she said as I opened my mouth to interrupt. "I haven't found anything yet."

"I can't ask you to do that."

"You didn't."

I hesitated, not wanting to take advantage, but I knew it was a lost cause. Around these parts, once help had been offered, it was damned near impossible to turn it down. We Hoosiers are a stubborn lot. "All right. But don't go to too much trouble, please."

She looked at me, her brown eyes serious. "Maggie, what is it you're looking for, really?"

I shook my head slowly. "I wish I knew. Something. I guess mostly I'm just looking for information. My, uh, new boss is related to Isabella Harding, and I'm afraid . . . well, I'm afraid she's been questioned in the investigation." I bit my lip, wondering whether I had revealed too much already. "Please don't tell my mom. She'll find out soon enough as it is, and I just really would like a chance to learn the truth myself before . . ." My voice trailed off and I gave a helpless shrug.

"Before your mom goes all hari-kari on you and tells you how you should have taken better care not to lose a perfectly good job, and maybe you should have had better sense than to take a job with someone of questionable background?" She put her arm around my shoulder and gave it a reassuring squeeze. "Don't worry, honey. Your mom and I have never seen eye-to-eye on everything. Besides, you're an adult. You make the decisions that are right for you. There isn't a thing your mom can do about it, and that's what makes her really crazy."

I couldn't help laughing. "You're right. It does."

We headed companionably for the stairs.

"So, what are your feelings about your boss?" Marian asked me. "It's Felicity Dow, isn't it? How serious do you think the questioning is?"

"I don't know. I just started there yesterday, and then this happens. It's thrown me for a loop," I admitted. "I like her—I really do. She's kind, and funny, and I felt from the moment I met her that I'd known her for ages. Does that make sense? I think this could be the perfect job, in a way."

"But—?"

"But I can't help wondering. What if I'm just seeing what I want to see?"

Marian nodded. "You want her to be innocent."

"But not only because I like the job and want to keep it. I'm not as mercenary as all that."

"You want to know that your perceptions weren't so far off the mark that you were able to trust someone capable of murdering a member of her family."

"I guess so. God, that does sound selfish."

"Human. That sounds human."

A group of middle schoolers had come in while we were downstairs and were congregating around one of the PC stations. Marian nodded toward them. "Looks like I'm going to have to go break that up. No telling what they've got up on that screen, but by their faces I'd say she's got one hell of a rack. See you later, kiddo. I'll be in touch if I find anything."

I was so ready to get home. A little peace, a little quiet, a little time to think about everything that had happened. It was just what the doctor ordered.

Turning onto Willow, I eased Christine to a halt beside the curb and switched off the key. Home again. The house was a large Victorian classic that had been broken apart into three decent-sized apartments back at a time when it had become less fashionable to have large families and the house had become an obsolete monstrosity. Still, when I think Victorian, I think cozy, and my converted basement apartment was anything but cozy. Maybe it was the closed feeling that being surrounded by dirt gives you. There were nights when I lay in bed scarcely breathing, the covers drawn tightly up beneath my chin in my clenched fists, because I had fancied I'd heard a heartbeat vibrating through my walls, as if the earth around me was a living, breathing entity. Then there were the nights when the wind screamed around the old house's myriad corners and coves, tossing dried leaves against the tiny recessed windows with a sound that was like the skittering of insects.

Creepy.

The house's saving grace was the fact that my lifelong best friend lived in the upper-level apartment. That and an affordable price tag, something that was next to impossible to find when you're living on a shoestring budget. My shoestring was already frayed from overuse as it was, so a nervous moment every now and then seemed a small price to pay for security.

I let myself in, set my purse and jacket on the chair next to the door, and stooped with a sigh to pick up the few dried leaves that had found their way in on the air currents. The apartment's sunken entrance was always accumulating a puddle of leaves in the landing, and a few inevitably accompanied my every homecoming. Dropping the bits of flotsam into the wastebasket, I went immediately to the tiny galley-style kitchen. A flip of a switch and the overhead fluorescents eventually blinked on, flooding that corner of the room with harsh light.

My priorities always arrow-straight, I made a beeline for the fridge and quickly surveyed the contents. After a few moments of hemming and hawing, I decided on a delicious gourmet meal of crunchy peanut butter and strawberry jam—on whole wheat, of course—and a bottle of water. After a few more minutes of soul-searching, I guiltily traded the water for a can of Coke Classic and closed the door before I could change my mind. Life was too short to worry about the little things. Better to let the moms of the world do that. They were great at it.

I carried my goodies to my favorite chair, a big, old down-filled wingback that used to belong to my grandparents. It was a barf green color that had been highly popular in the fifties and it really didn't go with my décor (Early Laminate Paneling—very retrochic), but the feathers conformed to and around my body like a kind of nest, and the color hid the stains and tatters of years of use. It was ugly, but I would pay to have the monster re-covered before I'd get rid of it, so I guess that's saying something. Kicking off my shoes, I settled in with a sigh and scooted the ottoman closer with my feet.

Ahhh . . . Paradise.

On the small table next to me, the message light on my answering machine blinked urgently at me. *Blink-blink-blink. Blink-blink-blink.* Three messages. I looked at the clock. Six thirty-one. *Mental countdown to* Magnum P.I.: *Twenty-eight minutes, forty-two seconds.* I let the message light blink a few more times as I tried to decide whether to listen to them now, or put them off until later.

It didn't take long. There were some things in this world I could put off indefinitely. A message on an answering machine was not one of those things. All it would take was one ignored message in an emergency situation, and boom, I'd feel like dirt for the rest of my natural life. You just never knew. Resigned to my fate as a slave to technology, I heaved a sigh and pressed the button.

Beep. The first, as expected, was my mother. "Margaret Mary-Catherine, this is your mother calling. Obviously, you are not home." This with a tone of reproach, as though I had missed her call on purpose. "Why you're never home at seven-thirty at night, I won't even hazard a guess. I'm assuming it has something to do with that woman who hired you. Why you felt the need to leave a perfectly good job to work for some person you had known a matter of *minutes* . . ." Her sigh was long and loud and meant to lay a load of guilt at my feet. My mother had endured a lifetime of regrets over my selfish choices. She liked to share the wealth of her suffering every chance she got. "But that's all water under the bridge now. We'll discuss this later, dear. Call me the *moment* you get in."

The machine's mechanical voice intoned the date and time. Seven-thirty-two, yesterday. Mother was probably fit to be tied by now.

I made a mental note to return her call last.

The second *beep* preceded a similar call from my sister, Melanie. Mel wanted to know what was going on, was it true what everyone was saying about Felicity Dow (my hackles went up at that), and how could I possibly keep all of this to myself? The least I could do is share what I knew. And wasn't it strange that Felicity had hired me, despite my lack of experience, just before all this happened? Well, she was sure it meant nothing, but I had to admit it certainly was *odd*.

Annoyed, I jabbed at the delete key. No return call necessary.

Third in line came a cryptic, three-word message: "Tell me *everything*."

I grinned, all of my annoyance melting away. The voice belonged to Stephanie Marie Evans—Steff to her friends—and the message was the opening to almost all of our conversations over the last eighteen and a half years. Steff and I first met when her family moved to town the summer I'd turned ten. I was riding my bike down her cul-de-sac—alone as usual—and she was sitting on the swing on her front porch with her big brute of a tomcat, Buttercup. Our eyes met and I saw fireworks—in my head, at least; I'd rammed my five-speed into an oak tree and flown over the handlebars. Being the kind, nurturing soul that she is, Steff rushed to my aid, eager to tend my scraped palms and skinned knees, and we spent the rest of the hot, hazy afternoon in the shade of her front porch, sucking down lemonade and playing Crazy Eights and gabbing like we'd known each other since infancy.

Over the years we'd traded up our lemonades, first for Cokes in our early teens, Diet Cokes at figure-conscious sixteen, rum and Cokes at adventurous twenty-one, wine coolers at twenty-five because we had become *true* adults and were far too sophisticated for the more hardline rum and Coke, and now fast approaching health-conscious thirty we drank bottled water as we once again warily watched our waistlines. But the flow of chatter was as constant as the change of seasons. Comfortable. Familiar. Jobs, men, fashion, men, mothers, men, hopes and dreams and fears, and . . . men.

Did I mention that we sometimes talk about men?

Picking up the handset of my cordless, I speed-dialed her number. The ring whirred in my ear less than a second before she picked up. I heard her pause to take a breath.

"Hello?" she said in a low, sexy voice carefully calculated to drop a man to his knees.

"I gotta warn you. Hot and sultry will get you nowhere with me, babe."

"Mags!" Immediately her tone settled into its usual light and airy rhythm. "Hiya!"

"Hey."

"I heard what happened."

"Yeah?"

"Yeah. Not many secrets at the hospital, you know." After an adolescence filled with tending to every sick or hurting pet that came her way, Steff had quietly assumed her role in life as an RN at our tiny local hospital. It was the only thing she'd ever done quietly. Gregarious and fun and full of life, she was able to fill a room with warmth just by walking through the door.

"I suppose not," I said thoughtfully. In a small town, keeping a secret was hard. You had neighbors, friends, neighbors of friends, friends of your mother's, neighbors of your mother's. Everyone talked about what they'd seen, what they'd heard, what someone else had said they'd seen or heard. Talk was the food of life. That was the way small towns had functioned from the time man had first come in out of the forests. Small-town secrets were very tricky to navigate. In an even smaller scale environment, like the hospital, I imagined it was nigh onto impossible.

"Wanna talk about it?"

"You know I'll tell you everything." Then: "*Magnum*'s on in twenty minutes."

"Down in ten."

She made it to my door in seven, armed with a flat square box that smelled like a little piece of heaven, fuzzy slippers, and a smile. "Am I late?"

"Perfect. What's that?" I asked, indicating the box with a nod of my head. Not that I really needed to ask. I was like a bloodhound when it came to junk food.

"Pizza. Giovanni's." She opened the box lid to display eight pieces of the local pizza dive's prize specialty, a deep dish smorgasbord of six layers of cheese, pepperoni, Italian sausage, red and green peppers, spicy herb enhanced sauce, and crust. She flapped the lid enticingly before me. "Your favorite."

My mouth instantly began to water as oregano-and-garlic-scented steam reached my pleasure centers. I thought for a moment about the peanut butter and jam sandwich waiting for me inside. Then I abandoned it gleefully, grabbing the box from her hands and setting it on the wrought-iron patio table-for-two that served as my kitchen nook. "You want it heated?"

"Nah. We'd just burn the roofs of our mouths on the cheese."

"Right."

Equipped with a plate, a fork, and a paper towel for a napkin, she plopped down on my sofa while I did the same in my chair. The muted TV changed images in usual rapid-fire fashion in the background while we took immediate measures to satisfy our hunger pangs.

"Yummm." Inhaling the first piece tended to take the edge off a person's hunger, allowing for the introduction of conversation to a meal. "I just love Giovanni's. Do you think he's really Italian?"

Steff waved her fork at me. "Cut the crap, Mags. You always try to turn the talk away from something that makes you uncomfortable. What's going on?"

She was right. Short, middle-aged Giovanni of the protruding tummy held no fascination for me. He made deep dish in a way that was almost sexual, but I had more important things on my mind than physical gratification. "Well . . . You know that my boss's sister turned up dead."

She nodded. "That's why I called. Among other things, of course."

"Did you know that they questioned her about it?"

"I had heard . . . but Maggie, as I heard it, she found the body. They had to question her."

Yes, but there was more to it than mere questioning. It was more than the nuances of attitude in the postures of the police officers conducting the questioning, more than the strange comments made by Deputy Fielding. It was even more than Marcus pressuring Felicity to try to piece together what she remembered. They suspected her. For whatever reason, they suspected her, and I acknowledged that now with a certainty I shouldn't possess.

But I couldn't tell Steff that. She'd think I was being my usual worrywart self. "Overly sensitive" was how my grandmother would so graciously have put it. Always getting *ideas* about people, imagining them guilty of all sorts of things. I could hear her voice in my head now, admonishing me not to be so fanciful. Don't butt into others' private lives. I should just be the good Catholic girl I'd been raised to be and not worry myself sick about what other people were thinking and feeling.

I shook myself in annoyance as I recognized the self-correcting pattern of my thoughts. Well, in spite of my mom's and my grandma's best efforts, I wasn't such a great Catholic. Not anymore. Not for a long time. I was just your average, everyday girl, doing my best to make sense of the crazy world around me. And I couldn't help the feelings I got. The ones that settled in at the pit of my stomach like a meal gone bad, or that clutched at my throat and made my skin crawl with fear and trepidation. I'd buried them for so long I'd almost convinced myself they were figments of an overactive imagination. And yet ignoring them had accomplished nothing beyond making me self-conscious and unsure of myself. Maybe it was time that I listened to them rather than smother them.

Maybe it was time that I took back my self-respect.

I was so caught up in my internal monologue that I forgot about Magnum until I saw the familiar red sports car zipping across the TV screen and the fun-loving lilt of Tom Selleck's famous mustache.

"Oooh . . . oooh . . ." Steff and I both said at once, snapping our fingers at the screen as if we could magically turn up the sound. More sensibly, I grabbed the remote and clicked off the mute.

The familiar strains of the *Magnum, P.I.* theme song filled the room, accompanied by the wondrous sights of Hawaii and, let us not forget, the fabulous dimples of Tom Selleck. With my eyes glued to the screen, I watched the opening credits, sighing just a little as his baby blues twinkled at me and only me through the magic of television. "I love this show."

Over on the couch, Steff had her knees drawn up to her chin. "Me, too," she cooed happily, a kooky little smile on her face. I was pretty sure it matched my own.

Magnum was another guilty pleasure Steff and I shared. When most people our age barely knew who Tom was outside of his brief but memorable stint on *Friends,* Steff and I often giggled and sighed over classic reruns of Selleck as Thomas Magnum, private investigator extraordinaire and dream man above all others. I mean, let's face it, the guy was perfect. Ice chip blue eyes that melted through a woman when he smiled, a sexy eat-me-alive-you-know-you'd-love-it grin, thick hair that begged the touch of a woman's hand, a sense of adventure, a sense of humor complete with a semigoony laugh that was wholly endearing, and a hole in his heart from the loss of his wife and child years before. Definite hero material. Never mind the fact that the man was probably now on the downhill slide from fifty. Thanks to a little TV magic, he was preserved in a state of perfect youth, perfect masculinity, perfect everything, all for me.

Us, us, I meant us.

We didn't speak again until the first commercial break a third of the way through the hour-long show.

Steff turned to me, instantly back in best-friend mode. "So you're concerned about your new boss?"

I tore off a chunk of pizza crust and started to rip it into bits. "Who wouldn't be? She's a nice person, Steff. She doesn't deserve this."

Steff's eyes fastened on my busy fingers. "I wasn't aware police questioning had gotten very far."

"It hasn't. At least, I don't think it has. I'm just worried, that's all."

"I'm sure they're just trying to gather as much information as they can. It's not every day we have a murder here in Stony Mill. Despite the element of tragedy, I'll bet our town boys are secretly elated."

The thought disturbed me, that anyone could derive pleasure from a person's untimely death, but I knew she was probably right. "The thrill of the chase, I suppose you mean?"

But Magnum's TV-land chase returned from a commercial, interrupting us. We gasped as Magnum was nearly forced off a rocky seaside cliff by the malevolent intentions of some faceless foe. We licked our lips as he kissed the hapless woman he was protecting, who seemed to be as powerless against his animal magnetism as we were. We watched in awe as Magnum returned to the Masters estate, and giggled when he insulted Higgins yet again for his stuffed-shirt pomposity.

Another commercial. Steff waved a cleanly picked pizza crust in my direction. "Tell me why you're worried about—Felicity, did you say?"

"I'm not. It's more the situation. I was there at the police station when they let her go."

"You were there?"

I nodded. "I went to pick her up. Lend moral support. It seemed like the right thing to do."

"So, what happened? Did they treat her badly?"

I frowned, picturing the scene in my head. "Well, not *badly*, per se."

"Then what?"

"Well, I mean, they were polite enough." I frowned, trying to find the right words to explain what were mostly impressions and feelings. "One of them, I think, had a bit of a thing for her."

"And that's a problem."

"No. The other cop was the problem. He made it very clear that she was not to leave town."

"She's at the very least an important witness as the first person on the scene. And I hate to say this, honey, but I want to be sure you've thought this through. What do you know about Felicity? Do you trust her?"

I was silent a moment, searching deep. "I think I do," I said at last. "I've been given no reason not to trust her. If it weren't for what happened yesterday, she's been the ideal boss. I think what bothers me most is what I see as a preconceived idea that she's their man, even before the investigation has had any real chance to get started."

"They must have some reason—"

"Not necessarily," I said, just a tad bit defensive. "You remember when Mike Coleburn was arrested for destruction of private property simply because he took his old pickup in for some body work and someone saw the dinged fender and a crummy old baseball bat in the back and decided to report him as the person who'd been beating the crap out of all those mailboxes."

"They must have thought they were doing the right thing."

"But that's just it. Haven't you ever noticed that people around here have a tendency to shoot first and ask questions later?"

Steff nibbled thoughtfully on a tough sliver of crust, considering this. "It's the self-preservation instinct. You know? Like the Wild West."

Somehow the images of pistol-toting gunslingers and baseball bat–swinging mailbox vandals just wouldn't mesh for me. "Okay, well, that's all beside the point anyway. The point is, they seem to have this preconceived notion that Felicity is guilty of *something*. Did I tell you what happened at the store?"

"Do tell."

Briefly I described the strange conversation I'd had with the dishy detective.

"I remember him!" Steff exclaimed, sitting up straighter as her male-triggered radar antennae went up. Steff was a first-rate connoisseur of the complex physical and emotional makeup of the opposite sex. Dr. Ruth had nothing on this woman. "We went to school with his sister Marla. He was a few years ahead of us. So . . . *intense.*"

I remembered his eyes and the way they had looked when he'd removed his shades. I had to agree with her there. "It was so strange, though. He was warning me away from Felicity. I know he was. But I can't for the life of me understand why. Unless . . ."

I trailed off, not ready to tell Steff about Felicity's strange beliefs. I wasn't quite sure how she would take the news. I wasn't even sure how *I* felt about it yet.

"Unless what?"

I shook my head. "Nothing. I don't know. I'm still trying to make sense of it all."

Steff was silent for a moment. "Marla moved away eight years ago. I don't know why, but I'd always assumed her whole family had moved. And yet here he is still. Huh."

I looked at her suspiciously. I knew that tone. "I think he's married, Steff."

She turned wide innocent eyes on me. I knew the look, too. "Why, I don't know what you mean."

"Stephanie Marie Evans, you know perfectly well what you were thinking about."

A twinkle of a smile twitched at her lips. "You mean the uniform they wear, and the way they roll the sleeves up around their biceps, military style?"

"Uh-huh."

"I just love those heavy gunbelts," she said with a sigh.

"Married," I reiterated forcefully as I tried not to think about the way his butt looked in those dark blue pants as he'd walked out of the store without a single backward glance.

She made a face at me. "Oh, tell me you didn't once think about his ass."

"Well . . . maybe once."

We dissolved into a barrage of giggles as we had countless times over the years our friendship had spanned.

We glanced up to see that Magnum had returned to the
screen, and the show was, in fact, almost over. For the last few
minutes, we sat enthralled as Magnum got the bad guy, tied up
all the loose ends, then kissed the girl one last time before he
said good-bye to her for good. The girl smiled wistfully as he
drove away, but even she realized that, as handsome and
heroic and perfect Magnum was, he was not meant to be kept
to oneself. There was a sense of right, of justice, a satisfaction
that things were exactly as they should be.

All was right in Magnum's world. How could I make
things right in mine?

Chapter 6

The next morning, I arrived at the store fifteen minutes early and used the key that Felicity had given me to open up. I couldn't say I was well rested—the events of the week had taken their toll on me, and I'd been having some trouble sleeping—but the sun was shining cheerily, the air was crisp, and I had a cup of coffee (large!) to brighten my outlook. This was as good as it was gonna get.

As soon as I set my purse down, I saw the note.

Frowning, I picked up the single folded sheet of paper that had my name written in a careful, looping script on the outside.

Dear Maggie,
   I've been asked in to the police station again this morning for further questioning. Don't worry about me—just stay at the store and I'll be in as soon as I can.
                                                              Felicity

Further questioning? A sense of foreboding shivered through me. I couldn't help wondering if Felicity had thought to seek legal counsel. I also couldn't help wondering if she needed it. Surely as a witch she could do something to protect herself. A spell or charm that would force the police to look for the true guilty party.

Unlocking the front door, I made a mental note to broach the subject as soon as she came in.

Yesterday's mail lay in a pile beneath the note. I flipped through the stack, sorting out catalogs, picking out the bills. When the phone rang, I picked it up on autopilot.

"Enchantments Fine Gifts, how can I help you?"

"Margaret Mary-Catherine, is that you?"

Damn.

I pasted a fake smile on my face and tried to inflect as much good cheer as I could muster. *"Mooooommm. Hiiiii!"*

Extra syllables kicked up the perkiness quotient nicely, I've always thought.

"Are you not returning calls to your parents these days?" Mom was too shrewd to be fooled by false gaiety.

"I'm sorry, Mom, I completely forgot—"

"I could understand it if you were married and had children and a husband to take care of, Margaret, but as it's only you, I just don't understand why you can't return a simple phone call."

"I meant to call you, really I did, but I fell asleep early last night."

"Your sister called me back last night."

Of course she did. Melanie always did what Mom wanted her to do—at least that's what Mom thought. I happened to know better, but it was easier to perpetuate the myth.

"Mom, I'm going to have to get going soon," I said, using my usual excuse. "I have work to do, and I feel guilty talking on the phone too long."

"And that's another thing: that job of yours. Is it true what they're saying? About the woman who owns the store? I tell you what, Margaret, I have a bad feeling about all this. You never had a head for business, really, and I worry about what you're getting yourself mixed up in—"

"Mom." I cut her off. "You don't need to worry. I'm fine. Felicity is being questioned, yes, but it's only because she was the one who found her sister's body. That's all."

"Yes, but you should hear the kinds of things going around town, dear. And you know, where there's smoke . . ."

"Mom, I have to go."

"You always have to go. I did have a reason for calling, you know."

I sighed. "What did you need?"

"I thought you might like to come over Saturday evening. Melanie has already said she and Greg and the girls would love to come, and of course your father and Grandpa Gordon. It's been an age since you've stopped by for a visit, Margaret. But of course the last thing I want to do is to pressure you into a nice family visit."

My heart fell. Not to worry, though—my blood pressure shot up to compensate. "Of course," I gritted out, pressing my hand to my newly aching head.

"What did you say, dear?"

"I said, of course I'd . . . love . . . to visit, Mother. Saturday, you say?"

"You don't have anything planned already, do you, Margaret?"

I wracked my aching brain, wishing I'd thought ahead. "Well . . . no. Well, I might later in the evening"—that was wishful thinking—"but I could probably make an *early* dinner."

Accent on *early*. Best to reserve time for a real live date, just in case.

"Wonderful, dear. We'll be eating at five."

I hung up feeling manipulated and grumpy. Dinner with my mother usually ended in either indigestion, irritation, or a combination of the two. And the indigestion rarely had anything to do with the food.

My good mood slipped a notch. Grumbling under my breath about my loving family, I finished going through the store mail. The last piece came in a nondescript manila envelope with no return address. Uncertain what it might be, I slid a letter opener under the flap, slicing it clean.

The Speculator. It appeared to be some kind of newsletter. I ran my gaze down the front page, pausing at a headline. CROP CIRCLE IN SW OHIO, one screamed; AUTHORITIES BAF-

FLED. Another read, STONEHENGE MIDSUMMER CELEBRATION, 1ST IN SIXTEEN YEARS—WHY? The rest of the newsletter seemed to contain similar messages. UFOs, fairy lights, the Reiki Connection (Jesus as Reiki healer, anyone?), divination techniques, and of course, the ubiquitous message that the government was somehow involved in covering up all evidence of the supernatural or paranormal in our daily lives.

Somehow I couldn't see Felicity setting stock in such tripe, but I placed it on her desk anyway.

Store traffic was slow, so I set myself up on a stool behind the counter with my coffee and the witch book I had been reading, a slick trade paperback titled *The Return of the Goddess*. I was determined to understand Felicity, and this seemed to be the best way to go about it since I didn't know her well enough to ask too many impertinent questions.

I was just beginning to dig in when the bell over the door tinkled. Swiftly tucking my book away, I glanced up to find a trio of women entering the store. My irritation level, already on overdrive from the phone call with my mom, went on the rise again as I recognized the expensive clothes and well-kept arrogance of women obviously suffering from that insidious, spreading contagion, Wannabe Chic.

Why did it not surprise me to recognize my little sister leading the pack?

Her companion, however, did surprise me. Just a little.

What the hell did Mel think she was doing, traipsing around town with Margo Dickerson, my high school tormentor and arch nemesis?

"There you are, Mags!" Mel exclaimed, storming forward between the displays with the same single-minded fervor as Sherman's march to Atlanta. She stopped just before the counter, her hands on her hips. "*You* didn't return my call," she said with a reproving twist of her lips. She paused, waiting for my apology. When it became apparent that one would not be forthcoming, she added, "I waited up until at least ten."

If there was one thing I had learned about my little sister over the years, it was that giving in to her, like mollifying a cranky child with treats, only reinforced the negative behavior. I was determined not to yield. I was also uncomfortably aware of the smug curiosity of her boon companions. Oh, Margo and her friends *pretended* to flip through a case of matted lithographs, but the avid watchfulness in their eyes made it painfully clear why the two were here.

I straightened my spine and lifted my chin, throwing on a sheltering cloak of aloofness. "What are you doing here, Mel? I thought Mom said we'd be getting together this weekend."

She waved a hand to dismiss the question. "Yes, but you didn't really think I could wait that long to get the scoop, did you?"

"There . . . is . . . no . . . scoop," I grated out between tightly clenched teeth with a pointed glance at her two cohorts.

She caught the glance and misinterpreted it utterly. "Oh, Mags, how could I have forgotten? I should have introduced you right away." She motioned her friends forward. "Have you met my neighbors, Margo Dickerson-Craig and Jane Churchill? Ladies, this is my older sister, Margaret O'Neill."

"Maggie," I corrected her, wishing I wasn't forced to by her outdated Miss Manners standards. After all, I seriously doubted that Miss Manners had ever been locked out of the girls' locker room wearing nothing but a towel.

Margo extended a regally limp hand, looking half as though she expected me to kiss it. "Maggie O'Neill. Maggie O'Neill . . ." She paused thoughtfully. "Did we go to school together?"

With anyone else, such a memory lapse was forgivable. With Margo, the smirk glittering in her hard eyes made it clear that she remembered me all too well. She just meant to be insulting.

Well, two could play at that game. "Did we? Sorry, I guess I don't remember. It has been a *loooong* time. Were you a few years ahead of me?"

She pulled her hand back as though I'd bit it and self-consciously smoothed her Mary Kay–perfect cheek. Score one for the Gipper.

"No," she snapped. "Same year."

"Jane and Margo live on my street, Mags. Margo's husband, Randy, is editor-in-chief for the Gazette, and Jane's husband works in the firm with Greg." Mel supplied the helpful details with relish. "We three formed a little coffee klatch of sorts a few months ago, because we have just loads in common."

"Ah." Somehow I didn't find that hard to believe.

"So. Mags." Mel moved closer to me, watching me with scandal-hungry eyes. "Is your boss here?"

I snatched away and began to tidy the stack of tissue paper beside the register. "No."

"Oh." Mel's face fell. "We were hoping . . ." Her voice trailed off, but then she brightened considerably. "But at least that gives us a chance to talk without worrying that she'll hear us. You can tell us everything."

"Such as?"

"Well . . . what's she like? Everyone's saying that she killed her sister."

If I kept my hands on the tissue paper, I would end up shredding it to ribbons to keep from throttling my sister. "Don't say that."

"Well, it's true. Greg heard they're amassing evidence against her."

It was as I'd feared. But why? Why would anyone suspect Felicity? Was it only because she was the first person on the scene? Or was there more to that story? Something I didn't know?

Despite my first instinct to boot all three of their scrawny asses out of the store, I decided to put up with them for the time being. I wanted to know what else Mel had heard.

I was a little new at this sleuthing bit, but a girl could learn anything if she put her mind to it. Even if it meant kissing up to her own sister.

"Mel, let me show you the new toiletries we got in just this week," I offered, taking her arm and leading her over to the display. "Direct from Paris. You'll love the scents. Oh, and try this lotion. It's absolutely magical." When she was nose deep in an amethyst-hued glycerine bar, transported to new heights with the pungent scent of lavender, I made my next move. "So. Tell me. What else does Greg say?"

"I don't know about evidence," Jane said, coming forward to lift the lid on a pot of Bee's Knees, a soothing balm for rough skin that smelled wonderfully of honey, "but it doesn't take a psychic to know there have been rumors going around for ages about bad blood between Felicity Dow and Isabella Harding. Not much happens in this town that can be counted secret or even private. I mean, when we were moving into our new house in Buckingham West, I called the utilities commission to make arrangements to transfer our account, and they already knew our new address. And here we'd just signed the papers!"

Mel dipped her finger into Jane's tester of Bee's Knees and rubbed it into her cuticles. Examining them, she said, "I heard Isabella had a fling with Felicity's husband, and that's what caused the split between the two."

If it was true, it was a piece of information I didn't have, one that I would have to pursue later with Felicity. But it didn't mean she was a killer. "What about other suspects?" I asked, trying to direct the conversation toward something a bit more useful. "Have you heard of anyone else who might have held a grudge toward Isabella? Other family members?"

"One husband. One adult daughter. I heard they were both out of town on business. Face it, Maggie," Mel said, placing a hand on my shoulder in what was supposed to be sisterly compassion, "Felicity Dow is simply the most likely candidate." She looked around the store, taking it all in, and I could see the questions moving through her head. "Maybe this job wasn't such a good idea after all."

"It's fine."

Mel just looked at me. Then she shrugged. "Suit yourself, but keep this moment in mind later, when I tell you I told you so . . ."

Turning away, she rejoined Margo, who had remained haughtily in the background since I insulted her, and motioned for Jane to follow. "Let's go, girls. We have loads of shopping to do. Maggie, I'll see you Saturday."

As they walked out the front door, I heard Margo say, "I told you she wouldn't know anything. What a total waste of good gossip."

Let it go, Maggie, I told myself as I struggled with my dislike for a woman I'd hoped never to see again. *Just let it go. Think about what's really important.*

For the next two hours, I dealt with the intermittent flow of customers and little else. I tried to go back to my book, but I couldn't seem to focus on the details. More and more I found myself standing at the front windows, watching for Felicity's car. By the time Felicity finally walked in the door, it was almost noon, and strain was beginning to unravel the edges of my composure.

"Liss! I was really starting to worry! Are you all right? What did they want? What did they say?"

She sat down heavily on a counter stool, letting her antique velvet purse drop carelessly to the floor. A full minute passed before she found the strength to answer. "They simply wanted to question me further."

"Yes, but how? What was it all about?" I asked, picking up her purse automatically and setting it down on the counter next to her. I was hovering, feeling useless, but I managed to stop short of wringing my hands.

"They wanted me to go over the sequence of events once again. Actually, several times again. I think they were waiting for me to slip up."

"Oh, Liss." It was just as I'd feared. There was no second-guessing this time. "I think it's time you consulted a lawyer about all this."

She peered up at me, considering this. "No. No, I don't think so."

"But—"

"Maggie. I'm not guilty of killing my sister. And while I'm not naïve enough to believe that innocence triumphs over all in the American judicial system, in this case I simply must believe the truth will prevail."

"Guilt is not the only reason for hiring a lawyer," I protested. "You need someone who can look out for your best interests, someone who can advise you and who can obtain information from the authorities that you don't have access to. You have to know what you're dealing with."

My voice had risen steadily in pitch throughout my impassioned bid for common sense, but I knew nothing I said would convince her until she made up her own mind. Felicity, it seemed, was as stubborn as I was.

As if to prove my point, Felicity smiled at me and held out her hand. "Sit down, dear."

I did as she asked, perching on the edge of another stool, my muscles so twitchy that I could scarcely make myself stay seated. Every nerve in my body urged me to get up and pace the floor.

"Maggie, I want you to know that I appreciate your concern. I do. But I also need you to understand there is nothing you can do."

"Maybe I can't. But there must be something *you* can do," I pleaded. "Look, I don't know very much about this witchcraft thing, but surely you have some way of dealing with false suspicion."

"What is it that you suggest?"

I'd gone this far. I might as well go for the whole hog. I placed my hands on my knees and gripped them hard to keep them from shaking. "A spell. Or a charm. Or even a hex, for God's sake! Anything that will make them back away from you long enough to realize that there might be another explanation. A better explanation."

Please, God, let there be another explanation. I did *not* want to think she could be involved.

Felicity's lips twitched. "A spell, hmm?" When I nodded, she patted my hand kindly. "Oh, Maggie. I haven't educated you very well yet, have I? You see, except in the most extreme circumstances, modern-day witches abide by Karmic Law, or the Rule of Three." At my blank look, she explained, "That, positive or negative, whatever we do returns to us three times as strongly somewhere down the road. We do not believe in manipulating the will of others in most circumstances, because we believe in treating others as we ourselves hope to be treated. And because our will is human and personal, we cannot possibly see the full ramifications of altering the plans the Goddess has set into motion. Now"—she patted my hand again—"do you understand why I'm telling you this?"

"Because you cannot cast a spell on our police force that will force them to look for the real killer."

"*Will* not. Not cannot," she corrected with a hint of pride in her voice. "They need to come to the conclusion on their own, else they'll be following my will. But don't worry. The Universe has a way of seeing that justice is done in its own good time."

Before I could voice my opinion that it wasn't much good being a witch if one couldn't defend oneself, she swept up her purse and began to dig within it.

"What time is it, what time is it. There you are," she said, withdrawing a tiny silver pocket watch on a fine chain. "Nigh onto noon, is it? Small wonder I'm famished. Tell you what," she said, taking out her checkbook. "I'll spring for a hopping-good lunch if you'll go out and pick it up for the both of us. After your boundless support, it's the least I can do. What do you say?"

What could I say? Fifteen minutes later, I puttered to a halt by the curb in front of a little restaurant I'd never tried before, a cute little café on Main Street called Annie-Thing Good. Outside, mix-and-match wrought-iron patio tables were pushed up against the plate glass window, tipped-up chair legs akimbo and laced together with chain, awaiting the arrival of summer so many months away. I waded through them to the pumpkin-and-cornstalk-flanked door and pushed my way inside. The fairytale tinkle of brass wind chimes sounded with the movement, mingling with the lilting soprano of some Celtic-style songstress and lifting my spirits.

Inside, the scent of baking bread just about bowled me over, yeasty, fresh, mouth-wateringly powerful. I took my place in line at the counter, nodding to Mr. Krieg, one of my old high school teachers who was nowadays tormenting a whole new generation of underachievers, and waving at Old Mrs. Hlavacek, who'd been postmaster at our outdated post office since before the changeover from the Pony Express and who was now having an enormous bowl of soup at one of the little side tables. For a newer restaurant, the café seemed to be doing brisk business. Usually it took a while for a new place to find a clientele, but the proprietor of Annie-Thing Good had somehow beaten the usual stick-in-the-mud tendencies of the good residents of Stony Mill. I'd lay odds it had something to do with the wonderful scents wafting out from the back kitchen. Nothing that smelled that good could be kept a secret for long.

Word of mouth travels like lightning around here.

Behind me, the door tinkled again. More customers. I hoped Annie The Proprietor was feeling up to the task. She seemed to be alone behind the counter.

There was a tap on my shoulder. I turned around to find Deputy Tom Fielding, standing in line just behind me, sunglasses, uniform, and all.

"Fancy meeting you here, Miss O'Neill."

I gulped, wondering if he had a permit to look that good. "I—I was just getting lunch. To take back to . . . to the store."

He took his aviators off and slid one earpiece into the front pocket of his leather cop's jacket. Right beside his badge. My gaze hit the glint of the badge, and it shocked me back into reality.

What the heck was I doing, making goo-goo eyes at the enemy? Tom Fielding had made no bones about his position regarding Felicity. Okay, well, maybe a few bones, but he hadn't hidden it much. It wasn't so much that he suspected her that bothered my sense of justice—hadn't I wondered myself?—rather it was the idea that he had convicted her in his mind without completing his investigation that didn't sit well with me. But that was the way our boys in blue operated. Imagination isn't what they're known for.

"So, have you eaten here before?"

Annoyed with myself, I turned my back on him, hoping he'd get the hint that I wasn't interested in conversation. "No."

"You'll love it," he said, oblivious to the fact that I thought he was a cretin. "I come here all the time now, but I don't know that I've ever appreciated the line as much as today. Must be my lucky day."

The comment was so unexpected and curious that I had to turn back to look at him.

He peered at me full on with a glint in his eyes that was unmistakable. There are few certainties in a woman's life. Unadulterated male appreciation was one of them. It also wasn't something I was overly comfortable with. My share had always seemed to be deflected somehow, rerouted toward my younger sister, or any number of more vivacious young women. I suppose that made me more like the ugly stepsister than Cinderella, but every once in a while I did find a guy who seemed to like me despite the fact that I was not blond, athletic, or rich.

"Is it?" I responded coolly, looking down my nose at him. I had to tilt my head back to do it, too. I'm sure it wasn't especially pretty.

"Well, it could be. How's that job of yours going?"

"It's fine."

"And how's that boss of yours doing?"

Ah, so that's what all this was leading up to. I must have been wrong about the level of appreciation I'd seen in his eyes. Apparently I was nothing more than a means to an end. He was looking for information about Felicity and thought I might have something to offer.

All of a sudden I was angry. Angry for myself, angry for Felicity, and angry for Isabella, whose murderer would walk free so long as such biased treatment was allowed to go on unchecked.

Riding high on the sudden surge of indignation, I whipped around again to glare at him. "You have some nerve," I whispered fiercely. "You know perfectly well how Felicity is, since you were questioning her all morning with your harassment-happy buddies down at the station. But since you're asking me, let me tell you. You're barking up the wrong tree. Felicity had nothing to do with her sister's death. Nothing. So if you're serious about looking for the killer who's out there on our streets as we speak, you might want to actually *look,* rather than pinning all your hopes on the easy target."

His mouth had fallen open at my tirade, and I was glad for it. I was mad enough to spit icicles. Another place, another time, and I would have walked out there and then, my chin held high, pride intact. The only thing that kept me in place was the check in my purse, made out to Annie-Thing Good, and the fact that the line ahead of me was moving and I was the next one up.

Good food wins out over the perfect exit every time.

At last, it was my turn to order. I stepped up to the counter and did a quick scan of the menu. "Hi. I'll have—"

My attention shifted from the menu to the woman standing behind the counter, and I did a double-take. Round of face and short on stature, this strawberry-haired dynamo did not exactly fit into the faded flannel and denim world of your typical die-hard Hoosier. She wore a cherry-red crinkled broomstick skirt that reached to her ankles and a lemon-yellow oversized T-shirt that screamed CHEFS DO IT TASTEFULLY! cinched around her comfortable middle by a frilly fifties-style apron. Though the gray in her softly curling hair suggested that she might have reached middle age, she wore it hitched up into a youthful ponytail, the ends bouncing with every energetic step. Stone-colored Birkenstocks and sensible white ankle socks completed the picture she made of an aging hippy making her way in life exactly as she wanted.

"First-time visit?" Her ready smile welcomed me as surely as a friendly hug. "It's cold outside and the forecasters are threatening a flurry or two this evening. Fall flurries are always the coldest. Why don't you try a nice, hearty bowl of baked potato soup? It's my specialty, with green onions and bacon and a helping of sour cream thrown into the mix. Trust me, it's pure soul food."

"That sounds great. I'll take two. Thanks."

"No problem," she said, eyeing me curiously as she doled out the man-sized servings of something that smelled like heaven. "It comes with your own miniloaf of homemade bread. Just what you need to take your mind off your troubles."

Lately my troubles seemed to be multiplying, and the man standing behind me, close enough that I could smell his spicy cologne, was not helping.

"And since you're a first timer, I hope you'll accept a little welcome gift from me. Caramel cream cheese brownies, my personal specialty. I'm Annie, by the way. Annie Miller. And you work for Felicity."

I stared at her in amazement. "How did you know?"

"Felicity called to tell me you were on your way over," she said with an impish wink.

I laughed, somehow relieved that there was a mundane, nonparanormal explanation for her knowledge. "Ah. I should have guessed. For a moment there, I thought you were going to tell me . . ." I caught myself just in time. "Never mind. It's not important. Thanks again."

I handed her the check and gathered up the two cartons and the bag with the bread. I had to stack one on top of the other, holding the topmost bag in place with my chin.

She helped me get my arms around everything. "That should do it. Oh, look who's here," she said, gazing past me. "Deputy Fielding, long time no see. You want the regular?"

"Hey, Annie. Yeah, the regular's fine."

"I'll have it for you in a jiffy," she said as she tidied my scarf around my shoulders like some sort of surrogate mother.

"No hurry."

In a slick, efficient movement, she whirled around, grabbed his already bagged lunch out of the warmer, plunked it down, and swept up the money he'd placed on the counter. I turned to leave, eager to get away before she finished with him.

"Tomorrow as usual, Tom? Oh," she said, as she noticed me trying to make my escape, "tell Felicity that I'll see her Saturday night, would you?"

"Uh-huh," I grunted as I backed out the door. The top bag started to slide, forcing me to grab it with my teeth before it could fall to its doom. *Got it—whew.* I looked up, bag in teeth, just in time to see the good deputy standing in front of me, a lopsided smile curving one side of his mouth.

"Allow me," he said, reaching a hand over my shoulder to hold the door for me. I took a quick step back, my heart scudding fast against my ribs with his nearness.

It wasn't fair, I decided as I tried to put space between us, that a woman should be so affected by a man the world had put forth in direct opposition to her. I hurried out into the brisk October air, hoping the wind that was scuttling dried leaves against the brick building would also cool my burning cheeks before he caught sight of them.

Now to get out of his way.

I hustled my butt over to Christine and tried to use my pinkie to push the chrome button release.

Locked. Damn it all to hell.

Muttering between gritted teeth, I turned momentarily back toward the café—long enough to intercept the grin Fielding didn't bother to conceal—then whirled away. Keys, keys, where did I put . . . My heart sank as I recognized the hard, cold object weighing heavily in my left hip pocket.

"Shi'," I hissed around the bag.

"Need some help?"

"No' f'om you."

He walked over and leaned a hip against Christine's flank, crossing his arms over his chest. I pretended to ignore him while I shifted the boxes and bags in my arms in the hopes that I could manage to free a finger and thumb. All the better to hook the key ring out of my pocket, my dear.

Except my key ring had slid to the lowest possible depths. No matter how hard I stretched my fingers, I couldn't manage to snag it.

To make matters worse, the topmost box began to slide.

"Shi'!"

With a movement so smooth it might have been choreographed, Fielding bent at the waist and almost leisurely stretched out his hand. The box dropped neatly into his palm.

He straightened and held it out to me. "Sure I can't help you?"

I gave up. Piled everything on top of Christine's sloped roof, then held them all in place with one hand while I dug in my pocket with the other. Retrieving the keys I jammed the right one into Christine's willful locks, yanked open the door with an embarrassingly loud creak of the hinges, snatched the box from his hand, and threw it all into the passenger seat in one fell swoop. "Thanks."

I all but leapt into my car. I would have closed the door, but Fielding put his hand on the frame and leaned down toward me.

"Miss O'Neill—"

"If you don't mind, I'd like to leave. Our lunch is getting cold."

"I'd like to speak with you further."

"In an official capacity?"

He hesitated, long enough for me to guess that nothing we discussed could possibly be determined unofficial. "There are some things I'd like to ask you," he admitted.

"About Felicity."

"Among other things, yes."

Exasperated, I crossed my arms and scowled at him. "Don't you have any intention at all of actually getting to the bottom of that poor woman's death?"

"I can hardly be expected to 'get to the bottom' of it if I don't have the full cooperation of all relevant witnesses, now can I?"

It made my hair frizz to admit it, but I supposed he was right. "Including me."

"I was hoping to . . . interview you later."

I hemmed. I hawed. I just didn't see a way I could refuse. I heaved a sigh of resignation. "Do I have to go down to the station?"

His lips curved up in a one-sided smile. "Not if you promise to answer my questions."

"Do I need a lawyer present at this . . . interview?"

"Do you feel you need one?"

"Not really."

"Then I think you should do what you feel comfortable with. Personally I don't think you need one—that's just my humble opinion, and should not be misconstrued as legal advice in any way, shape, or form—but the only purpose a legal eagle might serve in this case is as a chaperone."

Did he mean to suggest we might need a chaperone?

Get ahold of yourself, Maggie . . .

My gaze strayed down to the ring shining golden and warm in the cold sunlight on his left hand. I might be a lot of things, but one thing I was not was a homewrecker. I was a one-man woman, and as such, I felt the rest of the world should hold themselves to such high-minded principles as well. The world would be a happier place if more people did.

I narrowed my eyes at him. "It *will* be a short interview, I trust?"

"Scout's honor."

So why didn't I feel reassured?

I stewed about it all the way back to Enchantments, so much that my arrival there took me by surprise. It's rather disconcerting, when you think about it, to drive several miles and have no recollection of a single one. How many cars did I drive past that I didn't really see? How many people? How many other drivers were so caught up in their own private world that they didn't see me?

But at least the drive had accomplished one thing. By the time I arrived at the store, I had decided that meeting with the dishy deputy might be a good move. How many other opportunities would I have to pump for information the very people who had access to the crime scene itself? Because more and more it seemed that if I wanted Felicity to have a fair shake, I was going to have to do my part to help shake up our well-meaning, if shortsighted, boys in blue. Namely, Deputy Tom Fielding, whom I suspected to be a driving force behind the investigation.

Shake him up, hell! I'd prefer to throttle him.

Having learned my lesson back at the café, I purposely made two trips in with our lunch. Felicity was waiting for me in the little office.

"There you are. How did you like Annie's place?"

"Very interesting woman, that Annie. High energy. By the way, she says to tell you she'll see you Saturday night."

"Yes, she is that. High energy, I mean. Spirits seem to love Annie, you know. They flock about her like moths to a flame."

Ah. Important safety tip: Stay away from Annie Miller after dark.

To Felicity I just smiled and handed her a container of soup. "She certainly seems to know her soups. This smells wonderful."

She'd scarcely dipped into the creamy broth before she dabbed at her mouth with a napkin and pushed hers away. "Oh, my. That was delicious, but I'm afraid I can't eat another bite. Promise you won't tell Annie when you see her next."

I took in her container with but a few spoonfuls missing, then my own, with but a few spoonfuls remaining. I set mine down as well, ruing the loss almost instantly, but like everything else about her, Felicity's slender figure was a constant cause for inspiration. I couldn't look at her without having visions of salads, aerobics classes, and vegetarian cookbooks. The result was exhausting, but I could do worse than to emulate her whenever possible.

So I supposed that meant the miniloaf of bread was out of the question.

Sigh.

"I ran into Deputy Fielding at Annie's," I said to distract myself.

Felicity laughed and began to gather together the trash into a paper sack. "The ubiquitous Mr. Fielding."

"Was he—?"

"Yes, he was there this morning."

"He wants to talk to me."

"Does that bother you?"

"I'm not sure. *He* bothers me. But I think what troubles me most is that he seems so ready to believe the worst of you. It's his job to get to the truth of the matter, but it sounds as though the police aren't even following up on any other suspects. It doesn't seem as if the truth is all that important to him."

Felicity chuckled and wrapped her arms about me in a spontaneous hug. "Ah, Maggie, you are a dear. Thank you for worrying about me. But don't fret overmuch. I'm quite capable of taking care of myself. You do what you need to do. And I, I will go on with my life as best I can. That's all any of us can do, you know. The best we can."

She puttered around the office a few moments. I sensed that she had something else on her mind, so I waited in place, giving her time to form the words if she so wished.

I didn't wait long.

"By the way, Maggie," she began, uncharacteristically tentative, "I was wondering . . . but no, perhaps that is too much to ask. Forget I said anything."

"Don't be silly. What is it?"

"I discovered this morning that the police have released Isabella's body to the family."

Inwardly, I was glad for it. Isabella Harding had suffered enough indignities in death. It was time to allow her family to bury her and get on with their healing.

"I've spoken with Isabella's daughter," she went on by way of explanation. "There will be a viewing tonight, and then the funeral will be tomorrow afternoon."

In her voice I heard a quality that nagged at me but that I couldn't quite put my finger on. And then the clarity of it struck me like a bolt from the blue. Isabella had family to mourn her, a husband and daughter, but neither had thought to call Felicity until now, to ask how she was coping. Felicity appeared to be on her own.

"If you don't have anyone else to go with you to the funeral, I'd like to be there for you," I offered shyly.

"I was hoping you'd say that," she admitted with a telltale shimmer in her eye. "I'll pick you up at seven."

Chapter 7

What was I thinking? I hate funerals. There was something about them that would haunt me for weeks after, an aura of despair and utter melancholy that would hang around me like a swarm of bats, swooping back down at me just when I thought I had shaken off the oppression at last. And yet, paying one's respects to the dead is considered a duty of honor no one I knew would dream of forsaking. Parents taught it to their children through example, and in this way, generation by generation, the tradition of honoring the dead was passed on.

I can remember being brought to viewings by my parents as a small child. Hanging on to my mother's skirt as she dragged me along with her to view the body where it lay in a fancy, polished casket that appeared more a prison than a place of rest, my fingers gripping ever tighter with each step we took. A glimpse of a pale face, cheeks and lips ruddy with abnormal color. There were times when I thought I heard them speaking to me, hushed whispers in words I couldn't quite make out. I would dig in my heels, anxious to get away, terrified that one day I would get up to the casket and the eyes would open, the head would turn, and the cold lips would whisper my name the way they did in my head. And always, always came a wave of emotion that slammed into me like a tsunami, reckless in its hunger to consume, voracious with a power man was meant to revere. Anger, sadness, loneliness, fear. Inevitably I would melt down, unable to bear the weight of such raw, all-encompassing emotions, and my mother would smile tightly at everyone we passed as she steered me by the elbow to my father's big, sensible sedan, all the while scolding me for allowing my imagination to control my good judgment.

"Margaret, an undisciplined mind is a wicked mind," she would tell me briskly, "a tempting playground for Satan's minions. Never forget that."

And so I would sit in the car alone, stinging with the shame of a public loss of control, yet unwilling to risk going back into that chamber of horrors for anything. As I grew older, I learned to stay back when my parents made their walk-by of the casket, hiding behind a mask of teenage indifference with the rest of my cousins and friends, and I had remained in the car at cemeteries, pleading boredom. My mother had allowed this, in her own way even encouraged it, perhaps remembering the old days of tearful collapse.

I hadn't attended a funeral or viewing in years.

And now? Now I found myself preparing to attend a viewing for a woman I didn't know, freely and of my own volition, for the sake of a friend I admired but whom I'd known only a matter of days.

A noble sentiment, certainly. But in the back of my mind I couldn't help wondering if I'd outgrown my phobias about the dead.

My message light was blinking when I got home just after six. My mother again, I supposed. Rarely did a day go by that I didn't have multiple calls from my mother. It wasn't that we were overly close. My mother was a complicated person. God knows I didn't understand her, even after nearly thirty years.

I pressed the button as I slipped off my heavy coat and went to the closet to hang it up.

Beep. "Miss O'Neill, this is Tom Fielding."

The hanger missed the rod. Hanger and coat both fell from my suddenly tingling fingers and landed in a heap at my feet.

"I was hoping to find you in, but I guess I must have missed you. Hey, I . . . I wanted to apologize to you. I don't know what it was I said that set you off today—"

Hmmph.

"—but whatever it was, I hope you can understand that I didn't mean to offend you."

What he didn't know . . . Double hmmph.

"Call me. Please. My number is 555-9872. I'll be home tonight. Thanks."

I picked up my coat, replaced the hanger, and calmly hung it in the closet. Outwardly I was a model of serenity, but inside I was a mass of confusion.

Please . . .

That single word, so deeply masculine, so real, had lodged itself in my heart and refused to let go. I didn't know what to do. You see, driving home that evening, I'd come to a realization. I'd stopped at the grocery across town, then on a whim took the slow route back, traversing tree-lined streets golden with fall color. The season had been particularly lovely this year, and the evening should have been idyllic, but I couldn't shake off the feeling that trouble wasn't far behind. Of course it was the murder that had me on edge. I'd been thinking about Felicity. Once I had wondered whether she might have been involved in her sister's death, but I believed her now. I believed her, completely and utterly. The clincher had been the quiet sincerity in her voice when she spoke of her belief in the Rule of Three and a universe that had a way of exacting its own kind of justice. Beliefs so strong and unswerving that she felt no need to contact an attorney to look out for her best interests. She was innocent. I felt it.

But how on earth could I explain that to Tom Fielding?

I didn't have an answer, but I knew I had to try.

My fingers trembled as I picked up the handset of my cordless and dialed the number he'd given.

"Hello?"

My heart thundered in my ears. He sounded so good over the phone. I licked my sandpaper lips. "Deputy Fielding?"

"Miss O'Neill." I could hear the pleasure in his voice. "You called me back. I wasn't sure that you would."

All right, so it had been a while. Big deal.

"I wasn't sure that I would either."

"I, uh, wanted to apologize for whatever it was I said that annoyed you, but I'd rather do it in person. Maybe dinner."

"Dinner?"

"Yeah. Do you like Mexican? I know this really great restaurant. Looks like a hole in the wall, but the food is grand."

I gripped the phone tighter, staring at myself in the mirror next to my door. Flyaway hair, pale round face, open mouth. Yup, situation normal. "Let me get this straight. You're asking me to dinner."

"Yeah. I guess I am."

"Deputy Fielding—"

"Tom. Please."

"Tom, then." I didn't want to think about the consequences of even the minimal intimacy of using his given name. "If this is because you want to question me about anything, or even if it's because you think you offended me in some way, then let me assure you, it's not necessary." I paused a moment, then couldn't resist asking, "Is it?"

He didn't answer right away, and I had a mental image of him squirming. "Well . . . no. Not entirely."

"Not entirely."

"No. I mean . . . well . . . God, this is hard. I mean, yes, I did want to ask you a few questions relating to the case. And I do want to apologize. But that's not the reason I'm asking you to dinner."

"Oh." I didn't know what else to say.

He waited through a few moments of silence. "Does that mean you'd rather not?"

"I'm not sure. You haven't told me why you're asking me."

He laughed. "You don't let a guy off easy, do you."

"I'll take that as a compliment."

Was I flirting? My God, I was flirting. Oh, this was very, very bad.

"You do that."

"So?"

He blew his breath out, long and low. "All right. I'd like you to go to dinner with me because I think you're pretty, and you're interesting, and I'd like to get to know you better."

I swallowed hard. I hadn't expected him to be quite that honest. "Oh."

"Does that mean yes?"

"Well . . ."

"Oh. Hey. I guess I forgot to ask. Are you seeing someone?"

"No, it's not that. But you are forgetting one thing, aren't you?"

"And what's that?"

"Your wife. Gold ring, third finger, left hand. Remember?"

"My wife . . . ? Oh. God. I forgot about the ring."

"Men do tend to do that at times," I quipped.

"Uh, yeah. I guess for a while there, I still felt married, but . . . The truth is, my wife and I have been separated for two years. Once upon a time, I'd hoped we might work things out, but she served me with divorce papers three months ago. A new man. She wants to get on with her life and let me get on with mine. At least that's what she told me."

"I'm sorry."

"Yes, well, don't be. Sometimes things don't work out, even when you love each other. It just wasn't meant to be."

And that was how he got to me. I mean, how could I refuse dinner with a man who didn't choose to blame his problem marriage on the wife who left him?

"All right. Yes. Dinner would be . . . nice."

"What are you doing tonight?"

"Oh. Well, actually I do have plans this evening. The Harding viewing."

"I didn't realize you knew Mrs. Harding."

"I didn't. Felicity . . . well, she doesn't have anyone. I thought she might need support from a friend."

"Nice of you. How about tomorrow night?"

"All right." It would get me out of dinner with my family, too. That worked out beautifully. My mother would do anything to see me married with children, including letting me off the hook for dinner.

"Pick you up at seven?"

I gave him my address and hung up feeling giddy, and confused, and hopeful, and nervous. I went into my bedroom and flopped backward on the bed, my heart and stomach bouncing in time with the old spring mattress. Staring up at the shadows at play on the ceiling, I couldn't help wondering if I was doing the right thing. Too late now, though. I'd already said yes. And it was only one date, after all. Not a lifelong commitment. And if I could sway him in some small way, if I could make him understand what I had learned about Felicity, then it would be worth it.

Felicity needed a champion, whether she admitted it or not.

Reaching over my head, I grabbed my ratty old teddy bear from his nest in the pillows and pulled him in for a snuggle. He smelled like dust and fabric softener and memories. Comforting and familiar.

"What do you think, Graham Thomas?" I asked him, holding him out at arm's length.

Graham Thomas stared back at me with his black dome-button eyes, once shiny and now scratched and dull after years of falling out of my bed. He didn't say anything. That's what I liked about G.T. He didn't get mouthy. He also gave unconditional love, he never hogged the covers, and he didn't get too bent out of shape if I accidentally knocked him out of bed. G.T. was perfect.

"He seems okay," I told him. "I'll take it slow. I'm hoping he'll outgrow his suspicion for Felicity. If not, well, I guess he's outta here."

That seemed simple enough.

I switched on the small, frilly lamp at my bedside and blinked as the sudden light dazzled my eyes. The alarm clock showed the time as six-thirty-six. I deducted the fifteen minutes I habitually set the clock forward and decided I had thirty-nine minutes before Felicity would arrive. Settling G.T. back against the pillows with a loving pat, I went out to the living room and popped a tape into the VCR, set it to record *Magnum* at seven, then went through my bedroom into my Lilliputian bathroom. My makeup kit yielded up a compact of pressed powder and lipstick. I applied both, pulled my hair neatly back with a silver clip, then went to my closet. Somewhere in its depths, I knew I possessed a black suit. My mother had made sure I was supplied with everything I needed to meet her definition of a good Catholic. Good

Catholics attended Mass and weddings and funerals, and always dressed conservatively and appropriate to the occasion. Tonight, at least, the suit would come in handy.

I held it against me, wondering whether I could get by without pressing it. The austere cut wasn't the most flattering, but hey, it wasn't *my* funeral . . . and beggars can't be choosers.

"Maggie . . ."

The eerie whisper came from behind me, lingering on as though it had been spoken through a microphone and someone had set the synthesizer to echo. The fine hairs on my arms stood suddenly at attention. Clutching my suit to my chest, I turned toward the door, my heart in my throat with the thoughts of what I might see there.

Holy-Mary-Mother-of-God, what *was* that?

My first instinct was to back into the depths of the closet and pull the jumble of clothes about me, but I knew for a fact that I had shot the deadbolt, and the windows were too small to admit anything but the smallest mammal. Squirrels, yes. A cat? Sure. A psychopathic sex maniac? No way.

I grabbed my trusty baseball bat anyway—better to be safe than dead meat. With a semideadly weapon to boost my confidence, I tiptoed over to the bathroom doorway and peeped inside.

Nothing hiding under the pedestal sink.

Nothing slouching beside the toilet.

Nothing skulking behind the shower curtain.

Okay then.

I took a deep breath and pussy-footed my way to the bedroom door, holding the wooden bat back and ready to swing for all I was worth. All was still in the apartment. No sounds except for the ticking of the alarm clock and the soft low hum of the refrigerator. Standing in the open doorway, I shivered as a sudden chill permeated the weave of my loosely knit sweater. It was like standing before an open deep freeze. Frigid air tingled over my arms, raising gooseflesh wherever it touched. Adrenalin shadowed fear in a headlong tumble through my veins. I leaned close to the doorframe, peering carefully around the corner. I half expected to see my outside door standing wide open, the frosty night air clouding in around some hulking brute of a man standing threateningly in my living room.

The door was closed. The room was empty. The windows remained intact.

Where the devil was that cold air coming from?

With a death grip on my Louisville Slugger, I valiantly stepped forward to complete a walk-through of my tiny studio apartment, switching on lamps as I went until the entire room blazed with light. I needn't have bothered. The single greatest advantage of having an apartment the size of a postage stamp was that everything was visible at once. There was no one in my apartment.

No one.

Had I imagined the voice?

I bit my lip, my gaze darting back and forth as I tried to take in the entire room at once. I knew no one was there—that much was obvious—but I could almost swear I saw movement. A shadow here. A mirage-like waver of the air. A twinkle of light there.

Get a grip, Maggie. You're not a little girl anymore.

I made myself turn my back on the living room and return to my bedroom. It was my intention to push the incident to the back of my mind, but even though I knew there was nothing there, I couldn't seem to shake off the jitters. My pulse continued to race as I changed into my suit and squeezed into a pair of long-line control tops. When I had succeeded in making myself presentable, I perched on a hard wooden chair by the door, my back to the wall and a wary eye scanning every inch of the room as I tensely awaited Felicity's arrival.

Even so, the buzzer at my ear nearly made me fall out of my chair.

"Impressive," Felicity said as I opened the door. The corners of her mouth twitched. "Blowout sale on lightbulbs at the home shopping center, I see."

I shrugged into my coat and grabbed my purse. "Ready?" I said as I eagerly stepped past her onto the landing.

She hesitated behind me, one hand poised on the doorknob. "Shall I switch off the lights for you before we go?"

"No!" The panicky tone of my voice made her turn with a quizzical stare, so I amended, "I mean, it makes me feel . . . safer . . . to have a light burning when I get home after dark."

Her brows lifted as her gaze traveled from lamp to lamp, but she was gracious enough to keep her thoughts to herself. Instead, she followed me out and waited while I locked up.

Her car stood at the curb—warm, solid, safe. Real. I closed myself into the womblike interior and sighed with relief, not daring to look back at the house.

Felicity joined me a moment later. "Are you all right? You look white as a sheet."

"Let's just go, okay?"

I didn't want to tell her what I'd imagined. What I *must* have imagined. It seemed just too incredible for words. Even now—especially now?—having left the apartment and the situation behind, it seemed downright impossible. How could I help but doubting?

And yet, it happened. I knew it did. I hadn't been asleep. I hadn't been watching television or listening to the radio. Someone or *something* had whispered my name.

What that something was, was beyond my immediate comprehension.

"Maggie. *Maggie.*"

Someone was patting my hand.

"I'm sorry. Did you say something?" I shook my head, coming out of the haze of my thoughts with a start as I recognized the ornate Victorian building looming ahead of us, lights blazing not so much in welcome but more as a funereal rallying cry. "We're there already?"

"Actually, we arrived at least a minute ago." She peered at me with sudden interest.

"You're a bit of a lost lamb tonight."

She had enough on her mind. She didn't need my idiosyncrasies clogging up her brainwaves. It was bad enough that the terrors of my childhood were coming back to haunt *me*.

Of course there would be a perfectly reasonable, logical, *normal* explanation for what had happened. There must be. This was the twenty-first century, and I was no longer the strange, introverted child I once was. There was no real reason not to tell her, was there? We could laugh together over it. She could pat me on the head and tell me how silly I was being, and I could feel ridiculous and foolish and get on with things.

I took a deep breath. "Felicity, something . . . happened tonight. Something . . . I don't know how to explain it. I'm sure it was nothing, but—"

"At your apartment?" she interrupted.

I nodded. "A voice. Or something that sounded like a voice. It said my name. I thought . . . I thought someone had broken into my apartment—but—"

"But there was no one there." Her brow furrowed. "I knew there was something wrong when I arrived. I could see it in your face. I was, unfortunately, too preoccupied with my own thoughts to really listen." She shook her head ruefully. After a moment she patted my hand again. "It's quite likely there's nothing to worry about, however. Most spirits are perfectly harmless, as benign in death as they were in life. How did the experience make you feel?"

"Terrified," I said emphatically.

"Ah. Yes. Perhaps I should rephrase that. If this was your first experience with a spirit entity, your reaction is perfectly understandable. Man readily fears that which he does not understand, and what he does not fear, he typically ignores. What I want you to do is to close your eyes and think back. Reflect on what was happening in your body at the time. Feelings. Emotions. Smells. Random thoughts that might have popped into your head. Anything that might occur to you."

Skeptical though I was, I did as she asked, going back in time to relive the experience in too-vivid slow motion. What had I felt? Shock, initially. Incredulity. A mistrust of my own perceptions. I searched deeper, certain I was missing something. Felicity had mentioned smells. There was something . . . I'd assumed it to be fabric softener or some such at the time— but it wasn't that. Something flowery. Strong. Old-fashioned. Lavender, I think. Strange that I didn't take special notice of it at the time.

"Was it a male presence? Or female?"

"Female," I said softly, my eyes still closed. "I smelled flowers. Lavender. I remember that smell. My grandmother used to line the edges of her garden with lavender in a kind of minihedgerow. It kept the animals out."

I heard the creak of the leather seats as she relaxed. "Excellent. Your powers of recall are very good indeed."

For a moment there was nothing but the sound of our breathing. I opened my eyes, surprised at how calm I felt now.

"Maggie, have you had other experiences with things you couldn't explain? Now, or as a child?"

"I was afraid a lot when I was a little girl—seeing and hearing things that weren't there—but my mom always said I had a big imagination and not enough self-control to temper it."

"I see."

"I did have an imaginary friend. An old woman with long hair and a funny accent. Her name was Anna." I smiled, remembering how I would pretend that Anna would sit in the haymow with me, telling me stories about faraway people and places. "But that's not exactly remarkable. Lots of kids have imaginary friends."

"Of course they do. Has there been anything else? Anything since your invisible companion?"

"Well . . ." I cleared my throat uncomfortably. "There *was* the, uh, dog at your house."

She smiled indulgently. "I should have told you before, my dear. That was Cecil."

I frowned. "I thought you said you didn't own a dog."

"I don't. Cecil is my family's animal totem. A spirit guardian. When I moved to the States, he followed me."

Witchcraft, ghosts, animal totems. It was all just a bit too much. I tightened my fingers around the soft leather of my purse, because it, at least, was real. "I don't think I believe in any of these things."

"You don't have to believe. They can exist with or without your permission or acknowledgment." She eased off then, perhaps sensing that the conversation was straining the limits of my comfort level. "It's getting late. Perhaps we should go in now."

At that point, any diversion would have been a welcome one.

Hinkle & Binder Funeral Parlor was typical of many other small-town Midwestern funeral homes. That was to say, it was

a large, elaborate Victorian-era mansion, complete with tur-
rets and iron balconies, that had been converted over from a
private family dwelling midcentury, the whole of it lit up like
the Fourth of July by a covey of strategically positioned floodlights. For a moment I allowed myself to ponder the sheer
number of dead bodies that had passed through its halls over
the years.

*Maybe I'm not the only one who's a little bit afraid of the
dark.*

The steady flow of traffic spilling from the parking lot
should have prepared us for what we would find inside the
genteel old building. Inside the small foyer, at least forty
would-be mourners chatted elbow-to-elbow as they awaited
their turn inside the viewing room. I joined the crush gingerly,
squeezing into a small air pocket with all the enthusiasm of a
doomed inmate being led to the gallows. Large crowds were
not my thing.

*Panic is a sign of a weak constitution, Margaret. You
should pray harder to be relieved of such an infirmity.*

Prayer had been Grandma Cora's answer to everything.
Prayer and badgering. Each served a special purpose.

I knew I'd better find a distraction if I wanted to avoid becoming a quivering puddle of nerves, so I allowed myself a
good long look around the vestibule. The last time I'd been to
Hinkle & Binder, or any funeral home for that matter, had
been about fourteen years ago. The walls at the time had been
an ugly, outdated green that had gone out with shag rugs, lava
lamps, and macraméed anything. Now everything in my immediate view sported the sophisticated tones of a monochro-
matic color palette. No pea soup walls here. The paint chip
stand at the local hardware store gave these hues names like
Whispering Sand, Butterscotch Malted, Buttery Kiss, and
Willow Bark. The room oozed quality and refinement. Of
course, the slick, contemporary design of the interior was the
antithesis of the Victorian exterior, but I supposed that didn't
matter when a business wanted to attract a more upscale
crowd.

Slowly the throng moved en masse toward the more gener-
ously proportioned viewing room. Which, I noticed as we ap-

proached the door, was just as tastefully outfitted in shades ranging from sage to forest green. A noteworthy improvement over pea soup, I must say.

Felicity went stalk still as we reached the doorway and she put her hand on my arm. "There he is," she said faintly.

I followed her line of sight to a tall, well-dressed man standing near the high-gloss mahogany casket. I'd never seen him before—I would have remembered this one. In a professionally tailored navy suit complete with lapel kerchief and cufflinks—actual *cufflinks!*—he projected a kind of ultrasmooth appearance not often seen in our little town. "Who is he?"

Next to me, Felicity's gaze never wavered from her target. "Jeremy Harding. My sister's unfaithful husband."

Her breath was coming shallow through her nose, and her face had gone pale, except for the fever in her eyes and the flush of color at the centers of her cheeks. Lord have mercy, she looked *pissed*. This was a first. I'd never seen her look anything but a model of calm and composure. Somehow this little chink in her armor of English elegance made her seem more human to me.

"Cheating, hm?" I echoed speculatively as I let my gaze travel the length of Jeremy Harding. The carefully kept body. The lanky ease of movement. The tasteful dash of silver in black hair as thick and touchable as that of a man half his age. The relaxed confidence. Especially the confidence. He wore it like the mantle of a god, with the full knowledge that he was worthy of the admiration of all.

Felicity gave the merest of nods. "Don't let his looks deceive you. Jeremy may be attractive, but he's as shallow as a teaspoon."

"Wow. That shallow."

"What else would you call a man who brings his paramour to his wife's funeral?"

This was news. More than news, this was motive. I wondered if our good Deputy Fielding had uncovered the husband's . . . side interests.

I scanned the faces in the room, wondering which female was the guilty party. I was about to ask Felicity to enlighten me when a young woman approached us, her arms out-stretched toward my boss.

She gave Felicity a brief, stiff-armed hug then stepped back. "Auntie. So good of you to come tonight."

"Hello, Jacqui dear. I do hope my presence won't prove disruptive tonight. It's the last thing I want."

Jacqui said nothing. Not a single soothing word.

Charming.

"I'm so sorry about your mother," Felicity continued. "We may not have been on the best of terms, but this . . . this is an abomination."

"I'm sure Mother would appreciate your thoughts."

Felicity patted her on the arm. "Your mother's death must have come as quite a shock. How are you holding up, dear?"

The young woman shrugged, her shoulder-length sweep of ash blond hair shifting gracefully with the movement. "As well as can be expected, I suppose. I was out of town when Mother . . . when it happened. A business trip for Father. Imagine coming home to news like this. A terrible thing." She pushed her hair back, and her gaze flicked to me. "Hello. I don't believe we've met. I'm Jacquilyn Harding."

"Good heavens, where are my manners," Felicity exclaimed. "Maggie O'Neill, my niece Jacquilyn Harding."

Since she had not offered her hand, I kept my own closed tightly around my purse. "I'm so very sorry for your loss, Ms. Harding."

"Thank you."

"Maggie is my new assistant at the store," Felicity told her niece by way of introduction. "She's been a fantastic help for me already."

Though she did not move an eyelash, I could see Jacquilyn withdraw. "Ah. The store. How interesting." Her tone made it clear she found it anything but.

Felicity gave her niece a slight smile. "You know, my dear, I simply have to tell you. You sound more and more like your mother with every year that passes, did you know? What a blessing that must be for your father now."

The woman's pale eyes showed no emotion. "A blessing.

Yes." She cast an obvious glance over her shoulder. "Well. I'm afraid I must move on, Auntie—duty calls, and I would never forgive myself if I allowed Father to shoulder it all alone at a time like this. But I thank you both for coming."

She walked away without a backward glance, smoothly transitioning to another acquaintance who had come to pay his respects. I watched her for a moment from the corner of my eye. She was a strange one, to be sure. Young, almost pretty in a quiet sort of way, but the way she held herself was formal in the extreme and . . .

Subdued. Yes, that was the perfect word to describe her. Here she was, getting ready to bury her mother, and while she made all the right overtures and said all the right things, the words were dead. But then, people handle stress in different ways. Maybe hers was to withdraw from public displays of emotion.

One thing had not escaped my notice—her disapproval of Felicity had been readily apparent, even though she'd maintained that level of courtesy one kept intact when speaking with relatives.

Was it the store that she disapproved of? Or did she, too, suspect Felicity?

Felicity nudged me, breaking my train of thought. "There."

With the path of her gaze, she indicated a woman standing in a circle of polite strangers. A leggy blonde with permed curls teased high, she was striking in a hard sort of way, like a truckstop waitress wearing a pair of red satin shoes. And yet she wore clothes and jewelry that would have made my sister and her shop-'til-you-drop cronies sit up and beg. "Who is she?"

"Jetta James. Jeremy's personal assistant."

It didn't take much to read the writing on the wall, especially when it was written in such big, bold letters. What Ms. James lacked in polish, she made up for with a presence that was impossible to deny.

Or maybe it was just her teeny tiny black sheath dress with the slit up one thigh. It looked pricey, but that wasn't the issue. Evidently Ms. James did not have a grandmother like mine, who would happily have strung me up from the clothesline before allowing me to show any measure of my thigh in the presence of the dearly departed. But perhaps that was too harsh. She had, after all, covered her calves with a pair of knee-high leather boots, so maybe that made up for the funereal faux pas.

I tried not to be too obvious as I checked her out, taking careful note of her proximity to the mourning husband. "So. They're lovers?"

Liss broke her deathwatch to give me a sideward glance. "Well, I'm not sure love has anything to do with it, but they do seem to be all too familiar with each other."

"Do you know this for a fact?"

"Jeremy has all the subtlety of a hungry dog sniffing after a meal that's being kept just out of his reach." She chuckled softly, humorlessly. "There is a set of railroad tracks that runs along one edge of my property. A dirt trail follows along the tracks to the woods. Hunters used to use that trail before we bought the property. These days it's used more often as a lover's lane by young people when they think no one's paying attention. And evidently, by Jeremy. I've seen his SUV there more than once. Rather stupid of him, really. I have it on good authority he also has taken his lady love to Crooners, that country and western pub in Noble County—perhaps he thought no one would report back to Isabella." A sigh, long, weary. "I suppose that doesn't matter so very much now."

I turned my head to look back at Jeremy, calmly receiving his dead wife's mourners and looking all too much like the glib host of a cocktail party. "Do you suppose your sister knew about their affair?"

"I don't know. I never told her. What would have been the point? She'd had her share of . . . indiscretions . . . as well."

Including Felicity's own husband, if what Mel had told me was true. But a wife, even one who cheated, did not like another woman sniffing around her territory. What if she had found out about her husband's trysts? What if she had confronted him? What if he'd told her he wanted to be with his mistress and a violent quarrel had ensued?

Did Jeremy Harding have a motive for murder? *Oh yeah.*

"What about Ms. James? What do you know about her?" I whispered.

"Hush," Felicity said under her breath in lieu of an answer. Then she turned her attention past me, toward someone approaching on my left. As I watched, some part of her rose up, until it seemed to me that she had grown physically taller and straighter and more imposing before my very eyes. "Hello, Jeremy."

He sidled to a halt, his confidence turned aggressive. "Felicity." A curt nod.

From a short distance away, Jeremy Harding was the kind of man who made a woman suck in her stomach and touch a hand to her hair. Up close, the passing of years were apparent in the deep lines that fanned at the corners of his eyes and traced parentheses around his mouth, but I had a feeling most women over thirty would neither notice nor care.

Me? I couldn't get past the cold hard fury I saw in his eyes.

I knew that Felicity saw it as well, but honor ran deep in her veins. She was too much of a lady to acknowledge it. Instead she offered the proverbial olive branch.

"I've not had the chance to tell you how sorry I am about Isabella's passing."

"Are you?" He ran a hand back through the thick sweep of his hair. "I rather thought you might have come to enjoy the aftermath."

My mouth fell open. Even if the man was crazed with grief over his wife's death, no matter how unlikely that seemed considering Felicity's recent revelations, that was no excuse for a complete lapse in good manners and good taste. Recovering myself, I straightened my shoulders and prepared to leap to Felicity's defense.

But before I could do just that, Felicity placed a staying hand on my arm. "Fabulous to see you, too, Jeremy," she cooed in a soft tone that possessed all sorts of newly exposed sharp edges. "And may I just say, your assistant is looking particularly lovely this evening as well. Dear, sweet Jetta. Has she had her breasts done? They look a bit larger than I recall."

And the velvet gloves come off . . .

My respect for my boss deepened in spades.

An ugly look passed over Jeremy Harding's face. He threw a wary look back over each shoulder before snarling, "Keep your voice down."

"What's the matter, Jeremy? Don't you want anyone to discover the truth about your relationship with Jette?"

"This is neither the time, nor the place, witch."

Felicity drew herself up to her full five feet eight inches, looking every bit the queen in her understated wool suit. "I am comfortable with what I am. Are you equally at ease with what you are?"

Toe to toe and glaring daggers, they were beginning to attract curious stares from those closest to us. Jeremy became aware of the attention first. Like the flick of a switch, his face morphed into a mask of perfect, terrible respectability as he withdrew as unobtrusively as possible. Only his eyes showed the truth depth of his rage.

"If you had any decency at all, you wouldn't be standing in front of me," he hissed. "You're not wanted here."

Felicity shook her head in mock amazement. "Decency? Yet another word I never expected to hear coming from your lips, Jeremy. How you surprise me."

Someone cleared their throat nearby, the sound intruding upon the tension of the moment.

"Something I can do, Daddy?"

Jacquilyn had approached from behind, appearing quite suddenly and quite ready to come to her father's aid.

"Actually," Jeremy said, his ice chip eyes clashing with Felicity's calm stare, "your aunt was just leaving."

Felicity stood her ground, just as I knew she would. "Not," she persisted, "until I say farewell to Isabella."

Jacquilyn cut in and smoothly took her aunt's arm, effectively edging me out of the picture. "Let me come with you, Auntie."

Felicity allowed herself to be drawn toward the casket, leaving me to trail along behind. Until that moment, we'd remained along the fringes of the viewing room; I'd been able to forget that we'd come for more than people watching. Now the moment I'd dreaded had arrived, and I found myself doing something I hadn't done in nearly twenty years . . .

Approaching an occupied casket.

Chapter 8

The mahogany casket loomed before me, a remembered image that haunted me even as it drew me irrevocably nearer. So big, so polished, so black.

Breathe, Maggie. Just breathe, I told myself as I locked my gaze to the shifting shoulder blades of the two women walking just ahead of me. *There's nothing to worry about. Nothing to fear. Death is just a part of life. People do this all the time.*

Nothing to fear.

Step by step, moment by agonizing moment, I moved forward through the crowd that had gathered to pay their respects. There was something strange and otherworldly about my procession across the room. It was as if time had begun to shift and buckle, as if it were something physical and tangible that one could perceive beyond the abstract concept like a beam of light that could be bent or changed.

Oh, Maggie, honey, that does it. That flat out does it. You are going nuts. You're really losing it.

But even more unsettling than the sensation of time breaking free of its usually precise framework was the return of the anxiety I thought I had conquered. Six feet from the casket I slammed up against it—an invisible, impenetrable mass that called my name in a thousand whispered voices. I stopped in my tracks, frozen by the depths of an unreasonable panic even as Felicity and Jacqui paused by the closed casket, unaware of my distress. I'd been such a fool—there was no escaping this wall of fear and dread.

My breath came harder, faster, impossible to control. I opened my mouth to call out to Felicity, but no sound came.

I was lost. Alone in the middle of a crowded room.

Stars twinkled before my eyes. Perspiration stung sharply beneath my arms.

Terror . . . Complete, overwhelming terror.

I swayed on my feet and closed my eyes. I felt as though I were falling in slow motion, tumbling head over heels, wildly plummeting to an uncertain end. A shriek rose in my throat to echo the one I heard reverberating in my head. Raw and primal, it snagged there in my vocal chords, aching for release. Somehow I managed to hold it in, but the effort left me trembling and weak. The stars in my field of vision winked out, replaced in negative by pinpricks of darkness that expanded like the blooming of a terrible black rose.

Without warning I felt strong fingers wrap around my elbow.

"Easy does it. Here, let's just get you out of here. You look as white as a sheet."

An arm snaked behind me, supporting me at my waist. I surrendered without resistance, allowing myself to be led back through the multitude of bodies, and out into the bracing night air. It tasted wonderful. I sucked in great gulps of it, filling my lungs to bursting and blowing away the cobwebs that clouded the inside of my pounding skull.

The hands remained at my waist and elbow until I felt capable of standing on my own.

With an apologetic, if shaky, laugh, I ducked away at last. "Sorry about that. I don't know what came over me in there."

Just thinking about what I'd just experienced threatened to dislodge my tenuous grip on reality, so I turned to face my rescuer.

He was tall and well dressed, polished in a way I didn't usually associate with the men in Stony Mill. His tan was as golden and unnatural as a tanning bed membership will allow. Obviously another of Stony Mill's growing elite force. Perhaps because of the prep-school flip of his hair, I was reminded of a certain British film star whose boyish good looks and self-deprecating charm had masked a dark side few had imagined of him. I didn't recognize him, but I smiled my thanks anyway, all the while thinking how much he looked like a younger version of Jeremy Harding. Smooth. Unruffled. Confident. The kind of person who made me feel anything but.

"All better now?" He sent me a benevolent smile.

"Yes, thanks," I said, wondering where I'd put my composure. "I think so."

"I'm glad. We almost lost you in there."

He looked at me in a way that made me feel like a bug under the burning glare of a microscope. It didn't feel at all flattering.

I smoothed my palm over my hair, wondering if I looked anything at all like I felt. The prospect wasn't pretty. I felt like I had been run over by a Mack truck.

"I haven't introduced myself, have I," he said suddenly, extending his hand to me. "Ryan Davidson. I knew Isabella through hospital circles. Wonderful woman. Too bad, all this."

Certainly that was an understatement from Isabella's point of view, but from the standpoint of the living, what more could one say?

"Maggie O'Neill," I supplied. "So you knew Isabella, then. Of course you must have, being here." Well, I was there and I didn't know her at all, but logic didn't always make sense, now, did it? Not in my world. "Did you know her well?"

He shrugged and put his hands in the pockets of his wool flannel trousers, rucking up the front of his Harvard blue blazer. "We were business colleagues, Ms. O'Neill, nothing more."

His answer was quick and perhaps a trifle too firm, but I put that down to the situation. "I see. I'm sorry, I didn't mean to pry."

"Nothing to worry about. I didn't mean to be short with you. It's just that Isabella's death was such a waste. A damn shame."

I murmured in agreement.

"And how did you know Isabella? I thought I knew everyone here."

Whoops. So much for playing mum. "I, well, I accompanied a friend of mine. Isabella's sister, in fact."

"Aha. So you're Felicity's friend." He reached into an inner breast pocket to pull out a cigarette. From his slacks he brought out an old-style, fliptop lighter, the kind my grandpa was fond of carrying. "I had wondered."

The bug-under-a-microscope feeling intensified. I did my best not to squirm.

He cupped his hand around the end of his cigarette and leaned into his lighter. When a puff or two had the tip glowing hot, he waved it at me, a strange glint in his eye. "I probably shouldn't say this, but to hell with it. I didn't think Isabella and Felicity were on speaking terms. At least, that's the impression I got on the rare occasion Isabella spoke of her."

It was an odd, gossipy thing to say, and I wasn't about to satisfy his curiosity. "You seem to have known Isabella a bit better than you think."

He took a long drag on his cigarette, then laughed on the exhale. "I guess I knew her well enough. Isabella was a strong voice on the board. Fearless. Everyone admired that of her."

"The board?"

"Hospital board of directors. I've acted as legal counsel for the board for the past four years. Bella had . . . plans. Some of them required more of a legal presence than others." He shrugged. "We worked well together."

If his choice to divulge these things to me seemed out of place, it was the sort of thing I had gotten used to long ago. One of the peculiarities of my life thus far was an inexplicable tendency to be sought out as confidante by any number of people. I was a good listener, some had told me. Others didn't seem to realize what they'd shared at all. Whatever the cause, the personal revelations and secrets they shared seemed to leave them with a sense of release, but left me feeling troubled and ill at ease.

This time it was different, though. Ryan Davidson knew exactly what he was doing, and I had a feeling it had nothing to do with reminiscing about his board buddy Isabella.

Of course that didn't mean I couldn't do a bit of careful digging myself. Someone had killed Isabella. You never knew which of her acquaintances might hold the key to identifying the killer.

I pretended to be impressed. "Legal counsel for the board. That sounds terribly important."

"One never knows where the next lawsuit will come from," came his enthusiastic response, spoken with an unchanging smile. "My job is to advise the directors in every imaginable legal aspect. Frightening stuff, at times. Not for the faint of heart."

"And Isabella's heart?"

"Like I said. Fearless." Another drag while the cigarette tip smoldered. "She was absolutely unstoppable when it came to her pet projects. Never took no for an answer."

Isabella was a mover and a shaker? I'd had the impression she was just your average bored society wife. "What kind of pet projects?"

"Recently? Recently she was advocating the cause of the unwed mother. Quite vociferously, too. She wanted the hospital to create a special clinic for women. Family planning, pregnancy testing." He paused for a moment, then added, "Abortions."

I blinked at this. An abortion clinic, here in Stony Mill? Was she crazy? "Wow. That was some pet project."

"I see you understand the gravity of the situation."

That I did. Anywhere else north of the Mason-Dixon Line, that kind of clinic might not have been out of line. Anywhere else it might have been seen as progressive. But here, where the Bible Belt mentality was the order of the day, Isabella was lucky she hadn't been run out of town on a witch-hunt.

"She did have some of her regular opponents in an uproar over the idea," he continued, carelessly flicking his half-smoked and still glowing butt at the base of the tree that was providing us with shelter. "The Reverend Baxter Martin, for one. I think I can say without reserve that the old boy hated Bella's guts. In a purely Christian way, of course."

I smiled.

"He was always popping up at odd times with petitions against this or that. Tried to stir up trouble with his supporters. I *think* he even went a little crazy for a while. I know Isabella took out a restraining order against him a year or two ago, but then he stepped off the face of the earth for a time, and when he came back, I for one never heard another word about him. I always figured perhaps his family sent him away some-where, to get his head together." He took a moment to grind the smoking remnants of his cigarette under the heel of his shoe. "Anyway, Isabella had no sooner presented her ideas to the board two weeks ago than the whole thing was leaked to outsiders."

"Who would have done something like that?"

His lips twisted sardonically. "Who indeed?"

I was still pondering this a moment later when he cleared his throat to signal the end of our little discussion.

"Well," he said. "I'm glad you're feeling better. The crowd appears to be thinning out now, so I expect I'll go back in and rub some elbows. Maybe it is a little crass to use a viewing for a bit of down-home networking, but when you're shooting for a seat in Congress, you can't let yourself get squeamish about seizing the opportunities afforded to you. As my benefactor and primary supporter, I know Isabella would have understood."

I held out my hand to him. "Thank you for coming to my assistance when I needed it most."

"You can thank me by giving me your vote. Here's my card. Just to be sure you don't forget my name when the time comes." His toothy grin conjured images of the big, bad wolf. No doubt he meant to be charming, but then, so did the furry guy with the teeth and appetite. That kind of super-slick ma-neuvering never failed to send my antennae up. Somehow I doubted I would be moved to vote for Mr. Davidson when the next primaries came around. "Will you be going back in as well?"

"I think I'll stay out here awhile longer, thanks."

"Suit yourself."

There was no way I was going back in there. Instead, I watched him from the sidewalk, huddling beneath the wide-spread bowers of the massive old oak as he took the stairs two springy steps at a time. As he opened the door, I saw a flash of movement just inside. Someone stepped quickly out of sight and out of the way.

Had that someone been watching us?

I shivered, chilled as much by the thought as by the night air seeping through the weave of my thin sweater. My jacket would have been welcome, but it had been left behind, and like I said, there was no way in hell I was going back in there. Instead I tried to shake off the unease creeping up on me, rubbing my hands up and down my arms to chase away the goosebumps that had gathered there like scales of protective armor.

I must have been mistaken. There was no reason for anyone to be watching us. No reason at all.

Over my head, a freshening wind caught in the thick boughs of the tree, whipping them into a sudden frenzy of motion. It smelled of autumn, of wood smoke, of dried and dying things. I closed my eyes and listened to the sound of it, susurrant and hushed as it whispered through the remaining leaves, powerful and fierce as it whined past the bell tower of the church across the street. So wild. I lifted my face, expecting to see a gathering brace of storm clouds. Instead, through the maze of branches, I saw only a moonless expanse of velvety black sky punctuated by a million twinkling stars.

All around me the town had gone quiet. Not a single bird twittered. Not a single motor roared to life. Not a single dog barked. I was alone with the wind, the stars . . .

And the shadows.

One of them moved. I stared hard at it, willing it to stop, mentally demanding that it reveal itself as nothing more threatening than a bush or shrub or any other innocuous thing.

"Maggie?"

I nearly jumped out of my skin until I recognized the voice as Felicity's. With my hand pressed to my heart to keep it from tearing free of its moorings, I turned in the direction of her voice. "Jeez-Oh-Pete, you nearly killed me, Liss, coming up behind me like that. Why didn't you come out the front? I've been watching for you."

"Jeremy was holding court in front of the door. I didn't feel I could face him again, so I slipped out a side exit." She held my coat out to me. I took it with a rush of relief. "I didn't realize you'd already stepped outside until I couldn't find you."

"I didn't feel well all of a sudden," I said, responding to the unspoken question in her voice. The coat gave me instant protection from the relentless chill of the night breezes, but I couldn't stop shivering. The cold I felt went somehow deeper than that. "Someone saw that I was having trouble and helped me out for some air. Ryan Davidson was his name."

Her laugh pealed out, and she hooked her arm through mine as we walked toward the parking lot. "That man doesn't miss a thing. I hope you didn't let him hoodwink you. He's a right proper sham artist. A wolf in sheep's clothing."

I thought back to the gleam of his teeth in the twilight and to the shortage of character I had sensed—no, *known*—during our brief exchange. Call me judgmental, but I'd always been able to trust my first impressions, and I knew this impression was right on the money.

"I'll never understand what Isabella saw in the man," Felicity continued as we neared her Lexus. She pressed a button on her remote. The dome light came on, followed by the mechanical *click-crunch* of the locks lifting. "After Jeremy, one would think she'd have realized the problems associated with trusting a man whose only assets are a pretty face and misplaced ambition."

It took a moment for the meaning behind her comment to register. I stood there, my hand forgotten on the door latch. "Ryan Davidson and . . . Isabella?"

"Without a doubt."

Would wonders never cease? I don't know why I was so surprised, really. I didn't know Isabella, but if the last few days had taught me anything, it was that appearances and truths rarely coincide. Maybe it was just that I'd expected her to be more like Felicity—they were sisters, no matter how estranged, and since I had come to see my boss as both honorable and an astute judge of human nature, it seemed natural to assume that Isabella might have inherited those same qualities by default. Family resemblances, and all that. And yet what had I learned about her so far? That she had a unfaithful husband and an Ice Maiden daughter. That she served on the board of the hospital, advocated for women's issues, and dabbled in politics, if Mr. Davidson could be believed. That she herself had cheated at least once with Felicity's late husband. And that before her death she had had a thing going with her hospital associate, one Mr. Ryan Davidson.

We were silent for a moment as we got in the car and closed ourselves in, each preoccupied by her own thoughts.

"Mr. Davidson told me he'd hardly known Isabella," I murmured, still working through the details.

"Did he?"

She sounded amused. I, on the other hand, was miffed.

"Well, if that just isn't . . . Doesn't anyone believe in honesty anymore?" I grumbled. "Why would he lie?"

It wasn't the lying, so much. There was just no point to it. It offended that fastidious side of me that believed that the world should make sense. Somehow.

Always realistic, Felicity shrugged. "Who knows? Self-preservation is my bet. With Ryan, everything is about self-preservation. Darwin would have loved the man. He fully embraces the notion of survival of the fittest. Really, I'm not certain he even knows how to tell the truth. It isn't his nature."

I squinted at her across the dark womb of the car. "You seem to know a lot about him."

"He served on the town council with Gerald—my late husband—a few years back," Felicity said, her gaze never wavering from the road ahead. "Typical small-town affairs, but apparently Ryan let it be known he believed our little haven to be a mere stepping stone on the road to a much higher level of success. He may be young and he may be easy on the eyes, but he's no innocent."

I mulled this over as the Lexus purred through the residential streets of Stony Mill, and I tried to adopt her pragmatic outlook. So the man had lied. Big deal. People lied all the time, sometimes with good reason, sometimes for no reason at all. It wasn't nice, but it was human nature. His lies meant nothing to me. They were empty. He probably didn't intend for them to impact on me at all.

Just chalk it up to one man's bad habit and get on with your life, O'Neill.

My mother had a saying she was fond of repeating whenever she was trying to prove a point: *Let go and let God.* I didn't know about that, but I did know that within minutes of turning my back on the cause of my discontent, I felt a physical release as it all fell away, one piece at a time. Relieved of its hold on me, I began to relax as the gentle motion of the car and the familiar roadside sights worked together to lull me into a better mood. Felicity had switched on the heater to drive away the chill. Hot air blew from the front vents at full throttle. It sucked the moisture out of my skin and left my eyes feeling as arid and desiccated as the long-dead flesh of an Egyptian mummy, but I wouldn't have had it any other way. Hot and dry beat the hell out of cold and clammy any day. Cold and clammy reminded me of all those horror movies my mom had tried to keep me from watching, like *Horror from Beyond the Grave* and *Revenge of the Vampire Zombies.* I'd had enough of death and darkness for one night.

The car pulled up to the curb. With a start I recognized the looming outline of my Victorian apartment house.

Felicity shifted the car into park and smiled over at me. "Feeling better?"

A few days ago, I would have been ill-at-ease with her uncanny ability to read my thoughts. I'd come a long way, baby. "Much. Sorry. I guess the viewing got to me."

"No need for apologies. It was my fault. If I hadn't lost hold of myself like that . . . I'm ashamed of myself. I should have recognized . . ." She stopped abruptly and shook her head. "I'm afraid I was too caught up in my antagonism toward Jeremy to realize you were uncomfortable."

"It was the heat. I'm sure of it."

"Of course it was," she soothed, patting my hand. Then she looked up toward the house, where a single light shone through a gauzy curtain on the second floor. "I like your apartment. I meant to tell you that earlier."

"It's okay. I'd have preferred one of the upper levels, but the basement apartment is cheaper, and it was the only one available at the time. I was lucky to get it." I groped in the dark, wondering where the car manufacturer had managed to hide the door handle. *Ah. Got it.* "Will you be going to the funeral tomorrow?"

Felicity shook her head. "I've said my farewells. My presence at the gravesite would only present problems. And Jacqui, at least, deserves to say her good-byes in peace."

I paused, my hand frozen on the lever. "Are you sure? I mean, she *was* your sister."

"I'm quite sure. No one really wants me there. It would be . . . awkward."

"But . . ."

"But it makes me look guilty?" Felicity laughed softly as she glimpsed my stricken expression. "Don't look so horrified. It isn't a crime to have a mind, Maggie. You should never feel sorry for using it."

"I just don't want you to think—"

"I don't. I promise." She rolled her palms back and forth over the steering wheel. "But Maggie, I refuse to live my life by the rules and expectations of others. They're wrong about me—you know that. Someday, they will come to know it, too."

I nodded miserably. "Do you think they'll find Isabella's murderer, Liss?"

She turned to look at me, her eyes as stormy and impenetrable as Lake Michigan. "Good times three. Evil times three. Justice will be done. It's the way of the Universe. I *have* to believe that." In the blink of an eye, her expression softened, and she smiled at me. "Thank you, my dear, for coming with me this evening. I don't know what I'd have done without you."

We said our good-byes and I let myself out. As I stepped from the car, the wind picked up again as if by magic. It whined around the corner of the tower room and spun dried leaves around my ankles like the scuttling of crabs. I clutched at my collar to ward off its invading force. Felicity waited in the car as I made my way slowly up the walk and around the corner of the house to the narrow flight of stone steps that led down to my basement apartment.

I slowed instinctively as I approached them. I kept remembering the sounds I'd heard before Felicity had picked me up that evening. The whispered voice. And then there was the frigid air. I wasn't convinced I hadn't imagined the whole thing. It was possible, wasn't it? I knew it was silly, but a part of me wanted to hightail it back to Felicity for her protection. There was a safety in numbers that sounded like a pretty good idea right about then.

The grown-up side of me won out over more childish impulses. With my keys in hand and my heart in my throat, I deliberately descended the steps.

At the bottom of the sunken stairway, leaning up against my door, I found a sealed manila envelope with my name on it. I bent and picked it up. Not much heft to it. I slid my thumb under the flap and pulled out a note and a few photocopied sheets of paper.

Maggie, I read, *here are copies of all references to the Hardings that I have been able to lay my hands to so far. I hope they help you. If not, well, I will keep looking. The historian in me is having a blast. It's amazing the kinds of interesting information one can find in the local newpaper.* It was signed: *Blessings, Marian*

I flipped through them quickly. The first was an announcement dated January 9, 1991. Harding Enterprises opens its doors officially for the first time. The article named Isabella as new owner of a refurbished medical supplies company, with Jeremy Harding as CEO after the previous owners, Mal and Mo Rodgers, liquidated their local holdings and set out for warmer climes. My mind quickly latched on to the fact that Isabella was the owner. In other words, the person who controlled the purse strings. The one with all the power.

The second snippet was copied from the society column from 1993, the year Jacquilyn Harding graduated from prep school. The Hardings honored their daughter with a graduation celebration held at the local country club. The photo above it didn't photocopy well, but from the murky details I was able to make out a smiling father and daughter, arms wrapped about each other's waists. I had to laugh—Jeremy had the look of a yacht club reject, having chosen a nautical-themed sweater in lieu of his double-breasted blazer. Very early nineties.

On Jacqui Harding's right stood a good-looking young man whose arm was slung loosely around her neck. A silly grin split his flushed face as he jutted out his jaw to receive a congratulatory kiss from a fortyish Isabella on his right. Isabella, I noted from what little I could make out from her grainy profile, was dressed to kill in a wide-shouldered (love those Frisbee-sized shoulder pads) but slinky sweater dress that clung to her slender torso like a lover's embrace. The pic was nearly ten years old, but unless things had changed overmuch, Isabella had been quite lovely.

The caption beneath the photo identified the boy as Justin Marsh. The Marsh name was well known in Stony Mill, appearing on many buildings and historical placards, and common in country club settings. Very much outside my usual stomping grounds. A high school boyfriend of Jacqui's? Possibly. It was obviously a happier time in her life. I wondered what had happened to him, and to her.

The third and last piece was a letter to the editor, dated July, three years ago. My eyes widened as I skimmed the letter and went back to the top to read it again. It appeared to be a diatribe against the declining morality of Stony Mill, authored by one Reverend Baxter Martin. Though it didn't reference the Hardings by name, details within the letter itself made it clear that his disapproval extended to certain individuals and that he saw it as further illustration of the decline of the town and, more importantly, the world beyond. A notation from Marian, written in red ink: *Thought this might be of interest as well. Let me know if you don't understand. M.*

Maybe I should do just that. It would be interesting to see what Marian knew.

I began to stuff the pieces of paper back in the envelope. As I fastened the catch, the security light beside me blinked and fizzled, drawing my attention.

Just a power glitch, I told myself. *Old houses always have trouble with their wiring.*

The light winked out entirely as I turned my key in the lock.

Apprehension crawled across my skin. It prickled down my spine and lodged itself at the pit of my stomach. Cold as ice.

Stop it, Mags.

I made myself open the door. It swung noiselessly inward, bumping against the stopper on the wall behind it. The sound it made as it hit echoed the frightened thud of my heart. So far, so good. I stepped onto the rug just inside the door and stopped. Outside I could hear the retreating purr of a car engine—Felicity's Lexus. Enough time had passed that she must have decided I'd gotten inside, safe and sound. My sense of security disappeared, but it was too late for me to turn back now. Summoning up my nerve, I reached out to flip the light switch to ON. It hit me then, as I replayed in my mind my hasty departure—

I'd left all the lights on.

I froze where I stood, right there on the rug, my heart beating a thousand times a minute. The lights had been on; I knew it. Felicity had even offered to switch them off for me. That could only mean one thing.

Someone had been in my apartment.

Chapter 9

I wasn't stupid, and I wasn't crazy. Without further ado, I grabbed my Louisville Slugger from where I'd left it by the door and beat a hasty retreat. Christine beckoned at the curb, but even with keys, getting past her accident-prone door locks was iffy, at best. So, I did the next best thing . . . I raced up the back stairs to Steff's second-floor apartment.

I pounded on her door. "Steff! Steff, it's me. Let me in, hurry!"

Footsteps sounded inside, then the click of the deadbolt. She opened the door. Had I not been in such a panic, I might have felt my customary pang of envy. Dressed to the hilt in a clingy black dress and heels, her hair dressed up in a soft cascade of auburn curls, she made my sober suit look like a schoolmarm's getup. As soon as she opened the door, I barged past her, pulled her back inside, slammed the door shut, and turned the bolt.

"Well, hello to you, too," Steff said, her brows arched in surprise.

"Hey," I panted by way of greeting as I switched off her lamp and raced back to the window beside her door. I pulled the curtain aside, just a crack, and peered out into the dark side yard.

"Maggie, what are you doing?"

I turned to her, a shadow in the inky dark of the room. "Have you seen anyone at my place tonight?"

"I just got home. What's going on, Mags? Why are you—"

"I think someone was in my apartment tonight."

"What? In your apartment? Are you sure?"

Quickly I told her what I'd found when I returned.

Steff switched the lamp back on and we sat down together on the overstuffed sofa. "Okay, let's not lose our heads here. Think. Does anyone else have a key to your apartment besides the one you gave me?"

I shook my head grimly. "No one. I have one hidden in Christine, but no one else knows that."

"Not even your mom?"

I gave her a scathing glance. "Oh, sure. Let's get real. My mother would think a key gave her carte blanche to dig through every aspect of my life." I paused then, wondering whether I should tell her the rest. Guilt nudged at me for even questioning. I hadn't purposely withheld anything from Steff, *ever*. Why should I start now? "Steff, there's more. Don't . . . don't think I've gone over the deep end or anything, but there's something I haven't told you."

"Go on."

I bit my lip. "I think . . . no, I know . . . well, at least I *think* I know—"

"Just say it . . . whatever it is can't be all that bad."

"I heard a voice in my apartment tonight. Before I left with Felicity. It's why I had all the lights blazing and why I refused to turn them off before we left."

"A voice? You mean someone was in the apartment with you? Someone just outside? What?"

"I don't know. I was in my bedroom, getting dressed. Something said my name. I grabbed my bat and searched the apartment, but the door was still locked, and—well, you know my apartment, it's not exactly easy to hide in it. There was no one there. It was awfully cold, though. Almost as though the door had been left open long enough to chase the heat out. Except the deadbolt was still shot, so that's impossible."

Steff frowned at me, her lips pressed tightly together. "And you're absolutely certain . . ."

"Positive. I heard the voice. But there was no one there."

"It doesn't really sound like typical criminal behavior, though, does it. And I know you too well to suspect paranoid delusions." She got to her feet and went to the refrigerator, coming back with two cans of Diet Coke. She handed one to me. "Unless you want something stronger."

I shook my head. "This is good, thanks."

"You know, I hate to mention this, but has it occurred to you that it might not have been an actual person at all?"

"The TV wasn't on either, Steff."

"I'm not talking about the TV. Tell me, do you know how old this house is?"

I glanced around her apartment, which was as unlike mine as it could be. Whereas my basement apartment was outfitted in a terrible, dark laminate paneling and hand-me-down furniture, Steff had furnished hers with a flowery, overstuffed chintz sofa and coordinating easy chair, a dainty rocking chair, and decorated the pale yellow walls with framed posters of Monet paintings. Girly to the max, but all the furniture matched, and everything had been pulled together with an obvious overall plan that would have made Steff's interior decorator mom proud. "I don't know. Over a hundred years, I guess."

"One hundred and thirty-two, to be exact. It has a history all its own." She cocked her can in my direction. "Do you know how many people can live and die in a place within that kind of a time frame?"

"Yeah. Sure. A lot. What does that have to do with anything?"

"What if what you heard wasn't human? I'm serious!" she insisted when she saw me raise my brows. "What you've described sounds just like what went on at our house in Massachusetts before we moved here. I mean, I was just a little girl, but you just don't forget stuff like that."

"What do you mean . . . ghosts?" I said with a snort. "Devils? Things that go bump in the night?"

She gave me her laugh-if-you-will look, the face she made whenever she felt I was questioning her authority. Nurturing as Steff had always been, she could get downright testy when someone didn't respect her opinion.

"Foolish mortal," she said, shaking her head reproachfully as she patted my hand. "I know, I know, you haven't had the same experiences I have. How can I expect you to be open-minded when you're untouched by the unknown?"

I made a face at her. "Very funny."

"It wasn't meant to be. I was trying to make excuses for you, because obviously I was demanding too much of your unenlightened sensibilities. How can you understand what you've never seen, or heard, or felt?"

I let out a deep breath. She was right. I did owe it to her to at least try to keep an open mind. And besides, hadn't my mind taken me to that same dark place on its own? The difference was, *I'd* talked myself out of it.

Perhaps too soon.

"All right, then. Say it was a ghost. It seems ludicrous to even think that, but— for the sake of argument—let's just say. What does it want from me?"

"Who the hell knows? I never said I was an expert. But since you're asking, I'll tell you what I do know. Our spirit didn't seem to want anything, really. She just moved things around when we weren't looking, and then she'd put them back when we least expected it. Every once in a while, she might make some noise if you were home alone. Or if we had guests. I think she liked the excitement of our response. Oh, and she would sit on the end of my bed at night sometimes. Nothing too terrifying."

I gaped at her in abject horror. "Speak for yourself! Anything that sits down on the edge of *my* bed had better be male and plenty warm blooded. And he'd better have a pulse!"

She laughed at that and patted my hand. "Aw, honey."

"I'm supposed to be a grown woman. Don't you think I'm a little old to be seeing things and hearing things?"

"Oh, I don't know. It's not just kids. You wouldn't believe how many nurses at the hospital have experienced something out of the ordinary on the night shift. Heard something. Seen something. It isn't even confined to places where people have died. I read somewhere that it can happen even in newly built homes."

"But how? Why?" I gripped my can harder, my fingers leaving indents in the soft aluminum. "I don't understand any of it. Nothing like this has ever happened to me before. I . . . I don't believe in the supernatural."

"Looks like you don't have to believe."

Wasn't that the truth.

Steff slipped off her high-heeled sandals and folded her legs beneath her. "You said you went to the Harding viewing tonight?"

I nodded. "With Felicity."

"How did that go?"

"Before I nearly lost control of my faculties or after?"

She winced sympathetically. "Oooh. That bad, huh?"

"It was"—I paused, searching for the right word—*"interesting."*

"How is your boss handling it?"

"Okay, I guess. Matter-of-factly, which is pretty much her usual modus operandi. Except for when she had to talk to Jeremy Harding—Isabella Harding's husband."

Carefully I described the conversation that had transpired between these two charismatic people and the animosity that filled the space between them until it had seemed a physical thing, dense and impenetrable.

Steff chewed thoughtfully on her lip as I finished my tale. "So the family wasn't without its problems. You have the estranged sisters—"

"One of whom, if rumor is to be believed, had an affair with the other's late husband. Poor Felicity."

"You have your basic loathing between the remaining sister and her former brother-in-law."

"Not that either of them feels the need to apologize for it. And Liss doesn't seem the type to entertain petty feuds or jealousies, so I can't help but think she must have a good reason for her hostility. She did call him 'Isabella's unfaithful husband.' Oh! How could I have forgotten this? He brought his, um, lady friend to the viewing."

Steff's brows went up. "No. Not really?"

I nodded vigorously. "I saw her myself. Felicity pointed her out. Mid-thirties, I'd guess. Well preserved, but hard. Expensive black sheath dress that might possibly have been one size too small. Silk. It was slit up to . . . well, never mind."

"Interesting funeral wear."

"Yeah. I never saw them together at the viewing, but then again, she was never more than a few steps away from him, either. Oh, and then there was the daughter. If that was the face of grief, I'll never eat chocolate again. She worked harder at the role of hostess than that of grieving daughter, and she couldn't wait to get us out of there."

Recognition lit up Steff's eyes. "That would be Jacquilyn?"

"Uh-huh. Do you know her?"

"Vaguely. Actually, I, um, know her fiancé."

My ears perked. Now that was something new. Despite the graduation photo, somehow I was having a hard time picturing the ice princess I'd just met getting cozy with a guy. "She has a fiancé? I didn't see her with anyone at the viewing."

"Roger Foley." Steff seemed to take a sudden, studied interest in a blanket folded over the arm of the sofa. "His father owns a factory on the north side of town."

"I wonder why he wasn't there tonight." I couldn't help noticing how Steff's fingers worried the nubby weave of the blanket. Now, I might be a little preoccupied, but I wouldn't be much of a friend if I didn't recognize the signs that my best buddy was having a momentary crisis. "How do you know him?"

She was silent for a long moment before she answered. "I, uh, dated Roger—briefly—last summer. Not long. I met him at a party, and he pretended to be charming. It didn't take more than a date or two for me to recognize him for the playboy he was." She coughed self-consciously. "I, er, think he was engaged to Jacquilyn Harding at the time. I didn't know it until later, though, I swear. He really was a jerk."

Well. Isabella and her family certainly knew how to surround themselves with the best sort of people.

"It's just like him not to attend Isabella's funeral, though, so don't read too much into that. Roger's a twit, but I don't think he would have anything to do with murder."

I took her view of this point with a grain of salt. Of course she wouldn't want to think that a man she had dated could have been involved in a murder. Who could blame her? "At this point, we don't know enough to count anyone out." Except Felicity. Call it instinct, call it trust. Whatever it was, I still felt certain of that conviction. "Steff, have you ever heard of Ryan Davidson?"

"Have I ever. Everyone at the hospital knows *Mister* Davidson. Why? Did you meet him tonight, too?"

"He came to my rescue, actually. The viewing, the crush of people, the casket . . . it all started to get to me. I felt like . . . like a great wall of—I don't know—energy, I guess, was keeping me from moving forward. Panic attack, I suppose. Anyway, I was just about to completely lose it. He saw me and took me outside for a breath of air so that I could calm down. Just in time, too. What?" I asked as I caught sight of her face. "What is that for?"

"Nothing," Steff said with a little shrug. "Just that he doesn't exactly strike me as the benevolent savior type."

I thought back, remembering my first impressions of him. "No, he doesn't, does he." It did seem maybe a little too coincidental that he just happened to notice my little attack of nerves. "Well. Assuming that he had a reason for getting me alone, I wonder what he wanted."

"Well, if he didn't find it already, he'll be back," Steff said with a toss of her bobbing curls. "You can depend on that."

I shook my head. "I doubt it. He'll be too busy looking for another—shall we say, benefactor?—now that Isabella's gone."

Steff smirked. "Well, I could pretend that I'm surprised, but you know, nothing much surprises me anymore. The man has quite the reputation among the hospital staff. He's hit on too many Pretty Young Things for there to be any questions about his motives."

Motives. That was what we needed. Something, anything, that would demonstrate to the Stony Mill PD that Felicity was a dead end, and that they really ought to be investigating every aspect of the case. If this night had proven anything to me, it was that somehow I had managed to get on the right track.

"Did anyone else arouse your suspicions tonight?" Steff said, interrupting my train of thought.

"You make me sound like Brenda Starr, Ace Reporter," I complained, making a sour face. "But in answer to your question . . . *maybe*."

"Well?"

"Davidson let on that Isabella had taken out a restraining order against someone."

"Let me guess . . . her husband?"

"Nope. You'll never guess this one."

"Do tell."

"A Reverend Baxter Martin."

Her brows stretched high. "You're right. I can't believe it. A reverend?"

"I have no idea if it's true or not. But I intend to find out."

"How?"

Well, I hadn't gotten that far yet, but I had no doubt that if I was meant to find out, a way would present itself to me. I'd long ago discovered that if I stopped trying to rush things and let them happen on their own, they would do just that without my help. "I'm still working out the details."

"You don't have a clue, do you."

"Not even one. But what I do have is good, old-fashioned Hoosier resourcefulness."

"Uh-huh. That and a dollar will buy you a cup of coffee."

"Something will come up. I'm sure of it."

"I hope you're right. And I hope it's sooner rather than later. It makes me feel twitchy to know that there's a killer on the loose. The question is, is he a he? Or is she a she?"

"You mean, is it a husband, a lover, a mistress, or a whacked-out religious fanatic?"

"That about does it, yes."

"It is rather amazing, the sheer number of potential assassins Isabella had amongst her acquaintances," I said in all seriousness. Then I laughed in spite of myself. "Listen to us. We're either turning into a pair of honest-to-goodness sleuths, or else we're turning into a couple of old cats, gossiping and carrying on."

"It's a sad, sad thing."

I ended up spending the night at Steff's.

Calling myself a coward didn't change my mind. Neither did repeated self-affirmations. I'd psyched myself up for the eventual return to my place for hours while we talked well into the night. Every time I thought about it, the great black maw of my apartment opened wide in my mind's eye, jeering at me from the darkness and goading me to come down and play. Trouble is, I wasn't quite sure what I was dealing with, and until I knew by whose rules I was playing, the game was going to have to go on without me.

After all, a sleeping bag on a friend's sofa was eminently more inviting than a sleepover date with something dark and unnatural.

I woke up around eight after a long restless night of tossing and turning with the feeling there was something I had to do.

I sat up amid the bulky confines of the half-zipped sleeping bag and blinked away the sleep from my eyes. Steff was already up—I could hear the shower running, and from the kitchen wafted the scent of fresh-brewed coffee. Kicking my way free of the sleeping bag, I stumbled in the direction of the tiny galley kitchen. Not much bigger than my own, it was little more than a sink, a stove, a row of cupboards—up and down—and a small table. What it did have that mine did not was a killer cappuccino machine, a gift from a former boyfriend.

Like I said, Dr. Ruth had nothing on Steff. The woman was legend.

I found two cups set out on the counter, just waiting for someone to fill them. I was only too happy to oblige. The cappuccino machine made a lovely, foamy, sputtering sound as it shot the steaming liquid into first one cup, then the other. I had just buried my nose behind the rim of mine when Steff emerged from the bathroom, wrapped from head to toe in baby pink bath towels.

"Ahhh," she sighed as she accepted the cup I held out to her, "there's nothing like a hot shower to make a tired woman feel human again."

"Oh, good. There's still hope for me, then."

"Didn't you sleep well?"

I shrugged and ducked her question. "What do you have on your calendar for today?"

"The usual stuff this morning." Setting down her cup, Steff unraveled the towel from her head. Her auburn hair fell heavily to just below her shoulders. As she talked, she used her fingers to tousle it into curls. "You know. Cleaning the toilet. Laundry. Tonight I have a date with Danny."

"Danny?" I asked. She must have moved on. The last boyfriend I remembered her talking about was some guy named Paul.

Her lips curved in a secret little smile. "Dr. Daniel Tucker."

"Someone new?" And a doctor, too. Impressive.

She snugged her towel tighter around herself and then reached into a cupboard for a bowl. "*Very* new. Danny is a new intern at the hospital, fresh from med school in Massachusetts. How he ended up interning *waaaay* out here is beyond me. With anyone else I'd guess poor grades, but Danny is brilliant. Absolutely brilliant. Want some Sugar Smacks?"

I grimaced. "Er, no thanks. Not before ten."

"Suit yourself." She poured an overflowing helping of the sugary puffed wheat, added a dollop of milk, then settled herself into a kitchen chair.

I sat down across from her, bracing my elbows against the tabletop with my cup held hostage between my cupped hands. "*Soooo.* Tell me. What's Dr. Danny like?"

She licked a droplet of milk off her lips. "Dishy. Gor-juss. He's taking me out for dinner and a movie tonight."

"Aha. Which one?"

"I don't know. Either a chick flick or a spook show, that much we know. All the better for snuggling, doncha know." She waggled her eyebrows.

At any other time, I would have shared my own plans for the evening then, but at this point it was all too new, too uncertain, and in the end I chickened out. How could I tell Steff, the queen of Saturday night, that I *might* have a date . . . assuming I hadn't misread the interest in Tom Fielding's eyes . . . when in reality it was probably all my imagination, and that really, the evening would likely be no more than a way for Deputy Fielding to worm information out of me. Assuming that I knew anything he did not.

I took a sip of my cooling cappuccino. "If you don't have anything pressing this morning, I was wondering . . ."

I broke off, uncertain how to explain what had been running through my head since the moment I opened my eyes.

Steff glanced up from her cereal, took one good look at me, and set down her spoon. "What's on your mind, Mags?"

"Well, I was thinking. Isabella Harding's funeral is today. I thought I might . . . well, that I might go. Felicity won't be attending, and I just thought it would make sense to put in an appearance."

Understanding made her green eyes sparkle. "And you want me to go with you?"

I nodded, thankful that she could read me so well. "We'll be able to watch people's faces. See their expressions, observe their reactions."

"Nancy Drew time?"

"Exactly. Someone has to look out for Felicity's best interests."

She considered this, then pushed her chair back and stood up. "Right. Give me five minutes."

Chapter 10

One can always judge the caliber of one's friends by their readiness to sacrifice for you. Not only did Steff cut her breakfast short, but she also accompanied me back to my apartment so I could grab some clothes. In light of what I'd told her last night, I considered this above and beyond the call of duty.

But that was Steff for you.

My apartment was still dark, all the light switches flipped down, even though I knew I had painstakingly turned every last one on before I tore out of there like a complete scaredy-cat. Why I had expected things to revert back to normal overnight, I don't know. Wishful thinking, I suppose.

Steff walked around, antennae up for anything out of the ordinary as I nervously threw my suit on the bed. In the blink of an eye I had yanked on a respectable sweater and dark slacks, dragged a brush through my unruly hair, and tamed it with one of those handy-dandy toothy hair clips (a working girl's best friend). One blink more and I had pulled on a pair of loafers that were only minorly scuffed, then finally hurried back to Steff's side before the bogeyman could get me. I snagged her by the arm and pulled her toward the door.

"There. You see? Nothing happened," I told her, relieved to be turning my key in the lock and heading for the flight of cement steps that would carry me back to safety. To normalcy. "It *must* have been my imagination. There is no other explanation."

"Uh-huh. That would definitely explain the lights."

"Maybe I only thought I left them on," I argued, a little out of breath as we crossed the yard and headed toward the curb. Christine waited there like a faithful hound, a little tired, a little worse for the wear, perhaps even a bit temperamental at times, but there for me when the chips were down. I gave her an affectionate pat on the hood before scrounging in the depths of my purse for my keys.

"We could take my car," Steff offered too quickly.

"Oh, that's okay. Christine needs to be run regularly or she gets testy."

"Really, I have a tank full of gas. It wouldn't be any trouble. Really."

My groping fingers hit paydirt. "Found 'em!" I exclaimed, waving the keys around in triumph.

"Well, if you're *sure* you're sure . . ." When I turned to look at her, she shrugged. "I don't think your car likes me, that's all."

"Don't be silly. She's just a car."

"Hunh. Don't forget, I've actually read Stephen King."

But she got in anyway, settling into the worn passenger-side bucket seat without further complaint. While I revved the engine for a few minutes to heat up the oil and prime the pump, so to speak, Steff punched idly at the chrome buttons on the antiquated radio.

"Static. Always static." She sighed and flopped backward against her seat.

"She might like you better if you didn't always insult her."

Steff just didn't understand Christine. Sure, she provided constant challenges in my everyday, ordinary, plain Jane life. Sure, I might daydream about owning a brand, spanking, straight-from-the-factory new car, one that didn't try to lock me out on a regular basis and that smelled fresh and clean and not like a pair of my brother's old gym socks left out on the back porch overnight. But to tell you the truth, there was a comfort level to driving Christine that went beyond tangibles.

Christine was a real rock. You'd never find her spray-painted Day-Glo orange and spewing Marilyn Manson from her throbbing woofers and twizzling tweeters. She had a way of doing things that was unquestionably her own, and I loved her for it.

Oh boy. Was I waxing poetic about my car? I really needed to get out more.

According to the obit in the local paper, Isabella's family had chosen not to have a funeral service at a church, selecting instead a short graveside vigil that was more likely to fit into the busy schedules of the PalmPilot and cell phone set. Even so, the dearth of cars lined up behind the gleaming black hearse in the parking lot at Hinkle and Binders took me entirely by surprise. At this rate, we probably wouldn't even need a police escort. The viewing had been standing room only, and I had decided to attend the funeral based on the understanding that I would be afforded a certain degree of anonymity at the cemetery. Unfortunately it was fast becoming obvious that I would be hard pressed to remain in the background.

Despite what I'd told Steff, I'd had no intention of actually participating in the funeral. I figured I could stand back, maybe even watch from my car, as the words were spoken over the closed coffin and people said their final farewells. It would be interesting to see who attended, and who did not. Best of all, it would keep me from having to be anywhere near the coffin.

So much for plans.

We pulled off the state road we had followed south of town, into the quiet, tree-shrouded gravel lanes of Oakhill Cemetery. Christine was number eleven in a string of no more than fifteen cars, one of which was the hearse. There was no hope for fading into the masses, because there were no masses. Were it not for Steff's reassuring presence encouraging me to stay the course, I might have abandoned my place in the lineup entirely. Instead I found myself gripping the wheel tighter and trying to convince myself that all would be well. This was for Felicity, who would not do it for herself. I would see it through as best I could.

The morning had dawned sunny and clear of all traces of the previous week's mists and rains. It was the kind of October morning that persuaded one that winter was a very long way off. A day of warmth and wiles and wishful thinking. A day of promise. The perfect day to bury a person who had died under mysterious circumstances. I watched as the others in attendance left their cars and drifted toward the black-suited minister who waited, his hands clasped around a worn Bible, an air of solemnity worn like a badge of office.

"Welcome, friends. Welcome."

Steff got out first, before I could put out a hand to stop her. Without hesitation, she wandered over to the fringes of the gathering. In slim black slacks, ankle boots, a belted leather jacket, and shades, she looked every bit as if she belonged there. I watched from inside Christine, biting my lip and fighting down the apprehension that was turning my insides to Jell-O.

Apprehension merged with confusion when the group turned as one and wandered somberly through a legion of marble tombstones toward an imposing limestone building built into a hillside a short distance away, near the treeline at the back of the cemetery.

My heart stood still. *The Mausoleum.*

I'd been to it only once, when I was a little girl. Ten, maybe eleven years old. A bunch of us had been playing together when someone, I don't remember who, dared us all to go to the cemetery. We'd ridden our bikes across town that long, lazy summer afternoon. Laughing as we called each other good-natured names, we'd laid odds on who would be brave enough to touch the gated door of the mausoleum beneath the watchful gaze of its monumental guardian high above. The angel's arms stretched up toward heaven, but the eyes . . . pupil-less, blind, the eyes looked down upon you. Bore into you. Straight into your soul. It had scared the bejesus out of me then, and truth be told, it still did.

I never made it to the mausoleum that long-ago day; I never even made it through the cemetery gates. I had not thought of it in a very long time. Strange how things, memories, slip away from you. Maybe that was for the best. In the case of the voices I'd heard that day, unknown whispers that halted my progress and made me turn away in terror, I'd say that was definitely for the best.

I would not think of it now.

I forced myself to get out of my car. Forced my feet to move. Forced myself to take one step after another. It wasn't so bad once I got going. I could ignore the voices. They were faint, no more than whispers really. Much better than when I was a little girl. I could also ignore the feeling that I was being watched. It was probably just Steff, checking to be sure I was still following.

One foot after another, Maggie my girl . . .

There is a certain timelessness to cemeteries, a sense of being outside the everyday world combined with the perpetual passage of ages that I had nearly forgotten. Perhaps it would have been easier to remember were I not surrounded by the remnants of eons' worth of dead bodies.

Stony Mill, Indiana. Population: 6,841 living; 12,309 living-challenged.

I tried not to think of that. In fact, I tried not to think of anything at all. Reaching Steff's side, that's what I made my focus. It wasn't easy. Every time I paused, I could feel the energies creeping up on me, trying to get near.

When I reached Steff, I looped my arm through hers, as much to keep myself there as to let her know I had arrived.

We had stopped just outside the entrance to the mausoleum. I was glad for it, that I was spared the necessity of being inside that place of death that had once so terrorized me. Standing twenty feet from it was more than enough. I could scarcely hear the somnolent words of the minister as he spoke of Isabella's life. All the ridiculous things they say when someone dies.

She has gone to a better place.

No more pain.

No more suffering.

Taken in the prime of life.

The Good Lord called her home.

Ours is not to question why . . .

Pointless, meaningless, empty clichés.

I let them flow freely from my head, instead checking out my fellow mourners. The first thing I noticed: The elaborate closed coffin from the viewing was gone, replaced by a large, polished alabaster jar. It could only mean that Isabella must have opted for cremation. Not quite the norm around these parts, but hey, Isabella didn't exactly seem the type to be afraid of standing out in a crowd. At least, not if what Ryan Davidson said was true.

Speaking of the urbane Mr. Davidson, there he was now, hovering near the Harding family. Jeremy Harding looked the part of the mourning husband in a well-tailored black wool suit. He wasn't paying any attention to his daughter, Jacquilyn, nor the stocky young man wagging his tail so eagerly beside her. I didn't recognize him. He certainly appeared to be on friendly terms with the Ice Princess. This could only be the fiancé Steff had spoken of.

There were several people among the mourners whom I did not recognize—relatives, maybe, or friends, or even coworkers, I imagined. One I did recognize, however, was the unmistakable Jetta James. Attending the viewing had been bad enough, but hovering by the grave seemed oh, so much worse. I wondered if she realized how cheap and ambitious that made her appear.

Then again, maybe she just didn't care.

The minister droned on. Most everyone appeared to be listening, or were at least pretending to, and were making appropriate sounds of lamentation punctuated by the occasional enthusiastic *Amen*. As with most services, my mind tended to wander. I resorted to people-watching to amuse myself and to keep my mind off other, more anxiety-producing things.

People do the most amazing things when they don't think they're being observed.

Jeremy Harding, I discovered, kept surreptitiously checking his watch. Places to go, people to see, doncha know.

Jacquilyn, lovely, warm person that she was, looked more like a statue than a living, breathing person. Maybe her mother's death was finally hitting home.

Ryan Davidson pulled his credit card–sized cell phone from his pocket to check text messages no less than three times. Ah, the joys of living in a technologically advanced society.

Jetta James possessed the distinctive habit of pulling at the hips of her tight skirt, which kept inching its way up her legs every time she moved. Her fingernails, I couldn't help but notice, were at least an inch long. The mind boggles.

The fiancé—who Steff had earlier ID'd as Roger Foley—kept his hand on the small of Jacquilyn's back, and at first glance he seemed to be quite comfortable playing the part of supportive mate. Then it became evident he was darting glances at the hemlines and breasts of every other female present. Including me, despite the fact that I was wearing slacks and a loose, bulky sweater. Until his roving eyes hit upon Steff standing by my side. Then he went as stiff and pale as a corpse, turned his face away, and tried to pretend neither of us existed.

No one else appeared remarkable in any way.

At least, not until a flash of movement caught my eye as Jeremy came forward to place a rose beside the urn. Unobtrusively I let my gaze drift sideways, seeking the cause. When I couldn't immediately locate a source, I thought it must have been birds swooping from tree to tree. As a matter of fact, I saw a number of large crows hanging out atop gravestones and strutting across the grass. It could easily have been one or more of them that I noticed out of the corner of my eye.

Satisfied, I turned back to the proceedings and waited, wistfully, for them to be over.

But then I saw a long shadow stretching across the grass, loosely attached to another shadow cast by the trunk of an old red maple. The morning sun cast both shadows westward, extending them into almost mythic proportion.

A man was hiding behind that tree. I was sure of it.

Why would anyone come to a funeral only to hide behind a tree rather than to be seen out in the open with the rest of the mourners?

With a cue from the preacher, voices lifted all around me to the deep, sonorous lyrics of "Amazing Grace." I let my lips form the words, but all of my attention was focused on that lone maple. Who was it? Why did he come? To say good-bye? Or could it be to admire the results of his handiwork?

I stared so hard my eyes burned with the effort, but I could not look away.

"I see him, too."

Steff was staring at the tree as well. Together we kept a silent vigil while the hymn's solemn chords swelled around us, waiting for the private surveillant to let down his guard.

As the hymn drew to a close, the minister intoned the customary closing words over Isabella's alabaster place-of-rest . . . *Ashes to ashes, dust to dust* . . . which in Isabella's case turned out to be somewhat more appropriate than usual . . . and stepped back so that the Harding family might claim the remains. My attention jerked back to the proceedings momentarily as, for one bizarre moment, neither Jeremy nor Jacquilyn stepped forward. In fact, neither seemed to be overly excited about touching the jar at all. Finally, Jeremy reached out and gingerly carried the jar into the shadowy depths of the stone mausoleum.

He scurried out of the place as if his heels were on fire.

I was just thinking that I couldn't really blame him for it when Steff dug her elbow into my ribs.

"Look."

As the mourners began to wander back toward their cars, the person behind the tree cautiously tried to keep the trunk of the tree between him and them at all times. Thanks to our vantage point, we were able to catch a glimpse of him—it *was* a man—before he noticed us and ducked into hiding once again.

I didn't recognize him, but one feature was unmistakable: He was wearing the starched white collar of a man of God.

Could this be the Reverend Baxter Martin?

I started looking for a way to get from the mausoleum to the greater vicinity of the red maple without traipsing through an army of tombstones. But before I had plotted even the first leg, Steff and I found ourselves waylaid by a cool blonde who was being trailed closely by her frowning pet monkey.

Brought up short, I nodded a greeting. "Ms. Harding."

She stared at me. Her blue eyes were as warm as chips of ice. "It was Miss . . . O'Neill, wasn't it?" Her gaze flicked to the left to include Steff, dropped down assessingly, and narrowed as her gaze returned to Steff's pretty face. "And Miss—?"

"This is a friend of mine. Stephanie Evans, this is Jacquilyn Harding. Ms. Harding's mother—"

"Never mind that. My mother's funeral is not a freak show, Miss O'Neill. Close family and intimate friends only. And since you are quite frankly neither of those two things, I'm afraid I will have to ask you and your friend to leave us to our sorrow."

My cheeks burned with the full impact of her rudeness. "I'm sorry. I didn't mean to intrude."

"Oh, I'm sure you didn't." Like the Ice Princess I'd pegged her for, she turned on her sturdy, sensible heels, summoning her man with the snap of her fingers. "Coming, Roger?"

Jacquilyn's yes-boy lingered long enough to direct an unpleasant leer in Steff's direction, then he scampered along behind his fiancée.

Steff's lips were pressed together in a rigid grimace of distaste. Her fingers tightened on my arm. "Come on, Mags, let's go," she said, loud enough for Jacquilyn and Roger to hear. "It's quite obvious Ms. Harding is out of her mind with grief."

We turned to leave. Slowly. There was something about Jacquilyn and her high-handed attitude that really scorched my buns. I wasn't about to give her the satisfaction of hieing myself away like some flunkee to do her royal bidding.

By that time, the mysterious cleric had long since disappeared. We looked, but there was no sign of him. Quietly we made our way back up the lane toward Christine. With only Jacquilyn and Roger and a few cemetery personnel remaining, I had no reason to want to stay, and yet something made me hesitate.

"I don't think I've ever met a more disagreeable woman. The way she spoke to you. Ugh!" Steff paced back and forth in the gravel, her black ankle boots churning up little whorls of limestone dust. "I can't believe it. I just cannot believe a person could be so unutterably *rude*! Who does she think she is?"

"Forget Her Royal Highness. Were you able to get a good look at that man hiding behind the tree?"

"I think I'd recognize him if we happened to see him again. That collar is a dead giveaway."

"Reverend Martin?"

"I'd bet my date with Danny on it."

Now *that* was serious business.

We were interrupted by the sound of tires on gravel and the rush of an engine as a black SUV blew past us on the narrow lane, leaving a plume of dust in its wake.

The blonde behind the wheel was unmistakable.

"Damn!" I choked. The taste of dirt coated my throat and mouth, and it pissed me off. Royally. "What is the *deal* with her?"

"Maybe she needs to kiss a frog. Or even two," Steff croaked. "I get the feeling she could use a little magical assistance. I don't suppose you have a bottle of water?"

When she was in her element, Steff was rarely without a fresh bottle of Aquafina. I, on the other hand, usually made do with some sort of coffee bean and water combo. I happened to have just such a concoction on hand, but for some reason, a two-day-old latte in a soggy paper cup didn't sound like much help. Not even to me.

I shook my head. "Sorry."

"I'm almost certain I brought one."

While Steff dug around in my backseat, I found myself turning once more to look back at the stone Mausoleum. The cemetery staff seemed to have disappeared in the last few minutes, and in that moment I felt an almost uncontrollable urge to return to the gravesite.

Something was calling to me. Calling me back.

My feet started to move of their own accord. Before I realized what was happening, I found myself walking slowly back up the lane. It was nearly noon, and the sun was high overhead. Vital, golden, blissfully normal, the bright sunlight should have reassured me. Instead it only served to highlight the strangeness of the moment. What was I doing? I did *not* want to go back there. Why couldn't I stop? But my feet just kept up their steady pace forward.

For the duration of the funeral, at least, I'd found plenty of distractions that helped to temporarily shelve my fears and prevent my thoughts from turning inward. Perhaps those distractions had also lulled me into a false sense of security. Now that nothing else stood in my way, all my fears and anxieties came rushing back into my head like rainwater gushing through a storm drain, sweeping me out of my comfort zone and smack into the realm of the unknown.

Dread—the good, old-fashioned, get-your-heart-racing variety—pumped vigorously through my veins.

From what seemed a million miles away, I heard Steff's voice calling me. I couldn't answer. My vision narrowed until I could see only the open gate and the yawning space beyond. It was as though I were walking through a long tunnel and the Mausoleum was the only possible end result.

Strange, unearthly sounds filled my ears as I took that last step through the open gateway. Shadow closed in around me and the temperature dropped noticeably. I paused, shivering and blinking, just inside the door and waited for my common sense to return so that I could get the hell out of Dodge.

The air inside the tomb smelled stale with misuse, but not rank. Not . . . *dead*. Thank goodness. I hovered there in the doorway, wondering why I didn't just turn around and walk out, back into the light of day. Back to normal life.

So why then did I step farther into the darkness?

The whispers I'd managed to hold back were getting louder. Little more than susurrant undertones at first, they began to take shape. *To form words.*

touch it . . . touch it . . . touch it . . . touch it . . . touch it . . .
The lump of ice sticking in my throat got bigger.

I took a shaky breath and tried to get my feet to move. I wanted to go back, but they refused to budge. Around me, the quality of the air changed, from stale vapors into something tangible.

Something with shape.

Something with hands.

A lot of hands.

Oh God . . .

As if they belonged to someone else, I watched with a mixture of fascination and horror as my own hands stretched out toward the open bay. I could just make out the shape of the alabaster jar situated deep within the hollow in the wall. The sheer number of other such hollows, now closed, each with their own brass name plate affixed to the marble façade, made my blood run even colder. I tore my thoughts away from such worries and made myself look at the jar that held Isabella's ashes. A shimmer of light glinted along the upswept curve, just beneath my hovering fingers—so tantalizing, I ached to catch it in my hand. The flesh on my palms grew warm and began to vibrate, as though I had placed them on the casing of a computer monitor. Electricity, or something quite like it, tingled from my fingertips and up my arms. Such a strange sensation . . .

Screwing my eyes shut, I closed the distance.

The instant my hands made contact with the cold, polished surface, I felt it—sadness and anger in a sudden onslaught that came from so deep inside me that it might well have originated from the innermost caverns of my soul. With it came a cold, so vast, so profound, that I could feel it inside me, filling my lungs, clenching its icy fingers around my heart.

Murder . . . murder . . . murder . . . murder . . . murder . . .

I felt the word as much as heard it. Aftershocks rumbled through my body, so powerful that for a moment I worried they might tear me apart. Aghast, I tore my hands free of the smooth alabaster and scrabbled blindly for the door. A scream ripped upward but caught in my throat and stuck there. Gagging, I broke free of the tomb and stumbled out, collapsing to my knees at the base of a headstone fifteen feet away. My breath broke free from me at long last; I hadn't even realized I'd been holding it until it came shuddering out. I sucked in fresh air, only to choke again over the taste of the tomb, still coating my tongue and throat.

When I had regained enough presence of mind to ask questions, one very large one came to mind: *What the hell was that?*

"Maggie! Mags! Oh my God, are you all right?" Steff's footsteps thundered across the grass toward me, but I didn't have the strength yet to turn to her. Her hands closed around my trembling shoulders. "I saw you go down. What happened, honey? Why were you in that place? Did you trip over something? Fall? Are you hurt?"

As she shotgunned questions at me; her hands traveled over my feet, my ankles, searching for signs of injury. Finding none, she sat back on her heels, nonplussed, and took my hands in hers. "Maggie, honey? Maggie, look at me," she coaxed calmly. "Come on, just look up . . ."

I couldn't do it. I couldn't move, not an inch. I couldn't even lift my head. Whatever burst of adrenalin had carried me safely from that place of death was gone, and in its place was a total absence of life and an overwhelming sense of regret. In my head, I kept hearing the same refrain, over and over and over again, an echo that had followed me out the door of the crypt. *Letters, my letters, my letters, letters . . .*

Whatever that meant.

I didn't understand what had happened—*was* happening— but did that really make a difference? Not understanding didn't lessen the impact. I needed help.

I took another shuddering breath, reeling as the staleness of the tomb filled me again. My stomach clenched. "Call— Liss—" I rasped with difficulty.

Steff took one look at my face and lost her nurse's air of unflappable professionalism. "Stay right there. I'll—I'll get my phone. Don't move."

As if I could.

She tore back toward Christine, scrambling around stones and over graves to get there. She was back in a jiffy with her cell phone in one hand and my purse in the other.

"You must have her number in here somewhere, right?" she prompted, unzipping it and unceremoniously dumping the contents upon the grass in front of her.

I blinked, the closest I could come at the moment to a nod. If only the roaring in my ears would stop. . . . I was trying not to breathe any more than I had to. I just couldn't face that taste, the foul taste of decay. The short supply of oxygen in my lungs was making me even dizzier, but that was a small price to pay in my book.

Steff was pawing through my things, shoving aside a compact, lipstick, comb, the ever-so-discreet pink plastic tampon case, my wallet and checkbook, a couple of bills I needed to pay . . . Reversing her steps, she seized upon the wallet she'd passed over a few seconds before, fanning swiftly through it until she came across Felicity's business card in the change purse.

"Okay . . . Got it. Okay. I hope . . . damn it, where did everybody go, you'd think we were the only people in the world who had reason to be at this cemetery. You okay, Mags?" She didn't wait for a nod; her fingers had already dialed the number.

She sat very still with the phone held to her ear while a phone rang off the hook several miles away. Consternation carved itself deeper into her face with every passing moment. "Damn it, no answer."

She was interrupted once again by the roar of a car engine and the sharp bark of skidding tires as a sleek black sportscar turned too fast off the road into the semideserted graveyard, chewing up gravel as it thundered straight for us.

"Who the hell—?"

Chapter 11

How Liss knew I was in trouble I had no idea, but I wasn't about to complain.

Her door flew open and she burst out like an avenging angel, her forehead furrowed with worry. "Maggie, is that you? Good heavens, child, are you all right?"

Steff stood up as Felicity hurried over. "She just collapsed," she explained quickly. "As fast as she went down, I thought she'd twisted her ankle, but there doesn't appear to be any sign of injury. Her vitals check okay. It's possible she hit her head. Pupils look normal, but I think we'd better take her in, just in case."

I managed to shake my spinning head. "No, I didn't—"

"Don't try to talk yet, dear. Here, let's get her to the car. Mine might be a trifle more comfortable."

Together they managed to get me to my feet. My knees felt as watery as half-formed Jell-O, but supported between the two of them as I was, I made it to the passenger seat of Felicity's car, where I collapsed again. Nausea enfolded me in a smothering embrace. I couldn't remember the last time I felt so ill. So . . . overcome.

Felicity knelt in the grass at my feet without a thought for the mess the grass was likely making of her fawn wool slacks.

"Now, where does it hurt? Your ankle?" she asked, somehow managing to sound both businesslike and caring at once. "Can you tell us what happened?"

Felicity's presence proved to be exactly the medicine I'd needed. Far away from the cloying air of the Mausoleum, the fog that shrouded my eyes began slowly to lift. My thoughts cleared. My lungs expanded without struggle. "I didn't . . . turn my ankle." My lips were as dry as beach sand drying in the sun. I ran my tongue over them. A futile effort. Sand against sand. "I felt . . . something . . . in there. Heard something."

Her hands went still on my ankle. She lifted her gaze to mine. "Like yesterday? At your apartment?"

I nodded. "Yes."

Steff had been hanging back, her arms wrapped around her waist, but now she stepped forward, a question in her eyes. "What about your apartment, Mags?"

Tears sprang to my eyes unbidden, because as reason and logic filtered back into my aching head, I knew what all of this must mean. The smile I gave them was meant to be reassuring, but I knew it didn't fool either of them. Hell, it didn't even fool me. "I think . . . I think I might need to see a psychiatrist."

Felicity said nothing. Steff, on the other hand, spluttered in disbelief. "Of all the foolish things to say. Why don't you just tell us what happened."

I took a moment to gather my thoughts, then began haltingly to tell them what had happened. Everything, from the voice at my apartment, to the mysterious force I'd encountered at the viewing, and finally, to the strange events at the cemetery and, more importantly, the Mausoleum. I left nothing out. When I'd finished, I leaned back, a little breathless, and waited for them to agree with me. *Yes, Maggie my girl, you're right. You* do *need professional help. Only a complete lunatic hears voices no one else can hear.*

I mean, walls of energy holding you back? Come *on.*

I didn't have to wait long.

"Well. If you expected to shock me with your little . . . revelation . . . then you're sadly mistaken, Margaret Mary-Catherine O'Neill," Steff said, stiffening her spine in her best impression of my mother. She did a good job, actually. I'd never seen her so ready to squash my objections. If she'd had a wooden spoon within reach, I'd have quailed in fear. "You're one of the sanest people I know."

Felicity nodded. "I would have to say I agree with—er, terribly sorry, I don't think we've been introduced—but I do agree with you, in any case."

Steff held out her hand. "Stephanie Evans. But please, call me Steff."

"A pleasure, my dear. Felicity Dow."

"You know, I'm glad you're both getting along so famously," I interrupted, losing whatever shreds of patience I had left, "but if neither of you think I need a psychiatrist, then what *do* you suggest I do about all of this?"

Okay, so I sounded petulant. I couldn't help it. The psychiatrist had been my first and best solution. Without it, I felt as though I had lost my only hope.

"Well," Felicity said in a calm voice as she got to her feet and dusted off her knees. "First things first—it appears we need to convince you that you're not a candidate for the local lunatic asylum."

"Aren't I?"

"No," Steff asserted firmly, jumping right in. "In all the years I've known you, you've never once shown signs of being delusional. Except maybe when you were fifteen and you were so certain that you were meant to marry Johnny Depp. I think you must have written Mrs. Maggie Depp on every single flat surface you came into contact with."

I smiled in spite of myself. "Well, I still say we were meant to be together, but he hasn't come to his senses yet."

"That sounds like you. You must be feeling a little better."

"A little. But still having trouble accepting the whole woo-woo factor."

"You need to open your mind, just a little."

"It's just that the idea that ghosts . . . spirits . . . whatever you want to call them, walk the earth . . . it's a little too much for my poor brain to comprehend at the moment. I mean, I was brought up old-time Catholic in a world where modern, scientific thinking became a kind of religion all its own. You know what I mean, Steff. And just when I finally had come to terms with the disappointment that there is no God, no Devil, Heaven, Hell, nothing beyond a temporary life on this lonely water-covered lump of rock . . ." I shook my head, unable to keep on with that line of thinking. "I mean, so ghosts really do exist. What's next? Fairies? Elves? Pixies? *Trolls?*"

I giggled, but it was a nervous giggle, because from there, it sure wasn't a huge leap to witches and magic. Real magic. Criminey.

"Oh, I don't know, Mags. Is it so hard to believe? I mean, that woman we met this afternoon—what was her name, Jacquilyn Something-or-other?—she could easily have been a troll in disguise," Steff said, making a madcap stab at humor.

I winced. That was Felicity's niece Steff was roasting in such unflattering terms. Maybe I should have explained the connection . . .

But Felicity only chuckled. "She can be a bit troll-like, can't she? My niece hasn't quite gotten the hang of social niceties."

Steff looked stricken. "Oh. Oh, I'm sorry. I didn't know she was related."

"Never mind that. I would attribute it to her parentage, you know, but it isn't nice to speak ill of the dead. Though as for Jeremy, well, his behavior speaks for itself, doesn't it." She paused a moment as if considering her next words carefully. "Maggie, I have some friends I think it's time for you to meet. If you're of a mind to. It might help you come to terms with what's been happening to you. Do you have any plans for this evening?"

Dinner with my parents and a possible encounter with Tom Fielding, the prospect of which I found slightly more terrifying than the idea that I had been hearing the voices from The Great Beyond. "Kind of."

"Can you meet me at the store at eleven o'clock tonight?"

I agreed, but I couldn't help wondering what I was letting myself in for.

My mother wasn't expecting me until five, but I decided to go out just as soon as I'd dropped off Steff at the apartments. The old homestead wasn't my usual choice for a lazy Saturday afternoon, but just now I felt a strong need to be back among the world of the living. The normal. Back to where the sun rose and set, the dead stayed dead, and the living were as screwed up as they had always been.

There was something so reassuring about that.

I puttered to a halt beside the curb in front of the ancient, two-story farmhouse that had once belonged to my grandparents, and it had been old then. Grandma Cora was long since gone, and Grandpa Gordon suffered from emphysema and now lived in a little apartment that had been tacked on to the back of the garage in order to accommodate his electric motor-chair. Just within the official borders of town, the house had once been in the country but had since been swallowed up by subdivisions and minimarts. True, the old-style farmhouse with its carriage barn-cum-workshop-cum-garage looked out of place in the midst of the fresh, new, neutral-toned houses, all of which suffered from a dreadful Stepford kind of sameness, but it was sturdy enough to withstand ten decades of steamy Indiana summers and harsh winter winds, and no doubt it would withstand many more decades of the same, long after its high-style companions had dwindled to dust. To me it represented hearth and home, stability, a family that sometimes irritated the heck out of me but whom I loved just the same.

Normalcy.

I rolled my window down to ensure Christine's continued cooperation, then walked slowly up the brick path beneath the widespread bowers of three sturdy maple trees that towered over everything in sight. The strong afternoon sun filtered through the lacy cover of brightly colored leaves, dappling the path with flecks of light. Pausing there, I smiled, holding my hands out and watching the lights dance across my palms. A sudden breeze touched the windchimes on the front porch and sent a smattering of dried leaves skirling about my feet. I toekicked them, my mood suddenly lighter than it had been all day.

"There she is! Hallo, Maggie-May-I!"

Grandpa Gordon had a gazillion pet names for me, but

Maggie-May-I was the one I'd heard most often throughout the years. I turned toward the sound of his voice, a smile and a big hug at the ready. "Hey there, Gramps!"

My grandfather was one of my most favorite people in the world, and a dearer, sweeter man you would be hard pressed to find. Emphysema had hit him hard seven years ago, greatly restricting his abilities and forcing him to carry an oxygen tank by his side, but still he greeted each day with laughter and song, and a respect for the world at large. I'd often thought it sad that my mother had taken after her more austere mother than Grandpa. Perhaps Grandma Cora's stern influence had been too strong to oppose.

"Come to have dinner with us, have you?"

"Well . . ."

His rheumy eyes didn't miss a thing. "So you had a better offer, did ya? Hope the young buck's worth the effort. Your mother will be fit to be tied. You know how she gets."

"Yeah. I know." Boy, did I ever.

"That's all right, then. Watch out, girl, I'm coming through. Tally-hoooo!"

He barreled forward along the path with a clatter of rubber wheels and a mighty electric hum that forced me to skitter out of the way or be run down right there and then. At the last second he twirled his joystick control fiercely. The rotating seat of his wheelchair whipped around and he whooped like a kid spinning on a piano stool. The whoop brought on a hacking cough that racked his frail shoulders. When it was done, he inhaled deeply through his oxygen tube and sighed.

"Ya know, I love this thing," he wheezed with a grin as he gave the motor a fond pat. "Best invention there ever was. I could be laid up in there sick as a dog with tubes stuck up my ying-yang, moaning and groaning about my lot in life until the Grim came to claim my scrawny bones. Gettin' old's the pits, don't ever let anyone tell you different. But instead, here I am out in the glory the Good Lord gave us, a-wheelin' around like a young boy on a boxcart. Ain't life a wonder. Now where was I?"

"Mom's going to kill me," I reminded him.

"Well, you know yer mum pretty well. She's been slavin' away in that kitchen since before lunch."

Yeah, but I'd take a ticked-off mom over what I'd left behind at the cemetery any day. "It's okay, Grandpa. She'll get over it." Eventually.

"Best get it over with, I reckon," he said, setting his wheels into motion once again in a trajectory that would guide us both around the house toward the mud room outside the kitchen. "Want me to run interference?"

"Oh, Gramps." I couldn't help smiling.

"I'm gettin' pretty good at it, ya know. Years of practice."

"No, Gramps. I'm a grown woman. Besides, Mom would see right through you."

We had reached the bottom of the wooden ramp Dad had hooked up to the back porch to allow Grandpa easy access to the kitchen. Grandpa Gordon looked up at me as if he intended to say something more, then he shrugged. "Suit yerself." He started up the ramp. "Just don't say I didn't warn you."

I trudged up after him, steeling myself for the impending storm.

Grandpa rammed his motor-chair into the unlatched kitchen door. "Patricia, look who found her way home!"

A quick shuffle of feet met my ears as my mother rushed forward, her eyes flashing intent while she brandished a wooden spoon in one hand. "Really, Dad! Do you have to bash around like that when you come in the house? You know I have a cake in the oven!"

"Oh, put that thing away, missy. I brought your daughter in to ya."

My mom's eyes cut my way and her stance softened, if only slightly. "You're early, Margaret."

I cleared my throat. "I know. I—"

"I'm glad, actually. I could use a hand peeling potatoes." She walked back into the kitchen without waiting to see if I'd follow.

Grandpa Gordon arched a grizzled brow at me. *Are you coming in?* I mouthed to him hopefully. He held up his hands as if to say, *Sorry, little girl, you're on your own.* The coward. I squared my shoulders and followed my mom into the house.

"Potatoes are draining in the sink. Peelers there," she said, opening the drawer where the odd kitchen utensils such as potato peelers and rubber bowl scrapers and barbecue shish kebob skewers and turkey basters had been kept for as long as I could remember.

The thing was, I hated potato peelers. I could never get the hang of them, they never failed to pinch tender fingers, and the potatoes always ended up looking like they'd gone through a paper shredder. I selected a knife instead and grabbed a potato from the colander in the sink.

"What are you doing?"

I looked up. My mother was watching me with an expression of mingled incredulity and annoyance. "I'm getting ready to peel potatoes."

"With that?" Her eyes jabbed distastefully at the slender blade as she stirred a mystery concoction on the stove that smelled like nirvana. "That's why God made potato peelers, dear. It wouldn't be right to turn up our noses at something he put on this earth to make our lives easier, now would it?"

Just once, I would like to be able to do something without being reminded of God's wondrous interventions in our lives. And for something as trivial as a potato peeler, for Pete's sake. You'd think He'd have more important things to muck with.

Sighing, I set aside the knife and picked up the metal instrument of tuber torture. After only a few strokes, the knuckle of my first finger throbbed like a fresh bruise. By the time I'd finished one potato in teeth-gritted silence and let it slide into the battered pot already half-filled with water, I decided I'd best get my confession over with. Maybe Mother would get so irritated she'd cast me out on my ear, before I was forced to finish the entire pot of potatoes.

That almost sounded like a plan.

"Uhm, Mom . . ."

She didn't even look up. "Yes, dear?"

I cleared my throat. "Er, would you be terribly put out if I missed dinner this evening? Just a postponement," I hurried on as the big wooden spoon froze ominously in midrotation. "You know I hate to miss it." Was that my nose growing

longer? "I wouldn't even ask if it wasn't something important." That much, at least, was true. I did have some sense of
self-preservation. "Something really, really important."

"What is so important that it's more important than your
family?"

Ooooh. Good question. I scrambled my brains for an answer. "I, uh, have a date."

That got her attention. "A date?"

I didn't like her tone. I mean, just because I didn't have a
lawyer husband like Mel and just because I didn't have to
fight the men off with a baseball bat and a well-timed bucket
of ice water like Steff didn't mean I couldn't get a date when I
wanted to.

"Yeah. A date," I said, my tone just a teensy bit snappish as
I threw the potato I'd been peeling into the pan with a splash
and seized another.

"Margaret! Careful. I just cleaned the ceiling." She covered the concoction she'd been stirring and put it in the oven.
"Now, tell me. Who is this young man of yours? Have you
been seeing him long?"

Hmm. Maybe I should rethink this. I wasn't sure that a first
date would qualify as an important enough event according to
my mom's rigorous standards. "Well, I've known him a long
time, as it turns out. We went to school together. He was a few
years ahead of me. We're, uh, going out to dinner. And a
movie."

Actually, I had no idea what we were doing, or even if I
was still going to go through with it at all. I had my doubts,
and they were starting to get the better of me.

"How nice. You know how much your father and I hope to
see you settled. A nice Catholic man from a decent family. He
is Catholic?"

"Of course," I lied shamelessly.

That seemed to settle it for her. No longer did she appear
on the verge of telling me I was grounded and couldn't leave
the house. "What's his name, dear?"

"Tom. Tom Fielding."

"From the police department? How wonderful. Your dad
works with his father, you know. You should invite him to din-

ner with us soon. Just a nice, quiet dinner with your father and me. And Grandpa Gordon, of course. To get acquainted."

Oh-My-God. "Uh, no."

"Now, why do you say that? Honestly, Margaret, you'd think you were ashamed to claim us as family."

"Mom, I can't bring him to dinner!" The look on her face told me she expected an explanation. I bent my head to the task of properly shredding the potato I had in hand. "I don't know him well enough . . . I mean, that's something you reserve for someone you know you're getting serious about, and I just . . ."

"It's a simple family dinner. Just a friendly little meal. I don't think that's too much for a mother to ask of her oldest daughter."

I swallowed hard as guilt played havoc with my already queasy stomach. What was it about mothers that made them such experts at manipulation? "Well . . . I'll think about it."

"You'll ask him?"

I sighed. "I'll ask him."

"Wonderful. We'll expect you on Wednesday at seven o'clock."

I sighed inwardly, resigned to my fate, and I wondered if poor Tom had any idea what he had gotten himself into by the simple act of asking me out.

"Speaking of Dad," I said, changing the subject before I got myself into any more messes, "where is he?"

Her mouth tightened, passing judgment. "Oh, you know your father. He's probably out in his workshop, fiddling with something that's too old to be fixed." She looked down into the pot of potatoes, then at the potato I held in my hands, and her mouth twisted slightly. She stretched out her hand to cover my own and stop my abuse of the poor potato. "Why don't you give that to me, Margaret, and go out and say hello to your father before you leave."

Her hands were rough, work-worn, capable hands. I wondered how long it had been since she'd taken a moment to soothe them with lotion, how long since she had yielded to the temptation of a long bubblebath. It wasn't her way, I knew, but I couldn't help wondering if an occasional self-pampering might have softened her outlook toward others. Like me, or Dad, or Grandpa Gordon. The only two people I knew to have escaped my mother's critical eye were my brother Marshall, and Mel.

Pushing away that thought because dwelling on it helped no one, I gladly yielded the peeler to my mother and gave her a tiny smile. "Thanks, Mom. I'll do that."

"I'll call you to remind you about Wednesday."

I had no doubt.

My shoes crunched on the finely crushed limestone drive as I left the house for my dad's workshop. Mixed in with that sound and the whisper of dry leaves, I could hear the retreating electric whirr of Grandpa's motor-chair and his trademark call of *"Tally-hoooo!"* I turned to look, but he was already tooling up the road, an electric orange flag announcing his presence to the motorists of the neighborhood.

Shaking my head but smiling all the same, I returned my attention to the old barn. The door stood open, shadow reaching beyond, a cave my father had always holed up in when hiding from my mother. In the doorway I paused to give my eyes a moment to adjust.

"Hey, girl. Don't see you enough around here these days."

My dad moved out of the interior shadows, wiping his hands on a dingy old rag. He looked like a refugee from an L.L. Bean catalog in a light, buffalo plaid wool jacket, loose-fitting jeans, and a pair of beat-up old chukkas, but he could pass for ten years younger than his fifty-plus years and that wasn't a bad thing.

I slung my arm affectionately about his neck and planted a resounding kiss on his cheek. "Yuck. Sawdust. Hi, Dad."

He swiped his hand down his lightly stubbled cheek almost sheepishly. "Sorry. I've been working. Want to see?"

"Sure."

He turned and led the way over to his worktable. On it rested a two-inch-wide cross section of what was once a massive tree. The slab had been sanded until its irregularly shaped surface was as smooth as a sheet of glass. I trailed my fingers across it, awed by the hundreds of darker brown rings that gave proof of the passage of time. There was something reassuring about it. Life goes on, no matter what.

"Have a seat?"

"I can't stay long," I apologized, but sliding onto a tall stool anyway. "Date tonight. Don't worry, I've already cleared it with Mom."

He picked up a can of polyurethane. Popping the top with an old screwdriver, he began to slowly stir the viscous substance, purposefully, like a cow working over its cud. "Probably for the better. You know how your mother can be."

"I know." I indicated the slab of tree trunk with a toss of my chin. "So, what's that going to be?"

He patted the top of the wood, dusting off a speck of imaginary fluff. "Just a little project I've been working on. With retirement coming up—"

I clucked my tongue. "Don't be silly. You're too young."

"I am not. And believe me, I'm starting to think sooner is better."

My father was an accountant at Sea Breeze Enterprises, a manufacturer of pleasure craft. Speedboats, pontoon boats, and great, big, ultramanly bass boats. The company had been around a long time, the business bolstered by the many lakes and rivers in the northern part of the state. Dad had been a part of the company for as long as I could remember. "Is there something wrong? Did something happen?"

I crossed my fingers, a childish charm against a worrisome possibility. I wasn't certain I could take anything more being wrong.

He shrugged, frowning thoughtfully into the can as he stirred. "Nothing full retirement and a home in the Florida Keys couldn't cure. I'm getting old, honey, and business doesn't take kindly to old people. I don't know, maybe I am too old-fashioned. Too set in my ways. And I find I don't really care to accommodate all the changes the world is going through. Hey, so what do you think of this thing? Picture it with a couple of good coats of marine polyurethane, some stylized legs . . . I was thinking it might make a good coffee table or garden table or something. Rustic."

He set down the can, dipped a well-used but squeaky-clean brush in the clear goop, and began applying it in long, light strokes to the wood. Even though his face betrayed nothing, all at once I knew what this project meant to him. A possible future. Work he loved. Fulfillment. Pride. "I think it's awesome, Dad."

He looked up. For one brief, shining moment I saw joy and surprise and awe lightening the world-weary lines on his face. Then he recovered himself and bent his head to his task once again. "It might work, then. Perhaps it would provide your mother and me with a little extra income . . . when I do retire. Something to think about, anyway."

"You never did answer, you know. Have there been problems at work?"

He grunted, his face tightening slightly. "Only because that fool Foley is letting his son run us into the ground. An old fool and a young fool . . . two sadder things a body will be hard pressed to find. Painful to watch, after all these years."

Something clicked in my memory. "That wouldn't be Roger Foley, would it?"

"You know him?"

I thought of the attentive puppy with the roving eyes at graveside. "Not really. I've heard his name, that's all." I paused, not sure how to put my thoughts into words. "I understand Roger Foley is engaged to the daughter of the woman who was killed this week."

His brow furrowed. "That would make her related to your new boss, wouldn't it?"

"Her niece."

He went back to stroking on the polyurethane. At length, he said, "Your mother doesn't like your new job much, you know. I expect she'll be voicing her opinion soon."

I had no doubt. God knows my mother wasn't the type to hold her tongue for long.

"She's heard rumors," he went on in his slow, methodical way. "They make your mother uneasy."

"Mom forgets that I'm old enough to take care of myself."

"She feels better being involved in your life."

I shifted uncomfortably, caught between my claustrophobic relationship with my mother and the need to be my own person. There was a time when my mother had involved herself so deeply into my thought processes that I didn't know where her viewpoints ended and mine began. When I realized that, I'd moved out of my parents' house for good. That was eight years ago, right after my first and only engagement (Joby Turner, ancient history) had ended on a sour note and a bed of lies and recrimination. It took me a long time to redis-cover myself. To figure out who I was and what I thought about the world at large. I wasn't about to go back to the way things were. "Mom needs to get a life of her own and stop poking her nose into mine."

My dad nodded sagely. "That she does."

"What about you? Do you think I'm making a mistake?"

He didn't look up. He just kept stroking that brush back and forth. "You know, I've always thought you had a pretty good head on your shoulders. If you feel comfortable with what you're doing, well, then, that's good enough for me."

That's my dad for you. Supportive with a capital *S*. "Thanks, Dad."

"So, what do you make of all this hubbub? It's quite the story. Murder just doesn't happen every day around these parts."

"I don't know what to think about it—except that the town boys seem to have made up their minds that Felicity is responsible."

"You don't think so."

I shook my head. "I've only known Felicity a short while, but I've come to know her better than you might expect. No, I don't think she did it. Besides, I've been doing a little digging and it seems to me that the late Mrs. Harding wasn't exactly the most beloved person in town."

He stopped in midstroke and looked up at me, his eyes sharp. "Digging? What kind of digging?"

I shrugged nonchalantly. "Just asking a few questions of people who knew her."

The worry lines etching his forehead deepened. "Do you think that's wise?"

I slipped off my stool. "Someone has to," I said brashly as I stretched my arms around his shoulders for a good-bye hug. "Someone has to make them see. It might as well be me."

His troubled gaze told me he wasn't so sure.

* * *

Right up to the last minute, I thought I was going to go
through with my . . . *appointment* . . . with Tom Fielding.

As the clock ticked closer to the moment of no return, I got
a bad case of the jitters that no amount of feel-good affirma-
tions (anything from: *You are a beautiful, desirable woman,*
to: *There's nothing to worry about. He's not interested in you.
This is your chance to let him know what Felicity is really
like . . .*) could abolish. With fifteen minutes to spare and my
fingers trembling, I dialed Tom's home phone with the intention of begging off.

No answer.

I left a message on the machine, hoping against all hope
that I'd managed to catch him still at home. In the shower, or
with his head buried in the closet looking for shoes, or whatever it was men did in the last minutes before heading off on
a date.

Appointment.

Whatever.

I spent the last ten minutes squirming on the edge of my
seat and feeling like the world's biggest chicken. I switched
off my lights, my tension mounting.

Countdown . . . Five minutes . . . Four . . . *Please let me
have reached him in time* . . . Three . . . *On the other hand,
there was still time to change my mind* . . . Two . . . *He might
have to wait a minute or two while I change, but maybe he
wouldn't mind so very much* . . . One . . .

Right on cue, there was a knock at my door.

My heart leapt to my throat and stayed there, throbbing
madly.

Get up, a voice chided in my ear. *What's the matter? Are
you crazy?*

I must be crazy. What was I thinking?

*He's handsome. Strong. A good man. A police officer, for
heaven's sake. And he likes you. He said so. He might even be
Catholic, but you won't know if you don't ask. What are you
waiting for?*

Caught in the grips of indecision, I clutched the arms of

my chair. My knuckles went white, my face was hot, and I was torn between the need to protect myself and the desire to open the door, fling myself into his arms, and kiss his lips off.

Of course, he was a cop. That might be considered assault. That probably wouldn't be good.

The knock came again, louder this time. "Maggie? Are you there?" Long pause. "Maggie?"

Mother Mary, even his voice gave me the shivers. No, it most definitely would not be a good idea to mix business and pleasure with this man.

I sat on my hands and closed my eyes, and eventually he went away, leaving me alone in my dark apartment to wallow in the throes of regret and missed opportunities.

"Well, that's that," I said to the room at large. Thankfully, no one answered.

For a moment I sat there in the deepening shadow, wondering what I should do next . . . until the quiet in the room unnerved me like a predator that loomed just beyond my line of vision. A presence I could feel but not see. One day had passed since that strange voice called out to me from the depths of my apartment. Twenty-four hours. Not nearly enough time to reassure me that the voice I heard was nothing to worry about. It had been easy to ignore when my thoughts were wrapped up in a certain all-too-available hunk of male, but impossible now that I was so undeniably, irrevocably alone. I jumped up to flip on the overhead light, but that just cast long shadows that somehow seemed even more threatening than complete darkness. Then I remembered that I was entirely alone in this nightmare apartment house. Steff was long gone on her date with Dr. Dan, and the apartment on the ground floor still had not been rented out. Suddenly, calling off my date (*appointment!*) seemed like the stupidest thing in the world to do, and it was far too late to change my mind.

About Deputy Fielding, at least.

I grabbed my purse off the chair by the door and made my getaway, slinking out of my apartment before whatever force had poked a hole in this dimension found its way back. Christine waited at the curb, a familiar port in the storm. I sheltered there a moment, gazing uneasily back at the old Victorian exterior of my apartment house. Soon a time would come when I would have to face my fears and overcome the urge to skedaddle out of the apartment every time I was Home Alone. If sweet little MacCaulay Culkin could do it, surely so could I.

Soon.

But not tonight.

I took a single deep breath to clear my mind and turned the key in the ignition, making my way into the silent night.

Chapter 12

I drove for hours without a destination in mind. In a town as small as Stony Mill, that took quite some doing. After the third go-round of driving up the street my parents lived on, I came to my senses. If I didn't vary my pattern, old Mrs. Henderson was going to call the police. Having just ditched one member of our illustrious force, the last thing I wanted was to be ratted out by my parents' nosy next-door neighbor.

I found myself traveling down the Victoria Park Road without knowing how I'd gotten there. Once committed, though, I wouldn't have turned back for the world. When I'd first started asking questions of those who knew Isabella Harding, I'd been acting only on behalf of Felicity. That had always been my intention. My experience at the cemetery had made that stronger, but more, it had spurred an insatiable thirst to see justice done. Whatever the poor woman's faults had been, she didn't deserve to die, and her murderer didn't deserve to get off scot-free.

I drove past the fenced-in woods I knew to be Felicity's, paying more attention as the rough limestone barrier wall was exchanged for tall iron spikes. I slowed my car as I approached the imposing security gate, taking note of the difference in style. Where Felicity's had been curlicued and elegant, the

Harding gate looked more like the portcullis of some ancient keep—strong, commanding, and ultimately impenetrable.

I cut my lights and crept into the drive until my car was nose to nose with the gate. I hadn't met any cars in either direction on the six-plus-mile drive up the road, and with luck no one would come along while I played sleuth. The Harding property possessed far fewer trees near the road, and the drive made a straight line to the front of the house; I had a clear view. High-watt floodlights lit up the entire area like a used car lot. They made spying on the Hardings extraordinarily easy.

Whatever I'd expected, this wasn't it.

The difference between The Gables and Isabella's house was startling. Grand vs. grandiose. Whereas Felicity's home resembled something plucked out of a British tour guide, Isabella's might have been plucked from anywhere where there was a surplus of money and a shortage of taste. From the glass walls of the ultracontemporary, to Italianate villa, to New England shingling, the elements combined in a strange mishmash of architectural styles—like whoever had designed it couldn't make up their mind—and looked completely out of place in the Indiana countryside. Although, to be fair, I didn't think it looked as though it belonged anywhere.

No one appeared to be home.

Disappointed, I threw Christine into reverse (she gave only a single clunk of protest) and backed out of the drive, flipping my lights back on and letting her slowly idle forward down the road while I took in details. The woods were thick between the properties, the trees skirted with dense underbrush and ferns. I couldn't help remembering Marcus's comment about a flash of color as he and Felicity had approached Isabella's. Had someone been out there, watching from the woods? It was possible. But where had he gone from there? Through the trees to Felicity's? That seemed so risky. But . . . maybe a person who had sunk to the depths of murder was willing to take a few risks. Maybe he was so far gone that less consequential risks paled in comparison.

Yes, murder could make a person reckless. That made sense. And reckless people made mistakes by default. It was only human.

What mistakes had this murderer made?

Curiosity gnawed at me. What I really wanted to do was to explore the woods between the two houses . . . but not now. Killer on the loose or not, I wasn't about to brave these dark woods with my wits as my only weapon. Leave that to those poor hapless victims from the Gothic novels my mom used to hide in her underwear drawer, the ones whose covers portrayed beautiful young women wandering about some moldering castle, garbed in nothing more than a sheer nightie and carrying a flickering candle to light her way. Better to come back during the day when trees looked like trees and shadows couldn't hide homicidal maniacs.

Crazy I might be. Stupid I was not.

At first glance, Enchantments looked deserted except for a flickering light in the windows on the upper level. I parked Christine in my usual space out back and let myself in the store; the door was not locked. The pale light I'd seen in the upstairs windows shone as a glow beneath the closed stairway door. I opened the door and called upstairs.

"Felicity?"

"Up here."

I made my way up the stairs, my curiosity piqued. "What are you doing?"

"Waiting for you, my dear."

My skin began to tingle as I approached the landing. It felt as though I were entering an electrically charged cloud. Every hair on my body twitched and stood at attention. My eyes wide, I completed the climb and hesitated at the top of the stair.

The loft had been prepared for a gathering. Twisted wrought-iron candlesticks, each holding a thick white column candle at waist level, stood in a circle 'round the braided carpet that occupied the larger part of the loft space; enough to illuminate it entirely with a wavering, golden light. At the four quarters, like points on a compass, were candles of varying colors: green at north, yellow at east, red at south, blue at west.

Felicity stood in the center of the carpet, alone, holding a candle of deepest purple in her left hand and a long white taper in her right. She wore a flowing blue gown, a cross between an evening gown and lounging pajamas. Her hair glittered as though she had been sprinkled with fairy dust, making her look a bit otherworldly and years younger than I thought her to be.

"I'm glad you decided to come," she said, smiling in welcome.

I cleared my throat and gestured toward the empty room. "You said you had some people you wanted me to meet."

"They'll be along in a few minutes." She touched the taper to the purple candle and set it down by a pair of throw pillows beside her bare feet. Then she snuffed the white taper and turned to me. "First I had wanted to talk to you a bit . . . about what you've been experiencing."

I moved farther into the room. The sense of electricity intensified as I stepped onto the braided rug. I shrugged and tried to pretend I didn't understand. We both knew it to be a lie.

"It's okay to be nervous, Maggie."

"I'm not nervous," I lied, not looking at her. "Just very . . . alert."

"Well, why don't you come over here." She indicated the two throw pillows she'd set on the rug opposite each other. "Unless you're afraid."

I hung my jacket and purse on a coat rack and self-consciously settled myself on the plush pillow. Felicity had already seated herself, her legs folded elegantly to one side.

I gestured around us. "What is all of this?"

I'd seen the loft, of course, and knew well the items stocked here, away from the prying eyes of those who could not be trusted with the secret. But tonight it felt so different. I realized then that this was the first time I had been able to walk atop the braided circle. It had never seemed right before.

Felicity let her gaze sweep the loft, which I had to admit looked beautiful and mysterious with the candlelight and with the stars shining through the sky-high windows. "We meet here in the loft. My group. And I practice here some nights when the weather is too severe for safety in the place that is my preferred ritual space."

I spent a moment in silence, pondering what she'd told me. "That explains it then."

"Yes?"

"The reason I couldn't . . . the last time I was up here. I couldn't bring myself to walk across this carpet. And yet tonight . . ."

Her laughter tinkled around us, amusement crinkling at the corners of her eyes. "So, my wards worked. Good to know I'm not losing my touch. One hopes one's mind is strong enough, focused enough, but there is always the risk of distraction to muck things up."

So many things I didn't understand. And yet I was curious; I could not deny it. "What are . . . what are wards?" I asked shyly.

"Protection spells and charms, my dear. The one I use most often, the Invisible Threshold, is very strong, indeed. And very tricky. But amazingly effective when done properly."

Time for a confession. "I came up here alone, that first day. I didn't mean to pry. I thought the door led to a bathroom or something."

She kept smiling that patient little smile. "It wasn't too much of a shock?"

"Not really. To be honest, I was . . . intrigued by what I found here. I even borrowed a book from the used stock. I wanted to understand."

"Why does an otherwise normal woman fritter about with spells and charms and spirits and goddesses and all topics imaginary?"

I blushed at her intuition. *Got it in one.* "Something like that."

She rose gracefully and began to pace in fluid strides around me. "Tell me something. Do you think I'm crazy?"

I gaped at her, taken aback. "Of course not."

"No? Do you think me the type of person who fosters a belief in fairy tales because I cannot accept the harsh world I find myself in?"

"No."

She sank to her knees in front of me and took my hands. "Then perhaps you can accept that there might be a scrap of truth to what I believe."

Her eyes held me captive. Pale. Searing. Searching. I opened my mouth, closed it, opened it again. Had to stop that, I was starting to remind myself of a goldfish. "I—I'm not sure."

"Try." She squeezed my hand, and her intense expression softened. "Just try to keep an open mind. It will make things so much easier for you."

She released me and sat back on her heels. "Now. From the day you walked into Enchantments—"

"Fell in, actually," I couldn't resist inserting.

She laughed to herself. "Right. From the day you *fell* into Enchantments, I have sensed there was something special about you. A kinship, if you will. One sensitive to another. And I believe you felt it as well."

"Sensitive?" I struggled to understand what she was telling me. *A kinship, yes* . . . "I'm not—"

"I have reason to believe you're a clairsentient, Maggie. An empath," she clarified, when it became obvious the word wasn't sinking in.

"An empath," I repeated blankly.

"Yes. Clairsentients are capable of feeling the emotions of others, both in present time and remembered time, real and inherent. Some also receive impressions of people. Gut feelings, if you will."

It got me thinking. I cleared my throat nervously. "By gut feelings, do you mean something like listening to what a person is telling you and somehow knowing that person is lying to you, and why?"

She beamed at me. "Precisely."

Oh God. It couldn't be. I took a deep breath. "There must be some sort of mistake. I'm not . . . I mean, I might be a good listener, and I might be halfway decent at reading body language and other indicators. But there's nothing strange about that. Lots of people can do that."

Felicity shook her head. "They can't. How many people walk around, unconscious of others, their entire lives? It's a gift, Maggie. And there's nothing to worry about, nothing to be ashamed of. I have a theory that has been proven time and time again. Each of us is born with an aptitude for extrasensory abilities. In some, the ability is immediate, instinctive from birth. In others, the ability is delayed, sometimes a few years, sometimes a few decades before the gift makes itself known to them. Others never realize their ability at all. They travel through their life path oblivious to the wonders the universe has to offer, sometimes even purposely withdrawing from the realization. These souls are the least advanced and must work past all internal obstacles before they are ready to accept. To learn. To take that next step toward perfection."

It was all a bit much, but I was trying very hard not to slam the door of my mind shut. "Where does what I went through at the cemetery fit into all of this?"

"Emotional memory." Another blank look from me made her expound further. "Think back and maybe you'll understand better. When did the trouble at the cemetery begin?"

I did as I was told, closing my eyes to relive the moment. "When I stepped into the Mausoleum. It got worse—much worse—when I touched the jar that held her ashes."

Felicity went very still. "Ashes?"

"Yes, Isabella was cremated," I said, watching her. Something was wrong. Then I realized from the churning in my own stomach that the emotion causing the tension in Felicity's features was nothing less than pure, white-hot rage, and *I felt it, too.* It was deeper and more intense than anything I had ever associated with my heretofore mild-mannered employer. In a way I wasn't prepared to admit, it frightened me. "Didn't you know?"

She turned her head slowly to look at me, fury simmering just below the surface. "Isabella was terrified of fire. She had been from the time we were children. She would never have allowed cremation. Never."

"But if that's true . . ." I shook my head to clear it. My thoughts were spinning furiously, and my stomach was in knots. "Why? Why would they go against her wishes?"

Such disregard for the wishes of a dead woman was unheard of. Disgraceful. No, more than disgraceful. It was sacrilege.

"I can think of one reason, and one reason only," Felicity said, her mouth a grim line.

The candle flames flickered, all of them in unison. I was certain of it.

"Not to get rid of evidence," I said, reasoning my way through. "Our police force may be small, but they aren't entirely inept."

"No, not that. I think whoever killed Isabella would have been careful. No, I think this speaks more of Jeremy's will to be rid of *her*."

"They could be one and the same," I pointed out.

Felicity considered this, then slowly shook her head. "Much as I'd like to believe it, I'm afraid I can't see Jeremy putting that much effort into anything. Their marriage may not have been ideal, but for Jeremy I think it was a handy excuse. It allowed him to have his little flings without consequence. Without commitment."

She stopped a moment, cocking her head in a delicate sparrow-like movement, her posture watchful. "Ah, good. They're here."

Felicity held out her hand to me to pull me to my feet as the sounds of footsteps and voices began to drift up the stairwell. Within moments the loft was filled to bursting with an odd assortment of individuals who brought the chill night air in with them. A motley crew, I thought with a private smile as I watched the lot of them surround Felicity like a flock of mother hens. The women were quick to offer soft, cooing words of solace, while their male counterparts hung back with their hands jammed in their jeans pockets, their gruff words of consolation and apology all the more sincere for their apparent unease. Good friends all, that much was obvious.

A familiar face popped into my worldview, all sunkissed freckles and flyaway hair.

"I wondered if you'd be here. Felicity said you might need our help," Annie Miller said in her usual no-nonsense way as she swept off her fringed hippie poncho and hung it on the rack. Tonight she wore a long men's flannel shirt over an ankle-length denim skirt. Beneath its hem peeked her favorite Birkenstocks, her feet protected from the cold by thick, woolen socks. A red bandana held back her wild strawberry blond curls, but did little to tame them. Fresh-faced and looking younger than her years, she gazed expectantly at me.

I cast a quick glance at the others, still preoccupied with Felicity. "What is all of this?"

"We're the N.I.G.H.T.S. Northeast Indiana Ghost Hunting and Tracking Society."

"You mean like Ghostbusters?"

"Without that whole busting the ghost thing," she said with the merest trace of a smile. "We don't actually remove the spirits we find unless there is no other alternative, such as in the case of a dark entity bent on mischief. We promote a happy coexistence between the spirit world and the physical world, for the benefit of all."

"I see you've renewed your acquaintance with Annie," Felicity interrupted us, giving Annie's shoulders an affectionate squeeze. "I don't suppose you've brought along some of your world-famous brownies, my dear?"

Annie bent at the waist to pick up a foil-covered plate she'd set on the floor while she removed her poncho. "Have I ever let you down?"

"Not in a million years." While Annie set the plate on a glass counter along the far wall, Felicity turned back to the others and called out above the din. "Gather 'round, everyone. Let's get started, now, shall we?"

More pillows were hauled out of some built-in cabinetry that blended fully into the old-fashioned wainscoting. The cabinets had been invisible to me until that moment, their appearance a revelation. I closed my mouth and helped to empty the cabinet, wondering all the while what further revelations I would find here in this sacred space.

When the pillows had been placed within the circle, everyone took their ease—some cross-legged, some with their legs stretched out before them and only their ankles crossed, and still others (the men, natch) leaning back on their hands, their legs splayed out unself-consciously. Felicity stood in the center of the circle in her blue silk gown, surveying the lot of us with an open affection that rolled off her in shimmering waves. There was a feeling in the room of excitement and watchful awareness. The edge of discovery.

"I'd like you all to meet Maggie, my new assistant here in the store."

"Hi, Maggie," they all responded, reminding me of my elementary school days. I held up my hand with a sheepish grin.

"Why don't we start out with introductions, shall we?"

A man rose to his feet with an audible creak of his knees, grunting slightly with the effort. He was tall and built like an aging football jock with hands like hams. We do breed our football gods big in the Midwest. "Guess I'll go first, unless someone else wants to take a stab at it." When there were no objections, he nodded and looked straight at me. "Right, then I'm Joe Aames. I own a hog-farming operation out on 500 North. Nothin' special, but it's mine. I also have a degree in psychology, but the pigs don't do much talkin', and neither do I, most days." He tucked his battered hands into the pockets of an oversized quilted flannel shirt. "As to why I'm here, I also, uh, seem to have a knack for attracting ghosts."

"That's an understatement," a whipcord-thin college-age boy spoke up, taking the floor. "Our Joe has a whole mess of 'em on his property. It's a real trip. If you stay with this group, you'll see things most people only dream of. Things the establishment would like everyone to believe don't exist." He pushed his round Lennon-style wire rims up on the bridge of his nose. He had messy blond hair, an overly intelligent face and the burning zeal of a televangelist, minus the religion. Bending at the waist, he dug in the pack he'd kept glued to his side since his arrival. "I'm Devin McAllister, by the way. I go to school at Grace—you know, the religious college over in North Hamilton?—mostly because my dad insisted on it. But I'm not into that. Here. This is what I'm really into." He handed me a newsletter he'd pulled from his pack. "I put out *The Speculator*. Five hundred and twenty-two subscriptions strong. Editor, chief writer, printer, and mail boy. That's me. My dad would have a shit fit if he knew. He's not into any of that stuff. Just doesn't get it."

Next came a delicate young girl, high school age at most, I'd guess, with a dreamy, ethereal face and hair like spun sugar. She declined to stand, preferring to sit on her velvet pillow, her hands looped loosely about her updrawn knees. "Hi Maggie. My name's Evie. Evie Carpenter." She smiled shyly but didn't seem to know what else to say.

Felicity came to her rescue. "Evie recently became aware that the things she'd been experiencing her entire life were actually episodes of psychic abilities trying to break into her consciousness. She's been exercising her psychic 'muscles,' shall we say, with N.I.G.H.T.S. To refine them, and to learn to wield control over them."

Evie nodded to confirm Felicity's claims. "My parents don't know. They think I sleep over at a girlfriend's house on N.I.G.H.T.S. nights." She ducked her head guiltily. "They'd never understand."

Everyone murmured to themselves in agreement. I would bet every single one of them had that same worry with the majority of the people in their lives.

The woman who rose to her feet next would have looked out of place in most of the continental U.S., but was somehow especially so in the elegant confines of Felicity's store. She was the size of a man and dressed like a lumberjack: baggy denim overalls (overhauls, my gramps calls 'em), a big buffalo-plaid wool shirt, clunky boots, and a misshapen baseball hat pulled down low on her brow. "Well, it looks like it's my turn now. Hello, Maggie. It's good to have you with us. I'm Genevieve Valmont. Former nun at Saint Vincent's in South Bend, thank the good Lord, and firm believer in the supernatural. I left the church because I believed I could do more for others here on the outside than I could bound by its strictures. I'm here to discover as much as I can about the spirit world that the church would have us believe is entirely evil. I'd bet my old F-150 they're wrong."

"Amen," Felicity intoned softly.

Next up was, unexpectedly, a bearded man in the distinctive clothing characteristic of all Amish men. His accent confirmed it. "Eli Yoder, ma'am. Joe there, he's my next-door neighbor. Joe and I, we share the *geists* that populate our land . . . and there are many."

Joe Aames nodded. "Eli is a dowser. He has a special connection to the flow of earth and spirit energy. He's wicked with a pair of divining rods."

Annie rose then. "Annie Miller's my name, but you already know that. Clairaudience is my game. I hear spirit voices," she explained when faced with my blank expression. "And I can

sense the energy spirits give off. They're around us all the
time, you know. Sometimes they're chatty. Other times they
prefer to remain silent. You never know what you'll run into on
an investigation."

Annie was the last. When she'd finished, Felicity turned to
me. "These good people, my dear this group, is my touch-
stone in all matters metaphysical. There are many belief sys-
tems represented here in this room. But what we all share is a
strong and abiding interest in the paranormal. We share our
own personal gifts and abilities in a bid to investigate and understand as much about the spirit world as possible. And this
area"—she spread her hands wide and looked up at the
skylight—"provides us with an amazing amount of fodder."

I'd never thought of our small corner of Indiana as being a
particularly spiritual place, though I'm sure the church lead-
ers of Stony Mill would love to offer opposing views on the
matter. Spooky, though . . . spooky was another thing entirely.
When one ventured out of town onto more rural ground, away
from the reassuring reminders of civilization, the night swallowed whole farmers' fields with nerve-wracking ease. Wind,
a constant presence across land scraped flat eons ago by great
hulking masses of ice, spoke in an ancient tongue through the
creaking bowers of trees, the whispering leaves of corn, the
shifting stalks of wheat. Walk or drive down a gravel road,
surrounded by nothing but miles of fields of sky-high corn,
not a soul in sight . . . it was enough to give anyone the willies.

All right, so I was a bit of a weenie. As the saying goes, it's
a dirty job . . .

All eyes were on me. I was pretty sure I was expected to
say something pithy yet brilliant. Reminded all too much of
Mrs. Dumreddy's speech class, I cleared my throat. "Well. I
guess you all have heard a little about the trouble I've been
having. I, uh, don't know quite what to think yet. I don't know
whether I believe in . . . all this . . ."

"Hey. Maggie." Devin McAllister drew my attention to
him, his tone reassuring, his eyes intense behind his funny little glasses. "We've all had our doubts. You'll get over them on
your own terms. Take your time. It's okay."

I nodded, my throat tight with unexpected emotion. The

overwhelming sense of acceptance in this room humbled me. "Thanks. It's just a little overwhelming, is all. You know? I don't understand why . . . why me? Voices from the darkness, moments of debilitating emotion. Knowledge of things I shouldn't have. I thought I must be going crazy."

"I felt different," Evie confessed in a small voice, still hugging her knees. "No one else sees the things I see. No one else hears what I hear. All I wanted was to be like them. I didn't want to be different. I wanted to belong."

There was a moment of silence while I absorbed the truth of Evie's concerns. The trouble was, I've always known I didn't belong. Everyone else knew it, too. I suppose that's why girls like Margo worked so hard to keep girls like me out of their little cliques. People had a tendency to band together. Like meets like. Anything else made them nervous.

The question that had lodged itself in my throat refused to be swallowed. "Are you . . . are you all witches, then?"

Genevieve turned away from the brownie plate with a chuckle. "We are seekers of the truth," she said simply. "No one much cares about anything else."

"Maggie."

I looked up at Felicity's voice. Her eyes shone like candles in the dimly lit room.

"We all of us know what you are feeling," she said softly. "Use us. Let the group be your anchor as you travel the path of discovery. Of acceptance. We are here for you." Not expecting me to give her an answer, she addressed the room at large: "If everyone is ready, gather 'round. Time for Circle."

I stood up uncertainly as everyone rose from their pillows and held out their hands to their neighbor. The person to my right bumped my hand with the back of theirs. I looked over. Genevieve had taken her place beside me and gazed at me with a question in her eyes, and I knew she was asking me whether I would participate. Excitement zinged up my spine. Or was that apprehension? In the end I knew it didn't matter. I would never get past my fear by hiding from what frightened me. I would never understand by remaining in the shadows.

I hesitated only a moment, then calmly, deliberately, clasped her hand.

Felicity took her place at my left and closed the circle, and I started involuntarily. Something warm and crackling seemed to be flowing from person to person around the circle. Something like electricity. I could feel it coursing through my palm and up my right arm, across my chest cavity, then down my arm and on through to Felicity on my left. Charged by the strange energy, the fine hairs rose on my arms. My scalp tingled. I took a deep breath. My body felt weightless. I needed only to let go and I would go sailing off into space and time, slipping easily through the glass membrane of the skylight, straight to the stars.

Felicity's voice rang out, clear and strong:

> In the name of all that is sacred,
> we cast our circle 'round,
> By the turning of the eternal wheel,
> by friendship are we bound.

The carefully intoned words worked on my natural suspicion and wariness to elicit a response from deep inside me. I quivered, sucked into a dream world of Felicity's making.

> In this circle,
> Carefully drawn,
> Knowledge we seek,
> Truth be found.
> In this circle
> We form a connection,
> Shadows stay out,
> Light our protection.
> In this day
> And from this hour,
> Friendship is strength,
> Love is power.
> As we will it
> So will it pass.
> As we will it
> So mote it be.

She repeated the words twice more. Each time she ended with the words *So mote it be,* others chimed in with *Amen* and *Alleluia*. Strange, that it felt so natural. So balanced. So right.

As the ritual ended, I breathed deeply, letting the words, the electricity that in the blink of an eye had managed to infiltrate my worldview and turn it upside down, flow more slowly through me until it ebbed away completely, leaving me with only the memory still scudding in my blood.

When I was able to summon the gumption to open my eyes, I discovered I hadn't been the only one affected by the words spoken in candlelight. From Devin to Genevieve to Eli, everyone seemed to be blinking away the effects. The candles at the quarter points burned high, the flames leaping and dancing. I blinked repeatedly until the room started to look normal again.

Felicity appeared before me, the gaily painted plate of brownies held in her hands. "Everyone, take a brownie." To me specifically, she murmured, "You should eat something in order to ground some of the energy we just raised."

I took one, and—God, it looked luscious. I had only just taken a nibble when Genevieve began stamping her feet against the floorboards. I gaped at her. I gaped even more when the others started behaving in equally nonsensical ways, some sitting Indian-style, some lying full-out on the floor.

Genevieve intercepted my astonished look and she stopped her stork-like dance. "You need to release the energy." She stamped her feet again to demonstrate. "Send it back into the earth. Otherwise you'll be up all night."

Uh, yeah.

Feeling stupid, I just nodded and halfheartedly dashed my feet at the floorboards in case she was watching, then edged away. Now that the mundane world was starting to return, it was easier to deny that anything was strange or unusual about this entire situation except for the people I had met here.

The door at the foot of the stairs clicked and creaked, then came the tread of heavy boots up the steps.

"Sorry I'm late," a familiar voice called out, and with that Marcus Quinn came skidding around the corner in his clunky biker boots, his wavy black hair loose beneath a tight black do-rag. "I hope you guys went ahead without me. Hey, Liss." He caught sight of me then, and slow mirth touched his sensual lips. "Well, if it isn't little Maggie. I should have known I'd find you here with us sooner or later. Liss has that effect on people."

He shrugged out of his leather jacket with all its zippers and chains and tossed it to Evie, who caught it up against her nonexistent breasts with a blush and a breathy giggle. Walking past her to greet Liss, he chucked Evie under the chin, much to her obvious delight.

Seemed like Marcus had an effect on people, too. Women in general. Me, included, much as I hated to admit it. Under his jacket he wore jeans and a plain white T-shirt, undersized enough to have to stretch over the ridges and planes of his chest and to catch on the bulge of his biceps. Now, Marcus wasn't a big man by any stretch of the imagination, but he was lean and lanky and hard in a way that made me think of cowboys. Marcus was a cowboy with attitude.

He greeted Liss with a kiss on the cheek that completely deflated my appreciative little bubble. All for the better, I thought as I turned away. He obviously adored her. What I wouldn't give for a man to feel that way about me. And to feel that same way about him.

My thoughts turned unbidden to Tom Fielding, and the date I'd avoided by the skin of my teeth. I couldn't help wondering . . .

"So, Maggie, what do you think about our group?" Marcus asked, his arm looped 'round Felicity's waist.

Direct question. So hard to deflect. "I, uh . . . Well, it's been interesting."

"And?"

His eyes probed mine. I glanced away, but my gaze caught on his long fingers curved so attentively around her waist. "And . . . I guess I'm not sure. I'm not sure what to think." Everyone was watching me, curiosity shining from their eyes. I wasn't about to air my questions in front of the lot of them. Any questions I had could wait until I could talk to Felicity alone. "Thanks, everyone, for including me tonight. Sorry for leaving so soon, but . . . I have to go."

Felicity followed me around while I gathered my coat and purse. "Are you all right, Maggie?"

"Fine." I sent her a reassuring smile. "Really."

"You're sure?"

I nodded. "We can talk more on Monday, or even tomorrow if you like, but I should get home now. It's been a long day. I'm fine. Really."

"You said that," she pointed out. "If you have to go, I won't stop you. But we really do need to talk more, Maggie. There is so much you don't understand."

I nodded and escaped as quickly as I could, knowing her eyes followed my path down the stairs, and knowing that what I would see within hers, should I turn back to look, was concern. It was too much. *Today* was too much. But I didn't plan to go home. Not yet. I needed some air, some cool, autumn air to blow the cobwebs from my head.

The store was pitch black downstairs. I carefully picked my way through the merchandise I could by now see even with my eyes closed and let myself out the back door into the parking area. Christine was there waiting for me, the Tanto to my Lone Ranger. Or should that be Silver? Whatever. I paused by her door, wishing for light as I dug through my purse for the keys that had disappeared on me.

"Lose something?"

Chapter 13

My breath snagged in my throat. I whipped around, pressing my back to Christine, my hand clutched to my breast like a heroine in the best classic tradition. The wall of the building was shrouded in shadow. I blinked hard and stretched my eyes wide as I tried to find a point of focus on the murky darkness surrounding me. Then I decided self-preservation was a much better idea. Without further ado, I scrabbled behind me for the doorhandle, remembering at the last minute that I had locked the door securely against invasion. Mine or otherwise.

A darker shadow emerged from the gloom against the building, then straightened, assuming the shape of a man.

Mother Mary, mother, mother, pray for me . . .

I watched in horror, a scream clawing its way up my throat. I was half a second from letting it rip when for a moment I thought I recognized . . .

"Tom?" I squeaked, willing it to be true. I mean, it wasn't that I really wanted to see him—quite the opposite—but the alternative was too terrifying for words.

"Good guess."

On the other hand, it also meant I was busted. I cleared my

throat nervously as his head and shoulders emerged into the dim glow of the security light at the corner of the building. He didn't look happy. "Um, I take it you received my message?"

"That would be affirmative." He moved toward me. Just a step, but it was enough to make my pulse to do the two-step again. "After I stopped by your apartment to pick you up, of course."

"Oh. Sorry." It seemed to me that it would be in my best interests to try to steer the conversation into less agitated waters. "Er, what are you doing here?"

Another step closer. "You didn't answer your door."

Ripples of nervousness played havoc with my equilibrium. "I—"

His intense gaze locked with mine, his gray eyes near black in the weak light, daring me to look away. One more step and he stood in front of me, his hands slung low on his hips. I couldn't move. It wasn't that he had physically hemmed me in; more it was the overwhelming aura of masculinity that held me in its sway. Danger and desire and fear made for a decidedly potent brew.

Invisible air currents delivered the citrus tang of his cologne to my nose. A hint of soap, as though he'd just shaved. Elusive. *Seductive.*

Mother Mary, pray for me!

He leaned into me, perilously close. "You know, if you're going to play possum, darlin', you're going to have to remember the little details . . ." His voice, pitched so low I had a strange urge to lean in closer for fear of missing out, sent shivers trembling up my spine. "Like your car parked curbside on the city street."

Hot blood rushed to my face. "Something suddenly came up," I mumbled.

"You know, I have to tell you. I saw that *Brady Bunch* episode, and as I recall, Marcia didn't get away with it either. Why don't you just cut to the chase and tell me why you ducked out on me?"

"I didn't duck out on you." I was doing my best to remain calm and level-headed, but it's terribly hard to think straight when you have two hundred and ten pounds of male testosterone facing you down. "I just . . . thought it might be a bit premature for us to . . ."

"What? Have a cup of coffee? Chat? About the weather? About your boss? Or were you afraid I was going to have my way with you after a few hours of long . . . slow . . . kisses?"

Okay, well, there was that . . .

I swallowed the sudden upsurge of longing that made me want to throw my arms around his neck and ravish him right there on the street corner.

Easy there, Maggie my girl . . .

He was using seduction against me; I knew it. I couldn't give him the satisfaction of knowing he'd gotten to me.

"I have to go," I said, turning my face away.

He laughed softly. "Running away again?"

I reacted instantly, as he must have known I would. And then I thought about Felicity, and the way Tom had come into the store after Isabella had been found dead. It was obvious he didn't much like Felicity and had been trying to warn me away. Why would he do that?

I had to find out.

"All right," I said as serenely as possible. "What do you propose I do instead?"

The smile that quirked at the left corner of his mouth screamed pure victory. He was about to tell me when the door to the store opened behind him.

A cigarette tip glowed red momentarily from the shadows, then Marcus stepped forward. Shadow from shadow. "Sorry, didn't mean to interrupt. Need any help, Maggie?"

I licked my dry lips, grateful for the distraction because it gave me a much needed moment to regroup. "Thanks, Marcus, but I think I can handle it."

"You sure?" he pressed, his itinerant gaze busy sizing Tom up. Cigarette smoke wound around his head like a slithering silver snake. It made him appear just a little bit devilish and wicked. But then, everything about Marcus seemed just a bit devilish and wicked. That was part of his charm.

Tom straightened to his full height. "Miss O'Neill said everything was fine, Quinn."

They know each other, I realized with a start. *Know, but ot like.*

Why did that surprise me?

"Just had to make sure. You know I can't stand it when men ke their frustrations out on women."

Tom's brows came together like a clap of thunder and he pened his mouth to snap out a retort, but Marcus had already ded to black in the shadows. For a moment I thought he ight still be there, watching us, but the heavy silence reas- ured me he'd gone back inside.

I turned to Tom, whose brow was still creased with annoy- nce. He'd linked his thumbs through his belt loops, his fin- ertips playing a razzmatazz against his hipbones. "Do you ink that's what I'm doing?" he asked finally. "Taking out my rustrations?"

He looked so miserable that I couldn't help but want to re- ssure him. "He was just being protective, Tom." He didn't eem to like that answer any more than a straight yes, so I dded, "Did you want to go somewhere? Get a cup of coffee or omething?"

He just looked at me. "I thought you wanted to run away."

"Well, I figure that's a lost cause. You're not going to let e, so I might as well get a good cup of coffee out of it."

He coughed out a chuckle against his will. Still, the desire question me must have won out over his wounded pride. He lanced at his watch. "It's past midnight. Not much open. Do ou mind the truckstop?"

Ivy's Truckstop was one of the true abiding fixtures of wn. Ten years ago, Stony Mill had still looked like some- ing out of the *Farmer's Almanac.* Back in those golden days efore the fast-food revolution, Ivy's had been the town's only vatering hole that didn't actually offer alcoholic beverages on e menu, a place where farmers and truckers and good old oys gathered together for a bit of down-home cooking and onversation. Grandpa Gordon used to take me there, but I adn't gone since he'd had his driver's license taken away for aking out the gazebo on the courthouse square. It might be ood to see how things had changed.

"Sure," I said. "Why not?"

*   *   *

I insisted on driving. I figured if I had to be out on the town
into the wee hours with someone I didn't know very well, at
least I wouldn't have to depend on his good intentions to get
me home. "Hop in."

There is something about the way a big hunky guy looks all
folded up in a car built for midgets that never fails to strike me
as funny. I squelched a giggle and solemnly turned the key in
the ignition. "You can, er, move the seat back. If you need to."

He mumbled something unintelligible—that's pretty common when your kneecaps are jammed up against your lips—
and patted around for the release. Stretched . . . extended . . .
reeeeached . . .

I couldn't stand it. "Here, let me get that for you."

Our fingers closed around the lever at the same time. The
bucket seat went sailing backward on well-greased tracks.
Caught unawares, I lost my balance and pitched forward right
along with it. Tom reached out instantly to catch my fall but
missed as the seat thunked to a halt at the end of the track. My
nose bumped into his shoulder anyway.

"Ow," I said, my pride hurt more than my nose. Still, I
reached up my hand to rub it and used it as cover to risk a
glance up at him.

My stomach dropped to the vicinity of my toes, then made
a weak little wobble for good measure. He was looking at me
in a way that made my mouth go dry, an odd mixture of soft-
ness and awareness and good old-fashioned sexual charisma
that went straight to the heart of the matter.

*Margaret Mary-Catherine O'Neill, good Catholic girls
don't fall over themselves for a man on the first date . . .
Where's the mystery in that?*

But this wasn't a date. It was a race for the truth, with both of
us determined to outdo the other. Did that make a difference?

Confused, I straightened and pulled away, breaking the
connection. "Sorry."

"Did you hurt yourself?"

I shook my head and stared ahead as I steered Christine out
of the gravel alley and onto the street. For a moment, silence

filled the cold confines of the car, broken only by the occasional mechanical rap or wheeze emitted by the aging engine. I gripped the wheel harder, casting about for a safe topic. I for one have always hated the painful silences that occur when two people don't know each other very well. They never fail to make me desperate to fill the void. True to form, I broke it myself.

"So, why *did* you follow me tonight? I mean, most men would have given up and gone on to greener pastures, or . . . something."

"I figured you got cold feet, and I didn't want to let you go that easily."

The perfect evasive answer is one that can be construed in a variety of ways. Tom seemed to be quite fond of them. I, on the other hand, despise being manipulated, so I decided to guide the conversation toward a path *I* wanted to pursue. "You wanted to ask me about Felicity."

He hesitated a moment. "I won't lie and tell you the thought hadn't crossed my mind. I'm a cop. It's what I do. But that's not the only reason."

Sidestep needed. Duck and cover. "Why don't you just ask me about Felicity, then? Go ahead. Get it off your chest." Of course I wouldn't promise I'd give him the answers he was looking for, though. That remained to be seen.

"Not yet. Coffee. I need coffee. Don't you have a heater in this thing?"

I shook my head. "Not at this speed. It only blows cold air below sixty miles per hour. We'd have to hit the highway to have heat." I looked askance at him. "Except then I would be breaking the law, technically. Not recommended with an officer of the law sitting in the car next to you."

"I think I'd risk it for a little heat. My hands are like Popsicles. Cold night. Winter's on its way."

"There's a blanket in back."

"For just such an emergency? Thanks, but I can think of much nicer ways to warm up my hands." And he grinned in such a way that I could no more escape his meaning than I could my uptight Midwestern upbringing.

I laughed in spite of myself. "Why, Deputy Fielding, what

a perfectly wicked thing to say." I was blushing, but in the dim glow of the dash lights I could be reasonably certain that he didn't know. I was also flirting, but I guess he knew that. "My grandmother would box your ears for suggesting such a thing."

"I'll be sure to wear ear muffs when I meet her."

That might seem to suggest that he had intentions of some-day meeting my family, but I knew better than to make too much of it. Around here, that's just what people do. My folks have met every guy I've ever dated. They've had them to din-ner, to backyard cookouts, and to bonfires. In the end it meant nothing more than the friendly hour or two it was. I decided not to tell Tom that Grandma was already dead. For some rea-son, I felt more than a little off-balance with him, and any-thing that might help to make him toe the line would be more than welcome.

Lights flashed behind us in the rearview mirror as I drove up the deserted main drag. I adjusted it to night vision and wondered (*Pet Peeve #13*) why no one can remember to lower their brights as they come upon another car. I mean, common courtesy, people! Society advances, and boom, consideration goes down the toilet? At least I didn't have to suffer the thoughtless git for long. The truckstop loomed just ahead on the right, highlighted by dual roaming sky beacons that called truckers down from the interstate at the north edge of town. I pulled off the road into the rutted gravel parking lot and let the high-beam offender whip on past.

Even at one o'clock in the morning, Ivy's parking lot was not as empty as one might expect. Several big rigs were packed like sardines in a tin can against the back fence at the rear of the lot. The drivers didn't mind so long as they could get a little shut-eye. Nearer the building stood a nondescript sedan and a rusting old Ford pickup. The pickup was jacked up high enough that the driver must have needed a ladder to climb in and out of it. But the light shining from Ivy's win-dows was dazzling, and the music coming from inside was pure old-fashioned honky-tonk, bright and reassuring. I switched off the engine, took a deep breath, and turned toward Tom, but he was already getting out of the car. Before I could do the same, he had hustled around to my side and opened my door for me.

"Wow," I said, both surprised and, I admit it, more than a little pleased, "whoever said chivalry was dead?"

He flashed me a ten-kilowatt grin and held out his hand. "Obviously whoever it was has never been to Indiana."

Taking his hand produced a strange feeling. Everything about him felt strange and yet familiar, alien and yet comfortable. He would have kept my hand in his as we walked, but I pulled gently, self-consciously, away under the excuse of digging in my purse. Still, I couldn't help noticing the way he held the door for me or the way he helped me out of my coat before I slid into the first available booth.

"So," he said as we gazed cautiously across the table at each other.

"So." I decided to cut right to the point. "I've been meaning to ask you something, so I've decided I'm just going to come right out and ask."

"Shoot."

"The day Isabella Harding was killed and you came to the store to give me Felicity's keys, you said something that made me wonder what you meant."

"You mean, when I told you to find another job?"

"More the comment about Felicity's secret world."

"Ah."

"Well?"

His eyes searched mine. "Maggie, how well do you know Felicity Dow?"

With another person I'd known for a week, I'd have had to think about my answer, but Felicity was special. "By your standards, not very well," I admitted. "But I know what's most important. I know her heart."

We paused as our waitress, a middle-aged brunette wearing tight jeans, a T-shirt, and the requisite orthopedic shoes, interrupted us with two steaming cups of coffee, dropped two menus on the table, and bustled away with all the energy of a pint-sized cyclone.

Tom waited until she was out of earshot before he said, "I know you probably *think* you know her. But believe me, there are things about your friend that would scare you and the rest of the good people in this town to death."

All of this pussyfooting around was enough to drive even the most patient woman to distraction. "You mean because she's a witch?"

I regretted it as soon as the words left my mouth. While I'd never promised to safeguard Felicity's secret, I felt it my duty as a friend to protect her as much as possible. If disclosed to the wrong person, what I'd just said was tantamount to the worst kind of betrayal. And taking into consideration Tom's choice of profession, he was about as wrong as a person could be.

His lips tightened. "Yes. That's exactly why." He took a calming sip of coffee, keeping both hands wrapped tightly about his cup. "How do you know about that?"

I followed his lead with the coffee, because it kept my hands from betraying my nervousness. "I know because she told me. Before I started working for her."

"That surprises me."

"Because you don't know her. If you did, you could never suspect her. How did *you* come by this information?"

He shrugged noncommittally. "People talk. Heaven knows there were rumors." He paused a moment, then admitted, "I did a little digging. It didn't take much."

"Hm. You know, religious intolerance is an ugly thing, but persecution is far worse."

He looked at me, not saying a word, his thoughts shuttered behind his eyes.

"Does anyone else know?" I pressed, determined to know the full extent of the damage.

"On the force, you mean? The chief does, but I'm not sure about anyone else."

"Good. Let's just keep it that way. It's Felicity's life. She doesn't deserve to have it ruined simply because you don't like her."

Exasperation crackled in his gray green eyes. "Look. Maggie. There are reasons for Ms. Dow to be investigated as a suspect. You have to trust me on this."

The only thing to do was to call his bluff. "All right, then, tell me. Tell me what evidence you have."

"I'm not at liberty to say."

"But you're at liberty to hound a person because you have preconceived notions about her guilt thanks to her—shall we say unconventional—beliefs?"

He had the decency to look uncomfortable, at least. "Look. I realize they're calling it a religion now, which gives them certain rights—"

"Good of you to recognize that."

"—but you know as well as I do that's a result of liberals and the whole bizarre PC movement. It's invading every aspect of our lives. And witchcraft!" He shook his head. "That's about as bizarre as you can get."

"And Isabella's death indicates the use of witchcraft, is that what you're trying to tell me?"

"Of course not."

"No hocus pocus? No jinxes, or hexes, or even a psychic attack?"

He waved a dismissive hand. "You know there are no such things."

Gotcha. "Then you agree that it could have been anyone who killed Isabella? Anyone with a motive?"

He leaned back against the bench and assessed me quietly. "I can see you're trying to make a point."

Bet your ass I am, big guy. "Did you know that Jeremy Harding kept a mistress? Or that Isabella herself had a lover? I met both of them at the viewing. Lovely people, too."

Anger flashed in his eyes, swift as sheet lightning. "Jesus, Maggie, you think we don't know our jobs? In answer to your question, yeah. We asked questions. And in case *you* don't realize it, Jeremy Harding was in a business meeting at the time with six other prominent members of Stony Mill society. Didn't leave once, not even to go to the bathroom. As for Ryan Davidson, he was attending a deposition on behalf of the hospital. I guess that knocks both husband and loverboy out of the picture, huh?"

I stared at him, a little in awe of this sudden change in him.

And then I shook myself back to my senses. "All right. So they have alibis. They also have motives, and where there's a will, there's a way."

"What are you saying?"

I shrugged. "Murder for hire? It wouldn't be the first time."

"Okay. All right. That's a possibility, and it's one we'll check into further. Satisfied?"

"Supremely."

"Good. Now let's talk about your boss. In my book, she's every bit as good a suspect as the husband or the boyfriend."

"Oh, for heaven's sa—"

"They were estranged, and had been for over a year. Did you know that?"

"Sisters have arguments all the time," I told him. God knows I speak from experience. "Trust me on this."

"Let me test a theory out on you. Woman discovers, after the death of her beloved husband from causes natural, that said husband had a long-term affair with her own sister. The two sisters have words and refuse to have anything further to do with each other. But secretly the woman is consumed by rage and jealousy and denial. Suddenly, after a rift that has only deepened after more than a year, the sister ends up dead. Murdered. By coincidence, that very morning she calls the woman to her side, just in time to discover her body. Now," he said, arching a brow at me, "what does this situation say to you?"

I stared him down, my eyes as steely as my resolve. "Felicity is *not* guilty. I would stake my life on that."

His mouth twisted in a cynical excuse for a smile. "You know, if there's one thing I've learned, it's this: Best to avoid making sweeping statements like that in the middle of a murder investigation."

A sharp rebuttal leapt to my tongue, but it was stilled by the insistent electronic musicale of a cell phone. Tom put his hand to his waist.

Sorry, he mouthed to me as he flipped it open and spoke into it. "Fielding."

All I could hear of the conversation was a voice that twittered on at length on the other end of the satellite, but I didn't need to hear the words to know that whatever the news, it wasn't good. Tom's face said it all.

"Yes. No problem. I'm out anyway, and you're right. It's probably nothing. I'll head on over as soon . . . yes, right away. Gotcha. Right. I'll report back later."

He folded the phone closed with a *snick* and held it loosely in his hands on the tabletop. "That was the chief. Duty beckons, I'm afraid. I'm on call tonight. I have to go."

"Is something wrong?"

"No, nothing. Just a little Saturday night highjinks he asked me to check on."

He was lying. I knew it, without fanfare, the way you know that in the morning you'll have Cheerios for breakfast, shower, and brush your teeth, or that your mother will call you on Friday to ask after your latest boyfriend in the off chance that you've managed to get engaged in the preceding seven days. How did I know? Maybe it was his deliberately deadpan expression, or maybe it was the down-to-business way he stuffed the cell phone into his pocket. Body language is an important element of conversation, and I'd always tended to be more observer than active participant, so I had a lot of experience to back me up. Whatever the catalyst, I knew I was right.

"Gee, that's too bad," I told him, injecting just the right amount of disappointment into my voice. "I was enjoying our little talk."

His gaze slid to mine in a sidelong glance rife with disbelief. "Were you, now."

"Oh, absolutely," I said, wide-eyed and artless as he signaled for the check. Under the cover of the no-frills laminate table, I fingered my keys in anticipation. "*Sooooo.* Tell me. What kind of highjinks are we talking about?"

"*We* weren't discussing anything."

"Of course we were. What did your chief want you to check on? An accident of some sort? Teens out disturbing the peace? Domestic trouble?" He was doing the perfect impression of a deaf-mute. Obviously he needed convincing. Employing every bit of wile I had, I reached out and playfully chucked him under the chin. With any luck, my eyes had just twinkled. "Oh, come on. I'm not going to go blabbing about it. It's one-thirty in the morning, for God's sake. Who could I tell?"

He wanted to frown at me. I could tell. But he couldn't hide the slight quirk that tugged at the corner of his mouth. Finally he caved. "Well . . . all right. I guess it won't hurt anything." He lowered his voice to an undertone. "Someone called to report a drive-by." While I tried to wrap my mind around this, gingerly hoping the report hadn't originated with my parents' nosy neighbor, he remedied, "Shooting, I mean."

My brows shot up. "Here?" It seemed unthinkable. Things like that didn't happen in towns like Stony Mill.

He nodded in the affirmative just as our waitress hustled over, the table check waving in a breeze of her own creation.

"Got your total right here, hon," she said, dragging a pencil from its nest in her curly 'do. "You folks should sure try a piece of our pie before you go. Sugar cream and cherry are the specials today. No? You sure? I could wrap it up for you."

I swallowed convulsively over the thought of cherry pie, but I shook my head. "Thank you, no."

Tom handed her a five. "There you go, Jo Lee. Keep the change."

She looked at the cash. "A four-dollar tip for pouring two coffees? You're nuts, Tom Fielding. But a good kind of nuts. You must be wanting to get out of here real fast, huh?" She chuckled and gave me a saucy wink that had me turning five shades of red. "Have a good one, you two."

I ducked my chin before Tom could see my discomfiture and know it for what it was.

He held the door for me and put his hand on the small of my back as I walked through. I tried not to think about it, but somehow the gesture spoke to my feminine side, the one that liked to feel protected and pampered by a big strong man. I know, I know, the feminazis would have a cow, but hey, why fight nature? That's why I didn't argue when he helped me into Christine and closed the door for me before coming around to the other side.

"Where to?" I asked as he reached for the seat belt.

"Back to the store, so I can get my truck and head out."

"I'll take you."

"What? No. No, you won't."

"Why? It would be much faster if I drove you."

Mulishly he jutted out his chin. "We're wasting time."

"Right. We're wasting time. Now, where to?"

Exasperated, he looked at me. His chest lifted as he took a deep, deep breath, then let it out slowly. "You are one hell of a stubborn woman, did you know that?"

My lips curved slightly. "Thank you. I do try."

I could see the wheels of his mind churning. I had him, and he knew it. He scowled at me, a muscle twitching in his jaw. Finally he seemed to come to a decision.

"Fine. You're going. But you're not getting out of the car, and if I tell you to get on out of there, you're gonna do it as fast as this beast can take you."

"Fine."

He gave me the address. Regan Street, only six blocks away from the store. We drove back across town, a sense of anticipation giving the silence between us a palpable tension, one we both felt. We were alone on the street, stately trees arching their branches overhead. Headlights approached, far away, then turned off. We motored along through dark streets filled with equally dark houses. It occurred to me, then, how the night encourages isolation, and how isolation breeds fear. We were alone, but beyond that was a sense that there was something else out there in the darkness, something cold and without emotion watching our movements with predatory patience. As we turned left onto Regan, Tom reached over and touched my hand. The unexpected touch fortified me, reminding me that there was strength in numbers, just as there was comfort in shared experience. I let my hand relax beneath his, getting to know the size of his hand over mine, feeling the warmth of his skin, the tougher skin along his palm. Just being. I didn't dare look at him, but I knew he had been studying me. For some reason that knowledge didn't make me nervous, or embarrassed, or even awkward. It made me feel warm.

He drew his hand away then, and his whole demeanor changed. Hardened, somehow. Went on alert. I eased up on the accelerator, knowing we must be close.

"Two houses up. Slow down. Slow. Slow."

His eyes scanned back and forth, up and down, searching for movement. I pulled up in front of the house he'd indicated. It was ablaze with light from every window. A shadow flitted behind the window at the door.

"Stay here. Don't get out. I repeat, do *not* get out of the vehicle."

Nervousness had finally found me. "Do you, um, think, maybe, that, um, there could be—I don't know—someone—"

He paused with his hand on the doorlatch. "Lock the doors. Leave the motor running. Stay alert. Stay low. Anything happens, put your foot to the floor and get the hell out of here."

Well, that was certainly reassuring.

Before I had a chance to panic, the front door was flung open and a man came hauling butt down the tasteful brick walk, wearing nothing but a pair of boxers. He wasn't close enough for me to be sure, but from this distance I would swear they were silk.

It was Ryan Davidson.

Chapter 14

"So, let me get this straight. You were in your study, watching TV—*alone*—and the next thing you know there's a bullet hole in your wall, a spray of glass, and the squeal of tires. And that's all that you remember."

For once, Ryan Davidson looked anything but confident and self-assured. He sat hunched over the glass dining room table, face pale, hair rumpled from pushing his fingers through it. "Yeah. That's all I remember."

"Did you see the vehicle?"

Davidson's lips twisted into a snarl. "Well, it's kind of hard to see out the window when you've thrown yourself to the floor in a desperate attempt not to get killed."

"And you have no idea who might have a reason to want to hurt you or your property."

"Look. I'm not a saint. I've had relationships that have gone south, same as any man. That doesn't change anything. So are you going to do your job or do I need to go over your head?"

I yawned behind my hand. It wasn't that I wasn't interested in what Davidson had to say, but he'd said it three times already, and so far his story hadn't changed. And at three o'clock in the morning, a story had to be pretty damned scintillating to hold my attention.

Tom must have come to the same conclusion, because we were out the door five minutes later, leaving Davidson to seal the fist-sized hole in his window with a roll of duct tape while we hit the high road with the slug that Tom had dug out of the wall with his pocket knife tucked safely out of the way in a ziplocked evidence bag in the pocket of his leather jacket.

"Soooo," Tom said as we made our way out to Christine, our elbows bumping companionably against each other.

I smiled shyly at him. "So."

"Have any plans for the rest of the evening?"

I laughed. "In case you didn't notice, I think we're past evening and well into the wee hours of the morning."

He glanced at his watch and winced. "Ouch. Sorry. Some hot date I turned out to be, huh?"

Actually, despite my need for sleep, I couldn't stop thinking about things better left unthought, all involving the man in front of me. "What will happen with Davidson's would-be attacker?"

"I'll file a report. Poke around a little bit. See what comes of it. The lab will analyze the slug. Maybe we'll get lucky and the lab results will identify a weapon that's been used in a crime before by a known perpetrator. But other than that, unless someone from the neighborhood saw the car or the gunman, or unless the perp makes the mistake of bragging about their escapades to the wrong person . . ." He let his voice trail off and he shrugged.

"There's little chance of finding the person who shot out his window," I finished.

"You don't sound surprised."

I echoed his philosophical shrug with one of my own. "I know how this town works. People watch out for their own."

"That's pretty much it."

I let myself into the car and waited for him to follow before broaching the thing that had been bothering me since the moment Ryan Davidson had come tearing hell-bent-for-leather across his yard as if actual demons were nipping at his heels.

"Has it occurred to you yet that not only is Isabella dead, but now her lover has been shot at as well?"

"You're thinking the two incidents are related."

"Don't you?" And then, because he was so good at making his face a blank mask, I added, "Nothing else makes sense. It's too coincidental to be coincidence."

"It'll be interesting to get the results back from the lab," he allowed, cautious as ever.

Suddenly anxious, I pressed, "But you won't wait until then to ask questions, will you?"

"No. I won't wait."

That made me feel somewhat better. "What do you think of Ryan Davidson's claim that he couldn't think of a single potential assailant?"

"I think the man doth protest too much."

So did I. But . . . say that Davidson's attack *was* related to Isabella's death. Unless Davidson shot out his own window, which seemed a little too implausible even for me, the shooting seemed to throw Davidson out of the realm of possibility as a suspect. Didn't it? Who would have a reason for wanting both Isabella and her lover out of the way?

My bet was on the husband. Jeremy Harding had a motive for both incidents, by my reckoning. Rage over a wife's unfaithfulness has driven many a husband over the brink. Jealousy, too. Except . . .

Except something didn't quite fit. From what Felicity had said, Ryan Davidson was not the first of Isabella's lovers. I couldn't really see why Jeremy would have lashed out at this late date. And he'd had his own affairs as well. Their marriage seemed to be more one of mutual convenience than of emotional attachment. So why would he kill her?

Unless it was because of money. From what I understood, Isabella held the reins at Harding Enterprises. That left the execution of her will and . . .

I stopped for the stop sign and turned back onto the main drag. "Tom."

"Hmm?"

"Has Isabella's will been read yet?"

"We followed up on that, Maggie."

"Well, I hope so. That is your job. I'm not trying to be nosy—"

"Yes, you are."

"I'm not. It's not like I want to know how much she had in assets. I just want to know who will receive the bulk of her estate."

He narrowed his eyes at me. "You're not just going to stop, are you."

I raised my brows at him, waiting.

He sighed. "Her husband will receive some. Her daughter, more. Various minor bestowments. And lastly, a sizable donation to the hospital toward a certain project she'd adopted. Assuming the will isn't contested, of course."

She would have had life insurance as well, probably with the same beneficiaries. I thought a moment. The execution of an estate, presumably, could be an extended process. "I can't help but think that all of this points to one person in particular as a prime subject. I read somewhere that when a woman is murdered, most of the time it is by someone she is on intimate terms with."

Tom grunted. "That's true. Unfortunately, as I might have mentioned, Jeremy Harding has a convenient and ironclad alibi for the morning in question."

But I wasn't satisfied. What if he'd paid someone to kill his wife? What if he and Jetta had conspired together to get Isabella out of the way? Maybe things were more serious between the two of them than anyone knew. It deserved some thought, anyway, in my opinion.

I looked up to find a smirk playing about the corners of Tom's mouth. There was no mistaking it for anything but the wiseass sarcasm it was. I slitted my eyes. "Are you laughing at me?"

"Maggie. Your enthusiasm and your belief in your friend are admirable, but you have to admit you don't know what you're doing, and you're bound to get yourself into trouble."

"Is it wrong to explore all options when you're faced with a crime of this magnitude?"

He reached out gently to touch my hand on the wheel. "No.

But you're forgetting the first rule of psychological crime solving: The most obvious solution is almost always the right one. You're not thinking clearly."

Fear for Felicity tackled the doubt that his words instilled in me. "Well, at least I'm *trying* to think things through rather than relying on rumors and prejudice."

He took his hand away. "You know, you are damned sexy when you're angry."

"And at least I don't play with the affections of innocent women to get what I want."

A red light loomed. Riding the crest of my own indignation, I stepped on the brake a little harder than I needed to. Christine's nose took a dive.

"Whoa there. Is that what you think I'm doing?" he demanded.

I didn't answer.

"Honey, if I wanted to play with a woman's affections, you can be damned sure I'd be taking a more direct route."

The next thing I knew, his hand had curled around the back of my neck and he'd leaned over me, into me, his mouth firm and insistent upon mine.

Stunned, under siege, I did the only thing I could do. I melted into the seat while he made a feast of my lips, his strong fingers following the curve of my head, his thumb moving restlessly at the corner of my mouth.

I won't say that I saw stars, but I did see sparkling flashes of light.

Or maybe that was the headlights of the car behind us, flashing from dim to bright.

The long squall of a car horn finally permeated the fog of red-hot sexual intrigue that had somehow made me forget how much I was determined to dislike him. I started guiltily, breaking the liplock that had distracted me from my original purpose.

With a shaky laugh, I gestured toward the green light ahead of us. "Guess we'd better go."

The rest of the drive back to the store passed uneventfully with Tom watching me out of the corner of his eye while I mentally kicked myself for letting him get under my skin. So what if he was good looking and a really exceptional kisser. He was also bound and determined to put my boss behind bars for no good reason that I could see or understand, and as such could only be viewed as a threat to the status quo of my life.

I found distraction from my mental dilemma in the vehicle that had been behind us at the stoplight. It had followed us nearly all the way to the store. A little too closely, in my opinion, especially considering that we were the only two cars on the road. Probably the driver had had too much to drink at one of the local bars and was using Christine as a homing beacon to help keep itself on the road. Lucky me. In my current state of mind, the person was taking his life into his own hands. Finally the car swerved wildly off onto Main Street, two blocks away, and I headed downhill to River Street. With a sigh of relief, I pulled into the alley behind the store, and shifted out of gear.

"Hey. I'm sorry if I offended you."

Offended me. Oh, yeah. I'd nearly forgotten. For the last ten minutes, it had been all I could do to keep my hormones in check. "No problem."

"You never did let me ask my questions."

I risked a glance at him. "What could you possibly ask that we didn't already cover?"

"Did Felicity describe what happened out at the Harding estate that morning?"

There was no reason to keep anything from him. The truth could only help Felicity by demonstrating that his suspicions about her were way off base. "Yes, she did. We had just opened the store when she received a phone call—a rather agitated one, as I remember—from someone whom she said was 'a friend.' I didn't know her well at the time, and she had no reason to explain herself to me. She telephoned Marcus Quinn—"

"Ah, yes, Quinn . . ."

"—who met her at the store, and then they left together. For what I later found out was the Harding place. I think Felicity had been given the idea that the disturbances Isabella had described were supernatural in origin, based on what Isabella said."

"And what did she tell her?"

I shrugged. "I wasn't listening in on the call. Felicity mentioned that Isabella said there had been *disturbances,* and she said she was frightened. Oh, and that the things she'd experienced had worsened over a period of six weeks."

I could tell he didn't believe it. Skepticism is one of those things that most people don't hide very well. "Uh-huh."

"Look, you don't have to believe in it," I said, just a touch snappishly. "You asked me a question and I answered it. Besides, doesn't it seem more likely, in light of what happened to her, that perhaps someone had been watching her for a while? Categorizing her every move? Maybe to Isabella, explaining the things she heard as supernatural was preferable to explaining it as a real, physical threat."

He had the decency to look contrite. "Okay. Sorry. Go on. What happened next?"

"As they arrived at the Harding place—the gate must have been open for them, I guess—Marcus saw what he thought was movement in the woods. He went off to check that out while Felicity hurried inside to Isabella. Except Isabella didn't answer the door. She said"—I frowned, trying to remember—"she said that Isabella had been working in the kitchen having breakfast. Her laptop had shut itself down, but there were remnants of her breakfast on the table."

"Tea," Tom said. "She was having tea." He paused a moment, and I could sense him wrestling with a worry. When he spoke again, his voice was pitched soft and low. "Do you want to know why I think Felicity had something to do with her sister's murder, Maggie? Do you?"

I hesitated. Nodded, frowning.

"Whoever killed Isabella had wanted to make very sure that she wouldn't be able to struggle. Whoever killed Isabella had known her everyday habits. The teabag she had left in the sink—all of the teabags in the tin—were each laced with a large dose of Rohypnol."

Rohypnol. The word floated on my consciousness, trying to find a home in my memory.

"Rohypnol is one of the so-called date-rape drugs. It works to relax a person's inhibitions so much that they lose the ability to think on their own, walk on their own, do much of anything on their own. It also makes them very suggestible and utterly incapable of fighting off an attacker."

Every little thing in place. No better description of first-degree murder than that.

"I figure that Isabella had her usual cup of tea, and the attacker was there, waiting and listening. Isabella must have felt the effects of the drug but not understood what was happening to her. Somehow she managed to get upstairs to lie down. That's when the killer made his—or her—play. He—or she—took Isabella to the top of the stairs and"—he brought his arm up suddenly and swung it down with a force that startled me—"whacked her over the head, hard, before letting her body fall down the stairs. Which are marble, by the way. The poor woman had enough fractures to keep the whole staff at the ER busy. Luckily enough, she didn't feel any of them. Half her head was bashed in."

"I was going to ask you earlier," I said quietly, "whether you thought Isabella could have accidentally fallen down the stairs, but the Rohypnol certainly puts a damper on the notion of accidental death, doesn't it."

"Yeah. Maggie, you really need to find another job."

I made a face at him. "Really, what *is* it with you and Felicity? Just because she calls herself a witch does not mean that she is a threat to society. This is the twenty-first century. No one has hanged or stoned a witch for a long time. *For good reason.* It just isn't nice. Remember? Live and let live?"

"The tea was a specialty blend imported from England, Maggie. Date stamped this year. Enchantments is the only store in Indiana that carries it. I checked."

"That doesn't mean Felicity is the one who laced it with the drug. Anybody with access to the house could do that."

"Whatever," he said curtly. Then he jerked his head toward the store. "So, what was going on up there tonight?"

I squirmed, a little uncomfortable with the truth. *We've done nothing wrong . . .* "Felicity held a meeting for her ghost hunter group. She'd wanted me to meet her friends."

"Her coven, you mean?"

"She doesn't work with a coven," I said automatically. "She's a solitary—she practices alone."

"Jesus, Maggie! Don't you hear yourself? You're talking about a working, practicing witch. How can you be so blasé about it? Oh, I know it's all very politically correct to accept the New Age-y things like aromatherapy and psychics, but doesn't the Bible speak out against those very kinds of things? For God's sake, the next thing you're going to tell me is that you're into that stuff, too."

"She's not like that. If you could get to know her, I'm sure you would come to feel the same way I do." My words were calm, designed to direct his animosity away from my employer and friend, but inwardly I was fuming. What if I was into *"those things"*? What business of his was it? And whatever happened to religious freedom, anyway? Division of Church and State? How about good, old-fashioned *love thy neighbor*?

He stared at me, mental distance giving him an aloofness that belied the heat of the kiss we'd shared earlier. "I thought I knew you, but maybe I was wrong. Maybe I don't know you at all."

I gave him a stony look of my own. "I guess you don't." And then, because it gave me a huge amount of satisfaction to be able to dismiss him, I reached across him for the door latch and pushed the passenger door open. "Good night, Tom."

He opened his mouth as though he were about to say something else, then snapped it closed and got out, stalking down the alley toward the front of the building.

Damned pigheaded male.

Damned pigheaded male.

The phrase had become a personal favorite after several hours spent tossing and turning in my bed. Even Graham Thomas had given me a baleful look after being knocked to the floor for the sixth or seventh time. No use explaining to him about damned pigheaded males. G.T. would listen, his little ears perked up sympathetically, but he just didn't get it.

Being male himself, albeit a stuffed and furry one, he no doubt thought I was being melodramatic.

As soon as the sun was up, I dragged my sleep-deprived body out of bed and guzzled down a mug of instant coffee. I was still too agitated to relax with the tape of Friday night's *Magnum* episode, so I whipped through a load of laundry, descummed the shower, emptied all the trash cans, and vacuumed the entire floor plan of my less-than-substantial apartment. Ghostly voices? Ha. I was in no mood, and I'll bet my bodily challenged houseguest could tell. By the time I was finished, it was nearly nine o'clock. Not nearly as late as I'd hoped.

I sat down in my comfy green chair a moment, hoping to relax, but my mind refused to be quiet. I couldn't help replaying the information I'd learned so far. Unfortunately it was only that: information, and all circumstantial. None of it could help Felicity.

Sighing, I reached over and punched the Play button on my answering machine. Steff's voice filled my living room in a message dated late last night:

"Hey, Mags. I have to work tomorrow morning, so I thought I'd better leave this on voice. You'll never in a *million years* guess who Danny and I saw at the gardens tonight . . ."

The sunken gardens were the remains of a onetime gravel pit that, years ago, someone had decided to turn into a park and recreation area. At the floor of the manmade crater, a wild tangle of local flora and fauna wove between and around a number of bottomless lakes, the whole of it bordered by walls of limestone that rose like sheer cliffs from the foundation. Year after year, Stony Mill's teenagers used the gardens to answer the call of their hormones. Steff and Dr. Danny were a bit old for the usual crowd, but hey, whatever rocks your world.

"Ryan Davidson, for one," Steff went on. "But guess who was with him. The husband's girlfriend, that's who! I kid you not. They left before we did, but"—her voice took on a sheepish tone—"I didn't notice the time. Danny's a really good kisser. Anyway, I thought it was interesting. Don't know what it means, but you might want to check it out. Talk to you soon, sweets. B'bye."

The answering machine announced the end of the messages while I sat there, stunned. Ryan Davidson and Jetta James? What in the world was going on?

All keyed up and needing an outlet, I grabbed my car keys and headed for the door.

Outside the sun shone brilliantly in a sapphire sky. October had always been my favorite time of year, a time of bright orange pumpkins sporting jocular faces, crisp golden leaves, and spicy multitudes of chrysanthemums spilling out of fences. I'd been so caught up with Isabella's death and the ensuing chaos, I'd forgotten to take a moment to notice the beauty around me. Well, today I was going to make time if it killed me.

Christine beckoned from the curb. I jumped into my seat, revved her puttering engine, then took off with a soul-deep laugh and an appreciation for the moment.

The excitement was short-lived. As I drove past the courthouse and police station, who should be walking out the door? Uh-huh. Tom. He was wearing the same clothes and a full day's growth of beard that made me think he'd not gone to bed at all, yet instead of looking disreputable he somehow managed to look disgustingly, well, gorgeous.

He caught sight of me as I sailed past. I didn't wave. He didn't either.

Damned pigheaded male.

Well, who needed him? I had the whole day ahead of me. I could do whatever I wanted, with whomever I wanted. Footloose and fancy-free, that was me.

Trouble was, I still didn't know what I wanted to do.

Despite my determination to spend the day indulging my every whim, I couldn't help thinking about everything Tom had said about Felicity, which got me fuming anew. It was obvious that he wasn't interested in looking past his own prejudices . . . and they were many.

I picked up an ice-cold orange juice at Judy's Stop 'N Shop for a quick blast of carbs, then continued my tour of town.

Stony Mill was for the most part your typical Midwestern small town. That meant tree-lined streets, residential areas dating back to the mid-1800s, and the prerequisite modern-bland business strip where Stony Mill shoppers could buy groceries and run the bulk of their errands without leaving the same enormous (and psychotic) parking lot. Downtown renovations, on the other hand, had capitalized on the antiques craze and the river, bringing the two together in the old warehouses bordering its banks. I turned down River Street, but since it was Sunday, I wasn't expecting much. People were still conservative enough here that all the stores in town remained closed on Sundays. I drove slowly past Enchantments, but as expected, it was devoid of life. I'd hoped to find Felicity there, thinking she might know something about Ryan and Jetta that I didn't, but even she seemed to be honoring the Sabbath. So to speak. I guess even Felicity knew better than to break that rule.

So I headed out of town. The seed crops in the fields were drying now as autumn settled in for the count—miles of corn and soybeans, all golden-brown and wispy. As I meandered through the countryside, I saw more than one combine lumbering along in the fields, processing the grains in orderly spiral patterns that were as beautiful as the crops themselves. I rolled down my window and let the sun-warmed breeze stream in around me, enjoying the moment. Most of the trees were just starting to lose their leaves, and some of the vivid colors were fading to dusty shades of brown. Someone had set up a hay maze in one of their fields. Good, old-fashioned, disorienting fun. I hadn't been to one in years and made a mental note to try to get out this year. Maybe Steff could tear herself away from her dates for an afternoon.

Slowly, lazily, I wound my way through the rolling farmland and let the sights and sounds of the earth restore me.

Before I knew it, I found myself on Victoria Park Road, heading toward the scene of the crime from the opposite direction I'd come before. All around me, I saw more of the same fields, gentle hills, new-style farming operations, and the occasional old red barn. Only as I approached the Harding homestead were the farmers' fields exchanged for a mixture of woods and grassy meadow. I slowed as I passed, but there was no movement inside.

I wondered, not for the first time, about the security gate. It had to have been open when Felicity arrived, or how could Felicity have driven up to the house? Could Isabella have opened the gate as soon as she phoned Felicity, knowing her sister would be on the way? It was possible. But was it probable? Would she have had the presence of mind to do it? More importantly, would she have done that if she were afraid?

Reaching back to my experience at the cemetery, I decided to purposely try to put myself in Isabella's shoes. It wouldn't be easy since the only information I possessed had been filtered through Felicity, but if I truly had the kind of gifts Felicity seemed to think I did, then it stood to reason that I should be able to access them.

Closing my eyes, I walked myself through what I knew. She was home. Presumably alone. She's been hearing strange sounds for weeks. Threatening sounds. Sounds that made her uneasy. Anxious. Scared. That morning, she phones . . . Felicity, *the sister from whom she's been estranged for more than a year.* Why? Is it truly because she believes the problem to be supernatural in origin? According to Felicity, Isabella professed not to believe in such nonsense. I couldn't see why that should suddenly change. Even in the face of outright proof, I'd bet my beloved Christine that Isabella was the type of woman who would thrive in a state of denial. No, Isabella would have called Felicity, her *sister,* because she knew, in spite of everything, that blood is thicker than water. Because she knew she could trust her with her life.

Because she was afraid of someone close to her?

It had to be Jeremy. It made sense. Why else would Isabella have rejected her husband, her partner in life, for the sister she hadn't spoken to for at least a year? I didn't care that he had an alibi for the morning in question. There had to be an explanation.

All right, so back to Isabella. She sits at the kitchen table. Tea and cookies and her laptop. She has wealth. A beautiful home. Her choice of lovers. Life is good, except for the sense that she is not alone. Maybe she'd begun to suspect Jeremy of being a danger to her. Maybe she thought he knew about Ryan. What was that? Is someone in her house?

But wait. Why should she panic if Jeremy came home unexpectedly? He might have forgotten something. He might have spilled coffee on his tie. I couldn't see her panicking enough to call Felicity just because he'd returned home that morning.

I continued slowly down the road, bypassing Felicity's drive with its curlicued gate. I let Christine slow to a crawl while my thoughts spun in a whirlwind of suspicion. *Rohypnol* . . . How did the Rohypnol figure into all of this?

Tea and cookies at the laptop.

Rohypnol in the tea.

What if . . . what if Jeremy had never really left that morning? What if he'd laced the tea in advance, knowing Isabella would have her usual morning cuppa? He might have pretended to leave, only to somehow circle back. To wait while she sipped her tea, hovering like a vulture, passing the time until she had ingested enough to incapacitate her. Just enough to make her pliable. Unconcerned for her own safety. Suggestible.

Had he convinced her then to phone Felicity? She wouldn't have known what she was doing. Maybe he'd turned it into a joke. *Let's play a prank on Felicity, won't that be fun?* Maybe he'd fed the words into her ear as she phoned.

I rejected the idea almost as soon as it occurred to me. Too risky. But what if it wasn't Isabella at all? Felicity mentioned Isabella had sounded strange that morning. A female accomplice?

Could Jetta have played a part in all this?

I didn't see why not. It struck me that I had no idea of Jetta's whereabouts that morning. And after last night I couldn't exactly pursue the issue with Tom. Something to think about.

All right then. That left only the why. Why call Felicity at all?

I could think of a few reasons Jeremy might have called Felicity to the scene of the crime. To witness his handiwork. To pinpoint the time of death thereby guaranteeing his alibi. To cast suspicion on Felicity, the sister Isabella had wronged. His dislike for her had been unmistakable. The truth? Probably a combination of all three.

The more the thoughts played through my mind, the more they made sense. Jeremy could have opened the gate from within using Isabella's code just before he made his escape through the woods separating the two properties. The Rohypnol? Drugging Isabella ensured a pliable victim. No struggle, no embarrassing scratches or cuts to explain away. One vicious blow to the head and Isabella's world blinked out in a flash of darkness and pain.

I shuddered and gripped the wheel harder. Only after I opened my eyes did I realize I'd somehow closed them, probably around the same time I'd nosed Christine to a halt in the middle of the narrow country road. I blinked, queasily, as my own world settled slowly into place around me. Maybe there *was* something to this empathy theory of Felicity's. I felt—sensed—that I'd gotten close to what had actually happened this time. The focus I'd experienced had made certain sensations seem to be my own. Dizziness. Euphoria. She'd known something was wrong, out of place, but couldn't seem to help herself. The Rohypnol, I suppose. Confusion. A swooping sensation. Crushing pain. Then . . .

Nothing.

She didn't see it coming.

I couldn't quite allow myself to believe it. *Empath* seemed to be just another word for someone with an overactive imagination. And mine had been playing tricks on me for days.

But the theory . . . the theory was sound.

I shivered again and took a good look around to orient myself. I'd stopped just short of the railroad tracks, thank goodness. They stretched in both directions as far as the eye could see, a swath of order cut into the unruliness of woodlands and overgrown fields. To my left, the flattened grasses of a makeshift lane hugged the raised bed of the tracks, leading to the woods farther back. The same woods that skirted Felicity's property.

Furtively I checked the rearview for witnesses, but no one else seemed to be traveling the road with me. Before I could lose my nerve, I shifted Christine into gear and bounced onto the rutted path, offering up a fervent prayer that I wouldn't find anyone already utilizing the, uh, private space.

As it turns out, luck was with me.

Greatly relieved to find myself alone in a small, shady clearing, I switched the engine off and sat quietly in my seat, ears perked. The sounds of the woods surrounded me—the dry rustling of leaves stirring overhead, the drone of a bee as it buzzed around Christine's warm hood, searching for the last vestiges of food in preparation for winter, the lazy hum of an occasional black fly, grown fat and sluggish with the cooler weather. The breeze brought a wisp of sound from somewhere near, a tractor perhaps. My ears latched on to it gratefully as I ducked down to peer out at the swaying treetops above me. It was so reassuringly . . . normal. And yet, I found myself hesitating to leave the tiny sanctuary Christine provided.

The hand that clapped down on my shoulder nearly sent me through the roof.

"Looking for something?"

You know how, when you're watching a horror flick and the unsuspecting and of course scantily clad heroine walks toward the closed closet door, and you *know* that the killer is hiding there, just inside, a mask over his face and a butcher knife at the ready? And then she opens the closet door, and to your surprise no one jumps out at her. You heave a sigh of relief, letting go of the tension that had gripped you, and just as you do, just as your anxiety drains down through your toes and you're actually starting to relax, the killer grabs the poor girl and slits her open from stem to stern and you're left drowning in a state of shock and horror and amazement that you didn't see it coming. Now, picture me as the girl. Got it? Except in the role of the killer this evening, we have Marcus Quinn, ladies and gents. Face of an angel, body of a devil. Or should that be face of a devil, body of an angel? Oh well. You get the picture.

Once I'd stopped gibbering in abject terror, I was sporting for blood. "Jesus, Joseph, and Mary, what do you think you're doing, scaring the bejeebers out of me like that? Criminey! You don't sneak up behind a woman like that!"

"Sorry," he said, but his broad grin told me he didn't mean it. "Couldn't resist."

That I could believe. I crossed my arms, not ready to forgive him yet. "What are you doing out here?"

"I might ask you the same thing."

"I asked you first."

His lips curved. "So you did." He looked up at the trees, and I used the few seconds his eyes were averted to get a good look at him. Today he'd exchanged his black T-shirt for one that made his eyes as blue as the Hope diamond, but other than that and the leather thong that held his hair tied back at the nape, the look was pretty much the same. "It never fails to amaze me how quiet it can be out here."

"You've been here before."

The grin again. "Well, you know, this place was in use long before Felicity bought the property. It has a memory you can't miss."

I frowned. "What do you mean?"

"Why don't you get out of your car and find out for yourself?"

Well, I didn't usually rise to a dare, but . . .

Self-conscious, I reached for the door latch, trying very hard for aloofness. Marcus held the door for me like the gentleman he wasn't.

Once I stood upon terra firma, it took me a few minutes of soul-searching, but I think I knew what he was talking about. The place was secluded. Quiet, but with an undertone of movement. It had an all-over feeling of . . . intimacy. I drew a breath, looking up at the undulating motions of the treetops. I couldn't help wondering how many seduction scenes had played out here, surrounded by the dark witness of the trees, driven on by the urgent rocking of the passing trains.

Marcus placed a light hand on my shoulder and a flash of heat shot through me. "You feel it?"

My lips parted. *Easy, girl.* Embarrassed by my reaction—to the place, not the man, I reminded myself—I could only nod.

"These woods have always seemed a little magical. I used to come out here when I was a kid, back when Old Man Beverley used to own them. Lay a blanket out on the grass and stare up at the stars. Well, among other things," he added with a gleam in his eye when I'd shot him a skeptical look.

"Did you." I was determined to ignore that little ping of curiosity that made me wonder what lying next to him on a blanket might be like. For one thing, he was Felicity's man, not mine. For another, I was a little freaked out by being attracted to two men at the same time. Maybe it was my conservative Catholic roots, but I had always been a one-man woman. Anything else would have made me nervous. What was wrong with me?

"Yeah. The place hasn't lost its touch, either, from what I hear."

"Jeremy Harding and Jetta James?" I supplied.

"Among others. But, yeah."

"I've been thinking about that. Marcus, how far do these woods go? Toward the Harding property, I mean."

"All the way, baby. All the way," he said with a grin. "They're shaped a little like a crescent here, curving back behind Felicity's property and up in between. They actually continue on behind the Harding house, but more sparsely."

I thought for a moment, biting the inside of my lip the way I always did when I couldn't decide whether or not to share what was on my mind. "I've been thinking," I finally confessed, "about the morning Isabella died. About what you saw in the trees."

"And you thought that maybe it was her killer escaping into the woods."

I nodded, thankful for his quick intuition. Less explaining that way. "Whoever it was might have had a car parked back here, ready for him to make his escape while Felicity discovered the body."

"This area was crawling with cops within minutes."

"Not quite. Not until after Felicity had discovered Isabella's body and had gone to find you."

He seemed to be at least considering it. "You say him. I suppose you mean Jeremy."

"It makes sense. His affair with Jetta might have provoked

t. Or it could have been any number of things between him nd Isabella in their marriage that we know nothing about."

"I've been asking around. Hey, you're not the only one oncerned about Felicity. Harding was in a business meeting hat morning, and he has a number of witnesses to that effect."

"Including Jetta James, I suppose," I said, disappointed.

"Actually, no. Ms. James had taken a vacation day."

He purposely avoided my suddenly raised eyebrows. Was it ossible? Could it have been Jetta who struck the killing blow?

"You know," I said, "if Jetta is the person we're both look-ng for, that doesn't automatically absolve Jeremy of guilt."

"No, I don't suppose it does."

At least we agreed on that point. I was beginning to look at Marcus in a new light.

"The daughter, Jacqui? She was out of town on a business meeting that day. Left the day before and didn't return until he day after."

"Hmm, yes, I know. Too bad, too. Have you ever had the pleasure?"

He grunted. "I've seen her around."

"Yes, well, if it was from a distance, you didn't get the full ffect, trust me. The woman is unbelievable. She's one person wouldn't have minded seeing sent away for good. Totally ude, and apparently she didn't have a terrific relationship vith her mother, either. Anything else?"

He toed the roots of a huge oak with his sturdy black boot, sing his hand to steady himself. "That there was no love lost etween Isabella and one Reverend Martin, formerly of the irst Church of God."

"Reverend Baxter Martin," I confirmed with a nod. The ir was a little cooler than I'd expected in the shade. I vrapped my jacket tighter around my body and held it closed vith my crossed arms. "Did you know Isabella had a re-training order taken out against him? For harassing her, al-nost to the point of stalking, from what it sounds like. Ryan Davidson said he was always coming around to the hospital vith petitions and seemed to have a personal vendetta against sabella in particular."

"That might have something to do with the fact that she had him removed from his ministry a few years back."

I gaped at him. "Seriously?"

"You must not remember. There was a big uproar over it. It even made the paper."

"I, uh, try not to read the paper very often," I confessed. But that did explain the letter to the editor the good reverend had written that Marian Tabor had sent over from her review of the *Stony Mill Gazette*.

"And miss all of the reports of corruption and scandal? Tsk, tsk. You have to keep on top of things in this town."

I sure hoped Marian would be able to find that article. "Why did she have him removed?"

"Unwanted sexual advances. She said he made a pass at her. Who knows if it was true? According to the paper, the Hardings attended the church in question. I think Jeremy Harding was even a deacon of the church, if I remember correctly. People are always making plays for power in this world. Power and control. Maybe this was one of them."

"I wouldn't think a simple pass would have upset her. From what I've heard, she was fairly . . . worldly."

"You mean Isabella and Jeremy Harding were pretty well matched?" he asked with a grim smile.

"The perfect pair. Jeremy has Jetta, Isabella had Ryan Davidson. I somehow doubt they were first affairs."

"Yes, but from what I've heard, Isabella liked 'em younger. The question is, was Reverend Martin far gone enough to murder her?"

"He came to her funeral, did I mention that? At least I think it was him. Hiding behind some trees along the fringes. My friend and I both saw him. But to answer your question, I can't see it. However unstable he's become, he's still a man of God. Call me naïve, but I just can't see him killing her. Happy to have her gone, sure. And maybe he is the kind of man who is capable of killing. I don't know him personally. But I just can't help thinking that Isabella was killed by someone who knew her daily schedule. The timing proves that."

"Wouldn't hurt to check up on him. What about this Davidson guy? What do you know about him?"

"He's legal counsel for the hospital. Isabella was on the board of directors. I don't know how serious it was. He's very toothy. He's also running for Congress. I doubt Jeremy will be as generous with his funding as Isabella presumably was. I can't picture him killing her, either. Isabella was his meal ticket. Why would he have jeopardized that?" I paused deliberately, wondering if I had a right to say anything about last night, then decided, to hell with it. It would soon be out all over town anyway. "Besides, he appears to have made a few enemies of his own along the way. Last night he was the victim of a drive-by shooting. And that would have been *after* he and Jetta were seen together at the gardens."

His brows shot up. "Where'd you hear that?"

"Friend of mine was there. As for the shooting, I was with Tom Fielding when the call came in."

"And?" His eyes, icicle sharp, bore into mine.

"And I was allowed to be there while Tom questioned Davidson. Someone took a potshot at him through his living room window just after midnight, then squealed off into the night. He claims not to have seen the person who did it, or much of anything else either, since he dropped to the floor the moment the bullet went through his window."

"How inconsiderate of him."

"But prudent." I sighed again.

"Any speculation from your cop connection?"

"None yet," I said as vaguely as possible. I was *not* going to share anything about my pathetically nonexistent love life with this gorgeous man. My loyalty to Felicity did not reach that far.

"Too bad." If he suspected I wasn't telling him everything, he was well mannered enough to let it go. "I wonder what the connection is between Davidson and Jetta. I guess we're at a dead end, until we can find out more."

"Not quite." I'd already shared information about Ryan Davidson. Might as well go for broke. "The forensic tests showed that Isabella had ingested a large amount of a drug called Rohypnol shortly before her death."

He frowned. "The date-rape drug?"

"The very same. Evidently they found it mixed into the tea

in her teabags. Not just the one she'd used that morning, but all the rest in the tin to boot."

"Let me guess. A special blend available only from Enchantments?"

"How did you know that?" I said, amazed.

"Call it instinct. I suppose that's yet another nail in Felicity's coffin."

"What are we going to do, Marcus? Someone is making damned sure that Felicity is suspected in Isabella's death."

Marcus's mouth tightened. Without a word he stomped back and forth around the clearing, his emotion rising visibly with each step. Suddenly he stopped at a tree and drew his foot back as if to kick it. Then he changed his mind at the last second, stood with his feet planted at shoulder width apart, his hands pressed flat against the sturdy trunk, closed his eyes, and let his chin fall forward to his chest with an unintelligible uttering. To my astonishment, I saw the frustration, the anger, leave his body.

"What happened?" I asked when it was safe to speak.

His eyes flickered open. "Sorry," he said, his voice gruff. "I had to rid myself of that."

"Of what?"

"Excess energy. Negative energy. It was building to a dangerous level, so I grounded it. Sent it back to Mother Earth," he explained when I opened my mouth with the question.

"Sounds like a good trick."

"No trick. It's Craft training, and very effective."

Something clicked in my memory. "I had almost forgotten. You're a witch, too."

The grin he flashed was pure, unadulterated male mischief and damned attractive. "Are you afraid of me?"

"Should I be?"

"Well, you know. Demon worship. Black magic. Sacrificing virgins on the altar of my lust."

"You're joking," I said, hoping I was right.

"Yeah. Well, maybe not about the virgins." He waggled his eyebrows. And then he took pity on me. "You don't know much about the Craft, do you?"

"I'm reading up so that I can understand better, but—no

Not a whole lot. I understand enough to know that the old representations of witches aren't true. Witches are like people—some good, some not so good."

"That's good enough for starters. Hey, I'd like to show you something. Unless you really are afraid." He tipped his head to one side, assessing me.

I was, but not of his being a witch. Somehow I found his masculinity more threatening to my peace of mind. *Remember Liss* . . . I lifted my chin and leveled him a confident stare. "Lead on."

The woods were dark, cool. A thick carpeting of leaf humus muffled the sounds of our passing. Above us the treetops swayed and danced, filling the air with sylph-like movement. The afternoon sun barely reached us. I shivered. Wordlessly Marcus took my hand and pulled me along after him, gentle and yet relentless at once. The underbrush thickened around us, humus giving way to waist-high fern fronds that parted like the Dead Sea for Marcus as he led the way.

Without warning, we broke into a wide, circular clearing of soft, soft grass. Marcus let go of my hand and stopped just ahead of me. "Welcome to the glade," he said, spreading his arms wide and turning joyous circles in the stream of sunlight that spilled in from above.

I stepped into the clearing after only a moment's pause. Like the place we'd just left, this place contained a memory that was almost physical, palpable in the very air around us. This one, however, had nothing to do with sex. The farther I traveled within the circle, the stronger the impression became. A tingle of electricity. Energy.

Spirit.

"This is—"

"Where Felicity practices," I finished for him, my head filled with the sensation. I was new to the realization of what I was feeling, but once felt, I could never mistake it. "I know."

He just looked at me, his expression unreadable. "Sorry to underestimate you. It appears your abilities are growing." He nodded to himself. "Good."

"It's amazing. I've never felt anything like it." I held out my hand. Sunlight threaded in and around my fingers, glowing like a ball of backlit crystal. The sensation was heady, and—dare I say it?—magical.

"I brought you here so that you could understand a little better. Intellectually you knew that being a witch does not equate to being evil. I wanted you to feel it."

I nodded, still overcome with the fullness of emotion. "Thank you."

I was silent as he led the way back to my car, my head filled with the experience and everything we'd talked about. I was glad that I'd run into Marcus today. I'd felt so . . . so isolated until then. Like I was the only one who could see that the threat to Felicity was very real. I now knew without a doubt that I had an ally in Marcus, that I could trust him with anything when it came to Felicity. I knew we were both working for the same end.

But would it be enough?

Chapter 15

I was having that feeling again—that sickening, spiraling feeling that always came at times when I knew that control was just out of my reach, that no matter what I did or said, I had no more influence over the course of the future than your average, everyday palm reader.

Things were coming to a head. I could feel it.

The impression stayed with me as I drove in to work Monday morning. Felicity wasn't in yet, so I opened up on my own and set a pot of coffee on to brew. Friday I had decided to start boxing up some old files that were just taking up space and had discovered the filing system left a lot to be desired. So, after pouring myself a gigantic cup of coffee, I settled in for the long haul, keeping one ear open for the bell. The work wasn't exactly exhilarating, but it desperately needed to be done. Felicity was one hell of a businesswoman, but her filing methods were . . . well, creative. Everything was just kind of thrown into a number of very large expandable files. One per month. Or so. And they went back years! Before I'd flipped through a tenth of the first file, I realized I was going to have to completely resort them all. Taking a deep breath, I organized the office floor with a number of small boxes, all labeled for sorting purposes. Once I'd broken things down into these broader

categories, I could go further and break each pile down by
month and year.

For once, my accounting experience was going to come in
handy. If there was one thing I had down pat, it was filing.

The growing stack of bills of sale had given me a true eu-
reka moment. *The Enchantments tea.* If it truly was from the
store, then it stood to reason that *someone* had bought it. The
receipts contained itemized information about what was pur-
chased, the date of purchase, and the buyer's name and address
or credit card impression. My enthusiasm renewed, I began to
sort at a furious pace.

It was nearly nine-thirty before I realized that (A) it was
nine-thirty, and (B) Felicity had never arrived at the store.

I abandoned my piles and got to my feet. That bad feeling
was back, a cross between fear, panic, and the stomach-
wrenching antics of the flu. It settled at the pit of my stomach
like some slavering beast, waiting for me to show even the
smallest sign of losing it. I swallowed bravely, determined to
show the beast No Fear. Grabbing the phone, I dialed Felicity's home number.

The phone rang in my ear, jangling my nerves with each
electronic jingle. I counted to twelve before the canned opera-
tor came on the line, telling me my party was not answering.

Like I hadn't noticed.

Okay, so Felicity wasn't home. Maybe she was on the way.
Digging in my purse for her cell phone number, I dialed it
with shaking fingers.

Different number, same scenario, except this time her
cell's voice mail picked up my call. Did I want to leave a message? I did.

That done, I went up to the front of the store to peer out at
the street through the windows. No sign of Felicity anywhere.

I started to pace. What could have happened to her? An accident on the way in? An unexpected emergency? I felt so in-
adequate. I couldn't think of a single thing to do to find her
other than what I'd already done. It was too soon to phone the
hospital emergency room. And if they hadn't seen her and had
no admissions of a Jane Doe, what then?

I was quickly losing ground to that prowling beast when Marcus screeched his motorcycle to a halt in front of the store, thrust down the kickstand, then hit the door running.

"What?" I asked when he burst through the door, wondering if it was all right to lose it now that I had backup. "Where is she?"

Marcus took both of my hands in his. "Liss has been arrested."

"Arrested . . . ?" There are certain moments in one's lifetime, moments of such power and clarity that they somehow become lodged permanently in the fabric of your mind. I knew, even before the moment had passed, that I would remember this moment for the rest of my life. "How . . . ? When?"

He touched my lips with his finger, shushing me. "This morning. Bright and early. *Don't panic.* It won't do Felicity, nor you, any good."

I nodded. Deep cleansing breaths. In through your nose, out through your mouth. Again. And again. When I was calmer, I asked, "What happened?"

"Cops came for her as she was leaving the house. She phoned me and asked me to let you know."

I frowned, trying to take it in. I had a sneaking suspicion . . .

"Before you ask, yes. Fielding was one of them."

After our pseudo-date, after the connection I'd experienced with Tom, I felt the sting of his betrayal even more sharply. "So they charged her with Isabella's murder?"

"Yeah." He paused, then added, "And the attack on Ryan Davidson."

"*What?*" I blinked as a red haze overtook my vision. I pulled my hands away from him and stalked back to the office. "I can't believe it. I can't believe he would do that. How can you charge someone without evidence?"

He followed me, hot on my heels. "I guess they think they have evidence." He gave a pause that was almost delicate while I flung open the closet door and pawed for my jacket. "Felicity said they believe the bullet came from one of her husband's old guns. Now, guns are not my thing so I don't en-

tirely understand the specifics, but evidently Fielding and another cop served her with a search warrant yesterday morning,
confiscated a few things—her husband's collection of various
style guns, for one—then left. They must have pushed through
whatever testing they had to do, because they were waiting on
her doorstep this morning."

I'll bet. I remembered the determined look on Tom's face
when I'd passed by him yesterday morning in front of the cop
shop. He'd seen me as sure as I'd seen him, but he wouldn't
look my way. Was that before or after he'd served Felicity
with the warrant? I didn't even know Felicity's husband had
kept guns, much less been a collector, so the news had caught
me off guard. Damn it, why didn't she call me? I could have
contacted an attorney for her. "I'm worried, Marcus. Someone
is trying to set her up. It's the only explanation for everything
that's happened."

"Agreed. So we're back to square one. Who had the motive and the opportunity? Not Reverend Martin, as it turns
out. I found out last night that the good reverend has been
volunteering at Blackridge School, giving spiritual guid-
ance to the boys being held there as wards of the state. He
was there the morning that Isabella passed. No question
about it."

I sighed wearily. "Another prospective murderer bites the
dust. Where does that leave us?

"We know it has to be someone who knows her well.
Someone who has access to her house."

"And once again the finger points toward Jeremy Harding,"
I said firmly. "Their properties are connected. No doubt Jeremy has been inside The Gables countless times. He would
know Gerald Dow was a gun collector."

"We don't know what he was doing last night, do we?"

"No, but we know what Felicity was doing. She was here,
with the rest of the N.I.G.H.T.S."

He shook his head reluctantly. "The meeting broke up
shortly after you left with Fielding."

"Liss didn't go with you?" I asked, giving up any pretense
of discretion.

He opened his mouth to answer then paused, looking at me strangely. "No. No, she didn't."

Of all the times to go home to her own bed. "Well, that doesn't change anything."

"Not for us. For your boyfriend Fielding, that means she had time to take a potshot at Lawyer Boy."

"He's not my boyfriend," I said irritably. "And Liss was still here when we decided to get some coffee."

"Small town. You know as well as I do that it only takes about seven minutes to drive across Stony Mill the long way. Ten minutes at rush hour."

I was silent a moment, knowing he was right, but oh, I wanted to deny it. Except denying the truth was no way to help Liss. Right now we needed straight heads and clear thinking.

"Do you think Isabella had a key to Liss's house?" I asked him. "Because if she did, that means that Jeremy would have had access to it as well. Access to the house, access to the guns, and any number of things he could have used to implicate Liss."

He nodded slowly, the gears turning. "That seems a safe assumption. But then, anyone who really knows Liss knows that she doesn't bother to lock up her house. She uses wards to protect herself. Wards and the security gate."

And we both knew that the security gate would stop only the most superficial of house pests. Anyone with half a brain could find their way around it, even if it meant traipsing the long way through the woods. We'd proven that ourselves.

Damn it, Liss! I railed to the universe at large. I'd learned enough superficial witchy information in the past week to know that white sage and protection charms might work against your basic psychic interloper, but a locked door works a hell of a lot better to dissuade bad guys.

I began to pace. Not an easy thing to do with all my sorting piles. "This is ridiculous. I still say Jeremy is our best bet. The only one that makes any sense. Who else would have reason to shoot out Davidson's windows, on the heels of a secret rendezvous with Jetta?"

I couldn't take it anymore. I grabbed my jacket from the closet and threw it on.

"Whoa," Marcus said, catching my arm. "Where are you going?"

"To the cop shop. I have to see Liss. I might just have to kick Tom Fielding's sorry ass. And when I'm done with that, have a thing or two to say to Jeremy Harding. Wanta come with?"

His mouth twitched. "You're awful cute when you're pissed."

"You ain't seen nothing yet."

"What do you mean, I can't see her?"

The blond dispatcher-cum-officer-cum-receptionist stared at me. "I'm sorry, ma'am, but the prisoner isn't allowed to have visitors at present. She's entitled to legal counsel, of course—you aren't her attorney, I don't think?" She paused a moment, then pushed on before I even had a chance to shake my head. "But until the judge can arraign her, she really isn't supposed to have visitors, family or otherwise."

"And-when-will-that-be?" I gritted out carefully, the soul of politeness.

The girl's eyes twitched from my rigid face to Marcus over my left shoulder. "Well, not today, anyway. Judge Hardcastle's out of town and won't be back until tomorrow afternoon. Depending on his schedule, it could be late tomorrow, or possibly Wednesday, I guess. If you'd like to be present at the arraignment, ma'am, I'm sure you could call his office tomorrow and ask. Winnie—that's his secretary—she's real helpful."

"I'll bet." I let my fingernails rat-a-tat against the counter. "Well, if I can't see Mrs. Dow, perhaps you'd let me speak with Deputy Fielding. Surely *he* is allowed visitors?"

She blinked at me. "Well, of course he is."

"Then you'll call him for me?" I asked, sweet as pie, already anticipating the verbal tongue-lashing Tom Fielding so richly deserved.

"Sorry, can't do that, ma'am."

Now it was my turn to blink.

"He's out on a call, ma'am." My face must have fallen, because she added, "You're welcome to wait in the lobby, but it might take a while."

Drat and double drat. And I'd be willing to bet it might take all day if he pulled up to the police department and saw Christine parked out front.

My every attempt frustrated, I turned to Marcus. "Well?"

He shrugged. "You're the boss."

I turned back, just in time to catch the blonde giving Marcus the eye. "Thanks anyway," I said, past caring that I didn't sound the least bit grateful, "but we'll come back another time."

"Any time, ma'am."

If she called me "ma'am" one . . . more . . . time . . .

Outside, I stomped back to Christine.

"Where to now, Jeeves?"

"We can't see Felicity. Fielding's avoiding me, the coward." I jammed my key into the door lock. "Well, we have to do something. I'm going to see Harding."

"Do you think that's wise?"

I yanked open the door. "Either you go with me or you don't. But I'm going to Harding Enterprises. I have a few questions for Mr. Jeremy Harding. Now what'll it be?"

He shrugged his shoulders. "With you, of course."

We arrived at Harding Enterprises (early 1970s, glass and brick façade) just in time to witness the mass exodus of the lunch lizards. I'd seen this scene before, in my other life as an office slave. It wasn't pretty. Two hundred people make like lemmings toward the nearest fast-food establishment so they can gulp down their lunch in the prescribed thirty minutes and hurry back to their dead-end jobs with clogged arteries and roiling indigestion working together, along with monumental stress levels, to shorten their miserable lives. I knew it was pointless to try to buck the crowd, so I waited, blinker on, until it was safe to turn into the parking lot.

Marcus followed me, not saying a word. Obviously he knew a hot-headed female when he saw one.

The reception area was deserted, but I didn't let that stop me. I walked quickly up and down the aisles, past glass cases filled with undetermined metal objects, beyond something that was either a display rack or a twisted piece of modern art, peeking into darkened offices. The lower level contained no signs of life, so, determination intact, I continued up the stairs (utilitarian with nubby low-pile carpeting) to the offices above. This floor was different from those closet-sized offices below. The, stylishly decorated reception area opened onto a pair of offices.

Something cautioned me to quiet my steps as I stepped from the utilitarian carpet to top-of-the-line plush.

We heard voices as soon as we approached the nearest door, which stood slightly ajar.

"It must be an error, Jetta. I can't explain it any more clearly than that." The brisk voice belonged unmistakably to Jacquilyn Harding.

"Excuse me for saying so, Ms. Harding, but I thought the same thing. So I called the rental company, and they checked their records. They swear that the mileage is what you signed for."

"Then I made a mistake as well. I was tired. It happens. Now can we drop this? I'm really very busy. The last thing I have time for is stupid little details like this one."

"But if it's wrong, then I hate to just let it go. Unless I'm mistaken, the car was to be driven in Chicago. There's no way you could have gone over the allowed miles. The bill was several hundred dollars more than it should have been. We shouldn't be required to pay—"

"I said, drop it," Jacquilyn snapped, her voice sharp enough to cut glass. "It's not important enough for me to waste my time worrying about it. Why don't you go out and get some lunch, hmm? And bring some back for me while you're at it."

Marcus pulled me away from the door and through the doorway on the opposite side of the room. A quick glance around showed a darkly paneled office—real wood paneling, not the pressboard variety made so popular by the Bradys. The nameplate on the desk announced JETTA JAMES. I exchanged urgent glances with Marcus. Before we had a chance to make a hasty exit, Jetta stalked into the room.

Resplendent in a clingy green tube dress whose neckline plumbed depths not generally examined in business surroundings and strappy black sandals that made her nearly six feet tall, she gave us one irritated glance and held up a finger when I opened my mouth to speak.

"Jeremy," she called through the closed door on the rear wall of her office, "you have visitors. I'm on my way out to find lunch for Her Highness."

"Thanks, Jet," a muffled male voice called. "Hey, if you're going out, would you mind bringing something back for me?"

She started muttering under her breath, yanked her purse up by the strap, and stalked out of her office without a backward glance. When Marcus's gaze tarried overlong on the exaggerated sway of her hips, I gave him a good healthy nudge with my elbow.

The door swung inward. "Can I help—?" Jeremy Harding caught sight of us in the next moment, and confusion furrowed his brow. Annoyance replaced it a moment later. "Oh, it's you. You're my sister-in-law's friends, aren't you?"

I pulled myself up by the proverbial bootstraps. "I wonder if we might ask you a few questions, Mr. Harding."

He looked amused. "What are you, Jessica Fletcher? I'm afraid you're going to be terribly disappointed. I have nothing to say. I've answered every question the police posed to me. As far as I'm concerned, they have their woman."

I'd long ago decided that I was too old to keep walking around afraid of my own shadow. It was time I proved it to myself. "One question, Mr. Harding. Just one. Then I'll leave you to your afternoon."

He sighed and looked at his watch. "All right. One. Shoot."

Reasoning that a position of authority was the most likely to receive a response, I took a firm stance. "Did your wife have a key to Felicity's house?"

My strategy seemed to work, putting him on the defensive.

"What kind of a question is that? I have no idea what my wife did or didn't keep."

"Does that extend to . . . *friendships* . . . she may have kept?" Inwardly I was cringing, but it was too late to turn back now.

Color shot to his cheeks. "How dare you. My wife is only recently passed—"

"Your wife must have been very close with Ryan Davidson. I hear she was very generous to his upcoming campaign. I'm sure he'd appreciate your continued . . . support."

Marcus put his hand on my arm, but if it was a bid for caution, it was far too late. Harding's eyes flashed with anger. "Who have you been talking to? My wife was a respectable woman. I won't have you defiling her memory this way. You have no right. Slander is a very serious offense."

"Your wife is dead, Mr. Harding. And unlike you, I'm not convinced that the police have the real assassin in their holding cell."

"No?" he growled, advancing on me. "Well, let me tell you something about Felicity Dow."

Marcus, silent until now, moved forward to put his bulk slightly between mine and Harding's. "Careful . . ."

"You be careful," Harding hissed. "I know you. You're Felicity's creepy little friend. I have a good idea what you've been up to. Does she?" He indicated me with a dismissive flip of his finger. Then he turned to look at me. "Witches," he sneered. "Goddamned witches. Right here under our very noses. Town doesn't even know it." He paused, then added threateningly, *"Yet."*

Marcus didn't even blink.

I stepped forward. "Your wife is gone," I said carefully, "and there isn't anything anyone can do to bring her back. But Felicity isn't gone. She's right here, and she didn't do what you and everyone else are accusing her of. You hate her because she's different. Because she stands for something you don't understand. That doesn't mean she murdered Isabella." I'd come this far, so what was a little farther? It was the only way. "You want to know what I think happened?"

He crossed his arms and stretched to his full height. "I now I'm probably going to regret this, but you've captured ny attention. Enlighten me."

I was nervous, but he didn't need to know that. The trick as to keep him off balance and on the defensive as much as ossible. And then maybe, just maybe, the added pressure vould trigger off fissures in that ultrasmooth exterior.

I sat on the edge of Jetta's desk, letting my legs swing care- essly. "I think the killer planned that morning very carefully. think the killer knew Isabella's morning routine. That she vould be alone that morning. That she had a habit of drinking ea. I think he watched in the wings while she drank her tea, nowing it was laced with a drug that would render her pow- rless. He watched as she went upstairs to lie down after be- inning to feel the effects of the drug. And then, when he ndged the moment to be right, he deliberately and without re- norse *bludgeoned* her"—I slammed my hand down on the esktop for effect and was gratified to see him flinch—"and hoved her down the stairs to be sure the job was done. *Voilà.*"

His lips thinned. "I see you've put a lot of thought into it," e said tightly.

"I do try. Except that the killer wasn't done."

"No?"

I shook my head. "Huh-uh. The killer decided to frame Fe- city for the murder. I don't know exactly how, but somehow e must have convinced Isabella to phone Felicity *before* he illed her. The drug was especially important in the killer's cheme. I figure it ensured that Isabella would go quietly into aat good night. I figure it also allowed the killer to convince abella to phone Felicity herself."

Jeremy rolled his eyes. "That's about the most harebrained lea I've ever heard."

"And after he made certain that Felicity was the one who vould find Isabella's body," I said, ignoring his comment, "he scaped through the woods to safety, knowing that Felicity's :ory would sound ridiculous and that she would be the first erson investigated."

"You know, there's a reason we employ professional law

enforcement personnel in this country. It prevents rank ama-
teurs from pretending they are actually . . . competent."

"Only when it became apparent that Felicity's fate wasn't
sealed, the killer decided an added boost was in order, so he
borrowed a gun from Felicity's late husband's collection in
order to take a potshot at Ryan Davidson. Only that was a big
mistake. Felicity had no reason to kill Ryan Davidson. No
motive."

He stared at me, eyes narrowed, for a long moment. "Nice
try, but evidently the police don't agree with you. Let's not
forget that it's Felicity they arrested this morning."

"Strategy," I said with a shrug.

"You expect me to believe . . . oh, the hell with it. Look, I'm
not interested in your theories. As far as I'm concerned, the police have the person responsible for my wife's death. Now, if
you don't mind, I'd like you to vacate the premises. Or do I have
to call security?"

I exchanged a meaningful look with Marcus. He nodded.

"As you wish," I said, sliding off Jetta's desk with a light
bounce. The seat of my jeans caught the corner of a stack of
papers. Several floated to the floor as I found my feet. I bent to
retrieve them. "If you'd like to continue this conversation at a
later date, just let me know."

"Oh, believe me, Ms. O'Neill. If I change my mind, you'll
be the *first* to know."

The papers were a mess. I shuffled them together, clap-
ping the edges on the desktop to put them in order. As I did
so, my eyes came into focus on the topmost one—a car
rental bill in the name of Jacquilyn Harding for service dating last week. Could this be what Jetta and Jacqui had been
discussing?

Curiosity got the better of me. My gaze dropped to the total. This invoice was for over six hundred dollars. Pretty
pricey for a two-day trip.

Before I could find the line that related to the mileage, Jeremy held his hand out for the papers and I was forced to relinquish them. But I couldn't help wondering what Jacqui had
been doing on her so-called business trip. A secret affair of
her own? A few days ago, I would have found the concept

aughable, but now . . . maybe the Ice Princess wasn't as pas-
sionless as she appeared.

"What do you think you're doing?"

Marcus's annoyed question came as soon as we were out of
earshot.

"What do you mean?" I asked, playing dumb.

"Don't give me that. You were baiting the man."

"Me?"

"Purposely trying to antagonize him enough to lash out at
you. It's a damn good thing I decided to tag along. Goddess
knows what the man might have done in the absence of witnesses."

I waved my hand at him. I know, it's rude and dismissive,
and I hate it when someone treats me that way, but what can
I say? I was still high on the thrill of the hunt. "Don't be
such a man, Marcus. How else do you expect to flush a
killer out of his comfort zone? Besides, his daughter was
right around the corner. I seriously doubt he'd make a move
in front of her."

"She left," Marcus said, his tone blunt. "Several minutes
ago. I think she'd been listening."

I nearly stumbled. Had I really been so focused on Harding
that I didn't hear Jacqui leave? Chagrined, I risked a sideward
glance at him. "I must not have heard . . ."

He shook his head at me. "Maggie, I know how much you
want Felicity's name cleared. But you can't put your safety
on the line to see it done. You just can't. That's not helping
anyone."

I kicked at a loose piece of gravel with the toe of my boot.
"You're right. I guess I got a little carried away. But dammit,
Marcus, you saw the man. His attitude doesn't exactly scream
innocence, now, does it?"

"No. But we have no proof, Maggie. Just suppositions
and instinct. And gut feelings aren't gonna cut it. We won't
convince anyone until we have Jeremy's fingerprints on the
instrument of death and a confession signed on the dotted
line."

I knew he was right, and it irritated the hell out of me. I opened the car door and swung my purse into the backseat.

"Then we'll get proof," I said simply.

Chapter 16

drove Marcus back to the store so he could get his bike. I'd
intended to drop him off and go home—I was in no mood to
deal with the hordes of curiosity seekers sure to plague Enchantments this afternoon, once news of Felicity's arrest had
time to make the rounds and back again—but by the time we
got there, I had decided I would continue my search through
the store's sales records. It wasn't much, but maybe it would
spark something for me.

We were both quiet as I pulled into my usual space.

"What will you do?" Marcus asked quietly.

I jumped, wondering if he, like Felicity, could read my
mind. The thought made me uneasy. "I'm not sure. Keep
searching, I suppose. I've been sorting through store records
from the past few years. I thought maybe I'd find a record of a
sale to Jeremy, or even Jetta, something to tie him to the tea. I
know it's a long shot," I said before he could say it himself,
"but I can't think of anything better at the moment."

He just looked at me, his gaze dark and steady. "You're a
nice person, Maggie O'Neill."

Nice. He might as well have called me flat-out dull.
"Thanks," I said, keeping the flatness out of my tone.

Grandma Cora always said graciousness and good manners would save the world someday. "You, too."

"Want some help?"

I hesitated, and for a moment I actually considered taking him up on the offer. But I'd already taken up too much of his time, and just then I needed to think things through more than I needed companionship. I shook my head. "Thanks, but the time alone will do me some good. I appreciate the offer though."

There was a moment of awkwardness as we stepped out of the car and were faced with good-byes. Overhead in the sky the afternoon sun was being overtaken by a fast-moving wall of clouds. Front moving in. At the pace those clouds were traveling, we'd have rain before nightfall.

"I want you to call me," he told me, "if you decide to go anywhere. Do anything. Not that I don't trust you. I just really think cops were on to something when they decided to work in pairs. Promise me."

I promised. The promise was an easy one to make—I didn't anticipate anything more dangerous than the odd paper cut as I sorted through several knee-deep piles of receipts.

He strapped on his helmet and threw a lanky, leather-clad leg over his bike. The motor surged to life beneath his touch with a growl that made the cement vibrate beneath my feet. He revved it a time or two, grinning as I rolled my eyes at this overt display of the male affinity for power. Then he sobered.

"Be careful, Maggie. The veil between the physical world and the spirit world is thinning as we speak. Darker forces never need much encouragement to try to affect the actions of humans. A thinning veil makes it that much easier for them to accomplish their goals."

I nodded, touched by his sincerity even though the very concept of a conscious spirit world remained a difficult thing for me to swallow. It was so much easier to pass it off as the result of an overstimulated imagination.

"Come over here, would you?"

I moved next to him, too worried about Felicity even to wonder what he wanted.

"Close your eyes."

Okay, well, that caught my attention. I lifted my gaze, but his eyes were now hidden behind dark sunglasses, impenetrable in the shadow of the building, and his face gave away nothing. *It's all right,* I told myself. I didn't fear him. Well, maybe a little bit. But I found myself trembling as I obeyed his command. Moments ago I'd called him nice, and he was that . . . but there was an edge to Marcus I sensed but didn't truly understand, and it had been in stark evidence today. He was not a man to be trifled with.

My eyes closed. I had only a moment to prepare myself before I felt the touch of his fingers on my forehead. "What—?"

"Shh. Just breathe."

His fingers traced an intricate pattern on my forehead. *Breathe,* he'd said. My breath had caught in my throat at the first delicate touch of his fingertips. I forced myself to relax, to draw air inside my lungs, to allow him this moment. He repeated the pattern over and over on my skin. Hushed words rumbled from his lips in a tone so low and resonant as to be indecipherable. I might not be able to understand them, but I could feel them, buzzing along my nerve endings, filling my head. In my mind's eye I began to see a light. Just a dot at first, a twinkling star in a void of shadow. The tiny light expanded into a circle of whirling, twinkling light, a hurricane of stars. I could almost feel it encompassing us, encasing us in a blur of radiance.

"Now hold out your hand."

I felt him press something hard and warm and smooth into my palm. Then he brushed his fingertips across my cheek, the barest whisper of a caress.

Knowing somehow that the ritual had run its course, I let my eyes flutter open. Whatever spell Marcus had cast had left me feeling vibrant and alert, almost jittery. My blood was sluicing through me like spring flood waters along a creek bed. It was almost a sexual feeling, but not quite. It was, for lack of better terminology, raw energy. I looked down at my still-open hand. In my palm rested two stones: a piece of turquoise and another silver-black stone the size of a quarter, irregularly shaped, its finish reflecting my face like a fun-house mirror.

"I know the turquoise. What is the other one?"

"Hematite. Do you know anything about stones and crystals?"

I gazed in fascination at the stones, rolling them back and forth in my palm. Silver and blue. Sky and water. "Not much. What do they do?"

"The turquoise is a protective stone. It guards against danger and physical mishap. The hematite reflects negativity and prevents it from getting through to you. The mirrorlike surface, you know. It also promotes courage and mental clarity."

Amused, I asked, "Do you think I need protection, courage, or mental clarity?"

"After what I witnessed this afternoon at Harding's office, do you really need to ask that question?" He reached out and folded my fingers over the stones. "Humor me. Keep them in your pocket. I'm serious, Maggie. I have a feeling something is going to happen. At this point it could go either way. You don't want to get yourself caught up along with it, trust me. And call me if you go *anywhere*. Promise?"

I nodded.

The store was still and empty, just as I'd left it. Restlessly, I went up to the front and made sure that the CLOSED sign was prominently front and center, then returned to the dark office. I stood for a moment, staring at the piles of paper and wondering if it was all for naught. Felicity was in jail, and as far as I knew, she still hadn't hired a lawyer to get herself out of this mess. She needed my help, whether she knew it or not. I wondered if Marcus had given *her* any stones. I hoped so; as far as I was concerned, she needed them more than I did.

I settled down on the carpeted floor, the flood of papers in a half-circle around me. I had just grabbed a new stack when the phone rang. Sighing, I eased the papers off my lap and stretched for the phone.

"Enchantments Antiques and Fine Gifts."

"Police think your boss is a murderer," a quavering female voice intoned. "You like working for a murderer, missy? Ought to be ashamed of yourself, staying there. If you know what's good for you, you'll quit that place of shame and get yourself to church. Consortin' with killers, that's what you're doing. Ought to be—"

I dropped the phone in its cradle with a resounding rattle, my hands shaking. *Just an old nutcase,* I told myself.

The second nutcase was slightly less sane. At least, I hoped insanity was the reason for the irrational depths of venom and hatred the caller spewed into my burning ear. My eyes were watering and I could feel my own temperature rising with anger that a few *well-meaning* individuals could make me feel so used. Whatever problems they were suffering through in their own lives did not mean they should take them out on the nearest easy target.

When the third call came in, I was better prepared. I would wait for the caller to commence the attack, then stop the tirade in its tracks with a stern lecture about Sunday school lessons of tolerance and benevolence toward your fellow man. And what about those good old American values of a person being innocent until proven guilty in a court of law?

"Maggie, is that you?" a breathless female asked.

I frowned, trying to place the voice. "Annie?"

"Maggie, I just heard about Felicity. It's ridiculous, of course. But listen, honey, don't worry about Liss. She's a tough old bird and as wily as they come. If I know her at all, she has a half-dozen tricks up her sleeve to help the boys put things into proper perspective. Ten to one, she's gotten them to bring in her silk PJs from home, not to mention her pillow, a down comforter, and other necessities. By tonight they'll be laughing over a bottle of wine and sharing war stories. Just wait and see."

She meant to comfort me, but I could hardly bear to listen to her upbeat litany of goodness and light. Annie might well believe what she was saying, but Annie was a newcomer to Stony Mill. I was a lifer, so I knew better. Hoosiers were good people, but they could be as tenacious as pitbulls when their peaceful, ultraconservative lives were threatened. The best way to handle a problem was to root it out, isolate it, then eliminate it in whatever way necessary. I'd seen it happen before. "They wouldn't even let me see her, Annie."

"Tomorrow. Tomorrow we'll go together. They wouldn't dare refuse the both of us."

It was useless to argue with her; that much was obvious. "Fine. Great. Tomorrow."

"'Kay. And Maggie? Are the doors locked?"

Surprised by this sudden change, I looked up. "Uh, I think so."

"Make sure, okay? I'll see you tomorrow, hon."

It wouldn't hurt, I told myself, rising stiffly from the floor to accommodate Annie's request. Actually, considering the phone calls I'd just received, it was probably a damn good idea.

The stones Marcus gave me had been digging into my hipbone. I fished them from my pocket and laid them on the desk, then made my way up to the front of the store. As I thought, the lock was shot. I tested the door, remembering how it had given way under my weight the morning I'd first met Felicity, but today it seemed to be doing its job. I returned to the office and checked the back door as well. With both entrances secured, I sat down again and picked up my discarded stack.

I'd only eliminated about thirty receipts when the phone rang again.

"Don't these people have anything better to do?" I grumbled under my breath. I snatched up the handset. "Enchantments Antiques and Fine Gifts, and if you're calling to commend me to the legions of Hell or to pray for my immortal soul, or even to offer me a subscription to *Women's Wear Weekly,* I'm just not interested."

"Well, let me see. Legions of Hell, nope. Immortal soul, huh-uh. And I'm afraid I don't know what *Women's Wear Weekly* is. Hi, Maggie."

My lips tightened and I narrowed my eyes. "Deputy Fielding. Calling to gloat?"

"I guess you heard, huh?"

"I guess I have."

He fell silent a moment, cowed, I hoped, by my refusal to let him off the hook. "Listen, Maggie, I have a job to do. I'm sorry it gets in the way of your friendship with Felicity Dow, out there's not much I can do about that except to say I'm sorry. I'm sorry it had to be this way."

"Sure," I said. "You have a job to do, and you're doing it. You're doing everything you can to find out who really killed Isabella Harding rather than just listening to your own preconceptions about someone you don't like."

"Is that what you think I'm doing? Dammit, Maggie, a woman was killed. Right here in my hometown. I don't like that. In fact, I take that as a personal offense. And I will do everything in my power to see that the person responsible for the crime pays for the crime."

"And you think that person is Felicity?" I laughed coldly. "If only you knew how funny that really was. Felicity wouldn't hurt a fly. In fact, it goes against her code of ethics to hurt anyone, even herself. *If it harms none, do what you will. Harm none, Tom.*"

"Now *you're* spouting her psychobabble? Listen to yourself, Maggie. Your folks'd be horrified to hear you talking like that."

I stiffened. If he was only interested in cheap shots, then there was no point in furthering this conversation. "I have to go. Unlike you, I have work to do . . . like looking for a receipt for that tea you found in Isabella's home. I know you're not interested, but Isabella and Felicity had a falling-out over a year ago. There is no way Isabella would have Enchantments tea in her house. And unless she was irretrievably stupid, Felicity would never have implicated herself if she was intent on doing her sister in. So where did the tea come from? That's what I want to find out. And by the way, why don't you tell me what made you search her house for the gun?"

"That information is—"

"You had a tip," I guessed.

"Maggie—"

"Of course you did. Anonymous, too, I'll bet."

"Maggie, it was for her own good . . ."

"Oh, please. How much wrong has been done to the world by well-meaning individuals who set out to save us from ourselves?"

"We need to talk about this."

"I don't think so."

"Look, I get out of here in about an hour . . ."

"Don't bother. I won't be here." It was a lie, because I didn't have any intention of leaving until I had gone through every last receipt I could find, but at that point I didn't feel I owed him the truth.

"Maggie—"

"Good-bye, Tom."

Amazing how calm I felt, considering that I had been locked in a torrid embrace with the man less than forty-eight hours ago. I patted myself on the proverbial back as I quietly went back to the receipts, not realizing how much Tom's betrayal upset me until the print on the receipts swam before my eyes and a tear trickled down my cheek. He was a good man. An honorable man. A man who believed in law and order and justice. I trusted that. How could such a man fall so short of his ideals?

I waited a moment for my vision to clear, sniffed, then bent my head again. Nose to the grindstone. Work for what you believe in. Work will set you free, even when your heart is aching.

Sage wisdom from my Grandpa Gordon. God, I love that man.

I sat that way for hours, hardly noticing the crick in my back from sitting on the floor for so long. There had been no further telephone interruptions. After my conversation with Tom I'd decided to take the bull by the horns and switched the ring toggle to Off. Outside, afternoon turned to twilight. I didn't notice that either until I was forced to switch the desk lamp on in order to see the ink on the page. I transferred the current stack of receipts to the desktop then eased with a bone-weary sigh into Felicity's comfortable leather chair. It felt heavenly. I tried not to think about her sitting alone in a cold, utilitarian cell. Perhaps Annie's way of hoping for the best possible outcome was the right way after all. At the very least it helped to ease a woman's heart.

Night fell. I yawned over the stacks and paused to rub the weariness from my eyes. The hands on my watch pointed to nine-oh-four. From the height of the remaining piles, I estinated I had another two to three hours of sorting ahead of me—the summer's receipts. It disappointed me that I hadn't et found what I was looking for, but I'd known it was a long hot to begin with. And although there were still two piles to o, maybe it was time to prepare for the ultimate disappointment of not finding anything at all.

Or maybe I just needed a break. Something to help me think clearly.

Mental clarity.

I glanced over at the stones I'd placed on the corner of the esk. Marcus had told me to keep them in my pocket, but that was all a bunch of mumbo jumbo, right? Stones don't have the power to aid you on your path through life. Stones are just . . . tones.

Still . . .

Feeling guilty, I reached over and picked up the pretty sil-er one. In the low-power light from the desk lamp, it looked ke spilled mercury in my palm, fluid and graceful. Lovely. But probably not helpful.

I still had it in my hand when I heard the sound of a key be-ng inserted into the lock.

It's amazing how quickly adrenaline precipitates fear. My eart leapt to my throat in an instant, but even before that in-tant, my body had gone on full alert. My hair prickled at the ape of my neck and along my arms, and immediately my yes darted around searching out an appropriate defense. I eized the sturdy Celtic-knot letter opener from the pencil cup ust as the door creaked inward.

My mouth fell open. "Ms. Harding?"

Jacquilyn Harding's hand flew to her throat, her enormous iamond engagement ring catching and reflecting the light with n impressive flash. "Oh, hell! You startled me." She stepped nside and closed the door. "I didn't expect to see you here, Maggie. Aunt Felicity asked me to stop in and gather a few of er things before heading home tonight. She gave me her keys." he held up a set of keys and waved them around. "See?"

I scarcely looked at them. "They let you see her?"

She turned around and relocked the door, tucking the keys nto her pocket. She laughed self-consciously at my question.

"Of course. I am family, after all. Besides, Judge Hardcastle is a very old, very particular friend of my father's." She laughed again as she brushed at an imaginary smudge on her sleeve. "Never mind. I'm sure he's probably outside of your usual circle. You understand."

Oh, I understood, all right. I understood she had recovered from the initial shock of finding me here and was back to her usual high-handed self. "Of course," I purred right back at her. "How fortunate for Felicity that you have so many . . . connections."

"Oh, it's not just any connection. It's the kind of connection and what they can do for you."

She took off her nearly ankle-length black trenchcoat and threw it carelessly over a stack of boxes that stood along the shelving units, waiting to be unpacked. She kept her back to me, searching without a word through one voluminous pocket. I was glad for the reprieve—it gave me a chance to check her out unnoticed.

Common sense told me that Jacqui must be suffering over her mother's unexpected death, but her all-black outfit went way beyond mourning, especially since she'd exhibited little in the way of sentimentality before now. She was a reasonably attractive young woman in her mid- to late twenties, but as always she seemed to be hiding behind a cool, almost sexless façade. Witness exhibit A: her straight blond hair, which she had pulled up in a tight, high chignon that was straight out of *Little House on the Prairie*. Or how about exhibit B: her suit, impeccably tailored and top-dollar expensive, but in a style that was total middle-aged frump.

Serious hair. Serious clothes. Serious attitude problem.

Whatever she'd been searching for in her pocket, she seemed to have found. She turned back to me, a sphinx-like smile on her face as her gaze swept the mess in the office. "And what have you been up to?"

"Searching through the back records of the store," I replied, equally aloof.

"What on earth for?"

I set the letter opener down on the nearest stack of receipts

"It occurred to me that I might find something in store records that might help your aunt's case."

"Such as?"

"A bill of sale for the Enchantments tea that had been tampered with. You see, it occurred to me that your aunt and your mother hadn't seen each other, hadn't even spoken, for more than a year. Yet the tea that aided your mother's killer was fairly fresh. Date stamped this year, in fact."

She actually looked amused, in a way meant to let me know how far above me she considered herself. "Ah. That sounds reasonable, I suppose. Speaking of tea, would you like a cup?"

"Um, sure."

"Terrific. I'll have chai. I do love Auntie's chai. Well worth the inflated prices."

I guess that meant I was pouring.

She followed me out to the front of the store to where the coffeemaker held a constant supply of hot water for our personal use. I switched on the lamp that rested on the counter beside the cash register rather than using the overheads. I didn't want to draw too much attention to our presence in the event that any of my would-be phone terrorists decided to put in a personal appearance.

"You know, as much as I would like for things to be different, I have to say it's a relief to me that Auntie is behind bars. Not that I like having to admit that there has been a murderer in our family tree. But better to have her behind bars, safe and sound, than out here with the rest of us."

I gritted my teeth, wondering why I was doing this. Why was I forcing myself to listen to this wholly self-absorbed creature? "Your aunt *is* innocent, you know."

She waved her hand at me. "Yes, yes. You would say that, wouldn't you. Auntie Felicity always was good at picking up strays." She ignored the look of indignation on my face to continue, "But when faced with two evils, the lesser always seems the better choice to have around, don't you agree?"

I didn't know what to think, but I was rapidly tiring of her presence. I set her cup down on the counter. "I don't think I'll be having any after all," I told her. "I'm suddenly not feeling well."

"You really should. Didn't Auntie tell you? Tea is wonderful for the digestion. My mother was a great tea drinker, too. Several cups a day, starting first thing in the morning. The key to her girlish figure, so she said. I always hated her for that."

So the mourning attire *was* a sham. Good to know my instincts had been right about that much.

I wanted her out of there in the worst way. There was something about her that set my very skin to crawling. "I'm going to go back to the files, if you don't mind."

The smile again. "Be my guest."

Much to my regret, she trailed behind me again, brimming teacup in hand, as I returned to the office.

"Of course," she droned on as I started riffling busily through the receipts, "at least Auntie knew how to love. I believe she did truly love Uncle Gerald. Shame about that, but I suppose it can't be helped. I think Uncle Gerald loved Aunt Felicity as well, but my mother . . . Well. Water under the bridge." She set her cup down on the boxes and gave a cry as she accidentally overturned it. "*Fuck!* Well, don't just stand there, get something, why don't you!"

The F-bomb sounded so strange coming from her lips that under other circumstances I might have laughed. As it so happened, I was too busy scrambling to grab a towel from the broom closet as the tea ran down the sides, but with any luck not inside, the boxes. Annoyed, I began daubing at the cardboard with vigor. The top box, I knew, was a case of books, new releases from the publisher. Sure, they were just paper, but they didn't come cheap, and I didn't like Jacqui well enough—as in, at all—to want to help her, nor did I want to give her a reason to stick around longer.

"Forget about the stupid box. What about my coat?"

Assured that the books would survive, I tossed her the tea-stained towel. I'd had enough of her high-handed attitude. "Have at it."

Caught off guard, she lurched to catch it, but dropped her coat in the process. She shot me a dirty look, then stooped to wipe it from the floor. As she did, something metallic jingled as it fell to the floor from the deep pockets.

Felicity's keys.

Except on closer examination, they didn't appear to be Felicity's keys at all. I'd wielded Liss's keys myself and knew she only carried keys to the store, her car, and to her back door. This key ring held at least ten keys too many, and nowhere to be found was the elaborate silver Celtic symbol Liss was so fond of.

Something clicked into place inside my head.

Jacqui had lied about the keys. *She lied.* Could she have lied about other things as well?

She grabbed the keys and shoved them back into her pocket. I pretended not to notice. "Look at this mess. I hope this doesn't stain, for your sake."

"Sorry," I said, even though I wasn't.

"Apology accepted."

"So," I said, starting on the June stack. "What did Felicity say, when you spoke with her?"

She darted an annoyed glance my way as she slapped at her coat with the towel. "What does it matter, what she said? She asked me to get some things for her, and I said I would. End of story."

"What things?" I pressed, determined to draw her out. Her continued evasiveness had convinced me that she was using Felicity as an excuse to be here . . . but why? She hadn't expected to see me here; that much had been evident.

She didn't answer as she gave her wet coat a final daubing. Carefully she hung it over the back of my chair, then dropped the tea-soaked towel on the center of the desk with a grimace of distaste. Right on top of my neatly stacked receipts.

I snatched the cloth away, but I didn't let myself show my irritation in any other way. I tried again. "How did she look? I've been terribly worried about her."

"She looked the same as she always looks. Auntie Felicity has always been a rock. Nothing ever fazes her. I imagine she'll be just the same on the witness stand."

"You know, when I went to see her, I was told I'd have to

wait for the arraignment. You're very lucky to know Judg
Hardcastle."

"He was only too happy to help. As soon as I told him th
wouldn't let me see her, he called them then and there while
waited on the other line. He offered to come down with m
but of course I refused. His housekeeper was holding dinn
for him."

Another lie. Judge Hardcastle was out of town. There w
no way she could have spoken with him. Why was she here t
night? And how did she get a key? I had to know. In the o
chance Jacqui knew something that would help Liss, I had
find out.

All the same, I couldn't help wishing I'd kept Marc
around after all. Just the thought that Jacqui had withheld i
formation about her mother's death was really starting
creep me out. "Why don't I help you gather her things?" I su
gested in an attempt to steer the situation back to what h
prompted her visit.

She waved away my offer. "Not just yet." She went up fro
to the coffeemaker to pour herself another cup of tea in a fres
cup, leaving the other on its side on the carton. "You know
she called back to me, "I've always been curious. Mother to
me Auntie practices here. Upstairs. Call it morbid curiosit
but I've wanted to see it ever since. I don't suppose you
show it to me?"

I hesitated. The loft was special, to both Felicity and h
faithful customers. And for some reason, the thought of Jacq
invading that sacred space set me on edge. "I don't think—"

She reappeared in the doorway. "It will only be a minut
I'm sure Aunt Felicity wouldn't mind. I am family, after all."

I didn't dare hesitate too long. Much as I'd have liked to b
her way, I knew I needed to keep her talking to find out what sl
knew. Whatever the reason for the lowering of her guard,
couldn't allow this opportunity to slip away—I might never g
another. But I slid the letter opener from the desk and into n
sleeve just the same. Better safe than sorry. "Well . . . all rigl
Just for a moment or two."

I began to lead the way upstairs, cringing at the intrusic
of our footsteps, sharp raps that echoed clear up to the rafter

softened my own. "You know, I've been wondering about something," I said, trying to sound as conversational and nonthreatening as possible. "I think you told your aunt that you were out of town when your mother was . . . killed."

"That's right."

"That must have been terrible, coming home to such news."

"You can only imagine."

I made a sympathetic sound. "Had you driven out to . . . where was it?"

"Just north of Chicago. No, I flew. Puddlejumper from Fort Wayne, which I do not recommend, but it couldn't be helped. I had a very tight schedule."

We were almost to the top. I had to force myself not to double up the last steps. I would feel so much better once I had the reassuring safety of the loft beneath my feet. Maybe this wasn't such a good idea after all. My imagination was getting to me again. Best to get this over with and get her out of here. Tom . . . I was certain if I mentioned the car rental bill to Tom, I could somehow persuade him to ask a few questions. He might be stubborn as hell and a little biased, but he was a cop, and he did want justice to be served. Whatever that might entail.

I turned back as she rounded the bend at the top of the stairs. "Well, this is it," I said, stepping out of her way. A look or two, just to make her happy, and then we could go.

She was silent as she stepped onto the loft, her smallish eyes taking in every last detail. At last she frowned. "It's not at all what I expected." A self-conscious laugh. "It really looks very ordinary. Maybe Mother was right. Maybe Auntie can't do anything to us with her magic. I used to worry about that, you know. A childish fear, but one does wonder. Now I know."

I frowned. "Felicity wouldn't harm anyone. It goes against everything she believes in."

Jacqui shrugged as she walked along the gallery rail, head tipped back as she gazed up toward the skylights. "Whatever."

I knew that nothing I could say would change her mind, but her disloyalty to her own family rankled. My family might irritate me, but they were mine and I would do everything I could to protect them if I had to. Her views were too alien for me to comprehend; best to avoid difficult topics.

I took a deep breath to calm myself and tried again. "I've never rented a car, but six hundred–plus dollars for a two-day trip. Wow. Too rich for my blood."

She paused, her hand on the railing. "How did you know that?"

"Oh! Well, I, uh, happened to see a copy of the invoice on Ms. James's desk when I paid a visit to your father this morning." I paused, then added, "I overheard a little of your conversation with Ms. James as well. Accidentally, of course."

Get ouuuuuuuuutttttt . . .

The strange, whispered voice seemed to come from everywhere and nowhere at once. Tiny hairs jolted to attention all over my body. Another message from beyond? But somehow different from the bodiless voice I'd experienced at the cemetery. That voice had been full of regret, and anger. This one sounded urgent—even desperate—and it was enough to set my teeth on edge. *Not now!* I pleaded with the night at large. Please, now was not the time for otherworldly communication.

Jacqui walked back to the landing at the top of the stair and faced me, her whole demeanor changed. "It was an oversight. Nothing more. Jetta would spend days fighting a single charge, when she knows full well there's nothing to be done if a person signs for it. Mistake or no mistake, right or wrong, it doesn't matter."

I took an involuntary step backward, toward the circle, warning bells clanging in my head. "I was just thinking that the total mileage must have been pretty high, with a bill like that."

"I already told you. It was a mistake."

"But if you signed the receipt, that signifies that you *could* have driven it. Which presents a problem. By signing for it, didn't you also relinquish your alibi for the day your mother was killed?"

She looked at me sharply. "You don't know what you're talking about."

"Of course it was a mistake. But you know how the police are."

Get oooooouuuuuuuuuuuuutttttt!

I froze as the voice came again; I couldn't help it. Not a whisper this time. A cry in the night. And then I saw Jacqui's face. The instant the voice sounded, she turned white as a sheet and clutched at the railing for support, her eyes stretched wide with fear. And I knew . . .

She'd heard it, too.

"M-Mother?" she whispered.

Her shock lasted only a moment, then she turned on me, her face a mask of fury. "What is this, some kind of a trick?" She began to pace the floor in front of the stairs, her gaze searching out the rafters. "Where are they?"

I gaped at her. "Where are what?"

"The speakers," she said, agitated. "Where are the freaking speakers?"

I stared at her and took another step backward, onto the braided rug. "I don't know what you're talking about."

She snapped toward me. "Oh, no? All the questions. The creepy voice. Do you think I'm stupid? That you could get to me with your silly little games?"

That terrible sinking feeling in my stomach? Just my self-respect with a fear chaser. "I'm not playing games, Jacqui." Something told me now would be a good time to take some protective measures. Slowly, cautiously, I let the letter opener slip down my sleeve and pressed it flat against my thigh. "I'm sure this is simply a misunderstanding. Listen, why don't we just get the things Felicity needed. I'm sure all of this can be sorted out. I'll get a bag from downstairs to put them in, and—"

I stopped short as she withdrew a ridiculously small gun from her pocket. The size of the gun, I decided, didn't matter. I didn't know a revolver from a pistol from an Uzi, but I knew I didn't like being on the wrong end of one. Especially when it was being waved at me with the same level of caution with which one waves a flag at the annual Memorial Day parade.

"You can hand over the letter opener. Don't look so surprised. You couldn't have been more obvious when you took it from the desk. Come on." She gestured with the gun. "Unless you'd rather I took it by force."

Regretting the loss, I tossed the stainless-steel opener at her feet.

"I was worried something like this might happen. And here I'd planned so carefully. First Jetta, now you. What is the world coming to nowadays? Doesn't anyone mind their own business anymore?"

She pointed the gun at me.

Oh shit.

That fear chaser? It had just taken the lead. "Jacqui—"

"You strategize. You prepare. You plan ahead, down to the smallest detail. It doesn't make a damn bit of difference. Life refuses to be controlled, by even the strongest of wills."

She wasn't going to confess, was she? Oh boy. That was it. Curtains for me. I'd watched enough movies to know that a confession always precipitated the death of the woman who wasn't smart enough to use the cell phone in her purse to call for backup before she wandered into the dark forest when there was a psycho on the loose.

"How did you get a tape of my mother's voice?" she asked. "Never mind. It doesn't matter. I'm not sorry, you know. I'm glad she's gone." She motioned me away from the stairs, indicating the circle's center. "Over there."

I complied, keeping my gaze locked on the gun as she moved quickly to put herself between me and the only exit. "Where did you get that?"

"Where do you think?"

"Gerald Dow's collection?"

"An amazing bit of deduction. You're too good at those lucky guesses."

"It makes sense. The keys, you know. I knew someone must have had copies of Felicity's keys. When they said the gun that shot out Ryan Davidson's window had come from Felicity's home, I knew someone had access to her house." *Just keep her talking,* I told myself. *Whatever it takes.* "It wasn't easy, though, by any means. I thought . . . well, I thought it was your father."

She laughed. "My father? My father is a dear, sweet man,

but he is, after all, a man. He would have been perfectly happy to let mother carry on like the Whore of Babylon, sleeping with every Tom, Dick, and Harry who made the mistake of walking past her. But of course, he had found Jetta by then. Poor Jetta." She laughed again. I wished she wouldn't. The sound sent goose bumps chasing up my spine. "Too bad he won't have her for very much longer."

I cleared my throat. I had to know, but I didn't want to make her panic and pull the trigger prematurely. I was buying time and, with luck, prolonging my life. "Jetta suspected you?"

She shrugged with a haughty sniff. "She'd picked up a phone call for me from the company I was supposedly meeting that day. When she asked me about it later, I told her a stupid secretary had logged the meeting for the wrong date, and as I was running a little behind in traffic . . ." Her face darkened. "She didn't quite believe me, as it turns out. And then that stupid auto rental invoice with all that mileage. North Chicago to Stony Mill and back produces quite a lot more mileage than a day trip around the Windy City, you know. Now *that* was a mistake on their part, not mine. The bill wasn't supposed to go to Harding Enterprises at all. Dumb luck."

"And Jetta?"

"Jetta will suffer a tragic accident. Fell asleep behind the wheel. Can you believe it? She's waiting for me right now. She thinks she's in control of the situation. I let her believe that. She has no idea . . ."

She'd lost it. She'd truly lost it. First her mother—her own *mother!*—and then me, and finally Jetta. Who next? What if Jetta had told someone, like Ryan Davidson? "They'll know it's not Felicity," I pointed out with a calm I didn't feel. "Your aunt is in jail. They'll reopen the case."

"I've taken care of that. You know your freaky friend? The one with the motorcycle? Well, everyone knows you were with him today. Everyone knows he's friends with Auntie as well. He was with Aunt Felicity at Mother's that morning. Obviously he was a part of it from the beginning. A whisper here, a mention there. It shouldn't be too difficult to get the word started. People don't like his kind around here. Oh, and

I've taken the liberty of appropriating one of his gloves, which I will, of course, leave upon the stairs." She shook her head regretfully. "He really should learn to lock his doors. You can't trust anyone these days."

"But why your mother?" I asked as I felt her resolve growing. *Clear thinking, Maggie.* "So she was sleeping around. It's not exactly honorable, but it does happen. I don't understand."

"Why, because of Roger, of course," she said in a voice that implied it was all too obvious.

Her fiancé? "She—?"

"You know, you'd think once would be enough. I forgave her that. Justin—my high school boyfriend—was young, you could hardly blame *him*. Ah, but she must have thought I'd forgotten. She was selfish. She could only see what *she* wanted. I knew immediately when she started after Roger. She was so obvious," she sneered, her breathing coming fast and shallow, her face twisted with disgust. "She would flirt with him right under my nose. Wear low-cut blouses and bend down in front of him so that she could display herself right down to her navel. Do you know, once she fucked him at a dinner party we all attended together. I watched them. Neither of them ever knew."

On second thought, that word seemed perfectly right coming from her lips. I'd never heard it sound so cold before. "So, it was because of Roger that you wanted her gone."

"I wanted her dead. And it was because of the letters. Poor stupid Roger. He needs a strong woman by his side to keep him from making a fool of himself."

"I see," I said, though I didn't.

"She was writing him letters. God, she was so selfish! So freaking selfish. Did she think I wasn't sharing Roger's bed, too? When that was the only thing he was good for?" The wrong end of the gun was waving around erratically. "She said . . . she said she was in love with him. Letter after letter. She wanted him to leave me. To run away with her. Love," she spat. "My mother wouldn't know love from a hole in her head. Not until I showed her the difference."

I was starting to feel light-headed, standing there on the

braided circle. So much venom. So much hatred. The voice from the cemetery came rushing back. *Letters, my letters . . .*

"Your mother's letters," I said, desperate the shake the strange feeling from my head. "Someone will find them. Someone will put two and two together. Maybe even Roger. They're evidence—"

"Not anymore." The smile that touched her lips chilled me to the bone. "I burned them. Every last one. And I deleted them from her computer and e-mail that morning. *Poof.* No one else will ever have to know my mother was a whore."

Now I understood. Too late.

Something was burning in my palm. As if from a dream, I watched my hand open to display the hematite round within. *Mental clarity, Maggie. Clear thinking.*

"You know, I have to thank you," Jacqui was saying, her voice sounding tinny and far away. "They say confession is good for the soul, and they're right. I've never felt so marvelous."

From the windows above us I saw the dark clouds split open with a great, blinding flash of light. From there time seemed to shift into slow gear. I saw Jacqui lift her head momentarily to gape at the windows. The hematite flew up from my hand, arcing end over end toward the stairs. It clattered down the steps, making a racket I would never have suspected from such a small object. Jacqui's head whipped leeward in obvious confusion.

Before I knew what I was doing, I lurched forward, toward her. She seemed to have forgotten about the gun in her hand for the moment, and as WWMD (*What Would Magnum Do*) flashed through my head, I decided to take full advantage of the opportunity at hand before I could change my mind.

She saw my approach from the corner of her eye at the last second. Her head, and the gun, came back around toward me, her mouth wide in an O of surprise. But it was too late. As if I'd planned the whole thing, my foot swung up in the perfect imitation of a cheerleader's high kick. My boot connected with her hand, knocking the gun up just as a flash of light and a horrendous reverberation of sound filled my head. Glass shattered and bits of it came raining down upon us from a skylight.

Everything happened so fast. Before I could form a thought as to what came next, Jacqui took a single instinctive step backward in response to my charge. She threw up her arms, pinwheeling them for balance. I reached out to grab her, heedless of the gun now hanging limp in her hand, but my fingers caught air as she tumbled backward out of my grasp and thudded painfully down the stairs.

My mouth open in shock, I peered over the gallery rail at her body lying still and twisted in the open doorway. Slowly I became aware of a muted banging coming from elsewhere in the store. Another ghostly warning? The answer came seconds later as urgent voices filled the storeroom below and I heard someone calling my name just as my knees caved away beneath me and I sank to the floor.

Chapter 17

I came out of it to find a familiar face hovering over me. "Jacqui . . . ?"

"She'll live, unfortunately," Marcus grunted uncharitably as he helped me sit up. "A bit broken up, but bones heal. She got lucky. They're getting her into an ambulance as we speak."

"How did you . . . how did you know?"

"Evie," he said, cradling me against him and stroking my hair as though comforting a child. "She's been trying to call you for hours. She saw you. This room. A gun. The phone rang busy, no answer. She felt certain you were still here. She tried sending you a thought message, but apparently it didn't work."

I thought of the eerie voice I'd heard. "So she called you?"

"And me."

I turned to find Tom Fielding standing four feet away, watching us. I started guiltily. "Tom . . ."

He turned away, his gaze traveling in a slow circle around the room, his face oddly expressionless.

"Jacqui killed Isabella, Tom. Her mother was sleeping with her fiancé, and I guess she flipped. She blamed her for everything."

"A woman scorned," Marcus murmured. "Jealousy is a very strong motivator." Then under his breath, I heard him say, "Dark energy."

"She was also responsible for the attack on Ryan Davidson with a gun from Felicity's house. She thought she'd pull the noose around Felicity's neck just a little bit tighter. She even thought she'd bring Marcus into question."

I pulled gently away from Marcus and walked over to where Tom stood staring up at the night sky through the hole in the skylight, rain dripping down upon his head. "Tom—"

"I took her into custody for her own safety, Maggie. Maybe it was wrong of me; I don't know. It was obvious that something wasn't right about the whole situation, but I couldn't put my finger on it. I thought, maybe, if I could get the perp feeling comfortable enough, something would slip. I was trying to tell you that earlier. I just couldn't get you to listen." His eyes met mine. "Or maybe you just didn't want to listen."

Everything happened all at once then. Other officers came to take evidence. I gave my version of the night's events several times, and had to promise to come in the next day to give a formal, signed deposition. And then it was all over. The police wandered away, two by two, their popping, bubblegum lights fading into the night until it seemed impossible that they had been there at all.

Tom disappeared before I could thank him. The last time I saw him, he was standing silently by the long glass cabinet, arms crossed over his chest, one hip cocked against the glass as he watched the rest of us picking up the pieces with that same masked expression that drove me crazy. I knew a moment of regret when I discovered him gone. We had a lot to talk about, but it looked as though it wouldn't happen tonight.

At long last, needing to be alone with my thoughts, to make sense of what had happened, I sent Marcus away even when he would have stayed.

I wandered around Felicity's ritual space with a sense of awe and gratitude, touching the shelves of books, the cabinets full of treasures, the things she loved. I knew in my heart that my safety tonight had been somehow tied to this room, this sacred place, and to the words Marcus had spoken over me. I felt at a loss to explain everything, but what I did know I associated with Felicity's protective presence. For she'd been with me tonight, guiding me, watching over me. I'd felt her, just as surely if she'd stood by my side. I think I'd made her proud.

As for me, I felt somehow different. Had I been changed by the events of the past two weeks? Well, I no longer thought that living in Stony Mill meant leading a humdrum existence. And I was ready to make a few changes in my life. No longer would I lead my life worrying so much about what others might think, or suffering crippling guilt when I thought of acting on my own behalf. Tonight I'd thought for myself, and while it had been touch-and-go for a while there, everything had turned out just fine. It was high time I grew up, once and for all.

As for magic coexisting in the world around us, well, the jury was still out on that point. Let me just say that my mind had been . . . opened to the possibility.

They released Felicity that very night. I know because she showed up on my doorstep, as elegant and cheery as ever, even with the mist clinging to her hair and dampening her clothes. I laughed with relief when I saw her, threw my arms around her neck, and hugged her tight. So much in my life had changed in the past two weeks. So much of it could be attributed to this fascinating, honorable, wonderfully eccentric woman. In spite of everything that had happened, I wouldn't have it any other way.

Jetta James never knew for sure how close she'd come to her own unfortunate end, but I'll bet she suspected, once the whole story came out. I ran into her at the Java Hut a week later. Her gaze skated past me as she sailed confidently toward the door in a tight black suit and overtly sexual three-inch heels, but at the last minute she'd paused and glanced back. In that moment we exchanged a look of understanding and recognition, a look of shared experience. We'd each done the two-step with death and come away unsinged. That's quite something.

Jeremy Harding left town for a while, but I heard through

the grapevine a few months later that he was back in town and up to his old tricks with Jetta, who may or may not have cast Ryan Davidson aside. Who knows, maybe Jeremy and Jetta deserved one another after all. Lately I've heard rumors that he might be considering a bid for town council. A scary thought, but everyone knows it's the privileged few who control things for the rest of us. Such is the way of this crazy, mixed-up world. Maybe someday Jeremy and Ryan would get together and bury the hatchet. They had a lot more in common than either would admit to.

Or maybe not.

I wish I could say that things between Tom and me had been settled, but I hadn't seen him since that night. I wish I could say that our little town soon eased back into its quiet little routine as if nothing had ever happened. I'm sorry to say I can't. You see, something was awakened that fall, something dark and powerful that in these early stages only sensitives felt. Something I didn't completely understand but knew enough to fear. And I couldn't help remembering Marcus's words of caution:

I have a feeling something is going to happen, he'd said. *At this point it could go either way . . .*

Fresh on the wind was a sense of trouble not far behind, tainting the very air we breathed. Stony Mill old-timers gathered on weathered wooden benches in the park and complained about how much things had changed, and how isolated they felt from everything they'd grown up knowing. Farmers who gathered at the feed store for the combined pleasures of purchasing grain and shooting the bull ended up swapping stories about how the goddamned kids didn't respect property anymore; more than one had gone to dire straits to protect his roadside mailbox, first with bricks, then massive fieldstones, finally giving up entirely, trading up for a post office box in town to save himself the expense. And forget about respecting their elders—did kids even understand the word anymore? Road rage raised its ugly head unexpectedly on our quiet, tree-lined streets. But worse than all of that was the scope of evidence the N.I.G.H.T.S. had been quietly amassing that gave proof we were not alone on this physical plane. Even with my limited understanding of such other-worldly things, I knew this couldn't be good.

Because I, too, had sensed something big on the horizon. Something that went beyond the real world and that delved into a shadow world that until then had been hidden to me.

Real or imagined?

You be the judge.

The Kitchen Witch
by Annette Blair

When a single-dad TV executive hires
Melody Seabright, a flaky rich girl and
rumored witch, as his babysitter, she
magically lands her own cooking show—
and makes sparks fly.

0-425-19881-2

pc597

An entirely new supernatural mystery series from
New York Times bestselling author
CHARLAINE HARRIS

grave sight

Harper Connelly has what you might call a strange job:
she finds dead people. She can sense the final
location of a person who's passed, and share their very last
moment. The way she sees it, she's providing a service to the
dead while bringing some closure to the living—but
she's used to most people not really wanting to
know what they hired her to find out.

0-425-20568-1

Available wherever books are sold or at
penguin.com

b881